GIDEON'S ANGEL

❖ ANGEL ❖

Clifford Beal

SOLARIS

First published 2013 by Solaris
an imprint of Rebellion Publishing Ltd,
Riverside House, Osney Mead,
Oxford, OX2 0ES, UK

www.solarisbooks.com

ISBN: 978 1 78108 083 2

Designed & typeset by Rebellion Publishing

Printed in the UK by CPI Group (UK) Ltd, Croydon, CR0 4YY

For Lady Kay

Be not forgetful to entertain strangers:
for thereby some have entertained angels unawares.

Hebrews 13:2

...And no marvel; for Satan himself is
transformed into an angel of light.

2 Corinthians 11:14

Chapter One

HE DID NOT know me from Adam. Yet looking into his eyes, separated by the length of two old and pitted rapiers, there was no doubt that this man was fixed on killing me. It was not the usual expression I saw on those in the heat of battle: wide eyes, confusion, fear, elation. This was very different. It was deep hatred for everything I stood for. You see, for this young fool, I was the embodiment of a rotten and defeated Cause, a cause that had taken the life of his brother just a few weeks earlier. I was a king's man, a Cavalier. And for the simple purpose of feeding a grieving brother's revenge, I would do.

Never look too long into the eyes of your enemy. The eyes lie. They deceive you into thinking he will strike one way before he then strikes in another. I knew this, but still I had trouble taking my gaze from his face and putting it where it belonged: upon his legs and his sword arm. The look on him was enough to wither a field of corn. Maybe his friends in the regiment had wound him up tight, feeding his grudge. Telling him I was the one who had spitted his kin at Naseby.

He didn't need a grudge to give him the advantage. I had been stabbed on the same field that had claimed this fellow's brother and as I crouched, circling the man, I could feel the deep gash in my thigh splitting open again, the stitches snapping with a pop. This duel could only end one way the longer it lasted. I would falter, my leg would give out, and he would thrust me clean through.

His first attack exploded upon me. A stamp with the right foot and then a time-thrust to try and catch me out. I parried it and drew back on my rear foot, but his move proved he was no country clown with a rapier. He was half my age, well-rested, and filled with righteous rage. I drove in, catching his blade and running mine up along it as I twisted my wrist. He grunted and immediately threw his left leg behind his right, parrying my thrust. I recovered, but the lad riposted in an instant, leaping forward on his left foot and slashing with his dagger. I just managed to catch it with mine. He was more than a match for me with speed, but he was not used to playing against a left-handed swordsman.

He came in again fast with a flurry of well-aimed thrusts, leaving me untouched but heaving for breath. The assembled crowd of red-coated soldiers roared at the sudden exchange of steel, cheering the trooper. I tried to lure my opponent in, dropping my guard just a hair, hoping he would take a shot and give me an opening to counter-time him. It worked, but my bad leg seized up just as he struck. I twisted to avoid the narrow sword as it headed for my chest. I caught his blade on my quillons, but he was so fast he lunged in and stabbed my arm with his dagger. I fell back; the sleeve of my shirt instantly turned red in an ever-growing circle of blood.

His comrades jeered at me. They screamed for him to slit my belly, rip my guts and then cut my throat for good measure. And I... I had actually *asked* for this fight. A judicial duel. The first in more than thirty years. Parliament had given me a stark choice: repent and give them names, or be hanged, drawn and quartered. I gave them another option. Let God decide my guilt. And being sanctimonious canting Roundheads, they agreed. Now, on Tower Hill in the burning sun of a cloudless July day, my strength and blood ebbing away, the whole scheme was looking very stupid indeed. And the appointed champion, the champion of the Parliamentary forces, was beginning to look near as damn unassailable. Maybe God had already chosen the guilty.

He was smart enough to know not to give me the chance for rest. In a flash, he was on me again: thrusting, cursing, slashing. It was all I could do to parry each attack, limping as I moved to flank him, hoping to find an opening. I remember making a high parry out of habit, like the cavalryman I was. It was a fool's move. The next instant I felt that familiar tugging sensation followed rapidly by the dull deep pain of a sword as it pierced my thigh. I staggered back and found myself on my knees.

This is a charm I have made for you...

My little talisman, worn around my neck these twenty years, flew up out my shirt front and dangled upon my chest. A tiny linen pouch bound with red thread, I never had figured out what it contained. Crushed flowers and stems it seemed, that was all, but it had seen me into a hundred battles, cheating death a hundred times. And I could never forget how it came to my hand and who had placed it there.

Keep it upon your person—always. It will keep you from harm...

They were all laughing now. I would rather be jeered at than mocked as an incompetent. The boy trooper was sure he had me. He took a few steps to the side, swishing his rapier back and forth, smiling. He wiped his sweating brow with his dagger arm and just stared at me. He was savouring the settling of the blood debt. The crowd began to call out once again, urging him to kill me. I watched as the trooper took up his stance anew, levelling his blade at waist height, his dagger hand low.

My breeches were soaked in blood, cool against my thigh. I tried swallowing but my throat closed up, the lump just sticking halfway down like some wedged morsel of beef. I fought back the retching. But I resolved not to offer myself up to his blade without one last flurry. As he came towards me, I leaned back on my heels, raised my sword point up, tip towards his belly, and reversed my dagger, point down.

I know why he did what he did next. He was playing for the crowd, performing for the red-coated brethren of Parliament's army of saints. He was just at striking distance from me; I watched as he raised his hilt to chest height, swirled the blade twice in a wide arc, and then turned his wrist upwards as he came on his guard again. The long thin rapier sloped downwards, the point directly aimed at my throat. I knew that guard. He was going to ram that blade straight downwards, through my chest and out my back, pinning me to the ground. I could see him *thinking* this, marking his time, choosing the moment. And he let his dagger hand drop past his leg. Then he struck, struck like some hunter, ready to finish off this grey-bristled and bleeding boar.

I had let my sword hand fall low. His thrust was well aimed and powerful. I swept my dagger across and outwards, deflecting the rapier and running up the length of his blade as his momentum carried him forward. And as I parried, I dropped my rapier point and leaned in. I felt my sword go deep into his side, and then judder on a rib. He gasped and pulled himself off my blade, then staggered sideways before catching himself. His right hand opened and the rapier tumbled from his grasp. Half a moment later his knees gave way and he fell to the trampled grass. I could hear a slightly strangled cry coming from him, a long and low bleat of pain.

And then the redcoats were silent. Not just cheated of their sport but surprisingly robbed of it. I could see the Lieutenant of the Tower approaching and a loud murmur went through the crowd. Somehow, I pulled myself up to one knee, gave a grunt and stood up, leaning on my sword, the tip digging into the earth. I was tottering like a drunkard but I was standing.

The officer looked at me, mouth agape, unable to conceal his astonishment at the turn of fate.

"You must finish it," he said. "You or he. There is no quarter here. This is to the death."

This got the soldiers roiling again, calling out to the trooper to get up. But he was not getting up anytime soon. I stumbled over to my opponent who was still groaning like a stuck animal. He turned his head to look at me. No fear in his eyes, just burning anger.

But I had proved my innocence and I didn't give a flea's piss to finish the game. The dagger dropped from my hand. And then I weakly tossed the rapier across the green.

"Colonel Treadwell, you must finish the fight," said the officer. "It is the law."

Someone in the crowd shouted out "Cut down the damned rogue!" and the halberdiers started to force back some of the more wild Roundheads that pushed towards me.

I looked at the officer and shook my head. "I will not, sir. Judgement has already been given."

He stepped towards me. "Pick up a weapon, sir!"

"Go to the Devil. If Parliament still wants a life then one of you will have to take it. I am done with it." And my shaking hand closed on the talisman that swung at my chest. I could feel its little flowers and twigs crackling in my palm as I dropped it back inside my torn shirt. She had saved me once again.

Never take it off...

THEY HALF CARRIED me back to my cell. I remember seeing a man step towards me while I struggled to keep my shaking arms tight around the shoulders of the unwilling bearers. He had the face of a goat: long and thin, wispy beard, and eyes that seemed to bulge from his greying head. And as he reached me, he doffed his hat and fixed me with a most curious look. I could hardly keep my head up for loss of blood but I caught him smiling, and nodding at me. I saw his gloved hand place his hat back upon his head and then I was jerked forward once again and into the darkness of the Tower. Two days later they told me my fate. I was exiled, my estates forfeit. This final little gift of Parliament was wrapped with the promise of a traitor's death if I ever set foot in England again.

But that was a future I thought I would not live to see. Lying in my cell on a broken and sagging rope bedstead with a straw mattress the thickness of parchment, my wounds burned me into delirium. Shadows coming and going, day and night confused, I drifted. I remember sipping water and being fed gruel. At some hour I was awoken by the stab of needle and the tug of horsehair as they stitched me up, the pain strangely distant. By the third day I knew I was to live, for I was again lucid and near mad with agony. My thigh was swollen and red like a joint of gammon and stiff as a tree limb, but there was no stink of rot, thank the Lord. And it was that third day that my keepers thought fit to let in a visitor, seeing that I had not yet expired.

I had my cloak rolled up behind, propping me up on the rope bed, when the bolt shot open and the studded door creaked wide to admit him. It was the goat-faced man. He entered and took off his tall-crowned hat.

"Your brother gave me admittance, sir. He has been a constant angel over you."

I raised my head and shifted my weight on the bed, wincing. The voice was melodious and heavily accented: French.

"I should be grateful given he is a Parliament man," I replied. "But we're recently reconciled. Very recently. Do you know—in Paris—the adage about blood being thicker than water?"

The man nodded and smiled. "We say something much the same. And it was by Sir William's invitation that I witnessed your fight. And why I visit you again today."

William had risked his own standing in Parliament to get

me the gambit of a duel rather than a quick drop from the end of a rope. What was he up to now? I pushed myself further up on the bed, my back to the stones of the wall.

"Will you not introduce yourself, sir?"

Beard waggling, the man grasped his hat before him with both hands and bowed. "My apologies, Colonel. I had not considered that your brother has said nothing to you given your grievous state. I am de Bellièvre, ambassador of His Majesty King Louis of France."

"And what business does the King of France have with me?"

The ambassador smiled again and gently inclined his head. "Strictly speaking, it is by Cardinal Mazarin's authority that I propose to you an offer of employment."

My laugh turned into a retching cough. "And what service could a broken-down Cavalier on death's door do for the Cardinal?"

De Bellièvre waved his hat expansively. "Your knowledge of soldiering is considerable, sir. The war here. A few years ago in the German kingdoms and in Sweden. His Eminence would pay handsomely for an officer of your experience. Your brother is most generous in his praise of your skills."

"I think you're wasting your time, sir. I may not even walk again, let alone ride."

The ambassador laughed. "Nonsense. You will heal. My own surgeon will see to you. Besides, you are as strong as a cow!"

"I think you mean *ox*."

The ambassador moved to the foot of the bed, one hand toying with the elegant golden braid on his hatband. He gave me a knowing look with his watery pug dog eyes. "Colonel, you are an exile now and without a penny to your name. Would you go back to the Danes again? They are as poor as you. Hanover and Saxony are barren lands now. Come to Paris. Take the Cardinal's commission and find your fortune anew!"

One door closes, another opens. And that is how I ended up

in the service of a new master, plucked from the viper's nest to find myself in a different, but no less risky, employ.

For eight years I did good honest soldiering under the French. And I prospered. But then, I found myself again facing a man possessed of Righteousness and Vengeance in equal measure, like that young redcoat on the Tower green. And this time, it was a man guided by the Devil himself.

Chapter Two

HER HAND TRACED a path along my scar, a mottled indigo trench gouged out of my thigh in the summer of 1645. It joined another, slightly newer and higher up, forming appropriately enough a letter T. By the single candle flame that trembled in the draught of my bedchamber, I watched her as she examined me. I took in the sight of her full breasts, bronzed by the soft light and swaying invitingly as she moved her arm towards my hip.

"So many gambles with Death, yet you are still here," she said.

My hand went to the silver locket that hung on my chest, a trinket that now concealed a frayed and yellowed linen pouch, barely held together by the red thread that wrapped around it.

She snatched it deftly, and gave it a shake. "And what lies in this?"

"It's a charm, given to me a long time ago... in Germany."

"From a lover, perhaps?"

"Alas no. She was an old gypsy who took pity on a young soldier."

"But it's the secret of your survival," she teased. "True gypsy magic?"

I smiled, pleased with her intuition. "Aye, that it might be."

She propped herself up on her elbows, studying the pierced oval locket, looking for its catch. But I gently pulled it back from her and tugged the coverlet over our nakedness, gathering her up in my arms as I did so.

"I've spoken with those who have known you since you came to France," she said as she stroked my cheek. "They say you've not changed a whit since. Barely a grey hair on your head even though you're old enough to be a grandfather."

"Foolishness."

"It's a powerful charm, then?"

I kissed her full upon the lips and her fingers ran through my hair.

"It would seem to afford other powers as well, I see," she trilled.

"You're my charm, Maggie."

Marguerite St. John's father was an adventurer who had, like me, chosen the wrong side. He was a good Royalist still, and was even now off somewhere in the kingdoms of Europe trying to raise money for our new pauper king, young Charles II. This suited me well enough, affording the time to acquaint myself with his daughter unhindered, if not unobserved in so intimate a place as the Louvre Palace.

"I think that the one about your neck will outlast me," she said. "Something tells me you won't remain here at court much longer."

I hesitated in reply. She was a clever girl.

"No, you can't fool me, sir." She rolled over onto her back and sank into the mattress, one hand reaching down to play with my manhood. "If you *could* take me with you—I would don harness as well and fight alongside you! There's nothing left for us here. The money has run out and the cause is lost. I may as well become a whore and get paid."

"Don't talk of such things. Think upon Christmas a few weeks hence, my sweet. And remember that in London not one Yule log will be burnt nor a figgy pudding steamed. Copper Nose Cromwell has forbidden it."

She pulled her hands to her bosom and her fingers tugged the coverlet snug across her neck. "Christmas is just a child's diversion for a fortnight. We'll soon be back to the usual fare, short bitter days, and the endless bickering."

I reached over and ran my fingers along her cheek and she turned toward me, a smile broadening in spite of her huff. "One day," I said, "England will spit out the Puritan lump of gristle stuck in its throat and have done with the whole canting lot."

"My love," she said, stroking my chin and running her hand down my neck with the touch of a fairy, "you above all men must surely know, after all you've seen in this world, that people have a capacity to endure—to survive. To look the other way in the face of trouble. That is how they manage under Cromwell."

"Aye, well, I won't tell you otherwise. But where one door closes, another opens. And that's from an old soldier who knows." I leaned out of the bed and pinched the candle that guttered in the cold draught. Pulling her in to me once again, I drank in her perfume.

Softly, she spoke again. "I think it's time you told me what happened to you this summer—what you did for the king. What really happened. And why he *knighted* you. I know you don't have enough money to have convinced him. You must have done something else."

I sighed and lay back, falling into the pillow with her head upon my chest. "Very well," I whispered, "but there are good reasons why few people know what happened. You mustn't tell a soul lest you bring harm to yourself and others. There are enemies who would learn such things of the Stuarts."

"I swear to you," she said.

Like a moth, my bumbling, aimless flight had brought me back into the Stuart flame after several years on the Continent as a soldier in the pay of the French. Or to be more exact, His Eminence Giulio Raimondo Cardinal Mazarin. The French had gotten it into their heads to have a little civil war like we English and my skill at arms drew a good price. So I told her of that day last July, as the French rebel army retreated to the gates of Paris in hope of being let in by the city fathers. The Parisians were much too wise to let any army into the town so the rebel leader, Prince Condé, pleaded his case at the city gates while King Louis, the Cardinal, and the royal army closed in for the kill. Condé knew he was trapped at the walls of Paris, so he barricaded himself into Faubourg village, and prepared to fight us.

"I know all that," she said. "What was *your* part in all this?"

"Not so fast," I chided. "I will relate that soon enough. What you probably didn't know is that young James, the brother of our own good king, was also with us that day. Aye, the lad was doing good service as an adjutant to General Turenne, running messages and the like.

"It was late afternoon before what would prove to be a day of battle outside the walls," I said. "I was leading a few squadrons of the Cardinal's cavalry, harassing Condé's stragglers. Andreas Falkenhayn was with me."

"The loutish German fellow we saw today?"

"The same. My old comrade of many long years. There was a rebel musketeer behind every window flowerpot and every hedge and wall, all taking shots at us as we rode by. The whole afternoon we lay into them as they dug deep into the village like fleas on a poodle.

"Major Falkenhayn and I found a messenger waiting for us with orders to see the Cardinal at once. When we reached the summit of the hill above Faubourg, the Cardinal emerged from his tent, cassock flapping about him like an ensign on the field of battle.

"We had scarcely bowed and made a reverence before he barked at us to join him in his tent. His Eminence was not alone. There, next to a trestle table scattered with maps and documents, stood a soldier I had not met before.

"Mazarin's hand rested on a letter that lay half crumpled upon the table in front of his chair. He gestured at the soldier without even looking at us.

"'Gentlemen,' he said, 'May I introduce *Monsieur* d'Artagnan, of the king's company of musketeers.' He picked up the letter and waved it my way. 'And these two worthies are my trusted servants, Colonel Richard Treadwell and Major Andreas Falkenhayn, of my own regiment. Now then—listen well—we have little time.'"

"And who is this d'Artagnan?" asked Maggie, her voice quite muffled under the coverlet.

"He is some young Gascon of lesser nobility, come to Paris to find his fortune, and already a trusted emissary of Mazarin for such a tender age."

"Pray, continue," she whispered.

So I told her what Mazarin had told us, his Italian-accented French tripping so rapidly that I was hard-pressed to follow him. "'That young fool of a Stuart prince has managed to get himself captured—or killed,' said Mazarin, sinking further into his leather camp chair. 'If the rebels discover they have the Duke of York in their grasp it will give them a strong hand to play against King Louis.'

"'Where, Your Eminence? Where was he taken?' I asked.

"But it was d'Artagnan who answered my question. 'He fell off his horse in the main square of the village. He was seen to be dragged inside one of the houses by a group of rebel musketeers before the rest of his party could rescue him. Word is he was as limp as a sack of grain when they pulled him boot-first through the doorway. He might even be dead.'

"I looked over to Andreas who merely raised his eyebrows in reply.

"'And you, gentlemen,' said Mazarin, wagging a long bony finger at me and Andreas, "you are going to get him back—this very night. You *will* find him. If he is dead then we shall know. If he yet lives you will bring him back here. If you cannot get him out, then, in such an eventuality, I'm afraid for the good of the State you must kill him where he is.'

"I just stood there, dazed. 'Aye, Eminence, I shall assemble the squadron—'

"Mazarin jumped up, flapping like a puppet. 'No, man! This is work for three, not a regiment. Use your wiles, sir, it is what I have paid you for these last years!'

"'What three, Your Eminence?'

"'D'Artagnan will accompany you. He knows roughly where the Englishman was taken and you'll find he is a useful man in such circumstances.'

"D'Artagnan gave a slight bow but said nothing.

"'I pray that James Stuart has not opened his mouth to say who he actually is,' said the Cardinal as he dragged a lantern across the table onto one of his maps, his attention already moving to other concerns.

"I blinked in the gloom of the stifling tent, waiting.

"'You may go,' the Cardinal said without looking up again. 'God be with you.'"

It WAS NEAR to midnight before we could commence our plan, hatched as best one could on short notice and with barely a scrap of intelligence. I looked up at the moon, two days waxing full, and cursed our luck.

"Too much light," whispered Andreas. "We'll be as naked as a cuckoo at Christmas."

I don't know how long it took us to scale the low wall that confronted us, then skirt the gardens and make our way alongside the little abbey and so into the village. But at last, we entered an alleyway cut between two houses and followed it out to the street. And then, as one, we stopped. There were at least a hundred rebels, many around well-stoked braziers in the middle of the street.

D'Artagnan crossed to the far side and we followed, ducking into another alley.

"How long do you expect our good fortune to hold out?" I hissed.

"I'll find where the prisoners are. Don't worry," D'Artagnan said.

His arrogance burned brightly indeed. "I shall hold you to that, *monsieur*," I said quietly.

The Grand Rue held even more rebels. My Gascon musketeer sailed straight away across the street, carrying Andreas and me in his wake. After a few minutes it became painfully plain that d'Artagnan didn't have a clue where the prince was being held.

"This is near the spot he fell. I know it," he hissed at me when he saw my disdain.

"But near isn't close enough is it, my friend?" I shot back. It was time for other measures if our mission was to stand any chance at all and we were to get back alive. I reached into my pocket and retrieved something I had hoped not to have to use.

The brass device filled the palm of my hand as I raised it up, full in the moonlight. D'Artagnan recognised it straight away.

"That belongs to the Cardinal! How did you get it?"

Andreas grabbed my wrist to get a better look. "Why, it's a sun dial."

"It's no sun dial," I said. "It is a compass."

"And a rare one at that," added d'Artagnan. "You stole it from his field table today. But it will do scarce good. Just what are you playing at?"

I didn't answer him. I raised the compass up to chest height and held my other hand over it palm down. And then I started to recite what I had been taught.

"*In nomine Patris et Filii et Spiritus Sancti... In nomine Patris et Filii et Spiritus Sancti... In nomine Patris et Filii et Spiritus Sancti.*"

The needle, motionless and straight on north, now began to slowly revolve.

"Witchcraft!" whispered d'Artagnan. "Stop this now, you old fool!"

Andreas took a step backwards, his eyes big as supper plates. I continued the incantation.

"*Invenium... quem... quaera.*"

The needle began to quaver, slowing until it stopped dead. "Now we know where the prince is," I said. Andreas looked at me, shaking his head. "It's a little trick," I said. "One I picked up in your country a few years ago."

"And you'd better not show it to anyone else," said d'Artagnan, his face hard. "Not if you value your neck."

"We can argue the sanctity of it later. Now we must be quick. I don't know how long it will keep pointing the right way."

The whole of the village was stuffed full with rebels but most were too busy thieving what they could from the houses to bother us. We walked up the street. I saw the needle move again. It led us straight to a large house set back from the road.

Peering through the open door that rocked upon its hinges, I spied a table full of rogues playing at cards, illuminated by one small tin lantern. For the moment, the five contented themselves with cursing and laughing, their muskets and halberds stacked against a cupboard.

D'Artagnan gestured for us to move away and we crept along the side of the house, looking for a back way in. Fortune was smiling so far; the alley led to a tiny courtyard where at the back of the house was a door to a kitchen. The voices of the gamesters carried down to us from the front of the house and, in the reflected moonlight, I watched as Andreas and d'Artagnan felt their way forward until they found a staircase.

"Have a care, my friends," I said and we began our climb.

I heard d'Artagnan whisk his poniard from its scabbard. We reached the top, carefully shuffling forward in the gloom. Rounding a wall, faint candlelight now afforded us a view of the front room.

Three men lay upon the floor, feet bound with rope. The only furniture in the room was a little table and stool and it was here that another tin lantern burned, its tallow candle stinking and sputtering in the last gasps of life. One of the prisoners appeared half dead, his bloody head bandaged, face ashen even in the faint orange glow of the chamber. The other two spotted us, and d'Artagnan thrust out his open palm, ordering them to keep silent.

I stepped forward and, in English, whispered to them. "Are any of you James?"

One of them opened his eyes wider. "Who are you?" he said, in French.

"Colonel Richard Treadwell, of Mazarin's guard," I replied in English. "Are you wounded, sir?"

James looked at me for a moment, his long hair sweat-soaked and threaded through with hay. The English words followed, quietly and with hesitation. "I suffer no broken bones but my head is still hammering."

"If it's him," said d'Artagnan, "let's get out now!" He reached down and pushed the youth forward harshly, snipping his bonds in a trice and then sawing at the ropes that held James's bloodied ankles.

"And what of these fellows?" asked Andreas, already furtively looking over his shoulder. The half-dead man still lay unmoving while the other prisoner, agape at his turn of fate, had not yet uttered so much as a squeak.

"Free him," I said. "We shall deliver him as well. We leave the other to the mercy of God and the rebels." Andreas knelt down to cut the rough bindings as James tottered to his feet, his grip strong on my arm.

"I thought I was lost," he muttered, "but they don't know yet who I am. After they robbed me of my boots I was of no further interest."

"That is most fortunate, lad. For had they wrung the truth from you it's doubtful we'd be standing together now."

The tramping of feet upon the stairs froze my blood. Andreas snuffed out the lantern and backed into the room with d'Artagnan. I melted into a corner. A loud oath issued from a soldier as he walked into the door jamb and then into the room, cursing the darkness.

He may have been drink-addled, but he quickly sensed our presence and whirled to face me with a cry. Like a cat, d'Artagnan was upon him. His right arm hooked about the poor fellow's windpipe while he clapped his left hand over his mouth. I saw another shadow dart past—Andreas—who lifted the soldier's legs clear up. D'Artagnan and his opponent sank to the floor, a writhing heap of arms and legs which Andreas and I sought to pinion before the noise aroused the others downstairs. D'Artagnan had now managed to sit on the fellow's chest, his hand still clamped upon the man's face. A flash of silver and d'Artagnan's dagger descended. The man's strangled cries turned to a pig's squeal, but only for a moment. His legs shot out stiff in his death throes as the dagger found his heart.

We three leaned back from the corpse, regained our feet, and without a word, bundled our freed prisoners out of the chamber and down to the back of the house. Once out into the courtyard, we stopped.

"How do we find our way back with these two, half-naked and barefoot?" whispered d'Artagnan. He threw a quick look back towards the house as if we would be pursued at any moment. "In this moonlight we'll be spotted by the rebels quick as you like. We cannot return the way we came, that's for certain."

"*Schwartzer Peter*," said Andreas, half to himself, as if he had remembered something long since forgotten.

"Black Peter?" I asked. "What are you talking about?"

"The old tradition at the Feast of Saint Nicolas. Do you not remember, *Rikard*?"

He did not stay to explain but instead bolted back into the kitchen while the rest of us watched. Andreas reappeared in a few moments, his hands cupped together, bearing a dark substance.

"Soot!" he whispered as he reached our sides. "Get their shirts off and rub them down. Faces as well."

And then I remembered how in Germany at Christmas a blackened man would accompany Saint Nicolas, handing out sweetmeats—or a lump of coal—to the children. I understood what he had in mind. Sufficiently blackened to discourage all but the most sharp-eyed of rebels, we mounted a low wall at the back and fled to another courtyard and so on till we made the back alleys. And so, at length, and in the small hours, we crossed again the lines and to safety.

MAGGIE WAS LISTENING still, her eyes wide open in the dark, their whites all I could see of her. She had not interrupted me once since I had resumed my adventure, drinking in every detail of revelation. "So you saved the Duke of York! That was your worthy deed."

"When we finally returned to Mazarin, he said that he had sent us in search of a prince, not a blackamoor!"

"And what of your miraculous magic compass, then?"

"D'Artagnan returned it to the Cardinal, naturally. Not a word was mentioned."

"Convenient for your story, sir."

I shrugged. "A storyteller is allowed to embellish here and there, no?"

She was silent for a moment before she spoke again, her soft voice curiously on edge. "This French musketeer truly slew that poor soldier like a dog?"

"It had to be done that way, make no mistake, my dear. I beg you not to judge me on this business."

"*Monsieur* d'Artagnan strikes me as a rogue... I should like to make his acquaintance." She wrapped an arm about my chest. "If only to discover whether he looks as bad as he sounds."

I embraced her plump nakedness tightly and settled myself down in my pillow. I didn't have the courage to tell her that it was *my* dagger and *my* hand that had dispatched the unlucky rebel during my little adventure and not that of d'Artagnan. And as for the compass, better for her to believe it just an embellishment to my tale. So, even as I gave up some secrets, I wove lies to take their place.

Chapter Three

MY LORD MAZARIN, to give him his due, had outdone himself this night. I was holding up Marguerite as we stood in the balcony of the theatre behind the Louvre, watching what was unfolding below on the stage. We had been standing nearly six hours, having arrived at midnight to take our place among the other English exiles. It was now nearly dawn and the ballet was reaching its climax.

The performance told the story of the life of one night in the city, of the witches and demons that lurked in the darkness, of the mortals that struggled in the wee hours, and the arrival of Apollo and his cohorts to drive away the foul beasts and nightbanes. Marguerite had begun to lose interest after the departure of the frolicking werewolves at the witches' sabbath. For me, it was the play of light and fire, of cloud and rain which held me enraptured. Gods descended from above, moonbeams sprayed from out of clouds and spread across a starry sky that appeared from nothingness and hovered over the stage. Fire without smoke, rain without water, all was miracles. Marguerite's head popped up as the trumpets blasted, heralding the entry of Aurora and her handmaids to summon the day. And as the scenery parted, unaided by man, the goddess receded, beckoning a floating golden chariot upon which stood the young king of France himself. The sudden intake of breath of six hundred people, a collective moan of enchantment, drowned out the musicians who laboured below.

The king was dressed in cloth of gold, a golden breastplate strapped to his chest upon which the face of the sun was emblazoned. Sunbeams emanated from his neck, waist, and wrists and upon his flowing locks sat a magnificent tiara of golden rays a full yard in length. His face, painted gold, was fearless, and Louis descended the chariot as all bowed before him. And then the king danced. Without hesitation, without misstep, he moved to the strings of the viols, as dashing a figure and as fine a dancer as ever breathed, and he a boy of fourteen.

"By God, he's magnificent!" said Marguerite, gripping my arm as she stood on tiptoes to peer over the balcony rail. All around me the nodding heads of approval, the wide eyes of lords and ladies alike.

And then my gaze fell upon a group of spectators a few feet away: young Charles Stuart and his friends. And the look that was on my king's face was enough to bring tears from a stone. He was at that moment disarmed and transparent. I knew his thoughts as if he had cried them out for all to hear. His expression wasn't one of jealousy for his royal cousin, nor of anger for his own misfortune, but rather a look of such crestfallen weariness that he might die there as he stood. It was a knife to my heart to see the dark youth looking so terribly old and spent. His eyes drank in the vision of the bright Apollo before him, the rising dawn of France. Charles's flame seemed to wink and flicker, a poor tallow candle to the splendour of the sun.

"Do you not find Louis the most captivating man in this hall?" said Marguerite. "So handsome. So... regal. Well, isn't he?"

I was still distracted by my own monarch's distress. "He is hardly a *man*, my pigeon." I loosened her grip from my sleeve.

"Your eyes are misting over green, my love," she said. I watched the corners of her lovely mouth rise with mirth.

The ballet was ending in a crescendo of trumpets and the theatre exploded with applause and cries of "*Vive le Roi!*" But my attention was diverted as several men pushed their way through the crowd towards us. Quickly, I realized they were coming for me. And it was *Monsieur* d'Artagnan who was in the lead, a large tall-crowned charcoal beaver hat upon his head and dressed in a suit of grey velvet, a large blue sash across his chest. The lieutenant gave a flourish of his hand and touched the brim of his hat as he locked his gaze on Marguerite.

"*Madamoiselle,*" he said, bowing slightly. Then he turned his attention to me. "Colonel Treadwell, I hope you fare well and have enjoyed the dance?"

"Indeed, *monsieur*. We are all now basking in the warmth of the sunbeams of the king just as if it were a summer's morning."

He smiled again, but only to be polite. "I am come to say that His Eminence wishes to see you. At once."

"Then I shall not keep him waiting." I then felt Marguerite's hand clench my arm. I leaned in towards her. "I won't be gone long. We can take a saucer of *chocolat* together, no?"

"As you wish, my lord," she said, not convinced on either point.

"Fear not, Colonel," volunteered d'Artagnan. "I will escort your dear lady until your return."

I watched the crimson spread from her cheeks and down her neck like it was spilt wine. She gave reply in a quiet maiden's voice but with the steady eye of a hawk. "I would be grateful of your company, sir."

"Well then," I said, "where is His Eminence?"

I followed the guards down to the theatre floor and then down the stone steps of a torch-lit brick passage, down and around until we were in a subterranean world of grim machinery, more intricate than any clock tower. A dozen artisans, sleeves rolled, shirts undone, laboured to move little wagons set upon wooden rails that stretched the width of this dungeon. To these contraptions were fastened many ropes and pulleys and looking up I could see the slits cut across the stage floor. It soon became clear that this was the secret of the magic that unfolded above. These were the puppeteers that made the trees move and the heavens roil. And this was Mazarin's theatre. Despite the January chill above, it was damp and muggy below as we descended deep under the Louvre.

The passage, lit by torches, showed glistening walls that held dark alcoves on either side. The guards took me deeper down until the musty smell of a wine room filled my nostrils. At least it was not a dungeon—yet. We reached a large door, blackened with age and stinking of mould. The guard knocked once and I heard the command to enter.

"My dear Colonel!" said Mazarin, floating towards me. I stepped forward, briskly, bowing low and kissing the hand that was offered up.

"At your service, Eminence!"

We were in a large vaulted chamber; barrels of wine carefully stacked on massive racks surrounded us. The Cardinal raised me up by both hands. "It has been some time since we last conversed, has it not? I now find myself in need of your advice." He turned to usher me a few steps into one of the storage rooms that lay off the main chamber. "You may wait outside," he said to the sergeant behind me.

There was a rude table and chairs in the room but little else. Two lamps threw out a weak circle of orange light across the room. Mazarin spread his red skirts and gently seated himself.

"Forgive these surroundings, please, but you will of course understand the need for secrecy."

"Of course, Eminence." This was undoubtedly going to be grim.

"I've heard tell that my English royal exiles at the palace grow fractious. Or so my informants say. It would seem that young Charles's chancellor, Mister Hyde, finds himself struggling to keep the king's confidence."

His purpose was clear. I was here to be squeezed like an apple in a press. "Eminence," I began, trying to ease my way out of his grasp, "I'm afraid I do not have the confidence of the exile circles. I remain outside counsel."

Mazarin slowly shook his head. "Come, my dear Colonel, you do yourself no credit. Surely you observe more than that."

"I will say that in the court hope runs as scarce as daily bread, sir. That's no secret. And hungry, hopeless men are wont to squabble."

"And to plot, no?"

"Perhaps, Eminence, but not that I am privy to," I said, thanking the Lord that it was permissible to lie to a Papist.

"Well, at least Charles must be happy to have his brother back safe and sound. Thanks to your good work. His gratitude involved a knighthood for you. No small mark of trust."

"I am still but an ordinary soldier, Eminence. Not an advisor."

"Colonel," Mazarin said, worrying his crucifix in his hands, "I have kept you away from your regiment for some time now, have I not? You have the liberty to walk the Louvre for a reason. That reason being to inform me of the goings on in the English court. Do not dissemble with me or I'll have you in the trenches at Arras trading shots with the Spanish before the week is out."

"Your Grace, there is no grand plot, of that I'm certain. But there is complaint in good measure. Some of the exiles, Herbert and Gerard to name two, are agitating for some action in England. But Chancellor Hyde is of the opinion that this is a fruitless endeavour."

"And is it?"

The game was growing dangerous. I had balanced for a very long time between Mazarin and my own king but now I was on the verge of falling over into the French camp for good. I thought as quickly as I could of a way to smooth the Cardinal's feathers.

"All reports bear the same sad tune," I said. "There is no leader in England to unite the remnants of the king's supporters, and any plan to rise up doesn't stay secret for long under Cromwell's watchful eye. The Scots are useless and Hyde realises this now too."

The Cardinal nodded but I knew he was unconvinced. For more than a passing moment there was silence. I thought he might be weighing my words, deciding whether or not I was lying to him. But something else entirely was on his mind. "Colonel, I am questioning you for a reason... a delicate but serious threat may be arising among the English. And it is not an ordinary threat to the state but rather something more sinister."

"Eminence, surely the exiles present no threat to the French crown," I said, voice quavering. "It's hardly in their interest."

"I am using the word sinister in its truest sense."

I shook my head in ignorance. "Begging your pardon, Eminence, I am a little tired—"

"There is someone here you must meet. Someone who carries alarming intelligence." Mazarin barked to one of the guards outside the cramped room. "You may bring him in now!"

I took half a step backwards as a black-robed monk glided into our presence.

"Colonel Treadwell, this is Brother Anselm of the Benedictines of Saint Edmunds."

The monk drew back his cowl. He looked to be something over fifty years, with a round face and tired, hooded eyes that made him appear permanently penitent. His thick curly hair, yellowy white, looked like the backside of a sheep, straw and all. Dealing with one priest was bad enough but what news could this bedraggled cleric be carrying? I bowed curtly and watched as he studied me.

"At your service, Brother Anselm."

He said nothing in reply but moved closer towards me, never taking his eyes from me. And when he was before my face, he spoke—in English with the broad accent of a Lancashire man.

"Yes. You can truly see them. Indeed, you *have* seen them, that is clear to me now." He was nodding as he stared. Quickly, he turned to the Cardinal, speaking in flawless French. "Your instinct was correct, Eminence—as usual."

I knew exactly what he was speaking of. What bothered me was that the Cardinal appeared to have an inkling of my past experiences as well. I had never told him about my adventures during the German wars, nor of my glimpses there into dark places. That I could see the ghosts of men I had only ever confided to a few. It was no gift. More a curse. A touch that only certain others could sniff out on me—like that gypsy seeress had all those years ago.

I looked at Mazarin and it was clear he sensed my growing unease.

"Brother Anselm is the astrologer of *my* astrologer," he said. "As such, when he comes to tell me that the English are playing games with the Devil, I listen."

"I don't understand, Eminence."

"You will. Brother Anselm, tell the Colonel what you told me two days ago."

Anselm folded his hands together, close to his chest. "I have told His Eminence that I have drawn up charts for General Cromwell and for Charles Stuart. Once I had calculated these projections I drew them again... to be sure I had made no errors."

"What are you saying, sir?" I said.

Brother Anselm blinked and pursed his lips. "A calamity is soon to happen. Someone is about to unleash a great evil into the world. They will do this to affect the affairs of state and all men. The alignments are clear to me."

"And you're saying that Oliver Cromwell or Charles Stuart are intriguing with the Devil to win their war for England? Charles is above reproach and as for Cromwell, though Lord knows he is no friend of mine, he's convinced himself he's doing God's work and not the Devil's. It's laughable to say one or the other is involved in the black arts."

Brother Anselm shook his head. "I do not say that either man is the agent of this evil. That could be the case or it could be that there are those close to them that are invoking the Dark One. But I am not wrong in what I say—a powerful man is trying to change his fortune by other means."

Mazarin spoke up from his chair, his voice like a blast of icy wind. "Colonel Treadwell, you had better listen well to this because I am in no doubt. One of your countrymen is planning on opening a door that should remain forever shut. I mean to find out who that is and put a stop to it."

I stammered. "But... Eminence, what am I to do with all this?"

The Cardinal leaned forward and fixed me with a basilisk's glare. "I know that you possess a skill for finding the Underworld like a pig finds truffles. There is no one in my employ better than you to find out if this Satanist is among the exiles here in Paris. Once I can rule out the English court then I can decide what to do about General Cromwell and his faction. But I will have intelligence and I will have it soon."

"You can be our *compass*, sir, our lodestone to find these men," offered up Anselm.

I bowed to the Cardinal. "Very well, Your Eminence."

"The king needs to know what his royal cousin is up to and you are now in a situation amenable to that end. Do not fail in your duty to your king."

And it was plainly evident which king he meant. Mazarin slowly lifted his hand and at first I thought he wanted me to help him rise. But I realised it was the proffered hand of a holy Cardinal and I kneeled quickly and touched my lips to his cold claw.

I was dripping with sweat as I left the room, the Cardinal's guard eyeing me as I slowly walked back towards the stone staircase. An English voice behind me brought me round. Brother Anselm had followed me out of the room, one hand lifting the skirt of his robes so he could catch me up.

"Colonel Treadwell! A word, sir!" He drew close and put a

hand on my arm. "This is a dangerous errand you have been given. I'm sorry that I cannot give you better direction on finding who is behind this sorcery. Alas, that is the nature of divination—never as precise as one would want."

I must have flashed him a weak smile. "Direction? You've given me no help at all other than to say he's one of us. Tell me... how did you come to be so far from Preston?"

He smiled back. "Aye, a long way from the North that is true. Most of us at Saint Edmunds are English these days. My lord Cromwell has driven most of our faith into hiding or over here. Listen, I can't offer you much of use, I know. But remember that the enemy will be cunning and well-disguised. Maybe even godly in their ways. They will kill rather than be exposed."

I nodded.

"And one more thing. If they are successful, and they open some portal to summon infernal aid to their earthly cause, they may not be able to control what they bring forth. You know of what I speak."

I swallowed but did not answer.

"God be with you, Colonel."

I DISCOVERED D'ARTAGNAN and Marguerite arm-in-arm and conversing in earnest amongst the remaining theatregoers as they jostled to reach the great doors. I took a deep breath to regain myself.

"Your dear lady has been a source of delight, Colonel," said the musketeer as he lifted her hand to present her back to my care. "She has told me of her favourite scenes and I confess admiration that she in no way fades after such a rigorous spectacle. I'll miss her company, sir."

I looked into Marguerite's flushed face.

"Your audience was a fruitful one, I trust?" asked d'Artagnan.

"We discussed the Arras campaign," I said, drawing Marguerite's cloak closer about her shoulders as I propelled her ahead of me.

The musketeer's bronzed face opened into a full-toothed grin. "Perhaps our Spanish problem will have an English solution."

"Farewell, friend," I told him as I saluted with a touch to my brim. "I am sure we'll see each the other at the Cardinal's next play, and in short time."

Marguerite's heels clopped unsteadily across the cobbles as I held her arm through mine. She let out a sigh. "Richard, I would rather you escort me to my rooms. I am fully spent after such a conversation with *Monsieur* d'Artagnan. He has fair talked me to death, I think. A most intense gentleman. He has quite left me breathless."

I was saddened that I would not now have her to distract me from my darker thoughts, thoughts that now crept up fast on me. Mazarin was not a man to be easily fobbed off and would expect more than just a mean morsel—he desired meat. And so I took her to her apartments and then made my way into the freezing streets again, to a coffee house. Paris was roiling with the late morning swarm of sedan chairs and their huffing bearers, swearing drovers, footmen, and vendors bundled in their cloaks against the chill like corpses in shrouds. I blew inside the nearest establishment and finding a place on a bench apart from others, the bitter drink of the Turkmen soon warmed my bones and began to enliven me.

And then the Beast came.

Like a kettle filling with water, I could feel it rising up within me. And, as before, I knew there was nothing I could do to stop it. Welling up inside me was the most overwhelming sensation of cold sickening dread. My hands started to shake, my heart raced, and I drew breath as if I was being chased by a legion of monsters. I could feel the sweat dripping down my face. In a few moments, the sickness had embraced me in its terrible arms. I hunched over the table, hands cupped tightly about my drink, and tried to summon all my will to master the fear that was washing over me. It was all I could do to hold on.

It was my dreadful secret, one I had yet to share even with my Marguerite. I had faced Croats, Germans, Poles, Cromwell's

Ironsides, and Spaniards, all without flinching. When battle surrounded me, I revelled in the noise and clash, never once turning tail. But this curse, this unseen creature that pounced on me without warning, it froze me like a terrified lamb. The beast could strike for hours—or minutes. It had started only a few years before. And since then, it came again and again, every few months, even when nothing was troubling me. But I knew this time what had brought it upon me.

My jaw clenched as I stared into the Turkish brew. And suddenly, someone behind called out my name. With his usual habit of surprise, Andreas Falkenhayn was suddenly there in front of me, his churchyard cough echoing and raising heads. It was never lost upon me just how strange that we two, companions in some twenty seasons of campaign, were now again united under a common paymaster: the Cardinal. I had made his acquaintance in the German wars fighting under the Danish king when I was a lad new to soldiering. I latched onto Andreas and he made sure I stayed alive. If I was now around forty-and-six years old, God alone knew how old Andreas was.

"*Rikard*! You old bastard," he croaked. "I had given up hope that you would ever visit again whilst I drew breath."

I could already feel the Beast retreating, loosening its claws from me. "By God, you look like you've been whoring and drinking again," I said as he sat down on the bench next to me. In truth, he looked drawn, grey-faced, and very, very weary.

A rumbling laugh welled up from his chest, seasoned with a goodly amount of phlegm. "I suppose my looks give away my night-time frolics. And, well, I've slowed a bit since our adventures last summer. But, hey, what's this? You look not well either, my friend."

"It's nothing," I said. "Born of drinking coffee too quickly. But you, you're in need of a physician. Has the good widow not summoned someone to see to you?"

"Bah, there's little any barber surgeon can do that the goodwife hasn't tried already. I'll right myself by April."

The more he prattled the quicker the Beast fled me. Restored, I told him the tale of my conversation with our common patron and that I was to spy upon the house of Stuart for the Cardinal. But I left out any mention of the true quest I had been given: to find out whether King or Parliament was entreating with the Devil. He shook his head slowly and said, "You'll find yourself taking fire from both sides, *Rikard*. You'd better play this one with care."

"I know that, friend, and I think I would rather take my chances against the Spanish at Arras. At least there the musket balls come from just *one* direction."

"Surely there's some empty scrap of intelligence you could offer up, as it were."

"Not this time. The Cardinal has other spies at work in the court and he will quickly put to the test any fables I invent for him."

The Cardinal would need his report. Yet, perhaps I might buy some time to figure out my course of action. The two chief factions at the court, those gathered about Sir Edward Hyde, the more cautious lot, and those gathered about Lord Herbert, the king's Attorney-General, calling themselves the Swordsmen, had been angling to gain my support for months now. Perhaps it was time to show more interest.

"There's a damned good reason I've kept my head this long," said Andreas. "And that's because I don't commit myself to anything before I've reached the dregs of the cup. By that time, the path forward is usually clear."

"Even if one's head is not," I remarked, smiling at the old soldier. And I was dead tired, tired before my work had even begun.

Chapter Four

"WHAT SAY YOU, Colonel? Are you game?" Lord Herbert had just refilled my cup for the second time. He retook his seat and watched me, his rheumy old eyes narrowing, eager for my answer.

"A *promised* uprising in the West Country is about as good as a promise of payment from a pauper," I said. "Unlikely to ever happen and too late if it does."

"I told you not to waste time with this mercenary," said Herbert's companion. "He's managing well enough. He has a feather bed and someone to warm it for him."

I was too old and too hardened to rise to the bait on that one. I merely smiled and raised my cup. "You have not laid out a strategy, gentlemen, only a prayer."

Baron Gerard, a fire-eater who was at least ten years younger than me, neither liked nor trusted me. "Don't lecture me on strategy, sir. I speak of duty. I was in the saddle at Worcester, clouting Roundheads. But I don't recall *your* presence there."

Lord Herbert tut-tutted and shook his head in an attempt to calm the waters. "Give Sir Richard his due, my lord. He has done great service to the Crown."

They had revealed to me a plan to rise up simultaneously in Devon and London in the coming summer, the West Country rising to begin a week before the one in the capital, the better to lure Cromwell's regiments away from the city. Even so, it seemed to me less a plan and more wishful thinking. Ensconced in Lord Gerard's chambers, away from prying eyes and ears, these two had shown me that Mazarin was correct in his suspicions that the Swordsmen were quite willing to have another go at Mister Cromwell. But nothing I had picked up in the last few weeks had led me to a supposed circle of courtiers doing the work of the Devil under the noses of King Charles and his all-knowing mother. I was in danger of failing Mazarin's mission, and now, here I was being handed another fool's errand.

Gerard wrenched a chair back and plumped himself at the table, leaning in towards me. "My kinsman John waits in London even now, drawing more numbers to him. We need more old campaigners such as you to stiffen the spine in the west. This thing can be done, sir. Every report we receive tells us the country is ready to rise against the Tyrant."

I did admire Gerard. He, like me, had served in exile with the French under General Turenne. He spoke from experience hard-earned and fought. He was no idle fop. Yet even so, talk of rising was a forlorn hope—and I had finished with that a long time ago.

"How many men do you have between Exeter and Plymouth?" I asked him.

"Three hundred thereabouts. We have arms and can seize powder at will when the time is right." Gerard's eyes seemed to get bigger as he spoke. He was convinced of the moment, but he, unlike me, still burned with the Faith.

I sighed heavily at the woeful number. "This plan succeeds only where the blow falls in both west and east. You don't have enough men to fight the whole army. Timing is balanced on a knife edge. If too soon or too late, one or the other attack will fail."

Gerard's hand came down on the table, spilling the wine. His long handsome face, unblemished despite his many battles, shone with a determination that shamed me. "We don't have to defeat the whole of the army! The feint in the West will draw out enough troopers for us to take London. When that pin falls, the others will quickly follow."

Lord Herbert nodded. "We have a strong chance. The whole country is like a rotten apple. It only has to be cut open to reveal its corruption."

I then asked what had to be asked. "And what does His Majesty say to this enterprise?"

The pause, short though it was, told all.

"The king trusts in us to regain the kingdom," said Herbert. "But others prefer to sit upon their arses or talk of wishful purpose with the Dutch."

"So, Chancellor Hyde does not know your plan either," I said quietly.

Lord Gerard leaned back into his chair like a scolded schoolboy, his face in a sulk. "We thought you would see the world as we do—like a soldier. One who understands what must be done to set things to right again. But I perceive in this I was mistaken."

Lord Herbert was not so quick to give up on me. "Colonel, Hyde and his ilk are content to stay here until we all rot—or the French throw us out. Time is not with us, sir. We must act and soon, lest the folk come to believe their king has forgotten them."

I lifted up my head and looked him in the eye. "I shall not speak for the king but *I* have not forgotten them. I left my wife and my children—lost all that I possessed—to fight Cromwell. After Naseby, they banished me, but my family suffer in Devon still. I'll not hazard their lives in a new folly against the Parliament. You failed at Worcester in open battle—fairly fought. The next will bring much the same result. And more death, and want, and woe for those who resist." And I regretted the words even as they flew from my lips.

"If I had known that you believe the Cause is lost, I would not have shared my confidence," said Herbert. "I am heartily sorry for it."

Gerard stood. As far as he was concerned, the business was at an end. "Don't waste your breath. He's a beaten man... as I told you."

I rose, staring him down. "I have been to places and grappled with things that you have only glimpsed in your nightmares. I choose my own battles these days, sir," I hissed. "And I have suffered a bellyful of lost causes."

Gerard shook his head in disdain. "You're broken."

How could I even have begun to tell him I have spoken with the ghosts of men?

A WEEK PASSED. A week in which I contemplated throwing my lot in with Hyde and the other arse-sitters, in which I dreaded the arrival of a summons from Mazarin, and in which I very nearly returned to the regimental barracks to hide, besotted in drink. My dear Maggie, she who I could open my heart to, I spared the worry and the secrets. She knew I was distracted, but wouldn't press the matter even as she tried to comfort me. Yet, I suspected that she had guessed the cause of my strife. It could be timed to the moment I had met the Cardinal in his wine cellars. And so, I had finally arrived at that dark, deathly quiet place where no one in the world is to be trusted.

A summons arrived for me. But it was not from Mazarin even though it was brought by a runner from the Cardinal's regiment. He had found me at the barracks after asking for me in the Louvre. The lad, his face nearly purple from the cold and the brutal run through the streets, doffed his hat and gushed out the message in between gulps of air. "Sir... Captain Delacroix begs... that you come with me at once. Major Falkenhayn is gravely ill. He... the German, is asking for you."

When we reached the door to his house, I saw two dragoons standing nearby. I was halfway up the staircase to his chamber when the smell filled my nostrils. Sweet and metallic, it could have been a butcher's shop. I saw a figure sprawled upon the bed, hands clenched into the coverlet that loosely covered him. Captain Delacroix, a young officer of Mazarin's horse, touched my forearm as I stood in the threshold. "*Monsieur*, he lives yet... just. He has asked for you."

"Where is the surgeon?" I asked. The only other person who stood in the room was the old widow who owned the place, silent and expressionless.

"He left hours ago. It is God's will now... and the Major's."

My boots echoed harsh on the floorboards as I approached the bedside. Several candles burned, giving more illumination than when I had last visited. This time, I wished they had been extinguished to spare me the sight. Andreas was quietly gasping, fighting to take breath. His mottled face was puffed up badly, his eyes almost started from out his head. In all our adventures together, never had I seen him look so full of terror. And I had seen him blown off a rampart, beaten senseless by brigands, shot through, facing a hundred of the enemy with a smile of resignation. But I had never seen him like this.

I leaned over him. "Sweet Jesus, dear Andreas!"

"*Rikard*. I can't breathe." Andreas's words came out as a wheeze and the stench of death was already upon him. He released the coverlet and tried to grasp my arm, the bloodied bandages unwinding as he flailed. I pulled in a chair, sat, and gripped his hand. It felt like a cold slab of mutton, and slowly he tried a feeble press in return.

"I beg you," he whispered, and I leaned in to gather his words. "Help me... *Rikard*. Give me air..."

Andreas was giving battle, but how could he fight an enemy he could not see? And I, sitting there, a watcher only, was as helpless as any mortal who had seen Death lay hands on the chosen. No clever plan, no ruse, no entreaty would forestall the harvest of this poor soul. And few words of comfort could come to my mind. I told him to lie still, be at peace. I asked him if he could take a sip of strong water. Yet, I could not still his trembling, for all my soothing phrases.

Andreas turned his face towards me, his head lifting off the pillow. The cords of his neck strained as he fought for his voice. "I'm so frightened! Sweet Christ... I am alone!"

And my heart ached as I heard myself tell him to be brave, to trust in God. Those words rang hollow in my ears. And then he heaved his chest, fighting to gain breath. Alarmed, I rose, still clenching his hand. I heard him suck in another breath, rasping as he did so. He was suffocating as I watched.

"Not... like this," he whispered, his head shaking such that his knit cap slipped off upon the pillow.

A black-robed figure came across the foot of the bed and crossed to the far side, standing next to Andreas. It was a priest. As the old soldier caught sight of the man, he started as if he had seen an apparition. The priest kept up his cadence, the Latin quietly and firmly streaming forth from his lips. I saw him bend down and place a crucifix in Andreas's right hand.

I tried to calm my old friend, touching his shoulder, but it was to no avail. At my back, I heard one or two soldiers enter the room. The smell of the piss-soaked bed wafted strongly even as the prayers of the priest gained strength, his arm waving over Andreas in the sign of the cross. The priest leaned over, asking Andreas if he had confessed his sins.

"Tell me," said the young beardless priest, soft but insistent.

I took a few steps backwards from the delivery of the final sacrament, but even so, I know that Andreas confessed nothing, only shaking his head. Whether he took this as a confession or not, the priest shook the oil from his little phial and anointed Andreas's brow, then slowly, each hand. I heard him intone some prayer. When the priest had finished the prayer, all remaining in the chamber said an "amen." And so, too, did I.

Of his last words, I know not. He mumbled to himself for a

few moments and seemed not to be aware I was there anymore. Just before the end, I saw him fix his eyes on me. His lips moved but no words came forth. It was a look that shook me to my bones, a silent plea for rescue from what was carrying him far and away. My hand moved to cover my brow but a moment in grief, and when I again looked down, he was gone. I stood there for a time, very numb and very cold.

The regiment buried Andreas the next day. And as I walked from the churchyard, the thoughts whirled about: what did Fate hold for me? Dying an old man in my bed, gasping, drenched in piss and sweat? My lot was no different than that of Andreas. A few years away maybe, that was true, but my ship was on the very same course. And those same shoals of Death that he had foundered upon were looming fast for me. That wasn't the way I planned on leaving this world for the next. I had to steer a new course, one that didn't involve unmasking those in league with the Devil. I did not want to go down that path again. And maybe, maybe there was a way.

LORD HERBERT WAS curt but polite. "My lord Gerard has no wish to meet with you, Colonel. I am sorry."

"Well," I said, "I can't blame him for that. I acted the knave when we last met."

We walked together in the Tuileries, the bare branches of the pear trees rattling in the late winter air. The old man offered me no comfort.

"We misjudged your intentions, sir, which are most clear. So what further business can we possibly have?"

"I won't mince my words. I am your man for the West."

Herbert stopped short and turned to me. "Surely a jest, sir?"

"I am in deadly earnest, sir. I've reconsidered."

His head swivelled about, looking to see what other people strolled the gardens. "Your contrary nature does not give me confidence. And I doubt very much that Lord Gerard would consider your recruitment after you made yourself so plain before."

I nodded as I drew in a deep breath of cold air, tinged, even in winter's embrace, with the stink of the Seine. "That may be true. But I am the man for the West and my lord Gerard knows the soldier I am. If anyone can accomplish this miracle it is I. There is no one else at court who can do this deed."

"You are an artful adventurer, Sir Richard. That I give you. But the others may have their doubts."

"Then there is yet one more reason. I won't cost you a single shilling. I shall undertake this mission with my own resources. Soldiering in the service of the Cardinal pays well and I have little to spend the money on."

Lord Herbert pulled his cassock closer about his shoulders as a stiff gust rocked us, whiffling the brims of our hats. "That's a bold change of heart, sir. One that does not sit well with me."

I shrugged off his caution. "My regiment moves north in a matter of weeks—or less. If I'm to fly the nest it will have to be sooner than later, before orders are received. I am ready to leave the moment you give the word."

Herbert's hand reached out and touched my wrist. "Steady on, sir, steady on. Even if Gerard agrees—and I am in no certainty of that—you must receive instruction. There is the matter of contacts, of ciphers, of places of rendezvous... you'll have need of a travelling name."

I looked Lord Herbert square in the eye. "I am no stranger to these things, of that be assured. As for a name and a story, I have that too."

His eyebrows arched. "Have you now?"

"Call me Andreas Falkenhayn, wool merchant of Flanders."

"A foreigner? The redcoats will seize you in an instant. No, that would not do at all."

"The moment Richard Treadwell sets foot in England," I said, my voice as low as I could make it, "he's as good as dead if he is discovered. That was the bargain—if ever I returned,

Cromwell will hang me. So be it. I understood the terms of my banishment, then as now. I'm not afraid to return but by God I will give myself a fighting chance."

Herbert, flustered, strove to find the words. "But a Fleming? What... what will that accomplish?"

"Not a Fleming, a German. I speak the tongue well. A suit of clothes, the right hat, I grow my beard long, that is the trick," I said.

"The trick to draw attention to yourself, more like. Who is this Falkenhayn?"

"*This* Falkenhayn, my lord, is an arrow speeding to the heart of the Tyrant. I ask you to draw the bow and send it on its way."

Lord Herbert looked ahead again and began walking, a slow, measured pace. But he said nothing. I stood my ground there on the path and presently he noticed I was not at his side. He stopped and did a half turn to see what held me back.

"If our business is to conclude here," I said, "then it is to be now. Done and dusted, sir. I am the only one who will answer this call to arms and that you know already. Make me your instrument."

Lord Herbert looked at me and then off into the trees. "It is not for me alone to decide." He turned fully, facing me. "Why then, this change of heart, Sir Richard? Surely it was not Gerard's youthful taunts against your honour?"

I smiled. "It was not Lord Gerard. The example of a far older comrade has shown me my error. Unlike him, I still have the time to put things to right."

"And if your offer of aid is refused, what then?" said Herbert. "Will you sulk off to fight the Spanish instead?"

I slowly closed the ground between us, hands thrust in the pockets of my breeches. "No," I said quietly, "That was a lie. I think you know that I will go to England, just the same."

And Herbert's look of utter disarm was proof that he believed me too.

*　　*　　*

BUT THERE REMAINED one problem, one entirely divorced from the scheming of the Swordsmen. It was not my fear of how Mazarin would take the news of my sudden departure. I penned the resignation of my command knowing his fury would be swift at my failure to discover the Devil's pawn among the exiles. God willing, he wouldn't discover my absence until I was out of France. To further throw his hounds off the scent I let slip my intention to go to Sweden once again for employment as I had done years before. He was too crafty to swallow this whole so I sweetened the cake by making arrangements to send off a chest containing some worthless belongings by way of coach to an inn at Cologne, on the road to Stockholm. I was sure that distrustful musketeer, Lieutenant d'Artagnan, would quickly look for such arrangements, thereby buying myself a little more time to escape.

No, the problem was my mistress. She was far too sharp a pin to be fooled so easily as the Cardinal. Of my plans to fight the Spaniards, lavishly embellished by my yearning for the saddle, Marguerite drenched these with scorn. She knew that my regiment was staying put around Paris for the time to safeguard the king and she called me the bigger fool for thinking she would believe such a shallow ruse. So I changed tack, telling her that I would be going farther afield, to Germany, Denmark and Sweden, to find my comrades of old. She, better than anyone else, knew how the death of Andreas had shaken me. But this too fell upon stony ground and was met with a shriek of desperate outrage.

"You would leave me the discarded whore then?" She shook her head as if to answer the question herself. "No, you shall not buy me off with such a tale either, my love. There's more to this change of heart than mere soldiering, I swear." And she paused a moment, her eyes big and wet, before turning away. But then she turned back, looking at me hard. "You're returning to England. That's your clever plan, isn't it? But why?"

I stammered that she was wrong but she cut me off with an accusing finger.

"No! I shall guess it, sir. I shall puzzle it out, for I know your heart better than you do." And then a slow, grim smile crept onto her plump face, now bright pink with anger. "You're going *home*. You're going home to Devon. To find your wife and children." She was nodding now, and quickly closing the ground between us as we stood in her little bedroom. "*Memento mori*. That's why you've acted the baited bear these last days."

I could say nothing, and the colours fluttered down from my mast.

"You would leave me here alone to this drudgery," she said, "with my father returning in a few weeks to find I have been carrying on with you?"

"It's time for me to go home again, Maggie. That's the truth of it. And I don't know what I shall find there."

She seized me hard by the arm. "What you shall find? You shall find the end of a rope! You've told me that many times before. How could you think of such a mad adventure? You're no longer some mooncalf of a boy."

I moved to touch her cheek and she slapped my hand away.

"No emollients, sir! Your path is chosen and you're abandoning me to the laughter of the magpies here at court. And to face the shame of my father—alone." Those brown eyes had a strange glow, high-stoked rage and adoration mixed, enough to unsettle me. At that moment, she was poised to offer either a curse or a kiss.

I took her by the shoulders and gave her a shake as she tried to twist away from my embrace. "It is you who has my heart and no one else, woman! But I must return while there is still time to do so." Marguerite ceased her twisting but would not look at me. "There are things that must be done there, things that cannot wait."

"Then I shall travel with you."

"It's not safe there for you."

"And it's safe enough for you? You speak nonsense. Was it not you who told me before Christmas that the people would grow tired of Parliament's edicts and Cromwell's roar? 'Spit them out', you said. So wait!" She moved her hands to my neck. "Wait upon it, my love."

"I cannot. This must be done. But I promise you I will return." And I could feel her form sink inside my arms, the fight gone out of her.

"Then go if you must," she said, her voice steady. "But just as you know not what waits for you in England, you will not know what awaits you here when you return. Nothing in this life is certain except its ending."

Chapter Five

AT SEA, THERE'S time for contemplation even when the weather blows hard, lifting a vessel high and shaking it like some enormous mastiff would a rabbit. At times, I wondered if my life's labour would have been more rewarding had I become a sailor. Now, with little to do all day or night on the four day journey from France to the Devon coast, my time for quiet reflection was double-fold. And I had put it to good use, wrapped in a thick woollen cloak in my tiny cabin, kept company by a little tin carrying stove, stuffed with glowing coals from the forecastle galley fire.

The list of secret contacts that Lord Herbert had given me, I still worked to commit to memory, so too the false names that each was assigned for the purpose of corresponding. Herbert became 'Mr. Carson', Baron Gerard's cousin, Colonel John Gerard (already burrowed into London town) was 'Mr. Jeffreys' while the king himself was always referred to as 'Mr. Underhill'.

All the king's ciphers had each been broken in turn these last two years by Parliament men in the Post Office. It seemed pointless to tempt them again with yet another code, mathematical or otherwise. Ciphers or not, I had little faith in a letter ever ending up in rightful hands and so I resolved to pen not a single word to my co-conspirators.

Staring out of the leaded window of the stern cabin, its panes crusted with salt spray, the roiling grey sky and even darker sea moved in and out of view. Why in Christ's name was I undertaking such a foolhardy lark? The chance to smite Cromwell was the bait, but something else drove me as well.

I had never been much of a husband, I admit. Returning from the German wars I had married in haste, eager to become the man of commerce to equal my older brother William. But the war with Parliament had quickly put an end to that dream. I had foolishly penned a letter to friends in the Danish court at the insistence of the king's advisors, suggesting the Danes aid us against Parliament. Intercepted after the battle at Naseby, it was enough to crucify me. The trial by combat was my plan, but had it not been for my brother's help to get the army to agree to it, I would be dead by now. As dead as the king I had served.

For the last eight years, I had been pulled back and forth in the swirling currents of Mazarin's many fights in France, losing sight of all back in Devon. I had to return, to see once again those I had abandoned. I still did not know what I could do to alleviate my wife's suffering, though I was carrying a fat purse to deliver to her. But I would not be able to reveal my presence. Would my children even remember me?

Having beat our way up the Channel, clawing against wind and tide along the Normandy coast, we turned about and dashed northwards across to Plymouth. We made landfall on the twentieth of March and for the first time in many, many years, my eyes beheld the green of the Hoe and the rolling countryside beyond against a blue sky. We pushed along nicely under near full sail, whitecaps breaking all around, and slowly the land became larger and rich in relief. The spires of Plymouth hove into view and then the warehouses of the quayside down at Sutton's Pool.

It was only then that the practical concern of disappearing unseen into England came uppermost to my mind. I had taken what precautions I could: I carried no sword (only a small Scottish dirk) and wore no heavy boots, but instead, shoes and grey stockings. My dress was sober, my linen of Flanders lace. My hat, except for its black ribbon, was high-crowned and plain. My belongings were few and carried in a large sack: more clothing, a few small German books, and my copybook for my trade. All unremarkable, or so I hoped.

Slow headway around the old barbican, and then a gentle glide into the harbour. We touched in with just a bit of foresail and nudged by a lighter that stood at hand to help. And in short time I was down over the side, gingerly onto the dock, and finally once again on English soil. The first countryman to address me there was a Plymouth militiaman, sullen and stinking of stale beer.

"You—old man! Where is your pass?"

A group of redcoats, more militiamen by the look of them, also stood nearby, gathered around the master of the ship. And the officer, papers waving in his hand, hollered down to my interrogator.

"He's a trader from Bruges, you dolt! Let him pass!"

The militiaman waved back, cursing the officer as he did so. He turned to me and handed back my satchel that he had snatched. "Well, so long as you're not Dutch... sod off then. Go on, be off."

I nodded and walked on up the quayside and towards the cobbled square that led towards the Exeter Road. I watched a troop of dragoons enter from the other side, no doubt on their way to the quay, their mounts in a slow walk. Without a second thought, I moved closer to the houses, away from the centre, but did not alter my pace. My eyes instantly set upon the officer who led the dragoons. What struck me was how very young he was. He was hatless, and his close-cropped straw-coloured hair and deathly pale complexion made his eyes all the more blue, large and penetrating. He affected no beard or moustache; his shirt collar lay open even in the stiff March air. Unlike his troopers, dressed in their claret kersey wool coats, this man wore a sombre grey suit and black cassock, his figure made military solely by his large brown riding boots, pulled up high to his thighs, and his buff shoulder belt from which swung a good-sized sword.

I watched his face as we drew closer, about to pass on the square. There was something familiar in it, though I knew well we could never have crossed paths. Surely he would have been just a stripling when I fought at Naseby those years gone by. I felt that I *ought* to know him, and before I could help myself, I realised that I was staring. And then, his eyes met mine, only for a few seconds, before I turned my head down. It was long enough. He continued on, but the glance had near upon stopped my heart. I winced as the dangling silver talisman in my shirt caught and plucked a chest hair.

I was afraid to turn around and kept walking up out of the square to where I remembered Breton Side was, the better to find an inn. Plymouth had changed little in appearance from my vantage, the brown and black houses and streets and stables all the same. But the townsmen were not as I remembered. Their faces were pinched as they went about their business; a fug seemed to hang over all, a weariness that had sapped the place of its life. Over all there was a heavy silence. And Breton Side should have been a scene of bedlam, whores beckoning sailors to their arms. But there were none to be seen.

By the time I reached the lolling shingle of the Bell and Tun, I was more confused than when I had stepped off my ship. I pushed the door inwards and stepped inside the tavern's front room: low, dark, and hazy with blue smoke, which suited me well enough. The place was as lively as a funeral. I spied a few townsmen at the large table, smoking and drinking their beer. Near to the fire, a few sailors joked and sipped their rum. The scent of their salt-drenched jackets carried to me even across the room. This would do.

After I procured from the landlord a room the size of a cupboard, I shifted my little doglock pistol in the waist belt that lay underneath my coat. Downstairs, I took a can of ale and sat myself in the back to take in my surroundings and puzzle out what I should do next. As I walked past a wall, I caught a glimpse of myself in a little reflecting glass hanging there. My whiskered face, black haired and streaked with grey, stared back at me. It was a far cry from the neat little mustachios and chin fluff I had worn at the court in Paris. The ale soothed my fears by the time I had drunk down the last swig and the innkeeper, keen as always to pick up something new, engaged me when he refilled the cup.

"Just come in have you... from afar?"

I again tried to sound just foreign enough to a Devon man's ear to make the ruse but not come across as too much a queer duck. "In from France, yes. I hope to find some good merchants here to supply me in Worsted yarns."

The innkeeper nodded as he poured the bitter stuff from the jug. "You sound farther afield than France, I might say, though I admit you make good enough of the English tongue."

"I am German," I said.

"Aye, that would s'plain it, it would. Fancy some grub? I've got some roast pig that's up. And you'd consider yourself damn'd lucky to taste it after ship's fare, I should think."

"Perhaps later. Tell me," I asked before he could shuffle off again, "where is all the trade gone today? I expected to see more by way of commerce since coming into Plymouth."

"Where has all the trade gone?" he said with genuine surprise. "Probably where all the fish have gone, I should think, yes indeed. And there's the war. And there's—"

I took a long swallow of the ale. "A good many soldiers too," I said. "Led by some golden-haired fellow, not much more than a boy."

"You seen Major Fludd today then?"

"He seemed a very young man. A major you say?"

"If it were him you saw. Commander of our dragoons hereabouts. Gideon Fludd." And he grinned and nodded, half to himself. "Sharp young buck. Suffers no fools. I stay out of his way, I does."

The landlord turned as another patron barked for more drink and I was left to my own thoughts again. Gideon Fludd was preoccupying me more than I liked but I could not figure why. I was sure I had never seen him before but still something tugged. I intended to avoid him and his dragoons at all costs, keep to the shadows, and be quickly on my way to visit house and family. Lord Herbert had told me to search out a certain gentleman when I arrived at Exeter, most likely to be found at an alehouse, the Bishop's Mitre. This fellow was a local keeper of the flame so to speak, and it was in this establishment that meetings were often held and snippets of news exchanged. But I was in no hurry to get to Exeter, not until I had satisfied myself of what lay at home. The question remained: how would I approach my house and not be recognised?

I suppose my face had become very sober at these passing thoughts for I heard a man hail me from another table at the back.

"Why forlorn, Fellow Creature? Nothing be as bad as all that. Drink up with me!" And I turned to watch a youngish man, some mechanic fellow in a battered felt brimmer, raise his cup to me and then proceed to take a long swallow. Ale ran down the corners of his mouth and trickled down his unshaven neck and he slammed the cup down upon the table and rattled it as a signal for more.

I didn't know what to make of this rogue but I raised my cup to him in return. "Your health, sir!"

He raised his empty vessel to me and smiled. "We can only be healthy in the knowledge that we are all loved of God, each and every one. From the lowest sheep-buggering, cow-fucking rascal to the dirtiest whore in Plymouth town. We are all in the grace! We are in the Likeness goddamn it, the bloody Likeness of God!"

I watched the reaction of my fellow drinkers to this trumpet blast but the sailors only swore low and laughed amongst themselves while the landlord quite ignored the outburst. Drunkard, madman, or both, I knew not. But I had to smile at the boldness of this citizen of Cromwell's commonwealth.

"Laugh not! I am in earnest, sir. We are all saved no matter what the goddamned stinking prelates say. Goddamn Calvin's fucking bones! And rot those who parrot his creed."

"Rest easy, friend," I said, becoming alarmed at his rhetoric. "Have another drink with me." And I signalled the keeper to bring another pot.

The man smiled again and held his palm upward to reassure me. "I am in a fire of righteousness, sir, but don't be put off by my prattlings. I am at peace with my Fellow Creatures." He was not drunk, that I could see from his eyes, which focused readily enough upon the room. His lank greasy brown hair fell about his shoulders, framing a ragged face and a long nose, below which grew a wisp of a red moustache.

"He's a bloody Ranter," announced the landlord as he set down the pots of ale shaking his head in disgust. "Just a Ranter."

"I am of the party called My One Flesh, sir, the one true church of these times," said the clown, rising from his chair and, uninvited, taking one at my table instead.

"I don't care if you're the Antichrist so long as you keep paying," said the landlord, as he pushed up his soaking sleeves. "Ranters, Levellers, Diggers, Lord knows what they'll send us next but we have enough sects these days to please everyone, I should think." He shook his head again, as if long accustomed to this madness and returned to his bar.

The young man winked and clinked his wooden cup to mine. "Billy Chard is the name, sir!"

I had read the news of the Levellers over the years, and the Digger movement too, overheated radicals that believed in the abolition of all private property. But Cromwell had crushed them a few summers ago once they threatened public order and the ruling Council. *Ranters* however were a party I had not heard of, but it seemed they were aptly named.

Billy Chard looked harmless enough and since I had nothing better to do, I let him stay. "What is your creed then, if I might ask?"

"It's a simple one, Fellow Creature," he began, leaning back and seizing his mug. "And now that we have shared a drink, what is your name?"

"Andreas Falkenhayn... a trader."

"Aye, well, foreigner or not, He loves us all. Our creed is simple, sir. We are all made in God's Likeness, each and every one. God is in all of us, He is. He is in this here chair, that pipe over yonder... the dog by the fire, every thing. Therefore... there is no such thing as Sin, no act to be ashamed of. Even that which is evil was fashioned by God. We are in a natural state born into this world." He paused, as if waiting for my reply, but I was too amazed to say a word. "I shall now take a pipe of God myself," he announced reaching into his stained leather doublet and pulling out a tobacco pouch.

"We live in wondrous times, do we not?" I ventured.

"Aye, Mr. Falkenhayn, that we do. And hard times at that. The country has gone to ruin now after the wars. And why the hell did I bother trailing a pike for Parliament? It got us nowhere."

"And has your creed been persecuted like Mr. Lilburne and his Levellers?" I asked him.

He nodded and took another swig. "Most of the noisier of the creed get shut up in the gaols for a spell; even I was clapped up in Wells for a time... bad grub there, I tell you," he added, his memory now sparked. His voice grew lower. "All gone to ruin. The Council and Cromwell are now no better than the king ever was. Tyrants in their own right." His head swung around slowly to take in the occupants of the tap room. "Some of us think it was better in the old days."

I nodded sympathetically but didn't show my cards. "I am not from these shores and so know little of such matters."

"Oh, just as well, sir, just as well. All gone to ruin."

"They would have their king back?" I asked him. "After all that has gone by?"

Billy Chard's nubbled chin rested on his chest as he contemplated my question. And I could see his actor's mask drop for a moment when he finally replied. "Some of us would have our king back, I think. I'm just not saying who." He smiled again. "Trust is in short supply, Fellow Creature, that's for damn sure. And I do not know you from all the other fuckers out there."

I TOOK MY supper in my chamber that night and arranged for the landlord to have a stable hand sent around in the morning to take me to some horse trader nearby. It was all just silence and the occasional barking of dogs in the distance. But as I lay there, awaiting sleep, the Beast came upon me just the same. I thrashed about as the terrors ran over me, fists clenching and unclenching. After what seemed an age of agonies, I drifted off. I dreamt about seeing comrades from years gone by. The sort of dream that lingers, where the long dead walk past and even though you know they are dust, somehow it doesn't seem at all strange. And I conversed with my father too, in his grave these many years. He was telling me that my brother William wanted to see me and that younger brother Roger had left for the plantations in Massachusetts. And then he had just walked away.

I awoke early, dressed, and, guided by the stableman's boy, arrived at the horse yard. I bought an old bay-coloured mare, rather tired, but still with some life in her. With my satchel strapped to the cruppers, I decided to walk the animal to the town gate, only a short distance down the Exeter road. In the pillory near a church, two poor miscreants lay hunched over in sleep, steam spilling from their mouths and a blanket thrown over their backs by someone who had taken pity. Neither was Billy Chard, but I wagered he'd be there too before long. Around me trudged shopkeepers, peddlers, and apprentices, none of whom appeared to take notice of me or even one another. It was a procession of sad and sorry folk and I was sore surprised to see how far and how hard old Plymouth town had fallen.

My house lay between Plympton and Venton, a few miles distant. The weather held fair the whole of my journey but the sights that met my eyes were bittersweet ones. The lean-to sheds of tapped-out tin mines sat abandoned to fortune: no fires burned, no kilns smoked. And never had I seen so many sturdy beggars in Plympton town. They were a bold lot, following me with wary and covetous eyes. The war had laid the whole place low.

At last, I came upon my house, set up on a little bump of a hill, just off the road. I could see it four-square and large with its brood of outbuildings clustered around it. It was a good-sized place of cob and stone, sixteen windows to the front, and had been a place of much joy before the wars began and ruined my life.

How strange it would be to have to knock upon the door of my own house. I saw movement within, a woman in a bonnet. If she recognises me, how shall I play it? But it was a housemaid or cook that opened the door and not one I knew.

I raised my hat to her. "Goodwife, I seek Mistress Treadwell on business. I understand this is her house, no?"

The woman shook her head. "This is not her house, sir. You are mistaken. If you are selling something she lives down over there," she told me, waving her hand in the direction of the crofter's cottage down the hill. It was a cottage that I owned.

She must have taken notice of the expression on my face, struck dumb as I was.

"Down the road, sir! Begone. I have no business with strangers." She was already closing the door with both brawny arms when I finally regained my wits.

"Mistress, who *does* live in this house?"

She was already angry as a wasp and I was lucky to get an answer at all. "This is the house of Captain Israel Fludd. Now off with you!"

I swore a streak of curses as I walked back down the hill, leading my mount. I knew then what had happened. I should have anticipated it long ago before I had blundered into it. And that name again. Fludd. Sweet Christ, my Arabella had lost the house and the land. I knew it. Cromwell needed money and taking it out of the hides of the king's supporters was a painless way to get it. And then another wave of anger came sweeping over me. Why hadn't my older brother prevented this? He was the Parliament man in the family. He could have surely stopped the seizure. I stood in front of the weather-bleached door of the little cottage, my fist raised to pound, my breathing fast. What would I say?

One knock.

Arabella opened the door, looked into my face and took a few steps backwards. Before she receded into the shadow of the interior, I had seen the colour drain away from her. I took off my hat and entered. She had backed herself into the table, silent. My eyes quickly adjusted and I took in the room, its inhabitants, the contents. A young girl stood near the fire—she would be twelve, I knew. Next to her a maidservant, a woman I did not recognise. I did recognise the big cupboard, the table, some other sticks of furniture from the main house. And my wife, my poor wife, standing a few feet away and grasping the oak table that held her up. And she looked very worn and very thin of face. I stood there, hat in both hands, labouring to find words but only stuttering foolishness.

"Madame," I spoke quietly. "My name is Andreas Falkenhayn. I come from France with news of your husband."

She swallowed a few times but still said nothing. I knew she knew it was me and no other. The maidservant turned, the spoon in her hand dripping porridge onto the floor. And Ann, my little Ann, she turned towards me too. She looked at me blankly, no recognition, no fear, no joy. Nothing. And I could feel the tears welling in my eyes. The serving girl was soon at Arabella's side, guiding her mistress to a chair near the table.

She was searching for words to respond to the sight of a ghost. But when she spoke, her voice was much stronger than I had expected.

"You say you have news of my husband, sir. I would be glad to hear of it though you see we are in reduced circumstance here." And she looked straight into my eyes, playing her role. "There is little I can offer in way of refreshment, sir, but would you take a draught... and a chair?"

I nodded. The maidservant went and fetched the pewter and jug and I slowly eased myself onto a chair at the opposite side of the table. Ann walked over to stand next to Arabella, her hand upon her mother's shoulder. And here, I hesitated again, weighing the words that had to be spoken. In the end, I knew there was only one thing that could be said.

"Madame, I must tell you now, that your husband is dead, fallen in France. In battle."

It was a monstrous lie to utter with my daughter standing there frozen and wide-eyed. Having seen Arabella now, it was vital for the sake of them all that I *was* dead. For despite the lovely voluminous folds of her thick blue velvet dress, sadly out of place in a farmhand's hovel, she was clearly and truly, heavy with child.

Chapter Six

SHE NODDED SLOWLY, complicit in our little deceit. "It is as I have long feared, then," she said, never taking her eyes from me.

I swallowed hard. "I bring money with me... for you." And I dug out one of my purses, gently placing it on the table between us. "It should see you through for more than a few months."

Still she stared at me. It was a look of sadness but tinged with blame just the same. "I thank you, sir. Would that he had never left this place. We might not have come to where we are now."

"I am sure he would not have if he had known what would befall his family. And should more money of his come to light I will ensure that it too finds its way to you, madame."

Arabella was silent.

"Ma'am, should I take the child outside for a spell?" said the maidservant.

Arabella nodded her agreement, grasped Ann's hand and gave it a little rub. "Off you go child, with Lizzie."

We were then alone, facing each other across the table. And I truly felt that Richard Treadwell was dead and gone and that I was but the messenger of his passing. "I was told you have a son. Where is he this day?"

"He has gone to live with his uncle. A man who can better provide for his education."

I nodded.

"He's strong and already much in resemblance of his father," said Arabella, softening a bit. "He goes to the grammar school in Plympton. His uncle dotes on him and he is happy there."

"I am glad to hear of it, madame." And I truly was. "But did not this uncle seek to help you keep your home?"

She answered me straight away. "It was beyond even his means to stop the order of confiscation and sale. My good brother did what he could and looks after us still. I was the one who did not want to leave this land. I haven't much but I still hold this house. *This* he shall not have."

"Arabella..."

She reached across the table to me and I clasped her hand. "Arabella, who did this to you?"

She answered in little more than a whisper. "You mean, sir, my belly? Or the committee that said my husband's treason was beyond redemption and that his estate was forfeit to the republic?"

I held her hand between both of my own. "Who has violated you? Tell me."

"It was he who bought your house for a song from Parliament. The same who lives there now." And I felt her hand slip out of my grasp, her arm pulling back to her lap. "Captain Israel Fludd."

I could say nothing, but she could see the rage stoking within me.

"Do not seek to cause more trouble for us, I beg of you. Leave well enough alone and all will be well. We shall not want. But you must go. You must go before you're recognised." She pushed herself up from the chair and stood facing me. "You must go... Richard."

I got up.

"You did not ask me, husband, whether it was by my will or against my will?"

"I don't have to ask such a thing. And don't tell Ann the truth of me. You're better off a widow."

"I know this, husband. And if you still bear us love then you must leave again."

I left the cottage, my stomach in a rolling sick, and stood next to her. Her arm and shoulder brushed against mine; the closest we were destined to embrace. I looked back up the hill to the house. "I will see justice done, fear not."

She looked up at me, her mouth falling open in horror. "Justice? For the love of God, do not even think of it! You must not!"

"Very well," I told her, "you're right. I'll make sure you remain safe. Fare thee well." There seemed but little else to say. "I will send you more coin soon." And I took off my hat to her with a bow, cast one brief look to my daughter and walked to where my horse stood grazing. I looked back again.

Arabella had crossed her arms, still watching me as I picked my way down the rutted gulley of a path. "Good bye!" she mouthed.

It was time to visit my brother William. Perhaps from him I could find answers for the hurt done here, if not solace. I rode back to Plympton and stopped at the first tavern I spied in St. Maurice. From there, I sent by the taverner's son a brief scribbled message to Sir William Treadwell, who I hoped was at home at the old house a mile north of town. I asked him to meet me with all haste on important business concerning an old shared acquaintance. I signed it "Andreas Falkenhayn, recently arrived of France". And then I waited. I waited in the tap room watching the pale sun sink lower as the afternoon wore on.

At last, I saw the taverner's son return and close behind, there was William. He pulled off his hat and swept back his long grey hair, his eyes searching about the room. I saw the lad point me out, sitting where I was, back to the wall. Still, William had not recognised me. He walked across the room, winding his way around the benches and stools until he stood before me.

"You have business with me, sir?" I looked up and watched as it dawned on him who I was. His mouth fell open and for an instant he was frozen in his place. "Sweet Jesus! My sweet Jesus!"

I pulled him down next to me on the bench. "Hush, brother!" I hissed. "Do not give the game away."

He exhaled loudly and tossed his hat upon the table. "Have you gone quite mad? Why have you come? No, please... my heart sings to see you alive. I'm sorry."

"I will tell all, William, but not here."

We left and crossed the road, cutting through the churchyard and walking past the old barbican to the ruins of the ancient castle of Plympton Erle, following the foot path up the old motte. William had aged since we had last met, years ago. I knew that he had lost his seat in Parliament shortly after I had been exiled. I thought of all the fights we had had over the years, he for the Parliament while I stayed with the king. Now, he too was out of favour in this new world.

"I cannot believe it still," he huffed as we walked uphill, his stick stabbing into the soft pungent earth. "Why have you risked your life to come back here? Have you forgotten your sentence?"

I had not forgotten. Nor had I forgotten how William had loyally given me counsel during my trial. I would have been executed—suffering a traitor's death—had he abandoned me to the wolves. Yet I could not reveal all to him, not yet. "I had to see Arabella and the children again. That's the truth of it. And to see England again."

He stopped and looked at me. "Do I look like some calf-headed sot? You've shown precious little concern until this moment. You can't cozen me. You're rampant in some intrigue; I would stake a wager on it... You pitiful goddamn fool."

"Very well, then. I've been here but two days and seen more than enough. The country is gone to ruin. No work, no money, and men not free to speak their minds without fear of having their tongues bored through. And I've seen my home—and Arabella."

My brother shook his head in disbelief. "You're indeed a fool. That was a selfish prank, Richard. How could you have acted so rashly? If you've been seen, it is she who will bear the consequences."

"She has already borne the consequences! I have seen she is with child! Tell me you did not know she had been violated, brother."

He looked at his shoes, wordless.

"Tell me why you couldn't stop that? Or stop the house from being sold. Tell me!"

William started walking forward again, his head down. "She concealed the pregnancy from me until but a fortnight ago. I swear to you I've watched out for her. But she refused to leave the property she yet held. Your house and land was sequestered and sold before I could raise a hand. It was arranged quickly. You do not know how sorry I am for all that has happened."

"What's done is done. But you can tell me about Israel Fludd, then. I do not remember the name in these parts."

"He followed his brother here, a Norfolk man, Major Gideon Fludd, of Okey's dragoons. They both have fought for Parliament these last few years and Israel holds a captain's commission in the Plymouth militia."

I nodded, my mind already moving to dark places. "And this Gideon. I have seen him in Plymouth. What is his part in this villainy?"

"He holds much power here. I don't know how he rose so fast but he's the whip for all our backs. The mayor's in thrall to him and he does what he likes with his dragoons. The army is the power now. I've heard that Colonel Okey has sung his praises to Cromwell and the Council and given him free rein in Devon to establish order and stamp out any Royalist plans. Which brings us back to your intentions here, my brother."

I grunted in reply.

"It's better I don't know," he said as we reached the fallen stones of the bailey.

"This Gideon Fludd," I said, "he has the look of the overly righteous about him. And there's something in his face that unsettles me. I don't know what it is..."

I could still not forget how my talisman had tugged at my chest when I set eyes upon Fludd. As if it was trying to pull me away.

William gave a hoarse laugh. "You've marked him well. He and his brother are Fifth Monarchy men."

"And what are they? Another group of radicals bent on tearing down what's left of this place?"

"Aye, that is closer to the truth than not. They and those of their creed hold no church but they're convinced that we live in the end of days as was foretold in the Book. They believe that King Jesus will come and establish the new Kingdom of God here and now." He rubbed at his chin. "No, I misspeak—it's thirteen years hence—in 1666. That is when the Lord is to come again. But they have to get the house ready, you see, for the Second Coming. Gideon is convinced he is a saint doing the Lord's work."

"The world is gone mad." I looked out over the spire of St. Maurice, over all the houses that lay below and rested my back against the cold moss-covered wall of the long-perished stone keep. "I must see my boy. May I come up to the house?"

William mumbled some incoherent protest and then said, "Richard, that is not wise and you know it."

"Not this night. Tomorrow. I'll come around the back. To the window in father's old chamber."

"And what shall you do in the meantime?"

"Keep out of sight," I lied.

My brother pursed his lips in frustration. "Very well, then. I shall be waiting for you tomorrow eve. Richard, I pray your boldness doesn't bring the army down on us. I beg you not to stir the hornet's nest, for all our sakes."

"Brother," I said, "fear not. It is I that possesses the sting."

I CROUCHED IN a copse, enveloped in my cloak, and watched my house. The moon was still high and bright and I had waited until the last of the lights had been snuffed out. My horse I had tied up some distance away on the edge of the wood and I had walked onto my land, skirting the barns and cottage and flanking my way so that from where I hid, I could see the rear courtyard and pump. And there I had waited as the night grew old.

Israel Fludd had raped my wife and stolen my home. Yet I swear I had come to accomplish something other than revenge. I had come to regain something that was mine, something that *could* be regained. For underneath the tiles in the buttery, I had secreted a leather wallet before my last campaign. Inside it were letters of exchange, drawn from the Amsterdam goldsmiths and worth some five thousand gold ducats—a few thousand pounds at least. The fruits of my years in the German wars. Once redeemed, I could at long last do some good for Arabella and the children. But I needed no one to tell me what rashness my plan was.

The kitchen casement window lock was still broken after all these years, and I felt the frame swing inside as I pushed. With little elegance, I pulled myself up over the sill into the pitch black room and brought my knees up before slowly dangling my legs inside. I listened, my arse still balanced on the window frame. And then I was down, on my feet, and in my home once again. I waited as the pitch gave way to shadows, and then objects, as my eyes grew accustomed. I could just make out the little iron-strapped door that led to the buttery and I quickly crept across the kitchen.

The smell of musty wine and ale and old crockery filled my nose as I entered the buttery, moonlight spilling a shaft across the floor. I remembered which tile hid my prize and counted in from the outside wall. Dirk in hand, I stooped and worked out the tile from the floor. After what seemed an age, I felt a jiggle of movement and levered the blade underneath. The clay stone came up into my hand and I then reached down a foot or so into the damp earth below. It was still there. My fingers wrapped around the crusty leather and I drew it out of its tomb.

Thrusting the wallet into the little satchel about my shoulder, I replaced the tile as it had been. I brushed dust and dirt over the floor to conceal what had happened. A light startled me as soon as I re-entered the kitchen. Before I could make the window, a man filled the doorway. He held a horn lantern with one hand and a long cavalry pistol in the other.

"You've picked the wrong house to rob, thief," he said, almost amused, as if he had caught a child stealing pies. He took a pace forward and I stood fixed, my mind calculating whether I could make the leap before he got his shot off. "You were as quiet as a rat but not every man sleeps even at this hour. And I have very, very good ears."

He did not know me. How could he? But I had seen him before. It was the man I had seen in the square. It was the face of Gideon Fludd. But this man had long blond hair and it now struck me that though William had told me that Israel and Gideon were brothers, he had neglected to tell me they were twins.

"Do you know whose house you've broken into, little man?" Israel Fludd raised the pistol a bit higher. He was fully dressed, shod in his riding boots, and it was clear he had not been napping when I arrived. As I stood there, the anger grew. Anger because I had failed and because he had caught me.

"I do know. I am in *my* house, sir, and I have come for what is mine."

Even in the dim glow of the lantern, I could see a look of confusion cross his face. This quickly gave way to a smile and an intake of breath as the realisation broke upon him.

"Of course! The great Malignant has returned! Now the mystery of yesterday's visitor becomes clear. The foolish woman said you were some foreign fellow. You're a bold one, I give you that."

He stepped fully into the kitchen and I backed up a step. "I shall enjoy handing you over, sirrah, and this time you won't escape the Lord's justice. Get on your knees and be quick about it!"

I made up my mind there and then not to be taken alive. And if I was to suffer my end this night I would take him with me. I still gripped my dirk but there was little chance of getting to him without getting a hot pistol ball in my chest. He started babbling that a great burning brand was coming soon to scorch and cleanse this land of my kind. My left foot bumped against a milking stool and I knew I had but one opportunity to save myself. I started to bend my knees to obey his order, but as I went down, I snatched the stool and in one motion flung it high at his head.

Even as it left my hand, I was head and shoulders down and moving forward to take him. The pistol fired as soon as I leapt, but the sound and flash was not followed by pain. He had missed. And then I was upon him, throwing both of us down to the floor. He was half my age and even as I pinioned his right arm, he gripped my knife hand with his left. Straight away I could feel his strength beginning to overcome mine.

I sought to break his grip and plunge my blade into him. But the dirk was slowly turning in towards my own chest. I released his arm and seized his long golden locks at the top of his head. And I lifted and struck his skull upon the stone tiles. Again and again. His grip on my wrist faltered, and I dropped the dirk and tore another fistful of his hair, both of my arms yanking and then bashing his head upon the floor as I straddled him. The lantern, sent spinning, but still alight, shone against the far wall, and so I could not see his face. But I remember crying out, "This... is for... Arabella!" as I pounded and I heard the bones break in his head. My hands were wet and warm with his blood. Fludd had now let go of me, but still I beat his skull like some washerwoman on her rock. At last, I let his head drop with a sickening sound and feel, like a sack of pottery shards being set on the floor. It was only then that I heard his serving woman calling out from somewhere in the house.

The Lord Himself knows, I would have killed Israel Fludd sooner or later, but this was a matter altogether different. This woman had seen me yesterday. I retrieved my knife in my shaking hand and stood, leaning against the doorframe. The glow of candlelight spread into the hall and I crouched back into the kitchen, kicking the lantern across the room. I pushed myself back into the wall, not breathing. I heard her cry out as she saw Fludd lying there and then I glimpsed the woman, in her white linen shift, as she leaned over the body. I was on her in an instant, my right hand clamped around her mouth, and pulling her in backwards, against my chest. The candelabra crashed to the floor and I felt her harsh gasp against my hand as she screamed. And then I raised the blade towards her throat.

My head was shouting that I had to protect Arabella and the children, I had to. This thing had to be done. I hesitated, the tip already touching her skin. But I dropped the dagger, balled my fist, and struck her as hard as I could. And then a second blow that sent her sprawling. She didn't move. Now I had truly thrown the dice. So long as she had not seen me, I might yet make an escape. But I had to make this all look the work of some housebreaker, some masterless apprentice turned thief in the night—and murderer. I approached Fludd's corpse. Thinking to search his pockets for valuables, I found nothing. But his hand bore a signet ring which I tore off and pocketed.

I made my way into the hall, feeling through the darkness. I knew my house though, and reached the closet chamber at the front. The three windows afforded sufficient moonlight for me to rifle about the table and cupboards, and I seized two purses of coin, tearing up the room as I did so, pulling the rug off the table top and throwing drawers upon the floor. I shoved some silver into my satchel, and so too a good silver salter and tankard. In one of the cupboards, my hand fell upon a metal disc, too large to be a coin, and I picked it up. It was the size of my palm and rather thin, but heavy. I thrust it, sticky with blood, into the satchel and dashed out of the room back to the hall.

Out the back door, I was soon flying for the little wood a hundred yards away. My head reeling, I stumbled through the trees and down to where I prayed my horse still waited. It was still there, shivering in the night chill. I waded out into a little brook that ran through the copse, stooped down and splashed the freezing water upon my hands and then my face and head. I rummaged through the satchel, tossing away the pewter and silver but keeping the little purses of coin and the strange metal disc. Suddenly, I stopped and swore aloud. I had forgotten to retrieve my dirk from the kitchen floor. It lay there still, waiting to be found, its wooden grip stained in blood. But the blade bore no inscription, and not a soul knew that it was *my* weapon. I would have to leave it be.

Standing there, knee deep, I thought of Arabella. There was no doubt she would know in her heart the dreadful moment she was told, that it was I and no one else who had done this sorry deed. I prayed she would keep her wits if questioned by the militia. She would have to. And I would have to leave Plympton far behind, maybe forever. But not without seeing my son.

WILLIAM MUMBLED SOMETHING about skulduggery as he grunted and heaved me up through the casement into father's old chamber. "By God, you look fearsome," he said, finally getting a glimpse of my face. "Before you say a word, Richard, I need you to tell me you had nothing to do with Israel Fludd."

I did not answer my brother but instead walked to the table and sat myself in father's high-back chair, and removed the satchel from my shoulder.

"I feared as much," he said quietly as he joined me. "The militia was here this afternoon spreading the news. Asking questions."

My head snapped upwards at his words.

"They suspect Fludd had surprised some robber—or band of brigands. Had his brains beat out, they said. Tell me it was not murder, brother, I beg you."

As I told him all that had happened, I watched his face grow darker by the minute. After I had described the flight back to Plympton, I paused a moment, and then I asked the fate of the servant woman.

"She lives. But more important, she did not see her attacker." Then came that look I knew of old, the blank stare of condescension and judgement: "*That* should please you some."

His barb should not have stung me so, but it did. "I could not have wilfully killed her, you must know that. He, on the other hand, took little of my conscience. But I tell you, William, I had no choice. I swear it."

"No choice? You told me you would not go back there. And Arabella will not be deceived by this," he said. I pulled out the mildewed leather wallet, opened it, and removed the parchment letters, each folded and still sealed with wax and ribbon.

"Take these," I said. "Get one of your associates to redeem them when you can, though you may have to wait until this damned war with the Dutch has run its course." My brother picked up the letters of exchange and tapped them in his hands.

"Dearly bought, these notes. Pray that the price increases no further."

I reached back into the satchel, and pulled out the metal disc I had found on Israel Fludd's table. I had wiped it clean of blood to find it covered with strange symbols, its purpose a mystery. I handed it to my brother. "Fludd was in possession of this medallion. Have you seen its like before?"

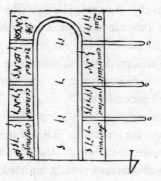

William examined it, his finger tracing over the etching. "Is it pewter?... no silver, I think. These writings here... this is... in Hebrew." His brow creased a little. "Some phrase about God, I think. As for *these* symbols," he said, tilting the disc so I could see, "unintelligible to my learning."

"But what is its purpose? Do you see the little hole at the top? Is it a pendant?"

William shook his head. "Perhaps some Fifth Monarchy device."

I pulled forth the ring, which had proved to be silver and equally strange in appearance.

William studied this too, but could only shake his head. "Similar strange devices, but different ones from the disc. But see here... it scribes a five-pointed star. And this phrase that

winds between the points—TETRAGRAMMATON—it is
Greek. It means... four letters." He shook his head and handed
the disc and ring back. "I'll tell you true, it smells un-Christian
whatever it is. My God, Richard, what have you dragged back
here with you?"

"A conjuring device of sorts?"

"I have not the science to tell you. But I know these Fifth
Monarchy men are a queer lot. Throw it away. It will only
serve to incriminate you anyway."

Brother Anselm's warning sprang into my mind and I leaned
forward with a start. *It could be that there are those close to
them that are invoking the Dark One... a powerful man is
trying to change his fortune by other means.* Maybe it wasn't
the exiles after all. I slumped back into the chair with fatigue
and ran my hand through my hair. William arose and fetched a
jug of wine from the sideboard to revive me.

"I had a dream the other night," I told him. "My first night
back in England. Father was there and spoke to me about
many things. He told me that Roger had left for the plantations
in Massachusetts."

William suddenly looked up at me as he pushed a goblet over.
"He *has*, Richard. Not even one month ago."

I lifted the wine and took a long swig. It had been many a
year since I had experienced dreams of foretelling. Now it was
happening again.

"A compass," I muttered aloud.

"What are you saying?"

I shook my head. "I have felt more than passing strange since
I set foot here again," I muttered. "Everything I once knew is
gone. The country is dying, I can see it. You can see that, can't
you? Your precious Parliament seems to have lost control of
the hounds."

William grunted, took a sip of wine, and set his cup down
again. "When the army threw us dissenting members out of
Westminster four years ago, I thought we would be returned

in a fortnight. I was wrong. The ones that remained in the Parliament were all lapdogs of the Army Council. Nothing good has come of them." And then he smiled weakly at me. "But we must forbear it until better days are delivered to us. There is now a rumour that Cromwell will dissolve the Parliament completely and rule by the Great Council alone."

I sat up in the chair. "He'll take the crown for himself next."

William leaned in towards me. "That is why you must return to France. The next ship, if you can. Get out of here before you are caught."

"Not every man is content to wait like you, William. There are those of us who will carry on fighting."

"Don't be a fool. The army holds the entire country in its grip. Its spies are everywhere and I can tell you that the new secretary to the Council, this Mister Thurloe, is a most efficient intelligencer and schemer. They will play you until you have revealed all of your co-conspirators and then they will close the net. Mark me!"

"Then I need to strike at the heart of the matter—Oliver Cromwell himself. I won't see my family suffer any further degradation in this land. If I cleave the head from the serpent than the rest shall die too."

William sank in his chair, instantly older. "You've been in exile for six years. You haven't any understanding of what's going on here. Oh, aye, you see the effects of the medicine well enough, and dire they are, but what you don't see is that it's Mister Cromwell and God's good Grace alone that are holding back the radicals from taking power. From what I've seen of some of those in the army, they make Oliver look like a Papist."

My laugh was sour. "That's rich indeed. No, the whole house of cards will fall tumbling down when Old Noll loses his head like the king lost his."

My brother again fixed me with the look of a circuit judge and for a fleeting moment I saw my father again in front of me. "You don't comprehend the truth of things here. Do you actually think it was my intervention alone that allowed your trial for treason to take such an unprecedented course? The Council was happy to condemn you outright and hang you straight away. But they gave in to your banishment instead. Did you think that was a *democratic* decision of Lord Fairfax and the others?"

I bristled under his harangue. "It was a trial by combat. I *won* it, by God!"

"Yes, you did, Richard. You did. And the Council was a hairbreadth from hanging you just the same." He paused a moment. "I will tell you now, that which I concealed from you these last eight years. It was *Oliver* who gave you your life. Oliver Cromwell himself who stood for your honour when the others bayed for your death. And Oliver got his way."

I felt myself falling back into the chair, leaden. The world had indeed gone mad.

"And with your hands still bloody," said William, "you would seek to murder the very man who spared your life?"

I couldn't give him an answer. Finally, I whispered in a hoarse croak. "Let me see my boy."

"THOMAS, MY VISIT must remain a secret, a very deep secret amongst the three of us here. You must not tell a soul, not even your mother or your sister, that you have seen me. One day I will be able to stay for good, but not now. Do you understand?"

My fourteen-year-old son nodded at me. "Yes, sir, I understand." He then glanced over to William. "Uncle has told me you were banished because of the wars with the king. Because you are a king's man. The boys at school say you are a traitor to the country—and to God."

I walked him over to the armchair and sat him down. "All of us who fought did what we thought best for the kingdom. But many of us could not turn against our king, who is ruler by God's will."

"But uncle turned against the king."

I looked up at William, who had a look that said 'you've dug the hole, brother, now climb out' and then faced my son again. "Aye, well... he did. He stayed true to his beliefs and I stayed true to mine. But see, we are reconciled again, are we not? One day all of England will be reconciled again."

He stayed with me not above an hour, and told me of his mother, his school and his friends, and a little of life without a father but with an uncle and cousins who treated him well. And I was glad of it. And when William ushered him out of the chamber, my heart was heavy but full. I could now give a face to my son again.

"You must know, Richard, that after this night, I can offer you no further help. If you stay—if you agitate—they will capture and kill you, be assured. And they are ruthless. For the sake of your children, go back to France. I will see that they do not want. You have my oath upon it."

"And Arabella... and the babe. They need your protection too."

"And they shall have it. Fear not."

I managed a smile. "I will not tell you my plans, brother. It would be unfair to hazard you so. You are free to believe what you wish as to my destination. And, one last request... I have need of a blade, a dagger."

He swore under his breath, looked to give an objection, but then turned and walked to his cupboard. He came back holding a weapon more suited to a surgeon—or an assassin.

"Here. A Venetian whore's toothpick. I would tell you to not to be rash with it but that would be a waste of breath."

I took the stiletto from him and placed it in my girdle where my lost Scots dirk had been secreted.

"Richard, I beg you to think again," he said. "Stirring it all up will only serve to push us over the abyss. Go back while you can."

I pulled out a leather purse with the coin I had stolen the previous night. "Take this," I told him, throwing it on the table. "Consider it blood money... Give it to the grammar school. For Thomas."

"If this is Israel Fludd's money, Richard, I cannot take it."

"*Sir* Richard, brother." I watched his eyebrows lift and I nodded. "Aye, I am still a king's man. God protect you and the family."

And I was gone.

Chapter Seven

I HAD MORE strange and vivid dreams that night at the inn in Plympton. The kind of dreams that roll around your skull long after waking, daring you to think it was something real. In the first, Israel Fludd stood before me, his long hair matted black with dried blood. He was handing me back my Scottish dirk as casually as a passerby would hand you back the hat blown off your head. I took the dirk from him and saw that the blade had my name etched the full of its length in elegant script. That vision alone brought me to wakefulness, covered in sweat.

The second was stranger still. I was back in Germany, sitting in the gypsy camp I had wandered into as a very young and very foolish soldier. And Anya, Anya the black-maned, blue-eyed seeress, was with me again. Never the hag I had told Maggie she was, Anya in rags had been more beauteous than any woman at the French court. It was she who had made me a gift of the talisman I had worn these past twenty-five years. But now, in this dream, she was handing me something different. It was the silver ring. The curious ring with the five-pointed star that I had taken from Israel Fludd. Yet her words to me were the same as spoken all those years ago in the deep of the forest.

"Wear it upon your person always and it will keep you from harm..."

And as I had taken it from her soft, browned hand, I was once again jolted to wakefulness. Out of my rack and rigged at dawn, I soon found that the quest for vengeance had begun sooner than I had expected—or was ready for. The landlord at the inn told me that the hand of Major Gideon Fludd had spread out to cover the town like the angel of the Lord against the Egyptians. The militia was rounding up every wastrel they laid eyes on between Plymouth and the Dartmoor—vagrants, peddlers, sturdy beggars—every man jack who ought to be doing honest labour. And, as some farmer had told him, word was that you could hear the screams of the wretches in the old stone gaol in town. Fludd was determined to find who had murdered his brother and if a hot iron would hasten the finding of the truth, then so be it.

I paid up my bill, slung my satchel and retrieved my mount from the stable. It would be a long ride to Exeter with every chance of being stopped and interrogated by the army.

Yet my luck held all that day, past Ivybridge and up to where the Exeter Road skirted the moorland. The sun had been warm comfort most of the day, but now that it was late in the afternoon, the wind picked up off the Dartmoor and low cloud rolled in. I could feel the chill settle down fast, blowing down my neck, even as the sun sunk low, obscured by grey mist. The road began to narrow and I was soon very near the town of Brent. I could just see a church tower in the distance and ahead of me, crossing my path, lay the river Avon. All along the bank, the oak and ash grew up thick and tall, the never ending winds of the moorland bending and twisting their branches into tortured forms made more visible in the barrenness of late winter.

I was now quite alone upon the road. Perhaps it was because I was tired, but I failed to look into the wood that lay either side as I approached the span. Before I saw anything, I felt the horse flinch beneath me. Looking to my left, I glimpsed a figure bounding from the trees close by, arms outstretched. Before I could kick the poor beast forward, the man had grasped the bridle to stop me. And he was aiming a long cavalryman's pistol with his other hand, centred on my chest.

I raised my hands and contemplated the brigand. He wore countryman's clothes and a battered hat and his face was nearly full hidden by a white cloth he had tied about his neck, leaving only his eyes visible. I slowly dismounted and spread my hands out to either side. With the muzzle barely a foot from me, he could have blown a fist-sized hole through me with no chance of a miss.

"Your purse! Give it over."

I reached up to my belt and began to unfasten the clasp that held it, all the while watching his eyes, bulging with the excitement of his capture. "There's little in it for you, sirrah," I said to him, softly.

"That'll be for me to decide, *Fellow Creature*. Even so, your horse will make up for the lack of coin, won't it?"

I hesitated, and then I closed the catch on my purse. "Billy? Billy Chard?"

The man said nothing, but his head tilted to the side, like a blackbird contemplating a crust of bread as he puzzled at my ability to pierce his disguise. I then saw that the hammer of his pistol was lying already down upon the wheel—spent. The trigger had been pulled some time before, loaded or not. This the buffle-head had failed to notice in his eagerness to rob me. I reached up and gripped the barrel with my right hand and stepped forward and clouted him with my left. He quick enough let go and clapped a hand to his smarting ear, much too surprised to do all else. I yanked down his mask and looked into the face of my drinking companion from the Bell and Tun.

"Beg your pardon, Mister Eff, sir! I had no blessed idea that it were you, I swear to the Lord!"

I held him by his jerkin and shirt, the pistol poised to pummel his brains if he tried to fight.

"You followed me up from Plymouth," I said, shaking him. "Then you rode ahead to take me here at the narrows!"

"Never, sir, I swear it!" He stood and pleaded, more embarrassed than eager for escape. "I've been in the wood there for hours—no horse—waiting on a lone traveller who looked to have a bit of money. It was God's will that brought us together!"

"And for all your godly words, you're nothing but a highwayman." I lowered the pistol butt, disgusted, but also amazed that we had indeed crossed paths again.

"There is no such thing as sin in the eyes of God. We are all in His image," said Billy, somewhat meekly.

I let go of his shirt and grasped the reins of my horse. "A neat argument, sir, and one you have told me before. But I'm sure the magistrate would be willing to dispute it on several points of the law."

"You're going to turn me over?" His flat voice said he was resigned to it already.

I looked him in the eye. He had suffered a hard few years of late and it showed upon him, from his scrofulous skin to his scrawny neck. He might be a poor recruit but I had to begin building the king's army sometime. Besides, he had shouldered a pike once and that alone made him brethren.

"No. I'll not turn you over to face the assizes—or the noose. I need a companion on my travels and you're in need of a legal vocation. What do you say, Billy Chard?"

He blinked a few times. "Are you in earnest—or in drink, Mister Eff?

"Just don't you run off on me now, and I shall make it worth all our whiles. If you leg it, I promise you I shall swear out a warrant."

He nodded his agreement. "I give you my word, sir," he said, the snot running down his prominent upper lip.

"Then let's get us to Brent town to make our supper. I'll tell you what I need of you and you can tell me what you know about King Jesus and the end of the world."

The light was failing fast but I could see his brow crease.

"You don't follow those Fifth Monarchy folk? What do you want from them?"

I shoved the hand-cannon under the satchel on the cruppers and then turned Billy around to face the road as I tugged the mare to follow us. "No, I don't follow them but I am curious to know more. If it will set your heart at ease, I think I can say that I have more sympathy for the Ranting creed. What was it you call yourselves again? 'My one flesh'?"

Billy Chard looked back over his shoulder and flashed a grin at me. "Aye, that be it, Fellow Creature!"

We were soon halfway across the old stone bridge, the sound of the river tumbling furiously below. Suddenly, as if someone had laid a cold blade on my back, I felt the urge to look behind me, back down the long road. In the grey gloom and sheep's wool mist that floated past the highway, pooling into the ditch on either side, I saw a black creature standing at the road edge, though still some distance away. It was a big shaggy cur the size of a pony, the largest dog I had ever seen. And it stood there, unnaturally stiff, gazing at Billy and me.

"What do you see down there upon the road?" I said.

Billy stopped, looked back, and then looked over to me. "I see nothing but the fog settling down."

And then I turned and looked again. The black dog was gone.

"We must find an inn before it gets too dark," I told him quietly. And Billy looked at me queerly, confounded at my strange and sudden unease. Old memories were stirring again in me. The memories of a young soldier once lost in a great, dark forest in the German lands.

BILLY CHARD WAS a Dorsetman, born and bred. As we wolfed down our supper at an inn on the edge of Brent, he told me of his sorry misadventures in the late war and what followed after.

He had dodged a musket ball or two in the Parliamentary forces and had his helm knocked off his head more than a few times. But after Cromwell's victory at Worcester, he had wandered off, hungry and without pay, working as a farmhand or drover where he could. And then, he joined a Ranter group that met near Saltash until they were finally sent packing by the Puritans a year later.

"They called us godless men, they did," said Billy, loudly scraping his spoon on the last morsels of his bowl. "But those of our creed make a damn sight more sense of the Lord's word than most of those army preachers, the sods." He shook his head. "Why did I bother to trail a pike? For what good? We're no longer free men, Mister Eff."

"Billy, I told you I need a travelling companion, someone to watch my back for me," I said.

"Oh, understood, sir," he said, breaking into a grin. "These roads ain't safe for no man." He then squinted and leaned towards me over the trestle top. "And what was that trade of yours again, Mister Eff?"

"I'm a wool merchant, bound for Exeter to meet with some other men of business. I could use your help along the way and while I'm there." I pushed two silver half-crowns across the table. "There's five shillings to see you right for a time. There'll be more if you keep the bargain—and if you keep thievery out of your plans."

He gawped a moment, then palmed the coins. "Aye, it's all the same to me so long as you'll not be asking anything that breaks the law of the kingdom," he said, all mock solemn. And then he let out a short laugh and reached for his beer. "So I'll be an assistant of sorts to you, the fine foreign merchant gentleman? You did say you was foreign, didn't you?"

I suppose my stage accent was wearing thin. Before long he would no doubt guess the truth. "And you can tell me about these strange countrymen of yours who preach of the end of the world and the coming of the saints."

Billy chuckled and spoke into his tankard. "For another shilling or two, Mister Eff, I'll tell you which hand they wipe their arses with!"

"There's more," I said. "I will compel no man to be my companion against his will. The truth is, you're free to go this night if you wish. The choice is yours."

"Very good, sir. Here's to goodly commerce in Exeter... and for you taking on an old soldier the likes of me."

We bedded down in the ground floor of the clapperboard ell of the tavern, the last free room. The wind blew in everywhere between the boards of the little place. The clay-tiled floor was strewn with fresh straw but the stink of the last occupant still lingered. There were two low bedsteads with dubious linen and I flung myself into one, fully clothed. Billy did the same and after a few of his stories about his wandering life I drifted off with a warm head full of ale and cider.

I was awake as soon as I felt the hand upon my arm. In one movement I clasped the thin iron grip of the stiletto at my side and thrust it out in front of me at the crouching figure. In the moonlight, I could see Billy's pale terrified face and I checked my blow.

"By Jesus, Mister Eff!" he whispered, pulling back. "It ain't me! Look out the window. There's a great beast in the yard just a-staring at us as cold as hell."

I approached the large, rotting casement and looked out into the courtyard of the tavern, the moonlight illuminating all with a crisp blue tinge. It was standing several paces from the window, and by God, its head was as high as the sill. It was the same black dog I had seen earlier on the edge of the road. But now, this close, I could see it was something more. Its eyes were monstrous huge, like those of a frog, and totally unblinking as if they were painted on its skull. But it stood unmoving as if frozen to the ground, upright as a post, steam pouring out of its long muzzle, dew glistening on its shaggy fur.

"It ain't goddamn natural," said Billy. "It be Old Shuck or nothing else, I swear it."

When I realised that it was watching me through the glass, I felt the hairs rise up on my nape. And then it took a pace forward, its great maw now grinning bared fangs. I heard Billy behind me shuffling further back into the room and I knew that if this fell creature leapt forward that it might well take the whole window and rotten frame with it into us. And without realising it, my feet too had moved me backwards. My left hand still clutched the stiletto—nothing more than a pinprick to this black thing should it lunge—but my right hand I placed upon my chest and felt the silver locket of my talisman. Then, the memory of that dream flew into my head. I plucked the ring from my pocket, the large, crudely fashioned silver signet in my balled fist. A man will clutch at any foolish charm in distress, but somehow I felt compelled to seize Israel Fludd's ring, not knowing whether it be for good or ill. The beast outside was even closer now and I watched in horror and amazement as the window panes began growing sharp fingers of frost. They started at each corner of the window and began reaching towards the centre, crackling loudly as they splayed inwards.

And even as Billy swore a stream of oaths, I raised the ring up to the window and the black dog. I gripped it twixt my thumb and forefinger, the seal pointing outwards, and touched the metal to the glass. I could not take my eyes from the creature's huge head, its gaping mouth, its lower jaw curving upwards into a hideous crooked smile. My legs shook as I stood my ground.

Billy finally yelled, "We've got to get out of here!" and made for the door.

Yet even as those words left his mouth, the hellhound stopped dead in its tracks, closed its jaws, and in one prodigious leap bounded across the courtyard and out of sight. Billy had by now tripped over the bedstead and lay sprawled on the floor, so terrified that his curses poured forth in a high-pitched squeal. I fell back away from the window, paused a moment in disbelief, and then sat down hard upon the bedstead opposite, my heart thumping against my ribs so hard my ears rang. "It's gone," I breathed. "It's gone."

Fludd's ring had somehow settled up to the knuckle of my forefinger. I pushed it down firmly and seated it upon my hand. I sat staring out the window, watching as the frost fingers slowly receded. At some point I became aware that Billy had risen from out of the straw and seated himself on the other bedstead, silent as a monk. Finally, he managed to find his voice again.

"We told tales as boys, but by God's precious blood I never... not in all my days, never did I see such a thing with my own eyes. That creature was straight from the Pit, I swear it."

I kept watching the courtyard, still bathed in moonlight. "I confess that I'm in agreement with you, Billy Chard."

Neither of us said anything else for the next few hours. The moon sank away, its light dying into pitch, and after a while more, the first glimmer of day appeared, purple in the east. I sat the whole of that night, my blade in one hand, the thumb on my right worrying the strange ring I now wore.

It was Billy who broke the silence. "What are you running from, Mister Eff?"

I didn't give him an answer.

"Come on, now. I'm no clodpoll and I've bought only about half your story since we met. Been a soldier long enough to know when a man is running from something."

I smiled and dropped my stiff and aching shoulders. "Aye Billy, you've foxed me. I was once a soldier too. For a long, long time. And my eyes have seen a fair few terrible sights, like you. And I've seen things no man should see. Strange, unnatural things."

Billy made a grumbling noise in his throat and shook his head. "Here now, Mister Eff, when I signed on with you I didn't expect to be chased by a beast like that one. That... that fucker was no farm dog, I tell you... I'm in sore need of some truth, Fellow Creature."

I nodded. "I'll tell you this. I killed a man the other day— in my own defence mind you—but I think this black dog is seeking revenge upon me. How it's found me I know not."

Billy whistled softly. "Wool merchant, my bollocks. My mother always told me a man can't spring from Delilah's lap to Abraham's bosom. I *knew* there was more to you."

"Aye, there's more. And I cannot tell you much. It is true I am going to Exeter town to meet some fellows. Perhaps once I'm there—assuming we make it—I can confide more to you. But not now."

"Where was you a soldier?"

"In the German lands for many a campaign. Fighting alongside the Danes and the Swedes against the Emperor of Rome. It was a long time ago, Billy."

"And that ain't the only place you've trailed a pike, is it? I reckon you've seen a fair amount of service on these shores, haven't you?"

I kept looking out at the brightening sky but when I looked over to Billy, his face wore a knowing grin.

"You was a fucking Cavalier. Maybe one of Prince Rupert's Germans?"

I returned to the vantage of the dirty window. "I told you I was a soldier—like you."

"Fair enough," Billy said, certain in his knowledge. "And you seen devils like that dog thing, over there across the sea? And demons and ghosts? He slowly shook his head. "Shit, my creed says that there ain't no Devil in this world, ain't no sin either. But I don't know what I saw last night."

I did not know whether it was wise to tell him of such things. He might think me a madman.

"I will tell you that I have seen things that I could not believe I was seeing. But I did see them. And the black dog we saw this night was not of this world."

He didn't reply. Christ, I had run in the opposite direction to avoid Mazarin's dark task and had blundered into it nonetheless. Was the Cardinal that clever?

"Will you still join me for Exeter?"

Billy looked up. He was clearly weighing the scales of risk and profit. "Is the money still on the table, sir?"

"It is."

"Then I choose to stay. Old Shuck be damned. These be hard times, Mister Eff, hard times indeed, and a body needs to earn a crust."

"I'm glad of it." And I was. I hardly knew him but it was good to have a companion on the road even if he was a mercenary. "Let's to the town and find you a mount. We must get on the road again without delay."

We were being stalked. And the fell beast's master must not be far behind. Worse still, my enemy now knew where I was. Gideon would come. And Gideon Fludd was involved in something; something far deeper and far blacker than anyone suspected.

Chapter Eight

I WATCHED BILLY as he bit into his pigeon pie, the crust tumbling into his jerkin. We sat on a bench outside the shop, watching the people of Exeter go about their business. It was our second day in the town and we had finally begun to settle in with little sign of danger. The black dog of Brent had not darkened our path again and I had already left word by way of the Mitre Inn. We would meet this evening.

I itched to confide in Billy about my mission, and God knows, he had probably guessed it as much already, but still I held back. If he reasoned the price on my head was worth the candle, he would be sorely tempted to turn me in. But how fair was it to lead him on if I should be discovered by the army? They would arrest him as my accomplice despite his protests.

"So, who's this cove you're meeting with today?" he said, wiping a bit of grease from his mouth with his sleeve. "You going to get down to your business then, finally?"

"God willing, yes. We'll meet at the Mitre, around the corner from where we billet."

"And what do you want of me in all this?"

"Just keep your eyes open. You're my bodyguard now."

Billy grinned at me. "You're a sly one, Mister Eff, I'll give you that. Never knew that the wool trade was this damned secretive." He paused, and then looked at me down his slightly bent nose. "You best not drop me in the privy, sir, if things go awry. I catch on fast I do—and I like the coin—but I don't fancy going back to gaol."

"Fair enough," I said. "I'll honour that, Billy. And I'll tell you what I can, when I can."

He nodded and turned his face to the street. Carts rolled by, followed by stray dogs and the occasional beggar. Exeter was arising for the day's labours and I was already worried how long I could linger in a place that had a full squadron of dragoons encamped in the castle at the north end of the town. And eating away at me was the worry that Gideon Fludd would follow me. And that he would arrive knowing who I was and what I had done.

I folded my hands, the silver ring almost burning into my finger. "Tell me more about the Fifth Monarchists. What does that name mean, for a start?"

Billy tossed the crust of his pie into the mud where it was set upon by three pigeons. A lesson in that somewhere I was certain.

"There have been four great empires on the Earth, Mister Eff. The first was all that with the great Whore of Babylon what enslaved the Jews. Then there was the Greeks and the Romans. Can't rightly recall the fourth, the Pope probably, but the fifth—the fifth monarchy, you understand, this fifth monarchy is supposed to be the kingdom of Jesus right here on earth. Leastways that is what these folks believe and pray for."

"So they are waiting for the Second Coming of Christ?"

Billy chuckled. "Waiting? Hell no, they're working to make it happen here and now. They reckon that they are the saints appointed to light the fuse, as it were. Half of the Commons is Fifth Monarchists now. They just don't sit and pray and shake like the others, they mean to change the politics of the land to get ready for Jesus. And I can tell you General Cromwell has his hands full."

I mumbled an oath. I had been away a long time. The late war had given birth to many monsters and this sect was but one. Was my brother in the right about Cromwell keeping the lid on a pot that was ready to boil over? I wound Fludd's ring around my finger. "Tell me what you know about these Fifth men and magic. Astrology and such."

Billy fidgeted with his clasped hands and cast a furtive look up and down the street. "I knew a few of 'em last year gone by. They was always going on about the stars and reading these little books on predictions. I don't know if it went beyond that—you know, conjuring and such. But they are a mad lot. Wouldn't be surprised if they were up to their elbows in the black arts. Anything to help get Jesus here in a hurry."

I was a little taken aback. "You *know* some of these folk?"

Billy raised his eyebrows and inclined his head. "Aye, well... truth be told, I fell in with a gaggle of them last year. They made a kind of sense to me at the time but after a bit I came to see them for what they are. Bloody tyrants and holier than thou. Scurried back to My One Flesh and my brethren. We make a whole lot more sense than those buggers, my Fellow Creature!"

I smiled. "I think I'm with you on that, Billy Chard. Let's go back to the inn. I'm feeling a bit exposed to the elements." Billy grinned again and laid a forefinger aside his nose.

We sidestepped the deepest of the mud and horseshit and worked our way up Fore Street to where it joined the old High Street, the castle and the cathedral hulking over that corner of the city. Our little inn lay not far off the church green. And the Mitre, that Royalist nest of conspiracy, was but a stone's throw away. I had decided better not to lodge there until I knew who my friends were. Assuming I had any.

We had not gone very far up into the High Street when we found ourselves in the midst of a great and growing crowd of townsfolk, all jostling to get a view of what was going on up front. Craning to see up ahead, I made out two figures upon some scaffold. Billy was already pushing his way through to the front, a steady stream of foul oaths upon his tongue. And like the Red Sea, the waters parted before us.

I pulled up short, my boots squelching in the mud. Half a dozen redcoats took up station at the foot of the stage, which now in plainer view proved to be the town pillory. Billy saw them at the same time and checked his advance, shooting a glance my way.

"I think it's a bad idea to stay for this entertainment," I told him as I reached his side, a child punching me in the bollocks as it squeezed past to get a better view. But Billy's attention was fast locked on the dreadful scene unfolding up on the platform. A constable was reading out the sentence of the accused even as they fastened his arms to the upright of the stocks. He was a youngish man, reasonably dressed if now soiled with the muck of the prison. His long brown hair was in disarray and this, plus his dirt-streaked face, gave him a sadly clownish look. Amid the shouting and murmuring of the crowd I heard the word "blasphemy" carry across the throng as the constable read out the sentence. Once the militiamen had pinioned the poor fellow and tied his head to the post with a leather strap, the executioner came forward, armed with his tongs and a red hot poker.

"He's one of mine," said Billy. "I know him."

The poor creature did his utmost to twist and squirm as the executioner rammed the tongs into his mouth, searching out his tongue. The crowd bellowed and laughed and I sensed Billy was about to start forward.

I reached out and seized him by the arm. "Hold! Leave it be!" He broke my grip and I grabbed hold of his jerkin, yanking him backwards. "It's no use, you fool," I said as he turned back to face me. And I felt the rage slip out of him as I held on. He let out an anguished groan and dropped his head.

"He is my one flesh, the poor sod. He is my one flesh."

"There's naught we can do for him now. Come."

The scream carried all the way to where we stood as the brand bored a hole through the Ranter's tongue.

Billy did not look back. I guided him by his arm as we pushed our way out of the crowd. Once free, he shook me off and kept walking, stamping his left boot with every step and shaking his head as if to drive out the vision. "Goddamn them all. Fucking Presbyterians and radical dogs."

"Let's take a drink at the inn. Come, away from here."

"They're all bastards, you know."

I nodded. "And is this what you fought the war for? Threw down the king only to end up with this tyranny instead?"

"It's damn well *not* what I fought for. By God, we did expect far better. Far better."

"We can change it—if we choose our battles with our heads and not just our hearts."

Billy stopped short and spun around. "Save your sermon, Mister Eff, I'll listen to no more talk of war. Not from your ilk. Your lot lost and that is that."

"So, you'll wait until they come for *your* tongue?"

Billy waved his arm and grunted as he turned and tromped off towards the cathedral green. "I need a tall can of ale. Now."

The drink took Billy's edge off. He did not wish to talk further of his Ranter brother and I did not wish to pursue it either. After a while, his good-natured self returned, but his mind was still on the scene in the square, that I knew. I left him with another full can and went up to our room to lie on the rack for a spell and to get my head cleared for the impending rendezvous with a certain 'Mister Black'.

When I entered my room my eyes were instantly drawn to the window. There upon the panes were stamped muddy handprints, as if someone had pressed in upon the glass while they peered outside. But I then quickly realised that these stains were on the *outside* of the glass and we were up two floors in the garret of the house. And it was the size of these hands which truly set my hairs up, prickling the back of my neck. The handprints were small, the size of a tiny child's, but with long slender fingers. Whatever it was, it had been looking into my room from a great height. After the night in Brent, I needed no one to tell me it had been looking for me.

I heard Billy come into the room behind me, and soon he was standing at my side, his eyes wide at the markings on the glass.

"Billy, can you wield a sword?"

"Aye. I'm no Ajax but I can hold my own in a fight... Tell me you don't see no fairy handprints on that window, I beg you."

I moved closer to get a better look. "Possibly a dog-ape, a monkey of sorts. I don't know."

"But looking for what? And sweet Jesus, what the hell was holding it up there outside?"

I started stuffing my satchel with my shirts and hose. "We're moving lodgings. Get your rig."

Billy swore.

"Here," I said. I dropped a handful of silver into his palm that I had dug out from my belt pouch. "Get to an ironmonger and buy us two blades—nothing heavy, mind. Hunting hangars will do. Bone grips."

Billy swore again. "I felt safer in the shitting army."

"It's not your army anymore, Billy. Just you and me. Hurry along and then meet me at the Mitre down the street."

It was clear to me that whatever was tracking us was doing so with sympathetic magic. I had long heard tales of how objects held their ties to their owners, even separated by miles. There was once even a corpse that bled anew when the knife that had slain the man was brought in contact with the body again. I believed now that my Scottish dirk, left next to Israel Fludd's body, had proved a lodestone pointing straight to me. It was guiding my pursuers just as surely as if I was leaving a bloodstained trail myself.

If Fludd knew his brother's killer was in Exeter, he could be on me within the day. I could not know for sure, but it was bad enough just knowing that I was facing someone who practised dark arts. Or was this all my own conjuring, disturbed as my mind was with my secretive undertakings? No, in my heart if not my head, I knew what was befalling me. I knew all too well from years ago the peculiar sensation once one is touched by the unnatural, the otherworldly. And it was cold dread. That goddamned black dog was too real. It was as if my own Beast, ever to rise up without warning inside my breast, had been made flesh.

We found another inn and with it another suspicious innkeeper, and this house even closer to the Bishop's Mitre. It was almost as if I was being hemmed in, cornered before the kill. This time, I took a room on the first floor—off the ground but within leaping distance if Billy and I had to get out quickly. I was keener than ever to meet my contact, if for no other reason than to find a reasonable safe house outside the city. Billy was already at the Mitre when I entered, seated at the rear of the tap room with his back to the wall. The tavern master smiled and bade me greetings (he had remembered me from the previous day) and I ordered a pot of ale at the bar and joined Billy, all the while casting my eyes around the room. No soldiers, just merchants and a few apprentice lads.

Billy said nothing but carefully and slyly drew back the canvas from the bundle perched on the table, revealing two rather stubby hunting swords, their iron shell guards pitted with rust despite the blacking they had been given. "I am sure you've had far better in your time, Mister Eff, but as they say, beggars can't be choosers."

I half drew one of the hangars out to eye its blade, which at the very least had a keen edge, if one sorely nicked. They were more suited to a butcher's shop than a fight one's life depended upon. "They'll do. But pray we won't need them." I covered the swords and took a swig of ale. Another two hours until my rendezvous.

Billy leaned back in his chair. "At what point did you think it would be a good time to tell me what you're really up to? When my head gets stove in or when I find a knife in my ribs?"

I cupped my tankard with both hands and stared into the dark liquid, looking for some wisdom. It was an honest question deserving of an honest answer. But truth here could kill me. I took a heavy breath. Billy's face was deeply lined, eyes fallen into his skull, and his red-tinged beard was still unshaven and patchy. I noticed now that he was probably far younger than I had thought, worn out by hard living and war. An honest answer for an honest rogue? Or would I be in the hands of the army by supper?

"You're right, Billy Chard," I said. "I suppose if you mean to stand by me you deserve a measure of trust. But that means you accept the hard part of the bargain as well as the good. First, I'll tell you I have a price on my head."

Billy laughed and wheezed. "Well, what wool merchant doesn't? No, no, Mister Eff, I reckoned a while ago you was up to no good here. I fancy that you're a Cavalier looking for a fight—here to meet a few other coves of the same ilk. And you're about as foreign as my old father." He took a drink and waved his cup towards me. "So it seems we both have the measure of the other, no? Both of us on the wrong side of the law as it stands. Both trying to stay a few paces ahead of the magistrates—or the army. It's all understood, Fellow Creature, all understood. And it's a trust safe by me, sir. Safe indeed."

"I mean to bring down the generals and the Council and bring back our proper king. Is that too much honesty for you?"

Billy's thick lips rounded in an O. "That is a heavy task you've set yourself, Mister Eff, a considerable task if I might say."

"And there is to be an uprising here in the West Country—and elsewhere," I added, my voice still low. "Is that a bit too much intelligence for you?"

"Well, there was bound to be a rising someday, that's no secret what with folks living under the yoke as they are. But what I'm still vexed about—by your leave—is that great black dog the other night. Is that some new pet of the Parliament men? And what do you figure this little dog-ape of yours who capered up our window is up to now? Seems to me you're more afeard of them than the army."

I set my tankard upon the table. We were apart far enough from anyone else that our words would not carry. "I'm certain that I am being pursued by a Roundhead officer of the dragoons who has some knowledge of the black arts. That is the truth of it."

Billy hunched his shoulders and pushed forward, his cup clacking into mine. "What you mean is he is pursuing *us*. And I remember that great dog was a real beast, big as a cow, but it didn't come after us, did it? There's no such thing as the Devil, or hell for that matter. That's what my creed says. Everything was put here by the good Lord. There ain't no bad and there ain't no sin."

I nodded. "That may be. And I could be wrong. But I tell you I've seen things with my own eyes in many dark places. Things that would turn your bowels to water in an instant and set your bones to ice. Whether it's Satan or not that I'm facing, I am being chased by the army and I mean to fight them. The question for you is will you be my bondsman and stand with me? Will you take back your liberty as a freeborn Englishman or stay under the heel of the Tyrant?"

"It's been a few years since I fought for any cause." Billy's voice dropped. "And the last one did me no benefit." He stopped as if he was still deciding what to do next. "I'll watch your back for you. I'll keep my eyes open for the redcoats. I reckon I owe you at least that much for not killing me on the road back there at Brent. Or taking me to the law. But I ain't fighting no black dogs and I'm not ready to die for fucking Charles Stuart."

I smiled at him. "You weren't a very good highwayman anyway, Billy."

He chuckled and burped. "Well, I guess that's true enough. At least now I'm in paid employment, eh?"

"That you are. And don't even think about betraying me for the sake of a few more coins, you hear? I assure you that you won't get the chance to spend it."

Billy looked all offended and crossed his heart. "Heavens no, Fellow Creature. There may be no such thing as sin in the world but betraying another is about as close a thing as there is to it. I give you my word, sir."

"Good! I'll take your word." And I reached over and gave him my hand, for which I received a firm grip in return. "Come, drink up and I will show you where we stay tonight. I need you to remain there and keep watch while I come back here and meet my man."

Billy pointed his chin at the weapons on the table. "You want one of these pig-stickers now, Mister Eff?"

"No, take them back to the room for now. But I tell you, I'll feel a damn sight safer tonight lying abed with a sharp blade next to me."

MR. BLACK WAS anything but. His skin was paler than pale, blue veins showing through his forehead, and he was as bald as an egg. The only hair that remained upon his noggin were two tufts above his ears. As a Royalist conspirator, he was well disguised indeed. He had about as much presence as a coat on a hook, a plain townsman of middling years and middling birth. As it turned out, he actually was a wool trader.

"We apparently have a common acquaintance in France," he said as we shook hands in the tap room. "How fares Mister Carson these days?"

"He is well and still in the employ of Mister Underhill," I said.

"I am glad of it," said Mr. Black. "Let us take a turn near the cathedral."

And so we strolled across the green, the great grey cathedral looking beaten and sombre in the fading sunlight. He told me in truth his name was Hugh Dyer, and that he had served as a captain in Hopton's regiment in the war. But I still kept to my ruse, and could only hope that Sir Edward had not revealed my identity. For no doubt, every government spy would now know I had returned.

"Exeter is pulling itself apart at the seams, sir," said Dyer as we walked. "Factions are now hard set and harsh words heard at every town meeting." He gestured over to the cathedral. "You know what they've done now inside there? They put up great wooden walls down the length of the nave. Why? So that the Presbyterians take the west side and the Independent preachers and their lot take the east. Christ, its sounds like bedlam in there with each side trying to drown out the other."

I was little surprised to hear his tale.

"And we Anglicans are now in the same boat as the Papists—proscribed under pain of imprisonment. It's bad, Falkenhayn, very bad indeed."

"How goes the planning?" I asked, eager to find out just how things lay.

"Oh, well enough. We have near upon thirty gentlemen from the county and they can promise between twenty and five and a hundred men for each of them. Aye, there are eleven of us leaders here in the city alone. We meet every week at the Mitre to discuss stores, weapons and the like. Just waiting on the word really. And your arrival." He looked at me and grinned.

"But don't you vary your meeting places," I said, "for safety? You're making it simple for the army to discover the undertaking, are you not?"

"I don't believe those up at the castle yonder have a clue as to what we're up to. If we went anywhere other than the Mitre then we'd have confusion each week. Besides, the Mitre has the best beer in town. It's a very good house, you know. And the landlord is a sympathiser too."

I'm sure I must have blinked hard in amazement at what he said. It took me a few moments before I could even speak. "When is the next meeting?"

"Why tomorrow night. Same as always. We take a back room at the Mitre and take our dinner together too."

"How amiable," I said, my stomach slowly sinking as the realisation of his words fully sank in. This western conspiracy had all the secrecy of a race meeting at Newmarket. It would be pure blind luck if the group had not already been infiltrated by Cromwell's spies. But if it had been compromised, why had they not swooped down upon these fools weeks ago?

Dyer and I soon parted company. I had little desire to confide anything to him after hearing of his attitude to clandestine endeavours. We agreed to meet with the rest of his companions the next day at eight of the clock in the evening, shook hands again, gave each other a little bow of courtesy, and Dyer turned back towards the Mitre. The whole enterprise seemed even more of a foolhardy lark than before. But here I was, walking into it with both eyes open wide.

I was sickened and sad, and instead of heading back to the little inn (where hopefully Billy was already ensconced), I wandered back south through the town, down the High Street. It was hardly a busy late afternoon; shopkeepers were already putting up their shutters for the night and a gentle quiet had descended upon the street. Yet I became aware after some minutes that a figure was shadowing me, although a long distance behind. I turned down a side street to make a few more turns before coming out again on to the thoroughfare. Sure enough, as I glanced back, the person was also coming around the corner. But it was no common footpad. It was clearly a woman. She wore a long grey cloak and wide hood, pulled down to cover her forehead and eyes. I kept walking, turned another corner into a street so narrow I could practically span it with my arms, and then ducked into a recess.

She passed by me, a whisker away, and I quickly leapt out behind her. Alarmed, she wheeled around, stepping sideways and almost tripping in her heels over the cobbles. And I froze as she looked up, eyes huge. There stood Marguerite St. John. Neither of us could stutter a word, and I fell backwards into the wall behind.

"Sweet Mother of God, Maggie—how?" I moved forward to grasp her arm.

She was nervous, hesitant, and gave a small laugh and smile. "Richard, I know it is foolish and bad. But I did tell you I wouldn't stay back there."

The initial shock and joy of seeing her face now dissipated as the reality sank in. "But how did you find me, woman? And how did you arrive here a day after me?" I seized her by both arms and shook her. "Who else knows and who is with you?"

She offered no resistance or her usual fiery tongue but just shook her head at me, quietly gushing out that she was alone and that no one knew where she was. She knew that I had gone to Devon, for I had told her as much. It had not been difficult to find my brother William in Plympton, she said, although he told her he did not know where I was headed. She had surmised it was north, to London town.

I gave her another shake as my anger boiled up. "What has gotten into your empty little head? Travelling alone on the road, in England? What are you trying to do?"

"I needed to be with you. It was only blind chance I saw you on the green earlier. I had no idea you were in Exeter. And I have found you again, my love."

I relaxed my grip on her arms and I shook my head, at a loss for what I should now do and rueing the day my vanity drove me on this hopeless adventure. "We've got to get inside. And you must tell me everything—I mean *everything*. Both our lives may depend on it."

Her hands reached up and pressed over my heart. "Richard, do not be angry. I will explain all. And your brother has given me a letter for you." And she pulled away, attempting to console me in her role as courier as she began to dig into the purse at her waist.

I stayed her hand. "No, not here. We're going back to my inn, and staying out of sight until I can think of a way out of all this."

Chapter Nine

As MAGGIE AND I entered the room, Billy's slack-jawed expression quickly gave way to a wide leer. He stood up from the bed with a jump and made a little bow of his head. "Ma'am!"

"Marguerite," I said, "This is Billy Chard—a friend." Maggie gave me a confused look, undoubtedly curious about the nature of my comrade. "Billy, why don't you go downstairs for a spell. Marguerite and I have... things to discuss." Billy said nothing but grabbed his hat and, giving me a wink, laid his forefinger aside his nose as he went out the door.

"Friend?" said Maggie. "He looks like a footpad."

"He is a footpad. Dangerous people for life in dangerous times. He's also my army, for the moment."

"Don't you wish to embrace me?" She looked hurt at my coldness.

I tried to soften what must have been now a longstanding mask of grimness. "Forgive me, Maggie, forgive me. I look at you and still cannot believe my eyes that you're here. But, sweet Jesus, it's great folly for you to have followed me. You don't understand the situation I find myself in, and now I must look after you as well." I did want to embrace her, to gather her up and melt into her bosom. But already, a hundred questions were running around my head and every one needed answer. "Maggie, sit down on the bed."

I dragged a stool over and sat in front of her, grasping her hands. "Now you must tell me how this all came about. Who has told you how to find me?"

Her face was already beginning to flush scarlet. "You believe I needed help to find you? It was not difficult to pick up your trail. I merely described you to the coachmen, said you were '*Monsieur* Falkenhayn', and made it to Rouen a day after you left that place. Not very many ships going to Plymouth and it was a simple matter to find out which one you had embarked on. As luck would have it, another was leaving in two days. And I was on it."

I shook my head in exasperation. "But why, for the love of God? I'm on the run, pursued by the army, and I've only been back one week. What did you hope to accomplish, woman?"

She pulled back. "I hoped to *accomplish* nothing. I wanted only to find you and to be with you. I told you that myself before you left. I said don't leave me in Paris. Did you doubt my resolve?"

"I did, Maggie, I did. And I wish to God you had thought better of it."

She fixed me suddenly with a cold eye. "I've come all this way to help you... to be with you. Don't you dare try to send me away."

"You have a stout spirit to have gotten this far. But I can't lie about how dangerous it is even now. And I can't tell any more about the business without putting you in harm's way."

She leaned forward again and seized my wrists in both hands. "I'm already in it. It's my fight too, and I possess the stomach for it. I was not about to sit in Paris while you lead the rebellion. Sit and wait for God knows how long."

I pulled back at her words. A good guess on her part? Or had my enterprise already been discussed far and wide? "What do you know of a rebellion here, Maggie?"

Her face flushed again, her brown eyes shining as she answered. "It's the talk of all the court. That our agents have been sent here to light the fire, to bring down the Tyrant. That is when I understood why you had left me."

I stood up and walked to the window. "Does no one know the meaning of secrecy anymore? For the love of Christ!"

"It is knowledge shared only in small circles there in the Louvre, not general news, my love."

I turned back to her. "And do you not think that Cromwell has eyes and ears in the court? By God, he does. And now they know all."

She threw her hands up and brought them down on her lap. "It wasn't I who spread the word! How dare you cast blame on me when all I wanted was to be with you." She ripped at the purse that hung from her waist, snapping the leather strap. "Here is the letter from your brother. Or do you want me to send that back too? He didn't even know if I would find you, but wanted to take a chance nonetheless."

I had forgotten the letter. I reached out and took the little square packet from her shaking hand and broke the wax seal. It was indeed my brother's hand, and I began to read. He addressed me merely as 'Sir' and proceeded to relay news of various business transactions and a goodly dose of how the weather was and if it would be an early springtime. It was signed 'William'. I held it out towards Maggie.

"Did he say anything more? Just this?"

"No."

It was only then that the scent of apples wafted up to me from the paper.

I grabbed the tinderbox off the little table on the other side of the chamber. Sparking it up, I lit the lamp that stood nearby. Maggie rose from the bed and followed me, despite her rage, curious about my frantic reaction. I gently held the opened letter just above the flame of the lamp, slowly moving it to and fro, the page rapidly heating. And sure enough, like the biblical handwriting upon the wall, words in pale sepia magically blossomed on the page, written in my brother's hand and between the lines of his black-inked nonsense about the weather. I heard Maggie's subdued rush of breath as she stood at my side. And I read the real message that now stood out boldly.

Brother:

The woman who bears this letter claims to know you. From our short conversation I do not doubt this. As you did not tell me where you were bound, I could not share this intelligence with her and if she has found you it is only by the grace of God. As we two may not see each other for some time yet to come, I seized upon the opportunity to pen these words. And they are heavy ones, I must tell you. I have learned that the estate of Israel Fludd has already been settled and that his will was most specific in the disposition of his land and chattels. He has left all to your Arabella. There, that is it then. She has regained the Treadwell home for her and the children, and the babe to come. This is a blow you must bear up under, my brother. Seek solace from the gentle lady who bears this note, one who claims great love for you, sir. And, if it is not too late, and God's hand still rests upon you, I beg you to return to France with all speed. That is where your life must take you. Farewell.

I placed the letter on the table and sat upon the stool. I felt very empty and very foolish for my pride. Arabella knew how to look after herself in time of war. How else had she managed without me for all those years? I was a cuckold who had assumed his wife had been taken against her will. I recalled her words to me not one week ago: *Leave well enough alone and all will be well.*

Why had I not listened with both my ears that day?

You do not ask me, husband, whether it was by my will or against my will?

I felt Maggie's hand upon my shoulder. "What's wrong? Tell me what he says."

"Wrong? Nay, it's good news about my wife. She has come into some money, it seems."

"I do not understand."

I rubbed my forehead and stood. "It's not important. We have more pressing troubles here and now. Such as what we're to do with you. You can't wander around the town, alone and unescorted."

She grabbed my arm and turned me towards her. "Then you will need to escort me, damn you."

I grasped her gently by the shoulders. "Look at me! I'm being pursued by someone. Someone in the army. He knows I'm in Exeter and... I have slain his brother."

She didn't bat an eye. She reached up and stroked my shaggy beard. "We're here to fight, you old fool. Not run. Tell me what I have to do but don't tell me to leave you again."

I was tired. I felt the tears welling up in my eyes and I pulled her into my chest as if to squeeze the life out of her. "I'm running out of schemes, Maggie. And time as well."

I felt her squeeze me back. "You are Richard Treadwell, not Andreas Falkenhayn. And you have work to do here. Let me be your helpmate."

I was silent as she embraced me, until finally I heard myself say aloud, "Very well. Tell me where you're lodged."

"I am at the coaching house, near the bridge at the south gate."

"Then I shall take you back there now. You must stay inside until I have a better idea of what is happening in the town. I have a meeting with the others tomorrow night. But you must stay out of sight, for now at least. Understood?"

"Tell me what I must do and I will do it."

* * *

How COULD I not have spent the night in her arms once I had brought her back to her chambers? I had precious little else to hold up my spirits while my enterprise crumbled around me with each passing day. Billy had shrugged when I told him she was my mistress who had followed me from Paris. "Better than a black dog," he said. I suppose little about me could surprise him at this point. I told him to stay around the inn and watch for the militia. "Aye, and then do what, Mister Eff?" he had said cheekily. I told him just to keep out of trouble and that we would meet up in the morning. "At least one of us will have a good night!" he called back to me as he walked down the stairs to the tap room.

All my fears and worries emptied into her as we tussled that evening, devouring each other as we had not for many weeks. But the whole of the time I held her, there was still the faint waft of distrust between us about what we each had revealed and what we had concealed. I finally drifted off, her head upon my chest, her long chestnut hair covering my mouth and chin. A deep sleep, undisturbed by my Beast, or nightmares, or any cares of the waking world. And come cock crow, we both awoke in the orange glow of sunrise, and she was upon me again. We lay there, afterwards, and slowly my reverie blew away and the stony truth of my situation invaded once again.

"Who was it that you killed?" she asked as we lay there.

"An officer of the Plymouth militia."

"My God, Richard, why?"

"Trust me, I had little choice but to kill him. And his brother pursues me even now. Gideon Fludd, an officer of Parliament's dragoons."

She reached for my hand. "And what is going to happen here, in Exeter? Where are the others in the conspiracy?"

"You should not know these things. It doesn't bode well, I can tell you."

"Are you telling me it's over before it has even begun?"

I swept the hair from her face. "Maggie, there's more to it. This Gideon Fludd is not just a Parliament man. He is deep into bad things. Dark things. He has some power of the black arts... conjuring and such."

Maggie giggled. "Surely not? You're saying he's in league with the Devil? What, a Parliament man—a Puritan no doubt—practising magic?"

"Maggie, I have seen—" and I had to pause, stumbling for the right words. "I have seen his creatures... his familiars. They're stalking me; I know it in my heart. I've never been more sure."

She reached over and squeezed me. "You're sore vexed, my love. The weight of these last days has tired you. It's no wonder you think you're seeing phantasms. But nothing has happened yet, has it? Only children and old women believe in goblins and demons."

I was sad for her in her ignorance. "I've seen such things in my life I do wish I had never seen. I am seeing them again now. You have to understand that there are things in our world that do not belong here, wondrous but terrible things. Billy Chard has seen the beast that follows us, he will tell you. This is no phantasm or fancy of the mind, my love. And I would spare you from it."

"You're frightening me."

"I know. And you need to be frightened. Don't underestimate this evil. Look, this evening I'll learn whether I can continue with my plans. That is why I need you to stay here today—do not venture out. I will come for you this evening. Promise me you will not follow me. If events go ill, I won't be there to help you. If they get me, for God's sake don't remain. Get on a ship for France without delay."

She pulled herself up on her elbows and stared into my face. She was delving into my mind, I knew, and few women could accomplish that. She was one of them.

"If that is what you want, then I will do it," she said quietly.

* * *

I RETURNED THAT morning to the little inn where Billy stayed, determined to obtain answers from Dyer and his comrades. But it would have to wait for the evening and Billy and I spent the whole of the day closeted in the little room, playing at cards and him telling stories.

"I'm hungry," he said as he played with his hunting hangar while he kept watch at the window of the room.

"What, again? You've already supped," I said. "You can eat again later." The sun was just dipping into the west, its rays reflecting into the room, a myriad of dust particles floating through the beams.

"You don't want me to go inside with you, Mister Eff? Meaning if they prove a rum lot you might want some help."

"I need you to watch the outside and if you see any redcoats you're to get to the back as fast you can and warn the rest of us. I don't think these fools have the plain sense to post any sentries while we meet."

"Aye," Billy said as he slid the blade back into its scabbard and placed it upon the belt that trussed his leather jerkin. And he pulled his black cloak over all and went to lie on the bed and wait for the appointed hour.

There was silence between us then, both of us buried in our own thoughts and fears. And like a piece of driftwood that insistently rises to the surface, I could not keep Arabella from my mind's eye, or Maggie. Maybe I felt that I deserved my fate. I had left my wife to the harsh contrary winds of war. Yet strangely, I admired her too, for surviving the tempest and getting the better of our enemies. What bothered me though, eating away at my guts, was the thought that maybe she *wanted* me to kill Fludd. Admittedly, she could not know that I was to turn up on her doorstep that day. But once I had, did a plan hatch in her head that I could speed a satisfactory conclusion to her situation? It was monstrous, I know, but I had lived in such a dark place for so many years that it was a suspicion that came naturally to me now.

And then there was Maggie. Was I being played again, and so very damned soon? Resourceful as she was, something was scratching away at the back of my head, whispering things I did not want to hear. Had she really found her way from France to Devon, all this way, without aid? Who else knew of her mission to find me? And it went around and around as I stared up at the cobwebs swinging in the rafters.

At length I got up and leaned against the wall near the window. How long I stood there, watching the empty street and rooftops, I know not. Eventually, the night came on, the light slowly retreating into twilight. I went to the table and reached for my blade, tucking it into my girdle. Resting against my hip, its presence gave me silent reassurance, like an old and trusted retainer who had lost his tongue. I reached over to the little shelf near the fireplace and retrieved my little French pistol, flipping the pan open to check the primer. I shoved it down into my girdle, the hammer and lock nestled against my belly. "It's time, Billy," I said.

We reached the Mitre tavern. Billy drew out his pipe and pouch and walked to the side of the house. He leaned back, crossed his legs, and proceeded to fill his clay bowl. I took a breath, pushed open the front door, and went inside. The tap room was awash with topers and beer while a great fire crackled in the hearth. I slowly weaved my way through the public, the stink and the smoke, towards the back and the private dining chamber. A crowded house has a mood—good or ill—and one easily read. Here were the merchants of the town, artisans, maybe a farmer or two fortifying themselves before the trip out of town. All was a jovial burble, though somewhat subdued, and an easy, downright lazy mood permeated the room.

And yet, and yet... It was a picture I had seen a thousand times, but something was amiss. Then, I hit upon it. There was not even one militiaman, redcoat or not, in the place. That was not the way of things. Still, I knocked on the door at the back, pushed it open, and stepped inside. There were seven men there, seated at a large round table, Dyer among them. And they all looked up at my appearance, and rose from their places.

The chamber was large, the only furniture being the table and chairs. Another door was at the back, presumably leading outside to the yard and privy. There were two windows on one side and a large brick fireplace on the other. And it was the most damn fool place to hold a conspiracy that I had ever seen.

Dyer smiled and beckoned to me. "Mr Falkenhayn, sir. Welcome to our little feast! Please, do come in and join us at table." The others smiled too, nodding their approval. I shut the door behind me and took a place with them.

"Gentlemen," I said, nodding my head and pulling back a chair.

Dyer poured me a tankard and pushed it my way. "Will you take some venison, sir?"

"I took notice that you place no one upon watch at the door."

It was not Dyer, but another fellow who answered me. He was a prosperous sort, well dressed, a brocade hatband showing off his wealth. "We're in no danger here in this place, rest assured. The landlord will always give us a signal if anyone suspicious turns up—like that fellow of yours who is lurking outside."

As I turned, I saw Billy dart out of view at the window. I gritted my teeth. "A measure of prudence, if you will indulge me that. I have always found that a drop of caution goes a long way. Forgive me if you take this as a lack of trust."

Dyer waved his hand, and went back to cutting me a slice. "Not at all, not at all. We have met here and dined for months, never anything amiss. Be at ease."

I must admit, I was somewhat flummoxed as to how to begin the discussion. I decided to let my hosts take the lead, but as the minutes passed by, the business of rebellion never once rose to the surface. All was frippery: talk of weather, wives, and gambling. As the time passed, I saw that at least two of this dining club were deep in their cups, eyes wandering and heads drooping only to start up suddenly at the next joke or jibe. As they licked their trenchers clean and reached for the great wedge of cheese and another loaf, I could wait no longer. I asked Dyer in a low voice when he wished to discuss the preparations for our mutual enterprise.

"And what would you like to know?" he asked, not fussed in the least.

"For one, numbers of men, horses, arms, powder stocks..."

Dyer laughed. Another gentleman, someone called Stubbes, a fat fellow in a yellowed collar, remarked, "That is more than one question!" and the others joined in the laughter.

"Gentlemen," I said, smiling, "My intention is to journey to London soon and it's vital that I brief Mister Jeffreys with exact details as to your preparations. Timing is everything."

"Who the blazes is *Jeffreys*?" asked Stubbes, still laughing and looking across the table from face to face. He was answered by one of the drunkards. "It's Colonel Gerard, you idiot! Have you forgotten already!"

And at that point, things unravelled fast. Someone stood up, started pissing into the fireplace and singing "The King will come Home Again," and the others joined in with the exception of Mr. Dyer, who looked mildly embarrassed as he tried to reassure me about the undertaking.

"My dear fellow," he said, "Don't fret about the details. I can provide you a list of everything and everyone."

I leaned forward, already worked into a lather by these simpletons. "A list? You mean you have committed these to *paper*? Your concept of secrecy, sir, leaves much to be desired."

"Falkenhayn," he said, waving me off, "You're among friends here in this town. The troopers stay cooped up in the castle and don't dare argue with a people they know to be loyal to the crown."

I stood up and cursed aloud. Not at them, but at myself for hazarding all on this pack of ignorant knaves. How badly compromised the uprising now was I didn't know, but anyone in Exeter would have to be blind, deaf and dumb not to know of its existence.

"They'll be no more talk of the enterprise here. If I'm to assist you we'll meet next time outside—in hiding. No more public houses, do you understand, sir?"

Dyer pushed back his chair with a horrible screech along the floorboards. "Do not suppose to tell us our affairs! I don't care whether you've come from the court or not. No matter what Lord Herbert has said."

My throat began to tighten as he spoke. These country clowns were in so deep they were halfway to the scaffold without even knowing it. And I knew then the whole plan was a shambles, indeed it had probably been instigated by Cromwell's spies to pull in bigger fish, like me.

"What was that?" said Stubbes, pointing to one of the windows. We looked over to where he was pointing, but there was nothing other than the reflection of our candles in the panes.

"What did you see?" asked Dyer.

Stubbes chuckled. "I don't rightly know. Not your man, Falkenhayn, but someone else. It was there for but a moment. Looked like the ugliest little nigger child. Had his nose pressed right to the glass, eyes rolling around like a lunatic."

And then, out of the corner of my eye, I saw movement at the other window. I turned my head to see the small black face of an ape peering into the room, its eyes locked firmly upon me. But the creature was near the top of the frame, looking in sideways and somehow clinging to the brickwork outside. And like that horrid black dog, it too had huge yellow eyes that betrayed an intelligence—and malevolence. A long spindly arm extended down the uppermost windowpane, its hand bizarrely elongated, ending in wicked ivory claws. And I swear I saw it point a finger at me.

I was on my feet in an instant, intending to rush out the back door and capture or kill it, but no sooner had I jumped up then the main door to the chamber crashed inwards. The latch blew halfway across the room and in poured half a dozen men, swords drawn and raised. We were betrayed.

Most men in such circumstances turn to statues. Dyer and his friends were no different. But I seized the table edge and flipped it outwards towards the intruders. Plates, cups, crockery and food went flying as the table upended, smashing on the floorboards. It gave me enough time to draw my pistol, cock the hammer, and level it at the lead man. None of the intruders were redcoats and in an instant I felt the hand of the Fifth Monarchy at work. The tumbling table barely checked their advance, and they pushed past a terrified Stubbes who had both hands raised and palms splayed. I fired my piece but was rewarded only by the puff and snap of the priming pan igniting. The main charge was fouled.

The first man came on, a big bearded fellow wearing a red woollen cap. I flung the pistol at his face. He caught some of it on his hilt as he raised his hand to block it and the pistol spun up and clipped his forehead. It checked him long enough for me to draw my sword and rush him. Only Dyer seemed to be putting up a fight. He too had drawn his blade and had just parried a wicked thrust at his chest. There was to be no quarter offered; they were here to kill. I jumped forward, left leg first, my blade hilt high and point down. I easily parried the bearded man's chop and simultaneously pulled back my tip and thrust down into the top of his belly. His leather coat ripped and I felt the blade nick him, but it had not gone very deep. I lashed out with my right fist and took him on the jaw.

The other attackers pushed into the room, coming around towards the left, as I stood to the right. Except for Dyer, the conspirators were crying out for mercy and as I backed up towards the rear of the room (and the back door) I saw that those giving least resistance got little more than a clout to the head. I seized a kicked-over chair and brandished it as I made for the door. Dyer, defending against two, took a well-aimed blow to his collarbone from a cutlass, and sank to his knees.

That was enough. I threw the chair, yanked open the door to the courtyard, and jumped outside.

Straight into the party of red-coated dragoons I had been expecting earlier. By the time I had counted five in front of me, I knew that my luck had run out. And then, a tall grey-coated man came forward. The man I had always known was behind the whole of this sad chase. Even in the poor lamplight, I could see that it was Gideon Fludd. He held one arm out low, palm outwards, as if to signal his men to hold back from engaging. I turned at an angle to cover myself from attack from the doorway, spread my feet and dropped into a high guard with my hanger. Gideon stepped forward, slow and measured, straight at me. His cropped blond head was practically white in the lamplight and his face was set as hard as old walnut. And when I looked into his eyes, I confess that the depth of his rage and hatred shook me. I could feel both courage and resolve draining through the soles of my shoes.

Gideon's eyes glanced down at my hand. I was holding my right arm poised in front of my chest, a secondary guard from attack. And there on the third finger shone the silver signet ring, the object of his attention.

His voice was strong, but chillingly, empty of either hatred or tension. "You have something that is mine, sirrah." He held out a thick-bladed rapier, lazily waving it at hip level, point down. "And you know what it is, don't you?"

I wondered where Billy had got off to. He had manifestly failed his first command. Well, I thought, even if he had given the alarm, the odds were very poor anyway. I hoped that he had gotten clean away; this really was not his battle. Three men spilled out of the back door, and I saw Fludd spread his left hand towards them in a gesture of restraint. Perhaps I was about to gain what I had sought at the beginning of this fool's voyage: a good death. I could never depart as Andreas did, rotting in his bed. This was the far better course. So I did something that Fludd probably had not expected. I ran straight at him.

He was surprised, but he was not confounded. No rustic at swordplay, he simply drew back his leading right leg and fell back with his weight on the left. He made a clean parry of my thrust, the two blades scoring each other loudly as mine ran up his, meeting his swept hilt. And I leapt back immediately; knowing the man closest on my right would take a swing. Sure enough, it came a second later and I twisted to parry this and then back again to take Fludd's counterthrust once he had regained his balance. I moved rapidly to the right, feinting a throat thrust at one of the men and then spitting him in the stomach. Even as he dropped, I whirled and brought my sword up to ward off the blow I instinctively knew was already in full arc. The blow I managed to parry high, but the force knocked my own hilt back into my cheek and a jolt of pain ripped through my face.

These things take but the blink of an eye. I didn't even get the chance to spin around again at the next attack. My vision became an explosion of sparks and light and the roaring pain in my skull told me I was too late. The blade or hilt—I didn't know which—had struck my head clean and I slowly spun around like a puppet. I could not feel my hands—probably had already dropped my blade—and I saw the faces of my enemies swimming in front of me. My head arched up, my last view of the world. I saw the heavens whirling and my eyes took in a dizzy view of the peak of the gable of the Mitre Tavern. I swear I saw the black ape sitting perched there, watching all, two great leathery wings sprouting out of its back, waggling in anticipation.

And all light and knowing failed me as I fell.

Chapter Ten

I WAS AWARE of voices around me. Something hard and unyielding pressed against my cheek. I was not dead—at least not yet, and slowly my mind rose up from the depths that surrounded me. I was sitting in a great heavy chair, my cheek lying against the carved oak headpiece. My eyes opened to take in a scene most strange. I was seated at the head of a table, a long affair, in a good-sized chamber of elaborate panelling and many leaded lights. It was still night. And I was not alone. Was this the magistrate's house? I raised my head and was rewarded by a thunderous clap of pain through my skull. Both of my wrists were bound to the arms of the chair. I then became aware of a dull but growing pain in my right hand. I could see that the silver ring was gone: my finger purple, bent, and probably broken.

In spite of the agony behind my eyes, I tried to focus on those who sat arrayed before me in the haloed light of the candlesticks. All five of them dour men, dressed in black, expressionless, tall crowned hats on each. And then, a sixth floated into my view, a man in grey, standing at the opposite end.

"Give him drink," commanded Major Gideon Fludd. One of his comrades stood and approached. He raised a tankard to my lips and I drank, gratefully, the beer soaking my beard and spilling down my shirt front and coat. "Now, sirrah," continued Fludd, his voice quiet and calm, "we must attend to the business at hand. I have taken back that which is mine but we are not yet satisfied." He came around the table and walked towards me. My eyes followed his progress. He was at first glance no more than a young man, a beardless boy even. But in his voice there was age, experience, and a note of self-assurance well beyond his years. He stood at the arm of the chair and studied me silently. I saw that this fair-haired man was fair-featured too, almost angelic. Unblemished; eyes, nose, and lips in harmony just like the statues of the ancients. And yet, looking at those eyes, I could see nothing behind them. No pity or high purpose, not even honest anger or hate. His eyes were dead.

He turned and held up my stiletto.

"We found this in your belt. Not the weapon of any gentleman who means well." He gripped it and thrust it into the table top. Fingers rubbing against his palm as if the stiletto had been tainted, he rounded on me again.

"I am in pursuit of the murderer of my kinsman. The signs that the Lord has shown me have led me to this town. And they have also brought me to *you*." He held up his left hand in front of me. "I now have a ring which I found upon your hand. This ring belonged to my brother and was stolen by the man who killed him." If he was fishing for me to blurt out a confession then he was going to be disappointed. Fludd began nodding thoughtfully at me, then turned to his disciples. "We now must appeal to the Lord for further signs of the presence of the guilty."

A murmur went through the five. "God be praised! His will be done!"

Fludd turned and walked back to the head of the table. "I had expected to find only a thief in Exeter, not a Royalist conspirator. And one in roost with other birds of a common feather. Will you tell me your name?"

I prayed he did not truly know it already and was merely baiting me along. I opened my lips and croaked out, "Falkenhayn... Andreas."

Fludd nodded, whether he believed this or not. "Your companions I have already turned over to the militia in the castle. Their fate is of little concern to me. Their plotting was already known and observed for some time. But you, sir, you there is more to than meets the eye."

I swallowed and licked my lips, already bone dry despite the sip of drink. "By what right do you hold me here? I don't know you or your companions."

Fludd smiled. "What *right*? By the right of retribution, surely. But we must make proof of our suspicions. You're correct in that you at least deserve that service, Mister Falkenhayn."

And I watched as he drew out another dagger. It was my Scottish dirk, the one I had dropped on the kitchen floor that wild night.

"This weapon was found alongside my brother's corpse. It did not pierce his body but it will nonetheless testify as to his assailant." He placed it upon the middle of the table, its point directed at me, the brass studs of the black hilt glowing in the reflecting candlelight. "If you are but a mere thief and opportunist—or conspirator—you'll be delivered to the Army Council for rightful prosecution. If a murderer you be, then I will take my own justice as I choose."

He then folded his hands in prayer, quickly followed in suit by his comrades. "Lord, continue to grant me Your divine favour and bestow the blessed signs. Give us Your divine wisdom to show out the guilty, the spillers of the blood of the saints! We beseech thee, Adonai!" A chorus of amens sang out along the table and Fludd opened his eyes again, settling that piercing gaze directly on me. It was just as it had been in the square at Plymouth. I felt him look right through me. He raised his right hand out over the table, palm down, face set in stone but never lifting his gaze from me. I heard one of the others start praying aloud, "Our Father, Who art in heaven..."

And after a few moments, a noise upon the table. A rasping noise, the sound of an object being dragged over the scarred planks. In numbed horror I watched as the dirk slowly moved along of its own accord, determinedly propelling itself closer and closer to me. It was returning to its owner.

In a low voice the man closest to me muttered, "He beareth not the sword in vain: for he is the minister of God, a revenger to execute wrath upon him that doeth evil.' So saith the Lord."

I could not take my eyes from the blade as it crawled its way to me. And it came on, inexorably, until it reached the edge, a hairbreadth away from my bound hand. Fludd lowered his arm and swept his other hand over his face as if a great weight had been hefted and set down again. He then looked at me again, and this time, rage stoked behind that saintly visage. He came around fast, pushing a chair out of his way and whisking the dirk from the table. He gripped it and pushed the blade up to my throat; the point bit into my flesh. "Base, foul creature," he whispered. "You have slain one of the appointed of God for no other cause than worldly greed and avarice."

The blade pulled back and he laid it on my right cheekbone. In a flash he jerked his wrist downwards, and I felt the tug of my skin as the blade cut in, and then the delayed agony as it sliced down, blood pouring out onto my shirt. Fludd raised the blade again, flicking it up to my nose. He then caught a nostril with the tip, and tore upwards with a swift pull. I screamed, the blood spraying out in front of me.

Fludd tossed the knife onto the table. "We will wait for the direction of the Lord's messenger to decide your fate. If God wills it, and He accepts our prayer, then His angel will come among us this night. As he has before. The hour will soon be at hand."

I was drooling and spitting out blood as he made this pronouncement. "You clever bastard," I muttered. "Where is your black dog and that winged ape? Are they too messengers of your God?"

He wheeled on me in an instant. "Blasphemer!" And his balled fist struck me so hard I saw lights dance, my head colliding into the wing of the chair. And he struck me again, and again. I felt him seize my forelock, and my head jerked up as he wrenched my skull. "For you, sirrah, the agonies of hell await!" And he drew back his fist to his shoulder before sending it crashing into my face. And for the second time that night, I was thrown into oblivion.

I WAS ON the floorboards. I could feel my left eye swollen up so tight I could barely see out of it. But I was still alive. The floor was sticky with my blood and I was stiff and aching, my nose on fire. They had dumped me out of the chair, trussed me like a hog, hand and foot, and thrown me in the far corner of the room. But this time, as far as I could tell, I was alone. The hard varnished floor stank of blood and soap mixed, and the cold went right through me. I started to shiver as I lay.

From my vantage, head upon the floor, I could see a doorway in front of me, slightly ajar. I didn't know whose house I was in, but from my surroundings, it was surely that of a man of wealth. And was I still in Exeter? It must be so. My ears kept ringing, high and low, around and around. I pulled my bound wrists close to my chest as I pulled up my knees, crawling on my elbows along the floor like a wounded worm. The doorway began to loom larger. I rested a bit, my face lying flat, and then pushed forward again. I finally reached the threshold of the open door and with one final push, found the upper half of my body in the next chamber, a darkened hallway. But at the opposite end another doorway lay, and this too, was open.

I had to find the stairs without making a sound if I stood any chance of escape. I pushed into the hallway a few lengths, but then stopped. There were many voices coming from the next chamber, and one of them was Gideon Fludd's.

"He comes not," said someone in the room.

"We have not prayed hard enough, or followed the conjuration to the letter!" said another.

Then Gideon: "Silence, all of you! On your knees again, and resume the prayer!" I could hear the rustle of garments as the others obeyed. And then Gideon Fludd spoke, voice raised almost as if in song. "Here are the symbols of secret things, the ensigns and the banners of God the conqueror and the arms of the Almighty One, to compel the aerial potencies. I command you, by their power and virtue, that ye come near unto us into our presence, from whatsoever part of the world ye may be in."

The prayers of the others tumbled out, in differing cadences and tones, all the while Gideon's steely voice raised high over all.

"I conjure thee, by His Almighty power and by the light and flame which emanate from His countenance and which are before His face... by the angelical powers which are in the Heavens and by the most great wisdom of Almighty God; by the Seal of David, by the ring and Seal of Solomon which I bear here... Eistibus... I demand thy presence!"

And suddenly, the light emanating from the room grew in intensity. It grew so bright, and so quickly, as if it was daylight contained inside four walls. I squinted as the door frame was bathed in whiteness. It slowly dissipated, but the light remained as bright as a thousand candles. And then I was struck full by the overpowering scent of blossoms, as if summer had somehow come upon us by stealth. I heard a sound like rushing waters, a waterfall or a wellspring coming from the room. The men had stopped praying aloud and I knew not what had happened inside. Then a voice spoke. A voice so clear it rang like Bohemian crystal. It was neither male nor female but a strange combination of the two sexes, and it filled my ears so full it was as if I was in the chamber with them all.

"Gideon, thou callest me forth, this, the third time. What would thou knowest of me, son of man?"

Fludd's voice fluttered with apprehension and whatever manner of thing had manifested itself in that room, it had filled him full with terror. "I would know more of your telling, Eistibus. We seek to know what we must do to hasten the final days. You have given me the signs before and I beg you to give them unto us again."

"I will tell you this: the end of days is not far and the new kingdom is near upon the tide. The rule of the Saints is upon us."

I heard the others exclaim and cry out hosannas and amens, but Fludd kept his head to his task. "Angel of the Lord, what must we do to bring about the day? Do we take the sword?"

The voice of Eistibus seemed to merge with the sound of the rippling waters that bounced from the walls around me. "The Great Captain will drive out the wicked from the house. This he will do inside the next moon."

"Cromwell will dissolve the House! I knew it would be so!"

"But be not cozened by the Great Captain... He who would usher in the rule of the Saints would also set himself up upon the throne before the year is out! He is false and does not serve the Light."

Fludd stuttered a reply, so terrible was the import of this prophecy. "The Lord General... a traitor to the Saints? O great Spirit, you give us Hope and Despair mixed. What must we do?"

"After the house is cleansed, he must die."

"He has delivered us from oppression, he is our captain..."

"He must die, that the kingdom may come."

Neither Fludd nor any of his companions deigned to reply to the entity. The water gushed unseen all around and the sweet smell became nauseating. I pushed myself upon my elbows to the side of the corridor that I might somehow catch a glimpse of what went on inside the chamber. I managed to press myself against the wall, crane my head upwards, and just was able to get a look beyond the partially open door.

What I saw took away all my pain, so sudden was the quickening in my chest. I could see the far wall of the chamber, now a roiling cloud of milky substance from floor to ceiling. It tumbled onto itself and swirled like smoke in a bottle, indeed, the whole mass seemed to push forth from the wall and enter the room only to recede back again. But that which stood upon the floor in front of this cloud froze me with dread. I saw the angel, white with great eagle's wings, tall as Goliath, standing over all of Fludd's men. I was spared its terrible visage for its head was turned away from my vantage, but such a white light poured out of the creature that the glow was almost painful. I could just make out Fludd and two others upon their knees, just inside a great white circle painted on the black floor.

Gideon Fludd must have pricked up his courage again; I heard him cry out: "Will you give us aid? You and the other Seraphim of the ether? Tell us what we must do!"

"Gideon," answered the angel, "My power in this sphere waxes with the moon and in the day of Saturn. Call upon me then and I will give you the instruments you desire. My servants will continue to do you service even as they obey me."

"Cromwell shall be slain," said Fludd, his voice choked.

"Fail us not!" the angel warned, its voice rising to a near screech. That was more than enough for me. Though pressed against the floor, my bowels turned to water, I somehow crawled backwards, away from that terrible sight. I regained the chamber I had been in before and swivelled my head, looking for a way out of the nightmare. All my pain had now returned, and my head spun with delirium and disbelief. I placed my cheek upon the floor and shut my eyes. The boards were cold on my chest and belly but I still felt myself drifting away, falling again.

An instant later my heart was in my throat. I felt a hand press into the small of my back and another cover my mouth. From the corner of my eye I saw someone lean over and look into my face.

"*Ca va, Colonel?*" came the words in a near whisper.

The man who knelt over me *looked* like d'Artagnan, that same swarthy face I knew of old, but I could no longer trust my senses which were fast drifting away.

"*Monsieur* d'Artagnan?" I croaked. "You have no shoes on your feet."

I felt his hand roughly grasp my chin and move my head, as he leaned over and examined my face. "*Merde!*" was the only word I could comprehend.

I felt a tug on my wrists and then they came apart. So too with my ankles as the musketeer cut loose my bonds. Then I felt my shoes coming off. He shook me and my head must have lolled like a doll's. He swore again and smacked me upon the cheek with the palm of his hand. "Colonel, get up!"

It was d'Artagnan. Here, in England. Here with me. I slowly crawled up to my knees and I felt him raise me swaying to my feet. Barefoot, and he practically carrying me, we somehow made it to the stairwell. Whatever still went on beyond us in Fludd's chamber, I did not know. Whatever prayers they were saying, they did not hear our escape. Outside it was darkness except for a sliver of moon. In my dizzy state, the trees swayed like monstrous Hydras and I could not tell whether we were in town or country, farm or estate. We hobbled across a courtyard, then mercifully onto lawn and towards a thick stand of oak. I glimpsed horses under the trees, and someone else. I felt myself pushed into the withers of a mount, and then someone had grabbed my legs and was hoisting me into a saddle.

"Blessed God, Mister Eff! Give us a hand, sir! Can't budge you on my lonesome, Fellow Creature. There now, up you go!"

Billy Chard pushed my hips round and I slumped over the saddlebow. Next I knew he was behind me and grabbing the reins. I looked up to see d'Artagnan, already mounted in front of us, raising his hand and giving a short whistle. And we were off at a fast trot, Billy's hand gripping the back of my coat. My stomach rolled and up came my accounts over the horse's neck.

"Sweet Jesus, Mister Eff! You're in a bad way. Hell of a banquet by the sounds of it."

I should have been thinking about how d'Artagnan had magically appeared. Or how Marguerite had lied to me. Or how Billy Chard had reappeared after abandoning me earlier. Or even of the miraculous vision I had just witnessed in that house. But what kept rolling around my mind was the thought of what Gideon Fludd would make of two empty shoes lying on the floor of his dining room.

Chapter Eleven

W̲HEN I CAME̲ to, it was in more comfortable circumstances. I lay on a proper feather bed, the curtains drawn back full. At my left sat Maggie, the vision of a proper country maid, dressed in plain dark wool skirt and bodice, a linen cap upon her head. At first, it was a slightly jarring sight. I had never before glimpsed Marguerite St. John in anything other than silks and taffetas. But looking into her face again, cheeks pink as budding roses, my spirits rallied.

But even as I opened my eyes into what I took to be early morning light, all the memories of what had gone before came swimming back to mind. And a new sadness quietly closed on my heart. Across the bedchamber I could see Lieutenant d'Artagnan standing near the large casement window, absently watching the world outside. Unlike Maggie, he was rigged to the height of gentlemanly fashion, and a Paris gentleman at that. His rapier sat low, slung across his hip, his jet black coat dripping with silver frippery, two huge lace cuffs protruding from the sleeves.

I spoke, my top lip feeling thick and swollen. "Where is this place?"

She looked up at the sound of my voice. Her green-flecked brown eyes suddenly gleamed. "Richard, rest easy. We're safe and outside of Exeter now."

I tried to raise my head off the two commodious pillows I lay on and was rewarded with a horse-kick to my skull. I must have winced visibly in pain for she reached out and laid a hand softly on my shoulder.

"Lie still. You still have a lump on your head like a goose egg." Her hand moved to my face with a caress. "But the boss and bruise to your cheek is already much improved and I think your nose will heal on its own in time. And God bless Billy Chard, he was able to set your finger while you were still senseless last night and put a few stitches into your face wound."

I looked at her, my head sinking back again into the pillow. "Why did you lie to me, Maggie?"

She looked straight into my eyes and spoke without hesitation, almost as if she had been expecting the question. "I did it to save you. I don't regret it... for the moment at least."

"You led him here to Devon, to me." By now, d'Artagnan had heard me speak and was standing next to Maggie, an arm upon the bedpost.

"Yes, I did lead him here. But I also told him that before he killed you he would have to kill me."

"That was very clever stagecraft you managed," said d'Artagnan in French, looking at me with a soft smile. "The Cardinal thought you were playing your role well at the English court. Too well as it turns out. You have forgotten your orders, sir."

"And His Eminence is a man who does not like being made the fool?" I mumbled.

"*Tout a fait, Colonel*. He knows of your part in this hare-brained uprising against Parliament. He knows, and he does not approve. You should have known better than to run out on your employer and benefactor."

"You may piss off back to France."

D'Artagnan shook his head slowly. "No, I cannot. Not without you. You might recall our orders the last time we served together, 'If you can't bring him out, you must kill him'. I'm afraid these orders are unchanged."

I said nothing.

"Don't be upset, Colonel. Consider this all a mark of great respect for your skills. If anyone could make this rebellion against Cromwell happen, it is you. The Cardinal knows this and the Cardinal does not want this to occur. Not before he knows the alternatives. It's not in the interest of France."

Maggie spoke up, and it was clear she knew I was wounded by her betrayal. "And he saved your life last night... with Billy. He could have let those Parliament men finish you, but he pulled you out just the same."

She was right, but so too was d'Artagnan cunning. Maybe he thought they would *not* kill me and I might later escape to do some damage after all. But no, I knew in my heart that she had convinced the Lieutenant to fetch me out, back to her, and back to France.

"How did you know where they had taken me?" I said.

She reached out and grasped my arm. "That was down to Billy. He followed at a distance and observed where they took you. Thank God it was not far out of the town. He returned, half-dead, to find me at my inn and tell me the news. The rest you have discovered for yourself."

D'Artagnan reached out towards me. In his hand was my Scottish dirk. "I recognised this from our little adventure last summer. It was on the table where I found you. Used it to cut your bonds... only fitting, no?"

I tried to smile. "That it is. But you have exchanged it for my shoes." Fludd could use any item that belonged to me to track me down. D'Artagnan gave me a puzzled look but his impending retort was interrupted by the entry of Billy, a satchel thrown over his shoulder.

"Good morrow, Mister Eff!" he said, noticing that I was awake. "Looking better than last night, I do see." He set down his burden and came over to the bedside. I saw that it was my own satchel he had somehow retrieved from our inn. "They gave you a mighty basting and I'm sorry I couldn't come to your aid in time, though the Lord knows I did try."

"Where were you when they burst in at the Mitre? You were at the window one minute and the next gone."

Billy nodded, his face more haggard, and suddenly, more grave than usual. "I saw that thing, sir. I did. That ape beast with wings. I was near the back of the tavern when of a sudden it swooped down, knocked my hat from my head and nearly took me down too. First I thought it was some night hawk or owl. But it came again and I saw its face. It was all teeth and claws." He held out his raked and torn sleeves for me to see. He then rolled these up to reveal huge red welts and scratches on both forearms. "Did my best to fend the beast off with my blade but I'm ashamed to say, I ran like a coward anyway. I'm sorry I left you to it, Mister Eff. Heartily sorry indeed."

I could not blame him for running. Even if he had managed to fight alongside me, the outcome would have been the same. "You did the right thing. If you had not followed and then fetched help, I would now most likely be dead and gone." I turned to Maggie. "Do you believe me now? That we're fighting more than men of flesh and blood?"

Maggie pursed her lips and said nothing.

"Have you told the Lieutenant what I told you about Gideon Fludd?"

"I have," she said quietly. "But I do not think he believes that magic is afoot."

I laughed hoarsely. "What? He's a Catholic, isn't he? Sounds as if the Cardinal has not confided *everything* to our dear d'Artagnan."

Billy was eager to lend support. "Aye, mistress, it's all the truth. I'd swear upon the Bible that it is so. You can tell that to the foreign gentleman."

"Those who do not believe must often see things for themselves to do so," said Maggie, almost apologetically.

D'Artagnan had wandered back to the window again, lost in his own deliberations and bored of the English patter.

"Whose house is this?" I asked, changing the subject.

"They are Catholics, merchants who compounded with Parliament to retain their house and business. We're very close to Topsham, I think. Somehow d'Artagnan knew of them and brought us here."

I nodded. "A safe house in Topsham known to the Cardinal? Christ, he does have a long reach."

"We can stay until you're better. The Lieutenant plans for us to hire a coach and make for Lyme Regis in a few days."

"As simple as that, is it?" I said, feeling like a runaway apprentice about to be dragged back to his master. "Maggie, whilst I was being held last night, something happened. Something terrible is being planned, something that I'm hardly prepared to face. Yet... you will have a hard time believing my tale. D'Artagnan will no doubt call me a liar or a fool."

"What is it, my love? What did Fludd say?"

I closed my eyes. "Not now. I hunger and thirst—and my head, Christ my head... Billy, fetch us some food from the mistress of this place, and drink, will you?"

Billy nodded and turned to go. He seemed as lost as me given this turn of events. We were more tied together than ever before, having both witnessed the unbelievable. And even Billy had not seen the awful and dreadful wonders that I had. He was still struggling with what he had seen with his own eyes, something that could not exist in his creed if there was no hell.

"Maggie, I need to shave off this beard and clean myself. Perhaps I could borrow a razor and some scissors from our hosts? And after I have downed some fare I'll tell all of you what happened to me last night, whether you believe it or not."

A remembrance of the night before, I could only bring myself to tell in the full light of the day, out of doors, in the warmth of the sun. My companions, both the invited and uninvited, sat with me in the herb garden behind the house. The master of the house, our gracious host, was an older gentleman and clearly terrified of our presence in his midst. One suspicious report to the mayor about his odd guests and he would lose everything. I could see him peeking from his larder window at our little gathering. Still, thanks to him I was fresh shaved and proper again in borrowed coat and breeches. But I looked a mighty rogue with the injuries on my purpled face, a great black scab running up the right side of my nose and a jagged welt where Fludd had flicked the dagger. God knows who this old man thought I was; I could smell the fear on him at thirty paces. He knew he was harbouring treasonous folk. That he allowed us to stay, it must have been, I suppose, from the duty of his Catholic faith or fear of the Cardinal. Whatever his motive, he was as nervous as a hen.

I told my tale in English for the benefit of Billy, asking Maggie to translate all to d'Artagnan. And when I had finished, after some minutes of recalling the horrors I had witnessed, there was silence. Billy swept his palm through his long greasy hair, muttering a low oath. Maggie seemed torn whether to believe or not for my sake, and d'Artagnan, ever the sceptic, wore a thin, parsimonious smile as he stared at me. He was obviously deciding whether I was plain mad or just devious. It was he who finally broke the silence.

"And what would you have me say then, Colonel, about your mysterious vengeful angel? I saw nothing of what you described yet I was there too."

"You were not in or near that room, sir," I said. "Perhaps it had gone by the time you discovered me on the floor. But the threat was clear. A foul outrage is about to be executed in London."

"But my dear fellow," said d'Artagnan, "You might have been senseless from your beating and have dreamt the whole visitation, no?"

"I was wide awake, and frightened for my very life."

"And what do you propose, *Monsieur*?"

I swallowed, still unsure whether I had made the right decision. "I must warn Cromwell of the plot to kill him. This is what His Eminence had an inkling of—what he had tasked *me* to uncover. Cromwell must be told that the Fifth Monarchists will strike in the next two weeks. If he dissolves Parliament as many already believe—and the angel foretold—then they will strike the sooner. You can help me warn him. Surely you carry a pass of safe conduct from the Cardinal. You could go to Whitehall or even Hampton Court."

D'Artagnan laughed as if he had just heard a good joke. "Tell the Lord General that the Angel of Death is coming for him? You came back to England to assassinate him, didn't you? It was an easy supposition for us to make and one the Cardinal has taken seriously." He slowly shook his head at me. "No, Colonel, I am no simpleton and neither are you. You cannot expect me to escort you to within arm's reach of Cromwell, carrying such a foolish story."

I looked down at the rosemary, thyme, and fresh shoots of lavender that sprouted in the garden bed in front of my borrowed shoes. "Very well. I confess it *was* my intention to kill the dictator. But that was before I learned certain truths, even before the other night's revelations. In my heart I know now that he is the only man who can keep England from destroying itself. As a comrade in arms, I beg you to believe me. I wish to save the Lord General, not destroy him."

D'Artagnan got up and brushed off his breeches. "Colonel, you know full well that there are plots hatched against Cromwell month in and month out. His intelligencers, including *Monsieur* Thurloe, are fully aware of what is afoot at any moment. The Post Office is an impressive collection of fellows. His Eminence is even jealous of their skills, I think. If these radical Protestants mean to murder Cromwell, it is no doubt already known. A web is probably being spun against them as we speak."

I stood and gently gripped the musketeer's arm. "D'Artagnan, no bodyguard can stand between the unworldly creature I have seen in that house and Cromwell. He needs to be warned. You must allow me to go to London, indeed you must come with me!" My plea sounded foolish even to my own ears. And if it was an avenging angel that served the Fifth Monarchists, what weapons could ever be raised against it? Was it God's will?

I need not have worried that d'Artagnan would ally with me to face the beings of the ether. He placed his hand on my shoulder, clearly convinced that I ought to be taken to Bedlam. "Sir, we will have you convalesce another day or two yet, and then we will return to France. These last days have overwrought you, admit it to yourself. The Cardinal seeks no punishment against you. You're too valued a servant to the Crown. Come, end this fantasy, sir. Accompany your good lady back to Paris and leave all this nonsense behind."

I nodded slowly. Not in agreement but in recognition that I had failed to convince him. "I am hurt and tired, d'Artagnan. You're in the right, sir, in the right."

Maggie was then at my elbow. "Come, Richard, let us go back inside."

I turned and caught Billy's gaze. "He doesn't believe you, that much I can understand at least," said Billy. "Don't you worry, Mister Eff, I believe. And even if only half of it's true, then God help us all."

I smiled back at him. "What can a man do, Fellow Creature, when he is but a man."

"Amen, sir." But something in Billy's eyes told me he was far from ready to give up on things so soon. A certain look, maybe a flash of intent he let slip, that said he was still willing to take revenge for himself, for me, and for the kingdom.

I was as meek as a lamb the next two days. D'Artagnan and Maggie somehow managed to find me some new rig to replace that which was bloodied and soiled and, marvel of marvels, produced a fine pair of black boots for me too. I'd never been comfortable in those shoes. Maggie didn't trust me to go back to France of my own free will, that I could see in the way her eyes watched me. And her words were carefully chosen ones, meant to elicit from me even a subtle hint that I intended some rash escape. But I kept my counsel to myself. It was late in the afternoon on the second day at the safe house before I had the opportunity to find a moment alone with Maggie. We strolled through the walled garden of the big brick house, along carefully tended pathways of slate flags and beds of marjoram, parsley and chives. Pushing down further into the garden in the full, warm sun, we entered a stand of box and yew, musty and fragrant. I pulled her in after me and embraced her in the green shadows and cool darkness of their thick canopy.

"I was angered when I discovered you were with him," I whispered. "But my heart could not stay cold—a few days ago I thought I would never see you again, and then, thank God, you were here with me."

"I would follow you again, my love, to save you if needs must. I have my father's doggedness in such things."

I brushed her cheek and caressed the locks that lay hidden beneath her linen cap. "Do you believe me? About what things I have seen. About what the angel foretold."

Her smile was one of pure, sweet faith. "Richard, I do believe you."

"Even so," I said, looking down and brushing my lips over her bosom, "the Lieutenant is sound in his judgement. There's nothing more I can do here. Cromwell must fight his own battles with the monsters he created. We have to go back. And I must make amends with the Cardinal somehow."

She stroked her hand along my now smooth chin and mouth. "I've uncovered a new person entirely here under that beard. It's a change for the better, I think. It will be as it was before."

"*Monsieur* d'Artagnan has treated you civilly, I hope... I mean, as you travelled together."

For just an instant, one eyebrow arched, and I knew I had ventured too far.

"He has ever been the gentleman, Richard. Is this jealousy I hear?"

"No, Maggie," I said. "It's just that I must know that you have confidence in him. He's your protector on this voyage, is he not?"

Maggie laughed. "Well, I suppose I have had to look after him here in England as much as he has looked after me. He speaks barely a word of English."

"Just make sure you stay with him at all times... for safety's sake."

She squeezed me. "But I will have two gentlemen to escort me back to Paris, not just one!"

"Of course, you will! We three will escort one the other."

BILLY CHARD'S PACING across my room worried me. "Here now! Are you settled in your mind with all this? If not, I must know now, not later."

The host was out in Topsham to market, d'Artagnan had gone off to make final arrangements about a coach and two, and Maggie was safely tied up on the bed, gagged, and as furious as a cat in a sack.

"Look here, Colonel... Mister Eff. I mean to keep my bargain with you. You know it's what I want, sir. And I'll pay back whatever fucking thing it was that cut me up and anything in league with it. But this is a buffle-headed plan as ever I heard."

"Aye, not a clever plan, I warrant. But I'm afraid I can't think of any other. If I can gain us but a few hours start, we'll confuse the hounds. Don't you worry. Are the horses out of sight of the front of the house?"

Billy grimaced. "Goddamn it, Mister Eff. What do you take me for, somebody kicked once too many times in the head? I've got the provisions and kit strapped to the saddles. Even stole a sword for you from the downstairs hallway."

"Billy, I should have given you more credit."

We were both quiet for a minute or two. Then he said, "I'm not ashamed to say I'm afraid. Fear is what's kept me alive many a time, it has."

I nodded.

"But," he said, absently rubbing his wounded forearm, "I have to know, sir. I have to know what is out there. If it's all true then my creed is wrong—I'm wrong. And the world is about to end."

"I don't know about the end of the world but I do know I owe General Cromwell a blood debt from long ago. I mean to warn him and pay it back." I walked over to the bed and looked at Maggie. She had stopped struggling now, just lying motionless, eyes wide open. When she fastened them upon me, she could have turned me to stone.

"Do not despise me, my love. There is no other way. I can't take you to London with what is about to happen there. D'Artagnan will take you back to France and out of harm's way. Stay with him. You alone have my heart and no other, Maggie."

Her eyes held both rage and hurt but little else. I would not find forgiveness that day.

My voice fell to a whisper. "Maggie, please forgive me for this."

"Mister Eff! He's coming now."

I had Billy's pistol pressed to the Frenchman's temple as soon as he passed through the doorway. He slowly raised his hands.

"And now, *monsieur*?" he said.

After Billy had relieved d'Artagnan of his rapier and bound him at the foot of the bed, he then went about stripping off a pillowcase to fashion a gag. The musketeer looked up from the floor, almost comically holding on to his dignity as he sat there trussed up, as if we were in some game.

"Colonel, you are truly a greater fool than I believed if you think this will afford you anything. You surely must know me better by now. I shall not give you rest."

"I do know you, comrade," I said. "And I begged you as a sword brother for your help. You refused. I now must take what gambles I need to. I ask you, sir, to escort Marguerite safely to Paris to her father's house. That may not be your duty to His Eminence but it is your sacred duty as a gentleman."

"You can only expect to steal a few hours' march on me, Colonel. You'd be wiser to use your little dagger on me now."

I shook my head. "You may yet take my life from me, sir. Tomorrow, or maybe the next day. But I cannot take yours. Sometimes loyalty trumps practicality. And besides, I trust to fate to decide what the future brings."

D'Artagnan let out a little laugh. "Ah, Colonel," he said, "I always suspected you were a Calvinist at heart!"

I motioned for Billy to fasten the gag on him. Then I thought of something. I knelt down and reached into his coat. D'Artagnan glowered at me for he instantly guessed my intent. I pulled a small packet out of his right lining pocket: the Cardinal's red wax seal stood out proudly, the size of a Spanish crown. I hoped it was a letter of safe passage or some such diplomatic pass. As the Gascon's bronzed face went darker still, I felt I was probably right.

"Billy, go get the horses."

I got up and moved over to Maggie once again. I leaned over, and kissed her upon her forehead. This time, tears were spilling from her eyes, liquid pearls of trust, lost. Probably forever.

Chapter Twelve

"GOD, THE STENCH!"

"It's the tanneries a few streets behind, no doubt," I said.
"You'll grow used to it before long."

Billy's face wrinkled up like a dried apple and he swore aloud.
For my part, I felt relieved. We had made it all the way to
London without being caught by d'Artagnan or the redcoats.
I had taken the road to Lyme Regis assuming that d'Artagnan
would never believe I would go where he wanted me to. From
there, across to Southampton and then north to London; we
had made it to Southwark and London Bridge in a week.

I shot the wooden bolt home on the door to our chamber and
threw my satchel on the bedstead. We were now ensconced at
the Bear at the bridge foot. As we had arrived at the old inn,
Billy's jaw fell slack at the sight of the rows of pikes high up on
the ancient stone gatehouse that hulked across the road: upon
each pike a rotting, crow-pecked head. I needed no reminder
that a similar fate awaited me if I should fall into the hands of
the army. But that was the very reason I had chosen to make
Southwark our destination. People here knew enough not to
ask questions. It was and always had been a lawless place and
the Roundheads generally left it well enough alone. What with

the stink, the whores, tradesmen, pickpockets and bull-baiting rabble, it was hardly the chosen haunt of a God-fearing Puritan.

"Some grub?" asked Billy. I nodded, pulled a few coins from my pocket, and tossed them to him.

He touched the coins to his forehead. "Maybe when I return you can explain what we're doing here in this shithole."

"As soon as I figure that out myself," I said, and flopped down on the thin mattress of the bed, which creaked and sank like a dying animal exhaling its last.

Billy smiled and headed for the door. "I am sure you've it figured out well enough, Mister Eff."

In truth, now that we were in London I had thought of little else than what I was to do. And the more I thought about the best way to warn the Lord General Cromwell of the plot to kill him, the less sanguine I became. Neither he nor any of the Council would ever believe so fantastic a tale. Assuming I made it past all the guards, past *Monsieur* d'Artagnan (who I knew in my heart must be on my heels), past whatever dark creatures Gideon Fludd threw in my way, Cromwell would undoubtedly call me a madman or a liar and arrest me on the spot. Even d'Artagnan's passport from Mazarin (I had lifted the seal and read it) offered nothing I could make use of. At best, the loss of it might slow down the musketeer's progress in London. No, there had to be another way. A way to stop it all from happening.

I rose from the bed, and went to the window. There before me was the great river, the grand old bridge at my right, straight as an arrow across the flow, its tumbledown houses jutting out over the piers and the smoke from a hundred chimneys carrying upwards and eastwards down towards Wapping. A few wherries plied the currents, careful to avoid shooting under arches where the brown water gathered deadly pace. And just beyond, just out of my sight, lay the Tower, that place I knew too well and my sad home when I was last in London town.

Billy was gone a long while. He returned laden with a platter bearing half a roast fowl, some bread, and a jug of beer. We sat at a little table and some broken down benches, beetle-chewed and raining sawdust. Yet both of us tucked in, ravening down the fare after so many days on rutted muddy roads. Billy waved a drumstick at me and gulped a mouthful of bird. "We had a clear run of it this far. Do you reckon that Gideon Fludd has given up trying to take you? I mean, no sight of Old Shuck or any other ungodly thing."

"Fludd has other concerns on his mind at the moment. But I don't think for a minute he's given up on taking his revenge on me."

"So what's it to be then, Mister Eff? March over to Whitehall and have a chinwag with Noll Cromwell? We'll need a bit of help to manage that."

My fingers tapped on the beer jug. "Aye, going at it head on seems the worst of all possible courses. But perhaps, just perhaps, some outside help is no bad idea, Billy. We're in need of some allies—and some protection."

"What do you have in mind? Recruit some volunteers while standing on a barrelhead in the Strand?" Billy snorted like a rooting hog and ripped off another gobbet of fowl with his huge teeth.

"No, I mean seeking aid of another sort. You were here in London with the army a year or so ago, weren't you?"

Billy nodded as he chewed.

"Then, where would these Fifth Monarchists go to get their astrological pamphlets and such? You know, where they would seek out the fortune tellers and the like."

"I've heard tell the place for that is the Seven Dials market, just the other side of Covent Garden. But what good will fortune tellers and old books do us? We need shot and steel and more than a few ruffians who can wield it."

I shook my head. "No, you've *seen* what we are up against. We need the knowledge of magic craft if we're to get through these next days. I'm convinced of it. That, and the love of Almighty

God. I need someone who can tell me about the medallion. And what that ring means. Those symbols. Remember how the black dog retreated at the sight of it?"

I watched as Billy blanched at the memory of the beast. "I don't wish to think about such things, sir, if it be helped."

"That won't stop them from pursuing us. You know that as well as I."

Billy lifted the jug and took a long swig. He handed me the beer and laughed faint heartedly. "So, a few lucky talismans from Seven Dials and we'll ward off the fucking Devil? And what if Fludd really has an angel on his side like what you said? Who are we to fight angels, or demons for that matter?"

"We don't stand a hope in heaven or hell without the wisdom to know our enemies. That is for certain. And we're fast running out of time."

ABOUT MID-AFTERNOON, our bellies full, Billy and I buckled on weapons, threw on our cloaks, and walked to London Bridge. It was far darker and cramped than I had remembered it years before. The road barely one cart wide, the houses soaring up on either side four or more stories, it was like entering some enormous long ship, a quarter-mile from stem to stern. It was a mass of people, all selling something from the ground floor shops, traffic pouring across in both directions and an argument overheard every few yards as drovers fought over who had the right to pass first. It took us half an hour to get across, Billy cursing and kicking at the beggars that jumped in our path. Things eased up by the time we reached the last third of the span: a fire a few years before had burned up all the houses. It was now just a thoroughfare with great wooden palisades thrown up on either side to stop people and beasts from falling over the sides.

Once across to the north bank, we hove west towards the Covent Garden. The streets were crowded with all manner of folk going about their daily business. No one could have imagined that the kingdom was fast approaching disaster and that something otherworldly was stalking the Lord General of England. Cattle were being whipped north to Smithfield, apprentice boys hung about in groups looking for trouble, hackney coaches tore up the muddy streets, sedan chairs tottered precariously under sweating bearers, hawkers called out their wares, and all was pure London bedlam. At the piazza, I asked a passerby for directions to the Dials, which were cheerfully given. And when we finally arrived into the maze of cheek by jowl dilapidated dwellings, I stopped. I had no idea where to turn next.

Billy looked at me, awaiting some instruction.

"Very well," I said quietly. "Let's just follow this road in and hope that it takes us to the centre. If it's a Dials there must be a hub to the wheel. Come on then, let's leg it."

We came to a cobbled nexus with a little stone fountain dribbling water like an old man trying to pee. Along every outward spoke, a myriad of shingles hung over the streets advertising physik, palm readers, astrologists, ale and wine, or bawdy women. I could have chosen among a hundred magicians, conjurers, charlatans, and capering mountebanks, all promising the secrets of the world. But which? I leaned against the stone of the basin and watched the high and low trudge by me. To think that such a place was tolerated by the New Republic was astounding, until one noticed the large number of wealthy Parliament men hurrying by. And as I was to later learn, even Cromwell himself consulted an astrologer before making decisions of state. Bloody hypocrites, each and every one.

Billy was remarking on some woman or other, when I caught sight of someone moving quickly across the fountain court. There amongst all the hues of brown, black, ochre, and white, something different drew my attention. An embroidered headscarf of many bold colours floated in and out of the crowd, its owner making her way to one of the little streets. And without thinking, I followed. As I drew closer, I could see the white scarf had many flowers upon it—gold, red, green, blue, and black. The woman paused, half turned back towards me so that I caught a glimpse, and then continued on. My heart skipped a beat. But still, what my eyes saw and my mind imagined could not be possible. Billy was pushing his way through a crowd of drunken men, trying to catch me up. I waved him on but didn't stop. I could not lose sight of the woman.

She ducked through a shop doorway, and I saw her sweep away a dark red curtain suspended across the threshold. Without a second thought I followed her straight in. I was in a receiving room of sorts, a large table and bench at its centre, and suspended from the ceiling beams were hundreds of bundles of herbs, all arranged neatly and ready to be plucked down. A cabinet on the far wall had phials and jars filled with what I assumed were medicines and potions, most of an amber hue. A low cupboard in front of the large-paned window held many tiny drawers, each meticulously labelled. And as I stood taking this all in, a woman's voice came from behind me, the strangely accented English making me shiver.

"What is it that you want?"

I turned around and I was looking into the grey-blue eyes of my Anya. I had not seen her in twenty-five years. She had read my fortune for the last time in Gottingen in the kingdom of Hannover on the eve of battle. Every word she had spoken then to that poor lost soldier boy had come to pass. She was older now, but not aged. The same brown skin and jet hair that I had known. The woman who had given me the talisman that now dangled from my chest. And she, not surprisingly, recognised me. Her welcome was like the first time, a lifetime ago. As if she had been expecting me.

She reached out a hand and placed it gently upon my heart. "You still wear the charm, then? That is good. I told you never to lose it, didn't I?"

I nodded, too dumbstruck for words. A few lines around the corners of her eyes, a thinning of the lips I had kissed but once. But she was still very much the same as I had remembered.

"How did you come all this way? To come to England?" I was shaking my head now in disbelief, even as her eyes crinkled up in amusement. "How, Anya... and why?"

"There be no why, man," she said. "I have always gone where the road leads me. You remember."

I did. I remembered that she had unexpectedly crossed my path twice before, many miles apart, and always the same knowing looks. And now again.

"Anya, I am in need of counsel—in bad need."

She nodded, bade me to sit, and then went to shut the door to her little shop. She returned and sat next to me on the bench. I saw she was barefoot as I had always known her to be, her brown feet scarred and hard. I turned to look into her face and touched her hand, but she gave away no emotion. "Anya, I still cannot believe my own eyes." I stammered something and, again, words failed me.

Now, and only now did the faint outline of a smile cross her lips. "Do not dwell on it. What is meant to happen will always seem strange. I knew we would meet again even if you did not. But you're in trouble. That much is clear to me. Ask me what you will."

I nodded and reached to my satchel under my cloak. I drew out the strange medallion that I had carried all the way up from Devon and I handed it to her. Before she could have possibly seen the symbols that lay etched upon it, indeed the moment she grasped it, I heard the sharp intake of breath and she pulled away from me. The medallion slid from her hand, thudding to the floorboards. I picked it up and she slowly, indecisively, reached out to accept it again. She gingerly turned it over, looking at the markings on both sides. And then she spoke in German as when we had first met, her voice but a whisper.

"*Schmutzig*... Tainted," she said. "It has helped birth some evil thing."

"I need to know what this disc is and how it works. I can tell you it belongs to my enemy and even now I suspect he searches for it. I know it is purposed for magic."

She looked up at me. "That it is, man. And it should not be carried lightly by a soldier the likes of you." She paused, as if thinking. "Your comrade is coming in."

Sure enough, Billy appeared in the doorway looking suspicious and on guard. "Anya," I said, "this is Billy Chard."

Billy's heavy brows knit together but he gave a quick nod. She regarded him for but a moment before turning back to the medallion. "Get rid of this thing," she said, handing it back to me.

"That I could, Anya. But my enemy is seeking to kill not just me but others as well. He is in league with things not of this world, things... aye well, things of heaven or hell I know not, by God. Yet I need someone who can give me answers to this magic, and maybe protection too."

She stood up and tugged her bodice down squarely upon her hips. I could see her hands were still shaking a little. "I must tell you—the charm I gave you is no proof against what that device brings with it. I can offer you nothing more to keep you from harm if you stay to your current path."

"Tell her about the black dog and the ring," said Billy in a low voice from the doorway, his eyes big.

"I had a silver ring. It, too, was from my enemy. It seemed to possess some power to drive away..." I paused, running a hand over my chin. "To keep at bay creatures of evil. I saw them. Billy saw them."

"Describe the ring," she demanded, her voice very quiet.

"It bore a five pointed star and a Greek word—or so my brother said. Tetragrammaton."

Anya nodded. "I know it." She walked over to her cupboard and began rummaging around. "It is the Seal of Solomon, a device of protection and of great power," she said, her back still to us as she pulled open some of her little wooden drawers.

"You mean King Solomon?" asked Billy.

"Yes. The legend says it was he who first fashioned this talisman on the word of angels."

"Do you have one?" I asked her hopefully.

She turned again to us, something in her hand. "No. And I have not the art to make one that would stand the test. But I do know someone who might be able to help you. He has been known to me for several months. He is a gentleman astrologer of some renown in London. He is trustworthy."

"Is he a Parliament man or a Royalist?"

"Does that matter to you? If he has the knowledge you need then that is that, no?"

"Actually, it does matter greatly."

Anya tilted her head slightly as if remembering something. But it was something she could not have known. "Of course. Fear not, this man will not turn you in. And if truth be told he was a supporter of your king."

"His name?"

"Mister Elias Ashmole. Seek him at the house of John Tradescant in Lambeth village."

She opened her hand and I saw a small white linen pouch tied with red thread. "This is not for you. It is for your man Billy."

She walked over and handed it to him. Billy looked at me and I nodded, recognising the same little cloth pouch she had given me as a young soldier in Germany. "Wear it always and stay safe."

Billy tucked it into his breeches pocket and gave her a tug of his brim.

"If he is to follow in your footsteps," she said, turning back to me, "it is the least I can offer him. As for you, I can give you no more than I already have. If you are set on your present course you must search out aid greater than mine."

"I understand. Does this mean I will not see you again for another twenty-five winters?"

Anya's eyes sparkled though the corners of her mouth remained unmoved. "Who knows, man. Who knows." She took my hand as if to say goodbye, but slowly turned my palm up and traced her fingers along it, eyes intent upon the lines. "We two are not done yet," she pronounced.

"Payment?" I asked her.

"One silver thaler... deferred for the moment."

I smiled at her, as one of the few pleasant memories of Germany flooded back to me.

Billy and I were soon out into the deafening madness of the Dials, the experience of the past few minutes already seeming only half real. "Did you really know that woman?" asked Billy, as we made our way back to the piazza and towards the river.

"Billy, I still truly do not know that woman—nor am ever likely to."

"Sturdy, handsome creature, though," said Billy.

We arrived back at the Bear as the sun was sinking, the purple of twilight already settled upon the sky in the east. Even as we had walked quickly across London Bridge, I had suddenly felt the quiet teasing of my Beast, tugging at my gorge. My breaths started coming faster and shallower. By the time we reached our chamber, it had me fully in its grasp. I just managed to unbuckle my belt and promptly fell upon the rack, a shivering heap. Poor Billy must have thought I had been stricken with the plague. He kept asking what it was that ailed me, as he tried to pinion my legs that were kicking about, quite beyond my conscious control. I wrapped my arms about myself, turning upon my side, mouth open like a gasping fish. And I could hear my heart pounding on my ribs so hard I thought it might burst. I somehow cried out for Billy to leave me be, but he tried to cover me with a blanket and threatened to fetch a physician.

"No, do not!" I said between short breaths. "It's no fever. It will pass."

"Fucking hell, Mister Eff. You're causing me a fright like a fellow I knew in the regiment who had the falling sickness. You never knew when he was going to flop. What do I do?"

"Just stay," I said, teeth rattling. Billy nodded. And there were no further words between us for near upon an hour. Slowly, I felt the anxiousness melt away, the shaking stopped, and I fell asleep like a babe, worn out with the struggle.

The next I knew, Billy was nudging me to wakefulness, the room in darkness except for a single candle.

"Are you whole again, sir?"

"What's the matter?"

Billy's voice was strained, his words tumbling out almost in a whisper. "It's one of the kitchen boys downstairs. He's in the tap room telling anyone who'll listen that he saw a goblin out in the alley tonight."

I was up in an instant, flinging the blanket from me. "One of our winged friends?"

Billy shook his head. "Don't know rightly. Just said it was a black thing, standing upright like a man and skulking around the back, all hunched over like and grunting like a pig."

That we could have been tracked again so quickly since our arrival startled me and the remnant of my invisible Beast blew away. "Get our kit. We must leave this place now."

"But the innkeeper saw nothing and the men downstairs are laughing about it."

"I'm not taking any chances with the enemy we're dealing with," I said, strapping on my sword. "We'll find a place to hole up in somewhere out on the bridge."

Billy was looking at me, his expression a mix of concern and doubt.

"Are you whole again, Mister Eff?"

And in a flash I realised that I had revealed my weakness to him, the only man who knew of my malady. That this put me at a disadvantage there was no doubt. I had to take charge if for no other reason than to reassure Billy not to abandon me, or betray me.

"It was just a passing illness, some stomach gripe. But I'm not about to keep running away from Fludd's minions since it's clear they can track us whenever they choose. We take the fight to them now. Show me where this thing was seen in the alley."

Billy's eyebrows rose for a second, and then he nodded.

"I'll load the pistol."

WE STEPPED CAUTIOUSLY down into the little maze of alleys behind the inn, the stink of beer and piss strong in our nostrils. Dogs were barking a few streets away and I could still hear late revellers down on the High Street which led to the barbican at the foot of London Bridge. Our eyes grew accustomed to the gloom, the only light a crescent moon that played hide and seek with the clouds. The way was so narrow that we would not be able to stand abreast and fight. Billy took up position at my left shoulder and a pace behind. I walked forward, upriver, headed towards the Clink prison and down to the great church of St Mary's.

My eyes and ears strained to detect any movement. The occasional perpendicular passage spilled random torchlight onto our path, creating threatening shadows that took on diabolical shapes. And then, a new scent wafted towards me, a smell that stopped me full in my boots. I glanced back to Billy who was looking at me with fear written all over his sweating face. He had recognised the smell as had I. It was not the smell of the tannery vats. It was the stench of rotting flesh, a sweet and sickening odour I knew well from years of war. And it was growing stronger. I began moving forward again with my rapier extended, the only sound the echoing clop our boots made on the cobbles. And then, a new sound came to us. It was a sort of scrabbling, a scratching of claws on wood, like some cat scrambling up a door.

I was hit from above. Something big had pounced on me and I was thrown against the far wall and then to the ground. A deep squeal like that of a hog echoed in my ears as I shook my head and braced myself to stand again, my sword arm swinging wide and my blade whistling through naught but air.

As I raised myself up again, I could see it, standing three yards from my nose. There was just enough light to make out its face though I wish to God there had not been. It was naked, skin glistening like grey wet leather. It was manlike, standing upright, but there all resemblance ended.

It was as large as a bear, its legs bowed outward, the arms absurdly long and the slim fingers and claws drooping like the branches of an enchanted willow. And its head was that of a boar and man combined, a stinking creature whose eyes were large and white. In that instant we glared at each other and I saw some strange intelligence in its hideous face. A flash erupted from behind me and a loud report set my ears ringing. Billy had fired. The beast staggered back screeching, for he had found the mark, but then I quickly saw the shot had done the thing little harm. It raised its arms and crouched as if to spring at us. I cried out and ran forward to skewer it while I had the chance.

It lashed an arm towards me to ward off the blow, then turned tail and made off, splayed feet slapping loudly on the cobbles. And I without a second thought gave chase, Billy's cries echoing behind me. It was unnaturally fast and it was outpacing me further every second. The alley opened up onto some yard as we entered the outskirts of the church and I could just see it hopping towards the river, and it was grunting as it did so. I lost it near the high bank where the Thames lay and heard a terrific splash as the beast leapt into the swirling waters.

I leaned against a wall to catch my breath and Billy was soon at my side. "It's gone," I rasped. "Into the river."

"Mother of God, did you see it? Did you *see* it?" Billy's arms were shaking.

"Yes, I saw it. But why did it run? It was big enough to tear me in two."

Billy stood next to me, sucking in breaths. He leaned his backside against the wall, clutching his smoking pistol like some charm. "We must have given it a fright, you and me, eh?" And he coughed out a laugh.

"No, it was something else. It was almost as if it didn't think it had the strength to take us. I saw its face. The bloody thing was actually thinking—*calculating* what it could do. And it ran. But by Jesus, why?"

Billy just shook his head. "This is bad business, sir, black business for sure. Now what shall we do?"

I rested my blade in my gloved hand as I looked out onto London. The smell of death had disappeared. "Tonight, we stay on London Bridge. Tomorrow we search out this Mister Ashmole of Lambeth. And may God help us. We need to make some powerful allies before the enemy has a chance to strike at Cromwell, or at us again. And I don't reckon that time is with us, Billy, not with us at all."

Chapter Thirteen

"THAT WILL BE sixpence, my dear fellow."

I blinked, not really understanding what I was supposed to be paying for. As it was known to every passerby, we had been directed without too much difficulty to the house of John Tradescant in Lambeth. I entered the front door and was met by a gentleman a few years younger than me, sandy-haired with a handsome ruddy brown face. His large green eyes shone with an almost peculiar eagerness to welcome.

"I'm afraid you are mistaken, sir. I am seeking Mister Elias Ashmole."

"Aren't you here to see the collection? The Ark... The cabinet of curiosities!"

I shook my head. "I am unaware of any collection. I have business with Mister Ashmole, though."

"Ah," he said, taking a half step back and inclining his head. "I am sorry to have presumed. I am Elias Ashmole. And who do I have the honour of addressing?"

I hesitated. "I am Andreas Falkenhayn. A mutual acquaintance suggested you might be able to offer me some assistance."

"Mister Falkenhayn... I see. And who was it that directed you to me?" Instantly, his look shifted to one of mistrust.

"Anya... in the Seven Dials."

Now his eyes expressed not scepticism but instead, curiosity. "Come with me, sir, into the collection room. We can speak freely there."

I followed him into the fine, grand house. Walking past a window, I glimpsed Billy near the horses, marvelling at the massive archway in the courtyard formed from the ribs of a long-dead grampus.

"My host, Mister Tradescant, is away visiting relations," said Ashmole, striding across the corridor in front of me. "I am carrying on with my cataloguing of his collection... the one you have not heard of." We passed through dark-stained oaken double doors and were in a large chamber, very bright and lit by eight great diamond-paned windows. It was without doubt, the strangest room I had seen in my life and my widening eyes drank in wondrous, exotic sights: a stuffed salamander, a chameleon, a pelican, a flying squirrel, another squirrel like a fish, all kinds of bright coloured birds from the Orient. A whole fantastical menagerie of things looked ready to leap upon me. Another view brought to the eye an ape's head, seashells, the hand of a mermaid (said the label), the hand of a mummy, all kinds of precious stones, coins, a picture wrought in feathers, a little box in which a landscape is seen in perspective, two cups fashioned of a rhinoceros horn, many Turkish and other foreign shoes and boots, a sea parrot, a toad-fish, an elk's hoof with three claws, and a bat as large as a small dog.

"Mister Tradescant inherited much of this from his father. But he is himself an inveterate collector of curiosities, both natural and fashioned by the hand of man. Still, it all has to be identified and categorised, you see. It will take many months."

"I am told you are an astrologer, sir."

Ashmole stopped and turned to face me again. "I dabble in mathematics, in casting projections and in the alchemical sciences. Which is why I imagine you were in the shop of our common acquaintance." He clasped his hands behind his back and leaned against a cabinet. "And what is it that you require of me, Mister Falkenhayn?"

"Wisdom, sir, if you can provide it." And I pulled out the medallion that had weighed so heavily upon me. "Do you have any science of this object, sir?"

Ashmole took it from my grasp, inclined his head in interest or confusion, then took a few steps to a window to gain a better vantage of light. I could hear him breathing loudly as he contemplated the strange inscriptions. After a few moments he looked up at me. "May I enquire where you obtained this?"

"From these shores, sir. The circumstances I am not yet at liberty to discuss."

Ashmole smiled. "That sounds devious, Mister Falkenhayn."

"Can you tell me what it is? What it says?"

Ashmole returned his attentions to the medallion. "It is silver. But very impure by the looks of it. The design on the obverse I cannot really decipher, other than it seems to portray a portal or gateway. But I can tell you what is written along here. Along the right it is Latin."

I followed his finger as he spoke and traced along the script. "'He hath broken the Gates of brass, and smitten the bars of iron in sunder.' That is from the Book of Psalms. And here, down the left side of the gate, it is written in Hebrew. 'Schioel, Vaol, Yashiel, Vehiel.' Names, obviously, but I have no knowledge of them. And finally, here, at the centre, the Tetragrammaton."

I suddenly leaned in closer. "The Tetragrammaton!"

"Why yes, the Hebrew characters spelling out the name of Jehovah. And now, the reverse." He carefully turned over the disc. "I think this could be a maker's mark but it is not something I can readily identify. Very curious. If it is an alchemical symbol, well, I have not seen it before. Aye then, there you have it." He proffered the object to me again.

"But its purpose. What is it used for?"

Ashmole shrugged. "That I cannot tell you for I do not think I have ever seen anything quite like it before. It could be part of

Hebrew ceremonial practice but the Latin inscription seems to contradict that... I presume you are here to sell it?"

I could feel my shoulders slump at his words. I shifted my stance. "No. That is not my intention. But I can tell you that its derivation may be a matter of life and death. I will also confide that Anya says it is purposed for magic. Dark magic. I have more to tell you, sir, but you will understand that we scarcely know one another."

Ashmole raised a hand. "Say no more. I would not ask you to reveal that which you may not. But if Anya sent you here... Well, I trust her judgement in such matters. Dark magic, you say?"

"I can tell you sir, that I have seen things of late that would shiver you to your marrow. And I do not exaggerate when I tell you that lives are in the balance. Maybe the kingdom too."

Ashmole rounded his lips and exhaled loudly. "It's clear that you carry a great burden upon your mind, Mister Falkenhayn." He stared at me for a moment, taking my measure. "Very well. I do know of someone who might be able to offer more science of this disc than I. But I will need your solemn word as a gentleman that if I make an introduction you will exercise the utmost discretion and secrecy."

"I will swear it. Anything to help me in what I must do."

"And your servant outside. Is he privy to your quest?"

"Billy has witnessed much alongside me. I vouchsafe him."

Ashmole gave a nod. "Then we must go into London town. To a most excellent wine merchant I know."

My mouth opened to speak, but Elias Ashmole raised a hand to his lips. "All in good time, Mister Falkenhayn, all in good time."

BY THE TIME we reached Cheapside, it was late in the afternoon. Ashmole naturally plied me with questions the whole of the way, which I did my utmost to deflect. But he was certainly no believer in my identity and, worryingly, acted like a man who was on the verge of remembering some important fact, long forgotten.

"You have the look of a former king's man, sir," he said airily. I remained expressionless. "Fear not," he continued, "I was once too... an officer of artillery."

I nodded. Billy shifted in his seat uncomfortably and moved aside the leather curtain from the coach window as we wobbled forward.

"Long time passing, Mister Ashmole, long time passing," I said. Ashmole smiled and nodded in return, but the wheels were turning inside his head.

The coach slowed and came to rest. Mr. Ashmole leapt out and we followed. We came to a shop front on a small street off Leadenhall, clearly a wine merchant's from the bottles stacked in the windows. Ashmole turned to me, his hand upon the door handle.

"Will Billy Chard be waiting outside for us?"

"His own testimony is valuable to the present situation, sir. I would prefer he accompany us inside," I said.

"Very well. Let us find our man."

The shop, a large front room with a tapestry-hung doorway at the rear, was all dark wood and whitewashed plaster bereft of decoration. But the shelves were full of brown bottles and jugs of a dozen shapes and sizes, red wax seals dripping down their stoppers, some caked in months of dust. A large, high table stood next to the rear doorway, and behind this, I could just discern the head, shoulders, and chest of a man dressed in black. As we entered, he jumped up from the book he was struggling to read by the light of a single candlestick.

"Bless me," he cried out as he attempted to extricate himself from behind the table. "Mister Elias Ashmole! How pleasant a surprise, sir!" His accent was lisping, and familiar for I had heard it among Spaniards in Flanders.

Ashmole grasped me by the shoulder and brought me forward. "Mister Falkenhayn, I would like to introduce you to

Senor Roderigo da Silva, a man who imports the finest Canary and Malmsey in the kingdom."

Da Silva looked at me and inclined his head. "Mister Falkenhayn, my pleasure, sir." He was a little man with a balding pate which still boasted long white hair at least upon the back and sides and a scraggly sparse sort of grey beard that descended down his neck. As he stepped into the light at the centre of the room, I could see his face was deep-furrowed, a sort of map of a long and careworn life, easily read by anyone who saw him.

"*Senor* da Silva," said Ashmole, "we are here on some rather delicate business. Mister Falkenhayn has an object I was hoping you could help to shed some light upon. Mister Falkenhayn, can you produce the medal please?"

I pulled it out and handed it to the old man. He held it close to his face and made an irritated clucking. "I shall need more light to shed more light, gentlemen," he said as he scuttled back to his table and fetched more tapers, lighting them from the already burning one. We three stood on the opposite side from him, watching as he traced the etchings with his forefinger. Suddenly he stopped, looked at me briefly but intensely, and ordered Ashmole to put the bolt upon the door.

"Do you know who I am, Mister Falkenhayn?" he asked me, deadly earnest.

"No, sir. Mister Ashmole has revealed only your profession," I said.

"I am a *converso*, *senor*. From Lisbon."

I shook my head in incomprehension.

"I am a Jew. And I know what this object is. The question is, how did you obtain it?"

"I would rather hear first what you say it is."

Roderigo da Silva pushed the disc away from him across the table top. "I shall tell you nothing until you reveal the story of this thing in full. I do not think you understand the import of this object—or its danger."

Ashmole began to look alarmed.

I had come this far and it seemed the only way forward was to risk all.

"If I reveal the story of this object, I place my own person in grave jeopardy. I have already told Mister Ashmole that lives hang in the balance. So, I must place my trust in you gentlemen."

Da Silva's voice was quiet but firm. "And I have revealed myself to you, still a stranger, as a Jew. The few of us here are forced to live a lie—to preserve our secret—if we are to survive in this country. I ask you to trust me with your tale, and Mister Ashmole, whom I would trust with my life."

And so I told the whole horrid story, leaving out, of course, the purpose of my mission to England or any mention of d'Artagnan or Maggie. But I told them my true identity (and watched Billy grin a mile in self-congratulation). The whole affair spilled out of me over the ensuing minutes. Ashmole's face went pale, jaw slack, as he listened. As I reached the part where the black dog appeared, and then the winged apes, Billy exclaimed an "aye" or two to lend support. Roderigo muttered something in Hebrew, the same phrase, over and over. A prayer, I supposed. And finally, I told them of the previous night and the creature in the alley in Southwark. And when I stopped talking there was nothing but silence all around.

"Colonel Richard Treadwell," said Ashmole, softly. "Yes, I remember now. The duel at the Tower, then your exile to France. My God, sir. You returned to find your family."

I was glad I had omitted any word of Royalist plotting, as the present situation was dire enough. But da Silva had no words of admiration for me. He was as intent as a magistrate, demanding to hear the elements once again. In particular, what Fludd and his men had performed that night in the house outside Exeter—and what it was they had summoned.

"Colonel—"

"Mister Falkenhayn, if you value my life, sir."

Da Silva waved his hand and nodded. "Mister Falkenhayn, tell me the name of this angel that Gideon Fludd was speaking with. Be exact as you can remember."

"I shall not forget the moment. It's burned into me. He addressed it as Eistibus."

"I see. Let me now go back to this device and explain to you its purpose." Roderigo's voice was heavy, almost tired. He picked up the disc and held it towards us. "This is called a *lamen*. It was fashioned from instructions contained in the Key of Solomon, an ancient *grimoire* of magic. The Latin and Hebrew phrases are clear: it invokes the name of the Lord and mentions several angels by name—*Schioel, Vaol, Yashiel, Vehiel*. The *lamen* is meant to be worn by a magister, a conjurer, when he calls an entity of the ether."

"Dear sweet God," muttered Ashmole, leaning heavily upon the table.

"So Fludd did call forth the angel Eistibus, even without this disc in his possession," I said.

"No," said da Silva. "This side of the *lamen* is inscribed to protect the conjuror from harm. The other side tells me what creature he was attempting to conjure forth." He turned over the disc and pointed to the smallish symbol inscribed.

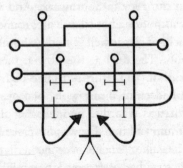

"This is also from the Key of Solomon. It is the symbol for Andras, reputed to be a powerful demon. That is what your Fifth Monarchists are playing with, sir."

I was strangely relieved in spite of this dreadful news. "I knew no angel of the Lord would demand the murder of a man. But how do you have such knowledge of these things, even if you are a Jew?"

Ashmole spoke up. "He is called a *rabbi*, a Hebrew cleric. He is greatly learned in this and more."

"I am no conjurer," said da Silva. "But I know the teachings of the Talmud and how to guard against wickedness and evil. And I am familiar with the Key of Solomon, which can be used for good as well as bad."

"How could Gideon Fludd magic up this demon without that there medal?" asked Billy, joining in, unbidden, in the best spirit of the Ranters.

The old man nodded. "He must have *another* pentacle, for that is what this is. They are easily fabricated but useless unless consecrated by the proper ceremony, by someone possessed of the knowledge of incantation. You hold here, Mister Falkenhayn, the First Pentacle of the Moon. It is designed to help call forth and to control a demon who is ruled by that planet and whose earthly power waxes and wanes as does the moon during the month. It can also be used with the right incantation, to open any locked door—it is the only such pentacle with that power. There are other pentacles, for all the planets. But Andras is a creature ruled by the moon."

"What does the Key of Solomon say about the demon Andras?" asked Ashmole.

Da Silva teased out his beard, nervously. "I have not committed that work to memory. It is frowned upon by the devout and if it was recorded by the hand of King Solomon then it was for him and him alone. I do remember that Andras is a Grand Marquis of Hell with many minions at his call. He can impart to those he favours the ability to pursue and destroy enemies. His chief desire is to sow discord and division among men, to breed war, to hide the truth, and to appear to the gullible as a being of goodness and light."

"A being of goodness and light... an angel," I said.

"Yes, an angel. And this fool of a man is dicing with death and eternal damnation. For it would appear that Andras is intent on having the Lord General murdered. Ironic in a way, this Gideon Fludd."

"What do you mean?" asked Ashmole, still not recovered from these waves of revelation.

"Why surely you remember your Bible, Elias. The name Gideon means destroyer. And Gideon was chosen by God to lead the Israelites against their enemies."

Ashmole turned to me. "Sir, upon your word as a gentleman, you have heard this conspiracy against Cromwell with your own ears? You have seen these hellish minions with your own eyes?"

"Upon my honour and my life," I said, "I have seen and heard these things."

"As have I!" piped up Billy again.

"What are we to do, then?" said Ashmole, turning back to the Jew.

"Whatever we are to do," said da Silva, "we have little time to do it. The moon waxes full in two days."

"Could the Craft be of aid?" asked Ashmole.

"It is possible," said da Silva. "You have brothers close to the Council. Perhaps they might be able to warn Cromwell if you can get an audience."

"What is the Craft?" I asked, completely at a loss.

"I am an Accepted Freemason. A brother of the Craft. As a secret society there is none older or wiser."

"But surely," I stuttered. "He is a Hebrew wine merchant, you are by your own admission a Royalist and you're saying you're in league with Parliament men too?"

"We seek to become better men and to understand God's wisdom," said Ashmole solemnly. "And these things surpass the petty politics of country and kingdoms."

It was only then that we became aware of cries and heavy footfalls outside in the street. We watched someone flash by the front of the shop, heading east. Billy moved to the door, clearly worried about riot, and volunteered to search out the disturbance. Da Silva nodded his assent and Billy went out, disappearing from view.

"But could Cromwell even be convinced of this plot?" I said. "Who would believe such things had come to pass? He will laugh it away."

"We count among our brethren Cromwell's astrologer," said Ashmole. "We can but try and warn him. But so too, we must protect your secret. You have returned here under sentence of death."

"I need no reminder of that fact, Mister Ashmole."

And at that moment the tapestry whipped back, revealing a young woman in a fury. A lace cap hid most of her jet black hair, pulled back tightly from her forehead, and her almond eyes were large and round, set perfectly in a face of sharp angles: chin, cheekbones, and nose. Her skin was deepest olive, almost polished bronze.

"Father, are you mad?" She had placed herself between me and the old man, her hands on her hips as if she was ready to fight us all.

Da Silva flew off in a rage, embarrassed by her eavesdropping. "Get upstairs! Now. You forget your place in this household."

"I will not! How can you think of aiding these men? Do you really think you will help our people by harbouring Cromwell's enemies? They will surely drive us out for this."

Da Silva's face flushed red and he suddenly gripped the girl by her arm, shaking her as he spoke. "Do not tell me my business, woman! My first duty is to serve God and to help those in need."

She shook off his hand and spat out what must have been an oath in Portuguese. "We are *marranos*. And we shall always be so. Hiding and running and lying. And now you're risking it all again."

"Enough." Da Silva looked away, shuffling again to the other side of the work table, shamed for his outburst and stung by her words.

She next turned on Ashmole. "How could you involve him, sir? You know our situation better than most." Her eyes were rapidly welling up with tears. She fixed me with a look of utter pleading but did not give words to her thoughts. And I could find no words either. She gave a short cry of frustration and fled the room and we could hear her feet pounding up the staircase in the back of the house.

Da Silva exhaled loudly. "I am deeply sorry for her behaviour, gentlemen. But you must realise her upbringing... she has faced great hardship in Portugal and in Antwerp. The loss of her mother two years ago, just after we arrived here, well, that too has taken its toll."

Ashmole and I nodded in sympathy, and I felt guilty for bringing this heavy burden into da Silva's house.

"She is only doing her duty to look out for her father's safety," I told him. "Don't chastise her for her devotion."

A pounding on the shop door brought us around. There was Billy, breathless and wide-eyed through the glass window. He hammered upon the door until Ashmole lifted the latch lock and he fell inside, ready to explode. "Well, it's done! The cat is among the pigeons now. Cromwell has chucked out the whole of the House. He is ruling by the Council alone. Parliament is no more."

"It is as the demon foretold," I said, my head swimming at the news. It was unfolding like clockwork, relentless and inevitable. "And now that he has abolished Parliament, Fludd will strike him down."

Da Silva placed his palms down upon the table. "And so it begins." And then he quietly said what Ashmole told me was a Hebrew prayer. "*Shema Yisrael Adonai Eloheinu Adonai Echad*."

I thought of the frightened girl upstairs, of all the people I was dragging into this nightmare, and my belly and bollocks tightened just as if I had entered battle. I now realised the mortal danger we all faced. I could read it plain enough in the eyes of Roderigo da Silva. He believed my tale fully—and he feared the outcome.

Chapter Fourteen

As a grizzled wherryman rowed us back across the Thames, we three were mostly silent, consumed by our own thoughts and dreads. Billy pulled out his pipe and tobacco and intently stuffed his bowl, grunting as if in some conversation with himself. For my part, I was glad of finding answers to the mystery but was now even more terrified of what lay ahead. Part of me wanted to let fate take its course as far as Mr. Cromwell was concerned, but I knew that was only one strand of the problem that I faced. Gideon Fludd would never cease hunting for me until one of us was dead. And our new comrade, Elias Ashmole, numerologist and astrologer, had yet to recover his rosy hue since hearing what was chasing us from out of the netherworld. He sat hunched and drawn, looking at his feet or blankly out onto the brown waters.

And my thoughts turned to Maggie. Was she now huddled below deck on some merchantman, bound for France? Or was she languishing still in Lyme Regis, awaiting d'Artagnan's return? I felt I had killed her love for me stone dead, and I prayed that as days passed her heart would forgive me for what I had done. The incessant squeak of the oarlocks was maddening, but slowly, leafy Lambeth hove into view once again. We bumped alongside the stone stairs slick with green slime, and the old boatman grabbed at the ring that hung there and pulled up alongside. We clambered out of the wobbling boat and up the stairs, prepared for the short walk back to the museum of Mr. Tradescant.

"Will *Senor* da Silva find us some way to protect us against this demon and his servants in this great book of his?" I asked Ashmole.

"I don't know. He says himself that he is no magician, but by God, he is a very learned man. If anyone can find some means to protect us from that evil, it's him."

"Christ, two days is but little time to find proof against the Devil."

Ashmole nodded. "I cannot disagree. And I am equally despairing of convincing the Council of the danger. But I must try. At least my brothers in the Craft will believe me. Together, we may be able to get John Thurloe to take it seriously. But it's an astounding claim and will be a difficult task. *Your* situation, sir, does not help that."

I stopped up short. "What do you mean."

Ashmole turned and faced me. "What am I to answer when I'm asked about who brings this incredible news of a conspiracy? Say that the news was fetched by a Cavalier running about London with a death warrant hanging over his head? A man who is claiming that demons are here to murder the Lord General and the Council of State? Cromwell will think you're mad or just looking for a pardon. And he'll think me a fool."

Ashmole's hand rubbed at his temple, his eyes shut tightly. "I have to think about this, and think hard. The worst is that they will believe nothing of it and swoop down upon you before you can get out of the country."

"I would go straight to Cromwell myself and tell him with my own words, if that is what it would take."

Ashmole looked up at me and smiled weakly. "What is it, sir, that makes you think you have such a duty to your old enemy?"

"A life for a life, Mister Ashmole," I said. "My honour demands it."

Ashmole nodded. "Ah, now *that* makes sense. So it was Cromwell himself who commuted your sentence of death to one of exile, was it?"

I watched as Ashmole's large green eyes suddenly widened a bit as some new idea flew into his mind. He wagged a finger at me. "Yes, it might do. It might do very well indeed. You are, after all, a gentleman of good character."

I looked over to Billy who shrugged his shoulders in response. Ashmole beckoned with his arm and resumed his pace back towards the house. "Come along, now! There is little time to be wasted."

"What is it that you propose?" I asked, catching him up. "Some means we can convince the Council quickly?"

"No sir, but what I propose will safeguard *you* at least and gain the trust of some influential friends. A Freemason must strive to protect his fellows in the Craft, to give them aid and to accept their word as oath. If I am to confide the existence of this conspiracy to the brotherhood—and your existence as well—then it is obvious that you must become an Accepted Freemason too."

"But I know nothing of this secret society, sir. Nor whether I want to join or even that your friends would tolerate it."

"Don't worry about that. I can instruct you in the history of the Craft straight away. The difficulty will be in gathering the Lodge for tomorrow. We need at least half a dozen of the brotherhood." And, his pace quickening, he forged ahead. "There will be little sleep for us tonight, Mister Falkenhayn! Much to be done."

I SENT BILLY back to Southwark to procure us a room on London Bridge, giving him a handful of silver. I told him I would return in the evening and instructed that he leave word of the new lodgings he procured at the Bear so I could find the place later. He mounted up and took up the slack on his reins. "Are you sure we're settled on the right course, Mister Eff? We don't know nothing about these men. We don't know their fucking secret society, and we don't know that we won't both end up in irons tomorrow." His face was particularly grim and pinched, even for Billy, and I was worried.

"Come now, Billy Chard. Are you thinking of running out on me now? After all we've been through?"

"No sir," he said, staring me in the eye. "I reckon I've got my own answers to find in all of this. If I've seen some wondrous bad things then it stands to reason there must be wondrous good too. I need to know that to make sense of this. Can you argufy against that, Mister Eff?"

"I cannot, Billy. I will see you after nightfall. Have a care back there at the bridge."

As he set off, I felt sad in my heart for him. He was a hard worn soldier who had become convinced that there was no such thing as evil in the world, only God's goodness. But now he had seen with his own eyes an evil that few men are faced with in their entire lives. As for me, I had no such doubts. My only question was why God seemed so uninterested in it all. If poor Billy had ridden off there and then for the west, I could not have held it against him.

Elias Ashmole was waiting for me in the chamber of curiosities, an open bottle of da Silva's Malmsey and two glasses on the table at the centre.

"Here. If you feel as I, you could use a drop or two." He pushed a glass over to me. I took a long gulp, palming the dainty vessel with both hands. It was difficult to keep my eyes from the stuffed crocodile suspended over Ashmole's head.

"Tell me more about this Craft you would have me join," I said.

"I can tell you some of the history but not all. The rest will have to wait until you are initiated. God willing, that will be tomorrow assuming I can get letters out by messengers this afternoon."

"Then tell me what you can if I'm to join this society in order to save my life."

Ashmole sipped at his wine and then began. "It is an old brotherhood, founded when the pyramids were but hazy dreams in the minds of the ancients. It is a guild of stone masons to be sure, those architects of immutable monuments, but it is much, much more. The Craft teaches us how to live as men and to serve the Greatest Architect—God Himself. And that is why there are fellows of the Craft that have never hewn stone themselves. They follow the allegorical wisdom of the Craft, aiming to discover the hidden truths of the world."

Ashmole held up a finger and dashed off to return in a moment with a black leather bound book. He opened the cover and spun the volume around upon the table so that I could see the frontispiece. "Look here. It is the best example I can give you of the deeper meanings of symbols. Remember, there is always more than meets the eye."

I looked upon the engraving and quickly noticed that it was a book he himself had written: *Theatrum Chemicum Britannicum*. "Is this a book of alchemy? A spellbook?"

Ashmole laughed and smoothed his sparse and trim little moustache. "Heavens no, sir. It is a book on occult philosophy."

I shook my head in ignorance.

"It *is* an alchemical text but in essence is about finding truth through mathematics and Hermetic science." He pursed his lips as he took in my blank look. "Don't concern yourself with the subject. What I am trying to point out is this example of *symbolism*. Do you see the intersecting mason's square and compass here at the bottom of the page?"

I saw a jumble of various objects engraved along the borders of the title page. Helms, armour, musical instruments, sun, moon, clouds, and a Greek goddess bearing a book at the centre of the page. But there, along the bottom, was the compass and square.

Ashmole looked at me and crossed the extended thumb and forefinger of his left hand over those of his right. "Compass and square, sir. The greatest symbols of our fraternity. The compass allows us to circumscribe all and to raise our expectations as to what can be attained through wisdom. The square, the measure of the right angle, reminds us to be honest and true in our dealings with our fellow men."

I nodded, for at least this much I could follow.

"But these objects signify something deeper and more spiritual: the compass signifies the heavens and the invisible world. The square is also a symbol of the earth, of matter fixed, the visible world. What you see here is nothing less than a representation of the marriage of heaven and earth."

"And this Craft you speak of would offer me fellowship and protection?"

"Absolutely, sir. It has flourished since the time the ancient Hebrews built Solomon's temple and the wisdom is held in trust by each and every Accepted Mason. The greatest precept is to do good by your fellow man and most of all to your brothers in the Craft."

"You're assuming they will let me in," I reminded him.

"Aye. I am assuming that. But I am hopeful my recommendation will carry."

"You expect me to risk my life by confiding my true identity to these Masons of yours? I have had little of the milk of human kindness these last few months, Mister Ashmole. And you demand much of my trust. Especially since some of your brothers are Parliament men."

Ashmole sighed. "I can understand your reticence. There is much evil in the world and in the hearts of men. But our oaths are not taken lightly in the Craft and most brothers would rather die than violate them... Richard, there will come a time when you will need to trust in your fellow man again—indeed, at the risk of your own life. If you do not, little by little, you will surely lose your humanity and your soul will wither away. Please take this chance."

And suddenly, right there and then, a vision of Maggie sprang into my head. Trust. I had shattered that belief for her well and truly. If I could ever find her again, would she return my love? Could she learn to trust me once again? I raised the glass to my lips and drained the last of the sweet wine. "If what you say is true, it would appear that the Masonic brotherhood alone will believe the story I have to tell. Very well then. I will hazard myself if it means gaining the help I need to stop Gideon Fludd."

Ashmole's face, now flushed with colour once again, beamed in full and he clapped me upon the shoulder. "Excellent! I'll fetch paper and pen and get word out to the brethren in the city. God willing, we can initiate you tomorrow and then get word to Thurloe to redouble the guard around Cromwell's house and to sweep the city for Major Fludd and his men."

I decided to ask him something that still itched. "Someone told me not long ago that Oliver Cromwell is the only man capable of stopping the radical Puritans from conquering what is left of the kingdom. Do you agree?"

"Sir, it's no secret. He is our only hope and many a diehard Royalist will grudgingly agree."

"But a regiment of his redcoats is no match for what Fludd comes to battle with, that is for certain. We need the help of a higher authority, Mister Ashmole."

Ashmole put a finger aside his nose. "Rest assured my dear Falkenhayn, da Silva will not fail us. We'll have the power of the Old Testament on our side against this evil. As a former artilleryman, I can tell you those are heavy guns indeed."

THE SUN WAS fast setting by the time I entered the hurly-burley of the Bear at the bridge foot. I quickly glanced about the tap room looking for redcoats or anyone who was taking an interest at my arrival. All seemed usual and proper, the normal mix of drunkards, whores, rivermen and wealthy gentlemen bent on good times. I sought out the landlord and asked if he had any messages for me.

"Yes, sir, I do. The word is: Billy says to tell you to go to the sign of the black glove, about halfway over the bridge."

Shop shutters were slamming hard as I walked out onto London Bridge. A day's worth of horse-apples covered the street, mixed with the stench of piss and burning charcoals. In the failing light I caught sight of the swinging shingle to my left. It was a weatherworn sign displaying a faded black glove and a large, oversized sewing needle resting against its thumb. The house, like most upon the bridge, was but one room wide though it soared up some three stories high. The ground floor's shutters were closed tight from the inside and I cautiously rapped upon the narrow door next to them. After what seemed a long wait, I heard a bolt being slid from behind and slowly the door opened inwards. Billy Chard's eyes and crooked nose popped into view between the door and the jamb.

"Come in, Mister Eff. You've found the place."

I found myself in an empty shop floor, a great workman's table still littered with bits of leather and a few tools. Billy stood, sword in hand, visibly relieved to see me. He quickly shut the door and threw home the bolt again.

"So you've found us some rooms, I see."

Billy snorted. "I've found us a whole fucking house, Mister Eff. The glover's wife is a widow these past two weeks and has gone to stay with relations. We have the place for a week for a few shillings."

I nodded. "Good. That means we can keep prying eyes away."

"Look at what we've got in here," said Billy, beckoning me into the back room. There was a large leaded window at the rear and not much else but Billy was pointing to the floor. He bent down, seized an iron ring, and gave a yank. Up rose a trapdoor and I found myself staring down twenty feet to the surging Thames underneath.

"There's some rungs set in the wall there to the left that lead down the side to the pier. Good for an escape if we need it."

"Good work, Billy. But the only escape here is by drowning unless we can get a boat moored down there. Show me the rest of the place."

We took our sup upstairs, sitting on the floor and eating cold roast mutton and some stale bread. Billy had managed to find a lantern and taper and we chewed away in its feeble, guttering light.

"So, you will join their secret society then? Tomorrow? What the hell am I supposed to do? Stay cooped up here all day?"

I washed down a lump of bread with a swig of beer. "Rest easy, Billy. I've got work for you to do. If da Silva is right, and we have only two more days before the full moon, we've got to prepare for battle."

"Battle? What fucking battle?"

"Look, we don't have a clue where Fludd is. But we know who he's planning on killing. Stands to reason that if we go to Cromwell, we will find Fludd and his men."

Billy leaned back and flung a bit of crust onto the plate between us. "And his goddamn monsters as well! You expect us to knock on Cromwell's door and ask him to let us wait in his parlour?"

"I admit I haven't figured the plan completely but I don't think we'll be standing alone. If Ashmole is right, we might even be able to convince the Council of the threat to the kingdom."

"How do you expect us to actually fight these creatures? You've seen that Devil hound... and the pig man—whatever the fuck it was. What good is iron against that?"

"I'm praying we'll get a little help from the other side. But in the meantime I need you to get us a couple of buff coats and gauntlets. Maybe a steel gorget would help too..."

"Jesus, you are planning on going to war! But why the armour?"

"You've seen the claws and teeth on those beasts, haven't you?"

Billy groaned and shook his head. "Oh Christ, we're well and truly buggered. What in the name of Mary and Joseph am I doing here?"

"We are going to save England. You and me."

I SLEPT FITFULLY, the house creaking and grumbling as the wind blew through every crack and crevice. The river beneath us gave out an unceasing, muffled roar. Both of us stretched out, fully dressed, swords naked on the floor with us. I felt that at any moment we would be caught out. God knows, there must have been any number of people looking for us by now. I was doubtful that Fludd would make another attempt until after his business with the Lord General was finished. But he still wanted his revenge. Then there was the chance that the failed West Country plotters had revealed my travelling name. A very good chance. The redcoats could even now be searching out Andreas Falkenhayn in the city. And that name was now slowly spreading here on the bridge and at the Bear. And most worrying was the whereabouts of *Monsieur* d'Artagnan. Maggie he ought to have safely ensconced aboard ship or in a hostel in Lyme Regis. But d'Artagnan would not abandon the chase when his master had given orders. No, he was bound to be on my scent whether his English was very good or not. And he could always call upon the French ambassador for help—and allies.

I awoke to the sun filtering through the filthy windows at the back of the house. Billy was already up and banging around in the adjacent room. As I walked in on him, he stood there bare-chested with his shirt around his neck. He saw me, and quickly whirled around, hurriedly pushing his arms down the sleeves. He was hiding something.

"What is the matter?"

He shook his head. "Naught. Leastways no concern of yours."

I pulled the shirt up off his arms as he swore bloody murder. Both arms were dripping with pus, the scratches he had received nearly a week ago burst open and weeping poison. "Sweet Jesus, Billy, you should have told me."

"It was that goddamn flying ape. The scratches scabbed up nicely after a day or so but they keep opening up again. They won't heal."

I fetched my other linen and tore it up to make strips to bind his forearms. "They are unnatural wounds. We must seek advice before things get too far along. Can you still feel your fingers?"

Billy nodded. "Aye, and not much pain... or maybe I've just gotten used to it. No time for the surgeon, Mister Eff. Just get them wrapped and let's be about our business."

We went south down the bridge and over to the Bear for breakfast. It was as we were finishing the last of it, tucked into the back of the room, that the landlord approached with a letter addressed to 'Andreas Falkenhayn.' It was Elias Ashmole. His only instructions: to meet him at twelve of the clock outside the Fountain Inn on the Strand. So, it seemed that he had met with some success. I gave Billy some more silver (now getting dangerously low) and told him to find us at least the stout buff coats to protect us, if nothing else.

"If a few scratches cause wounds like yours," I told him, "imagine what a deep gash from those creatures would do." This time, he agreed fully. Protection was best.

"I will look for you at the house by nightfall. Keep your wits about you, Billy. No slacking off. I can feel it in my bones that enemies are drawing closer."

Billy looked out across the half-empty room. "I've felt it too. The hairs on my neck are prickling like mad. I've already practically rubbed that gypsy charm down to bare threads."

"Then God keep you. I shall see you when I return."

"Have no fear. I'll get us the kit and keep low the rest of the day."

ASHMOLE WAS WAITING on the Strand as I approached, my broad-brimmed hat pulled down over my face and my cloak drawn tight about me. As soon as I reached him, he cupped my elbow with his right arm and began walking me quickly up the Strand towards Fleet Street.

"Good day to you, sir," he said, barely looking at me. "I am afraid that the plot is thickening faster than we can keep up."

"What do you mean?"

"I do not know how it has transpired, but Cromwell's spies now know that Richard Treadwell is returned and that he may be conspiring to uprising and murder. Mister Thurloe has already placed his agents out on the streets to find and seize you, and they know your alias as well."

I wasn't too surprised. "What I told you is the God's truth, Elias. I am here to warn Cromwell, not kill him."

"That is what I have told William Lilly, brother in the Craft and chief astrologer to the Council. He says if I believe your tale, he will believe it. As far as uprisings go," he said, half turning to me, a smirk upon his lips, "you did not really expect me to believe you risked a traitor's death by returning just so you could see your wife in Devon?"

I could feel my face grow flushed. "If any uprising did exist, it was only in the minds of a few drunken fools. The threat to the kingdom comes not from the Stuarts but from within the bosom of Parliament."

"So it would seem, so it would seem. But we are fast running out of time and the net is closing in upon you. Indeed," he continued, as if the realisation had just dawned upon him, "now I'm in the same boat since it can be said I have harboured you."

I threw an arm around his shoulder. "Then for the love of Christ, let's get some allies and end this thing before we are too late."

We came upon a fine house in the Strand, its carved timbers prettily painted. Over the lintel of the doorway was a Latin phrase in gold that I puzzled to translate. Ashmole helped me as he knocked loudly upon the door. "It says, *Ex Uno Omnia*, 'From the One, All.' Everything is connected, Richard. *Everything*. Astrology shows us how."

The door creaked open and we were ushered in by an old serving woman and directed up the main staircase to the dining room where, we were told, Mr. Lilly and the others awaited. I found myself in a large hall leading to another room behind closed double doors. Ashmole took off his hat and indicated that I should give him mine. He placed them on the side table and then reached into his pocket and pulled out a long strip of black silk.

"Now is the time for you to put your trust in your fellow man. I must blindfold you now before we enter the Lodge room."

I nodded my consent and was soon in darkness. Ashmole rapped upon the door in a series of knocks and pauses. I heard the door open and then felt Ashmole's tug at my arm as we entered. For all I knew there could have been a party of redcoats in the room, containing their laughter as the lamb was ushered in for the slaughter. But I resigned myself, the door shut behind us, and my ceremony of initiation began.

"Is this the candidate?" came a strong young voice from somewhere in front of me.

"It is he," replied Ashmole, at my side.

"And have you, Mister Falkenhayn, been instructed in the history of our Fellowship and will you take the oath to join with us, knowing that to break it will be your death?"

"I have and I will," I said, feeling a little foolish.

"Then upon the word and honour of Brother Ashmole, we shall proceed."

And then followed a bizarre interrogation by the lone voice, with Ashmole whispering the set response in my ear and me repeating it aloud.

"Where lie the keys to your Lodge Door?"

"They lie under the three-cornered pavement."

"What are the keys to your Lodge Door made from?"

"It is not made of wood, stone, iron or steel, or any sort of metal, but the tongue of a good report behind a brother's back as well as before his face."

"How many lights are in your Lodge?"

"Three. The sun, the master, and the square."

And so it went. Finally, I felt the blindfold being undone, and I blinked as my eyes adjusted to the darkened room, lit by but three candles upon a centre table. Far from a roomful of redcoats, there were but five men standing around the table. The master of the Lodge came forward, a man of my own age with a flaming ginger moustache. William Lilly then whispered into my ear the word of the Masons and gave me the secret grip. I swore an oath to never reveal the secrets that had been bestowed upon me and Lilly directed me to kiss the bible that lay open upon the table.

And that was it. Smiles all around as the solemn mood lifted like a passing summer storm cloud. Lilly and the others clapped me upon the back and welcomed me into the brotherhood. A brotherhood I scarcely understood anything about. Another set of doors were opened and we entered a further room, already laid out with sweetmeats, pies, cheese, and wine.

And all eyes were upon me.

"I do not know what to say, gentleman. Other than to thank you for accepting me into your midst. I must admit, I would not ever have expected to be in the same room with some of you."

Lilly's sad, drooping eyelids arched high as he laughed. "The Craft brings together all sorts, joined in fellowship. Fear not. Brother Ashmole has confided your news and we recognise the risk you take in coming here. Let me introduce your fellow Lodge brothers. I am William Lilly and these gentlemen are Thomas Wharton, William Backhouse, and Robert Childe." All three men gave a slight bow as they were named.

"May I bring in my guest now?" asked Ashmole.

"Yes, of course. Have *Senor* da Silva brought upstairs," said Lilly. "And now," he continued, gesturing to the table, "I suggest we take our meal and begin discussing the situation that our brother Tread– *Falkenhayn* finds himself in."

I had passed from stranger to confidant in less time than it takes to sneeze. And now these men, still blank pages to me, had undertaken to share my troubles or at least safeguard me from harm. I was dumbstruck.

"Let us get down to business," said Lilly as he poured out the wine. "I learned last night that Mister Thurloe's spies are well aware of an impending plot against the Lord General's person. Unfortunately, his hounds are on the wrong scent. You see, the French ambassador has claimed that *you*, Richard, are the chief conspirator, here as a rogue agent."

I kept my mouth shut.

"But as we have been advised by our friend and brother Ashmole, it is a group of rogue Fifth Monarchy men who are seeking to do murder, as discovered by our brother Falkenhayn. And these Monarchy men—it has been alleged—are in league with spirits of the ether." Lilly raised his hands as Mr. Wharton began to object. "I know that this point is open to contention, based as it is only upon the word of Mister Falkenhayn. But I must tell you that from the details given me by Messieurs Ashmole and da Silva, combined with my own recent astrological figures, I believe that we are facing a threat not altogether of this sphere."

Da Silva, who had just shuffled in and sat himself down at the table, was nodding vigorously in agreement. Wharton was frowning with scepticism while the others remained unreadable.

"Come now," urged Lilly, "we are all occult philosophers here in this room. We have all seen or read of the possibilities. And remember Doctor Dee's visitations with the spirits. Not least our own Holy Book that details many such encounters. I must tell you that the enemy is known to possess at least one Pentacle of the Moon for conjuring. Monday, I needn't remind you, is the full moon."

Wharton leaned forward. "You mean that these Fifth Monarchists are performing conjurations—of angels and spirits?"

"They are raising demons!" I said, unable to contain myself further. "And I have seen and faced them in the last few days."

A silence descended upon the table. The brothers of the Craft cast glances, one to another, some in full belief of the threat, others unable to decide.

Lilly rose and went to a cabinet at the side of the room. He returned with a rolled-up piece of velvet and took his seat again. "If we are facing an attack by the supernatural, by beings of the ether, then Thurloe's men and the army will never even see it coming. We must fight fire with fire. The enemy may have pentacles of his own to summon evil, but we have something more."

He unrolled the round piece of cloth, the size of a brass charger, and upon it was painted in painstaking detail a glorious calligraphy: a series of golden circles, hexagons, and Hebrew words. "Behold, gentlemen, the Grand Pentacle of Solomon."

The others all craned or stood to see the device as Lilly held it open upon the table.

"And, gentlemen... one of us must learn to use it."

Chapter Fifteen

THE HEAVY SILENCE around the table was broken by the sound of Robert Childe's stomach rumbling its discontent. And the silence made me despair that I would find help even among these men of magic and mystery. Not one had volunteered to fight against Fludd's demons, and Lilly, master of the Lodge, had not even offered to take up the gauntlet. But then, someone did finally rise and speak his mind.

"This is *my* task, gentlemen," said Roderigo da Silva, looking straight into my eyes. "As a man of God it falls to me and no one else here."

Nods all around the table.

"We are physicians and astrologers, whereas you are clergy, sir," said Lilly, somewhat awkwardly. "I mean, that is to say... clergy after a fashion."

Da Silva inclined his head in recognition of the fact he was no Christian. "I do have some knowledge of the grimoires and of Kabbalistic teachings as Mister Ashmole will himself attest. More importantly, I have my faith. I am not afraid."

I looked from face to face as my new brothers studied their plates and twirled their glasses. "And what will the rest of you do?" I asked. "Consult the stars or say a prayer?"

"Brother Falkenhayn," said Lilly as he stretched out his hand to stay my outburst, "we are still discussing the point."

"If I could show you the wounds of my comrade, inflicted by a hellish beast not a week ago, would you believe me then, gentlemen?"

"I believe you now," said Elias Ashmole, raising his voice for effect. "And though it may be small help I will accompany you and *Senor* da Silva in meeting the enemy when we must. I can still wield a sword."

This rather visibly unmanned the others and Doctor Wharton quickly spoke up to save his honour.

"The best course of action is for myself and Mister Lilly to pay call upon John Thurloe and convince him of the threat to the Lord General's safety. We do, after all, have some influence with the Council. Influence that is not universal even at this table."

Lilly nodded vigorously in agreement. "Then we have our plan. Brother Ashmole and Mister da Silva will accompany Brother Falkenhayn in directly searching out the Fifth Monarchy men while the rest of us will make a mission to the spymaster's office. Now, gentlemen, let us fortify ourselves for the days ahead."

It was mid-afternoon by the time we went our ways. Da Silva asked Ashmole and me to accompany him back to his shop that we might put meat on the bones of our thin plan of attack. I couldn't help feeling the suspicion that even Roderigo da Silva did not really know how we were going to defeat Gideon Fludd or the entity that he was playing with. It was almost as if now that he had taken the responsibility for the fight, the reality of the challenge had struck him hard. Back in da Silva's house, I watched as the Jew unrolled the pentacle scroll upon his work table and traced his fingers along the myriad of inscriptions that encircled it.

"I have but little time to learn the invocations for this pentacle," he said, his voice heavy.

"And what would these invocations accomplish?" I asked.

"Pentacles serve two main purposes," said da Silva. "They can raise spirits both good and evil, and they can keep one safe in the presence of these beings of the ether—of heaven and hell. But one must know what to recite and when, otherwise the pentacle is nearly useless."

"But how can we use this to stop Fludd and his demon?"

Da Silva's look chilled me. "I don't know if we can stop them. The power of this Grand Pentacle should trump whatever Pentacle of the Moon that Fludd is using... but I have never undertaken such a thing as this."

Elias looked at me, his face written with worry.

"*Senor*, you must learn to wield this," I said. "We have little else at our disposal and even less time to find it."

Da Silva nodded. "I can set up a ring of sanctuary to keep the evil ones at bay. That is documented well enough. But I have never tried to raise the spirits of the ether. I never dared to. Never had to."

"To create a magic circle would be help enough," said Elias, encouragingly.

"You must know now, gentlemen," said da Silva looking up at both of us, "that I will not conjure any demon, black spirit, or creature—even if it might help our cause. My religion forbids this and you must not ask me to do such a thing."

"What else can you think of then?" I asked. "Weapons that will do them hurt?"

Da Silva shut his eyes briefly, as if gathering the will, then started turning pages in one of the great books that he had pulled up from underneath the table. "Yes... yes. I remember in the Talmud there is teaching on charms of protection. If this Gideon Fludd is conjuring a demon like Andras, the creature is bound by the Moon. That means that the metal silver will be of aid to us." The wine merchant was flicking through the pages in a fury, mumbling to himself.

Ashmole brightened. "He is correct. Of the precious metals, silver rules the Moon and those agents that are bound by it. If we had some musket balls of silver..."

"Ah!" Da Silva stabbed at the page he had finally found. "We can use the Tetragrammaton and indeed all the names of God as talismans against Andras and his minions."

"I don't understand!" I said, my voice betraying my impatience.

Da Silva grabbed my arm. "It is powerful intercession. The letters themselves spell out the name of Jehovah, if applied properly to... to your sword... or your coat—to anything! These will banish evil for they cannot stand in the sight of the Almighty." Da Silva was on fire, caught up now with the revelation that we did indeed have some small armoury at our disposal. He looked at me again, worried.

"You say this demon's malignants pursue you and have attacked already?"

"They have sir."

Da Silva nodded, reached down under the table and rummaged for something. A moment later he handed me a small lump of chalk.

"Take this. I use it for marking my wine casks but you can use it to mark out a protective circle around you if you find yourself under attack again. And you shall need an incantation to recite once you stand within." He hurriedly scribbled on a scrap of paper that he snatched from under the book. "I write this in English for you, you understand?"

I took it from his shaking hand and read it aloud. "*Be split, be accursed, broken and banned, you son of mud, son of an unclean one, son of clay, in the name of Morigo, Moriphath and his seal.*"

Da Silva nodded vigorously. "Yes, yes, you must not let even a toe outside the circle and you must repeat the text until the creature flees."

Ashmole gave me a look that spoke both apprehension and disbelief. He was getting further and further away from his comfortable world of numbers and science. I folded the paper and thrust it and the bit of chalk into my breeches pocket. "I am not a Jew, *senor*. Will it work for me?"

"It matters not," replied the rabbi. "You are a child of the Lord nonetheless. Now memorise the words. It won't do to fumble with the paper when you are facing a demon."

I silently read the words of the incantation again. Somehow I could not even imagine reciting the prayer or curse or whatever it was if the black dog came at me again. But it seemed I had little else to fight with.

"Mister Ashmole," said da Silva, turning his attention to the astrologer, "we need pure silver—I have some but not enough. This I can bless as we cast it into pistol balls."

Ashmole nodded, recovering his enthusiasm for what lay ahead. "I can get this. Do you know a silversmith or goldsmith we can trust and do the deed this day?"

"I do. Mister Falkenhayn, we will have need of your sword—and yours too, Mister Ashmole. We need to have them silvered along the blade."

My hand automatically moved to my hilt. "I'll not part with my blade for even a minute, sir."

"It's all right," said Ashmole. "I will get us swords and accompany you to the silversmith, *senor*."

The rabbi straightened his hat that had slid sideways in his excitement. "Mister Falkenhayn, we must depend upon you to find the whereabouts of Fludd and his men. My art can only be of use if we are in the direct presence of the enemy."

"Call me Richard Treadwell, *senor*. My alias is no longer any cloak of secrecy. And as for Gideon Fludd, I know he will be where Cromwell is when the moon is full."

"The old royal apartments of the Cockpit, at Whitehall?" said Ashmole. "Surely not even he would have such boldness to strike there."

"Yes, he would, Elias. And that is where we will wait to serve him in full."

* * *

THE WHOLE WORLD was not quite right that afternoon. I walked swiftly up Fleet Street having left Ashmole and da Silva to their tasks, my anxious eyes settling upon every passerby and all the while praying I would not be challenged by a patrol. The sky was leaden grey, the light fast disappearing, and some trick of the wind had dragged down the smoke of all the chimneys, down, down from the gabled rooftops, sending creeping, wispy tendrils into the street. The acrid taste of sulphur entered my nose and mouth, my eyes burned, and all the time the low cloud roiled overhead. A certain strange heaviness permeated the atmosphere, an almost unnatural harbinger of something dreadful.

The street was full of people and horses and I weaved my way in and out at a steady clip, my eyes searching for redcoats. I would every so often pause, stand to the side with my back to the houses, and scan where I had come, just to be sure of what was following me. I had just done this for the third time when I bumped into a figure that was nearly wedged into a corner of a house front under the eaves. I quickly moved to the side and glanced down at the curious beggar. A dirty, battered felt hat obscured his face but as I took half a step back he raised his head and looked at me. He was a little man, old but not ancient, resting on a crutch. His left leg was missing below the knee and his ochre coloured breeches were practically faded dirty white, covered in road filth. His coat—a soldier's coat—had lost all of its buttons, kept closed by a leather belt, cracked and brittle with age. The creature regarded me and gave a toothless smile as he held out his hand. I do not know why, but I was not revolted by the poor man. Perhaps it was because he had been a soldier, one whose fate might someday be mine as well.

"Hallo there, brother," I said as I fumbled in my purse for a coin to give him. "Hard times, I see."

He nodded slowly, and I placed a sixpence in his grubby palm. That was when I looked into his eyes. Something was not right about them, or him. It was as if someone else's eyes had been placed in this grizzled old veteran's skull. They were the eyes of a much younger man looking out of a broken, old carcass. And it unsettled me greatly. "Where did you fight, brother?"

"Everywhere, brother," he replied, voice as melodious as a choirboy. "I have seen many battles. Like you have... but many more."

"You know that, eh? Well, looking at you I'd be inclined to accept that."

His palm slowly closed around the coin and he looked at me with those strange green eyes, bright as emeralds. "I was near to you when you took that pike in your leg at Naseby," he said, his voice quiet and firm. "And after that at Arras in Flanders... and your first fight at the gates of Nienburg—do you remember that?"

My blood ran cold. I could say nothing. I took a step back, my mind desperately working how he could know such things. This broken down creature *knew* me. I drew back further, nearly knocking into a cart.

The beggar raised a hand, a gesture of farewell. "Be ever watchful, brother! And trust in your God."

Warning or benediction, I was sore shaken. I hurriedly turned my back to him and scurried up the street. I glanced back over my shoulder for a moment, but he was already gone from view. By the time I reached the north end of London Bridge, my head was swirling with dark fantasies and conspiracies. And I could feel myself sweating like a pig. It was then I spotted a dozen dragoons gathered about a brazier in the last of the twilight, hard by the rutted cobble lane that led up to the bridge foot. Their short muskets were slung over shoulder or balanced in the crooks of their arms. They were carefully eyeing every man that set foot upon the bridge; clearly relishing their power to challenge whoever they chose. They were looking for me.

Asking a boatman down at the steps near Blackfriars to ferry me across was one way around the problem. But then it quickly occurred to me that the army would by now have every waterman in its employ too. So I stood across the street, pulled my cloak up tight around me, and waited to see what might happen. As an old soldier, I knew the value of patience and, again, it rewarded me for my prudence. Three whores had wandered down to the bridge end, looking to cross over to the taverns in Southwark. But finding a dozen likely customers on this side of the bridge convinced them it was worth a go to remain where they were. As they struck up a merry banter with the soldiers, I slipped closer to the bridge. Now the whores were performing a song and as one bared her tits to show what was on offer, the soldiers formed a tight circle around the ladies, rapt in their attention. The sergeant, a fuzzy-bearded barrel-chested man, shouted and began cuffing one of his men who had tried sampling the wares. It was time to make a move.

I walked deliberately, but not too swiftly, down to the right of the bridge entrance and up past the wooden palisades. And I kept on walking, walking into the narrow roadway and into the jostling crowd that fought their way backwards and forwards in the gloom. The road on the bridge was dark—it was always dark because of the close overhanging houses. In a few moments, I was safely lost in the jumble of the bridge dwellers, the shops and the crooked little houses. Yet this was temporary respite from the tightening noose. It was only a matter of time before the army would find me, but I needed one more day to wait for Gideon Fludd. There was only one thing for it: I now had to stay all that night and the next day in the glover's house with Billy. Time to wait and to pray.

I reached the house, watched suspiciously by an old man who was shuttering his shop windows next to the glover's. I reached for the latch on the peeling and blistered red door. It lifted and the door opened inwards. It was not locked. I hesitated, my hand resting upon the jamb as the hinges groaned. There was lantern light coming from inside so I assumed that Billy might be napping or else upstairs. But for Billy, twitchy at the best of times, leaving the door unbarred was an unlikely oversight. I stepped inside and slowly closed the door behind me, letting my eyes grow accustomed to the faint light.

I undid my cloak and threw it upon the work table.

"Billy, Billy Chard!" There was no reply. It was only then I saw the crumpled figure upon the floor. Billy was face down in the corner, his tangled brown locks glistening and wet.

"*Bonsoir, Colonel.*"

I slowly turned around, towards the doorway. Lieutenant d'Artagnan stood just four paces away, his pistol levelled at me. I swore under my breath, mainly at my own stupidity in letting this all happen. "Did you have to kill him, you bastard."

D'Artagnan shook his head. "I brained him with the flat of my blade. The rascal has a skull like an ox. He'll live. Mind you, I should have killed him for catching me out in Exeter—taking my sword and my horse."

"And I should have killed you when I had the chance. Sometimes I take comradeship a little too seriously."

The young musketeer chuckled. "But Richard, that is why I have spared you. We have served together, and will again I am certain. But you must come back with me now, or else. Cromwell's army is closing on you."

"Thanks to you, *monsieur*." I slowly knelt near Billy to see that he still drew breath. He did. "You went straight to your ambassador to tell him the traitor Treadwell was here, didn't you? And he told John Thurloe, Cromwell's spymaster." I stood up again, my fingers slick with Billy's blood.

"We've had this conversation, Colonel. His Eminence has no wish for General Cromwell to come to harm and your little sojourn was never sanctioned by him. You expected me *not* to warn my ambassador that a rogue agent of the Cardinal was here? Don't you think it would have been far easier for me just to kill you? I am trying to save you." D'Artagnan took another step into the room. "Now, unbuckle your swordbelt, sit down in that chair, and be reasonable. I can reunite you with

Marguerite shortly and we three can be off for the coast—with an escort from the ambassador's retinue."

I took a step towards him. "Where is Marguerite? Don't tell me you brought her here with you, you fool."

D'Artagnan pulled back slightly even as his arm shot forward, the hammer of his doglock clicking loudly. "Stand down, sir!"

I balled my fists until I could feel my nails cutting my palms. I had trusted him to keep her safe. "You trumped up Gascon peasant. Where is Marguerite? Where did you leave her?"

D'Artagnan inclined his head and narrowed his eyes. "Now, *monsieur*, my patience is truly at an end. Give me your word of honour to yield or I will blow your brains out here and now."

I had not time to answer him. The door crashed inwards and strangers were upon us. The Frenchman was fast, wheeling towards the intruders, but he had only half turned in a crouch at the sound before a cudgel struck him upon the head, dropping him like a stone. His pistol bounced on the floorboards but did not discharge. I possessed only half the reflexes of the young musketeer but went for the pistol on the floor anyway, even before looking at my attackers. If the redcoats were to take me they would have to work for it. I had one knee on the floor, one hand bracing me up, and the other wrapped around d'Artagnan's firelock, all the while the sound of crashing boots rang in my ears. I had just picked up the weapon when I felt the cold heavy steel of a pistol barrel poking me at the back of my head.

Gideon Fludd's voice was close to my ear, that same quiet measured cadence I remembered from when he had slit my face. "No, no, no, that will not do, sirrah." I felt a hand on my collar pulling me up while someone seized the pistol from my grasp. "You've been a trickster, my friend, very difficult to find. Not so your comrade here. He was easy to follow."

Fludd pulled me backwards sharply, throwing me across the floor. I looked up to see him standing over me, two of his Fifth Monarchy men flanking him. And I was staring into the muzzle of his cavalry wheel-lock, my heart in my throat, wishing now that they had been red-coated dragoons instead. I pushed myself backwards and slowly gained my feet.

Major Fludd was bareheaded, his close-cropped white hair almost aglow in the dim light of the room. But I could clearly see his eyes. They fairly started from out of his pale face, burning with keenness to kill me for what I had done. "It is bad enough that you've slain my brother, but that you still hold what does not belong to you, now *that* rubs salt into my open wound, old man."

He knew I held the Moon Pentacle. I bumped into the wall behind me. Gideon Fludd raised his pistol towards my head. "Do not make me hunt for the *lamen*. Surrender it and then I will kill you quickly, I swear upon my God. The blood debt must be paid."

"At least most canting Roundheads believe they're serving God, sir. Not the Devil—like you are. Are you so blind not to see what it is that you truly serve?"

Fludd's booted foot slammed hard upon the boards, bouncing the entire floor. "Enough of your blasphemy! Where is the device?"

"It is no angel that you treat with." I still had my sword about my waist. But the room was too small for swordplay and he would either blow a hole through me or all three would jump me, or both.

"You are going to die anyway. Just give me what I ask for." His voice had regained its quiet certitude.

Here he was, within reach of me. I could end it all here, perhaps. Was this not what I wanted, to have him in my grasp? I smiled at him. "Why not ask your angel Eistibus where it is?"

Fludd started towards me but one of his men grabbed his shoulder. "Hold, Major! What has he seen of us?"

Fludd stepped back, digesting my little morsel. "So, you're a spy too, it seems. Did you see the Holy One when we had you tied up?"

"I've seen enough. And I know what the creature has bid you

to do. You will not succeed. Even now the army surrounds the Lord General to guard him from your attack."

Fludd hardly blinked at my sally. He shook his head slowly as if truly saddened for me. "Little old man, do you really think any mortal can stand before the Will of the Almighty? How many soldiers Cromwell surrounds himself with does not concern me. And your little efforts have only served to annoy me. This night, the angel will bestow upon me all that I need to accomplish the task. And King Jesus will follow."

The silver pentacle lay heavy in my pocket. "Very well, sir. It is my wish to serve God. I will reveal where it is hidden."

Fludd seemed to relax a little, but kept the pistol levelled. "Play me not, sir. Just tell me where it is."

"It is right *there*," I said, gently pointing my finger towards the opposite wall. And thank God, they all looked over their shoulders. I ducked fast, swatting his hand cannon away, and bounded into the next room. Even as I slammed the door shut and threw home the wooden bolt, a shot blew through the door, ripping wood splinters across my face. The pistol ball went wide. I backed into the room, my mind racing to think of an escape. And then the floor under my feet rang hollow. I was standing on the trap door that Billy had shown me, the hatch leading down to the river. I stooped to grab the iron ring, even as the door to the room was cracking off its hinges as Fludd bellowed at his men.

If Billy had somehow managed to find a boat and tie it up... I heaved again and the hatch groaned as it gave way. I peered down into the darkness and the roar and smell of the river rose up to engulf me. Then I saw it. It was hanging from the rungs of the ladder. Even as I jumped backwards, its arms reached up into the hatchway, and its long-fingered hands hit the floor, claws scrabbling on the boards, trying to find purchase. And as the head and shoulders of the thing came into view, I felt my guts go to water.

It was the pig man. The same I had fought off on the south

bank. The hellish creature pulled itself up, its huge baleful eyes never leaving me. It opened its wide maw, hog tusks yellowed and dripping, and let out a squeal that went to my marrow. It was far bigger than I had thought, glistening grey, its back covered in long bristles. I turned and ran for the stairs leading up to the next floor. When I reached that, I kept going, the narrow little staircase twisting up and around to the loft above. And below me I could hear the flapping and scratching feet of the creature as it pounded the staircase after me, the walls shaking as it bounced and pushed its way through the narrow stairwell. And all the while that terrible cry like some creature being scalded alive.

By the time I reached the loft my chest was heaving. I didn't have the balls to start drawing a chalk circle and reciting a prayer while that thing was nearly upon me. So there was no place to go but out. I burst open the dormer window frame with my shoulder, lifted my leg over the sill, and climbed out onto the roof. Christ alone knows how I managed to scramble up the peak of the dormer, but I somehow perched myself, heels slipping on the slates. I could hear the creature hissing and snorting inside the room beneath me, and although it seemed to have few brains it somehow knew how to sniff me out.

And it gave me no respite. I felt the peak of the dormer shudder under my crotch and realised the beast was battering the window frame like a ram. I heard the wood crack and several slates went sailing off a hundred feet below into the Thames. My perch was fast disintegrating beneath me and then a black, spindly hand twice the size of any man's appeared next to my boot. I swore and pulled my legs up and with only the moonlight to aid me, craned my head upwards, looking to see how I could climb further. The roof was steep but there was another dormer just higher up that I might reach. If I could get to the peak I could crawl to the next house and enter through a window there. Already, the dormer beneath me was sagging inwards, about to collapse. I balanced as best I could, stretched out and was just able to grasp the second dormer above.

As I began pulling myself upwards, my knees and boots scrambling for purchase, the pig ripped the dormer to pieces. I looked down to see its head and shoulders rising up from the hole it had torn in the roof. Its arm was beginning to reach upwards so I raised my left boot and gave it a thumping kick to the head. It howled in rage and while only annoying the thing for a moment, terror gave me the strength to pull myself to the next window with the grace of a baboon.

I was now perched on the second, smaller dormer window, the peak of the house some six feet higher up. Straddling it like the wooden hobby horse we used to punish drunken soldiers on, I tried to pull my blade out of its scabbard without sending myself tumbling over sideways. I watched the unblinking eyes of the pig thing as it heaved its bulk up, desperate to come out and join me. I was gasping now, my sword across my lap, and I knew I had little strength left to fight the thing off once it climbed out. My arms were shaking and if I tried to climb higher I knew that I would lose grip and fall.

So I sat there and watched as the pig scratched away at the roof slates and slowly managed to pull itself free of the hole. Once it had gotten its long feet up on the edge of the hole, it regarded me like some dog about to attack. The rotting scent I remembered from before wafted up to me: its fetid breath. Bracing itself with one arm, the other shot up to me, grabbing my ankle. I slashed down with my sword even as I held on to the peak with my other hand. My blade nicked its wrist and it howled and let go. Its head shook and flecks of foam from its snout splashed out across the roof. Again it grabbed for me and I swung again, weakly glancing off the slates and missing. Either I would fall from my own frantic struggles or it would pull me down and savage me. That was about all there was left. But something made me remember the pentacle—and the words written upon it. Da Silva had said the name of God held power in itself. I pulled it forth from my pocket, palmed it and thrust it out towards the pig man.

"Is this what you want?" I yelled.

And even as I did so the thing leapt upwards, pushing with its mighty legs, both arms stretching out to seize me. I fell backwards against the roof as it landed on top of me. My sword went spinning but somehow I kept the pentacle in my hand and thrust it out. The pig's jaws snapped and it raised a clawed hand ready to slice me open like a rabbit. And I pushed the pentacle into its chest. Instantly, a white flame erupted, the searing sound loud in my ears and that terrible cry of pain from the beast. It leaned backwards, limp as a doll, tottered for a moment, and then slipped sideways, rolling down the roof. It disappeared over the edge and fell to the river below.

I can barely remember getting down off that roof. Somehow I crawled through the hole the creature had made, regaining the room below. I staggered down the stairs, only half caring whether Fludd and his men waited below. My heart was still beating a rapid tattoo when I reached the bottom. All was quiet. I stumbled in the gloom into the front room to find both Billy and d'Artagnan still upon the floor. Gideon Fludd was gone.

Billy was groaning, his boots scraping along the floor as he tried to rouse himself. I helped him sit up but his head lolled like a drunk's. Then I heard d'Artagnan cry out in pain. I turned to see him pulling himself up off the floor, holding his noggin. I was on him in an instant. Practically straddling him, I hauled him up by his shirt front and shook him like a hare.

"Where did you leave Marguerite? Tell me!"

He was mumbling about who had struck him the blow.

"You goddamned fool! You've led Fludd here. To us. Where is she?"

He looked up at me, eyes beginning to focus. "She's at the inn where you stayed the other night... The Bear."

"Bastard!" I threw him backwards onto his arse and moved back to Billy who was moaning softly and cradling his broken head. "Billy! Billy Chard!"

He looked up at me. "The fucking sod crowned me good, Mister Eff. I'm poorly."

I cupped his face with my hands. "You'll be right as rain, Billy. Now listen to me. Are you listening?"

He nodded.

"Good. I need you to make your way back to da Silva's house. Tell him that Fludd is on the move. He came here after d'Artagnan struck you. Do you understand?"

Billy was rapidly clearing his fog. "He was here? In this house? Oh, Christ."

"I've got to go find Maggie. I will try and get back to da Silva's later. Don't wait around for d'Artagnan to get up. Get out of here now!"

"I'll kill that French bastard first."

"Just leave him. Come on. There's a lad... up we go."

Billy steadied himself, hands gripping the table edge. "The... the buff coats... I brought them."

"Fetch them if you can, but get out now. I don't know who will be on our doorstep next!" I clapped him on the back and made for the threshold. D'Artagnan was retching in the corner. "And you," I said, stabbing a finger in the air, "you I'll be back for if she has come to harm!"

It was all unravelling. I knew that as I emerged from the house to see several folk standing by, alarmed at what had been going on for the past half an hour.

"Here now! What's all the ruckus in there?" I could see in the lantern light it was some bloody-aproned butcher coming towards me, cleaver in hand.

I must have looked a sight; my coat ripped open, shirt undone and breeches caked in slime and seagull shit from the roof. "Mind your own business!" I blustered, tottering along the cobbles, away towards the Southwark end.

I reached the Bear and made my way to the stairs, ignoring the challenges of the serving boy and landlord as I entered, pushing past the drinkers and whores. Up the stairs, bouncing along the walls of the hall, I found the room. The door was wide open. Wheezing and panting like a spent hound, I entered, already knowing that I was too late.

She was not there. But—sweet Lord—her valise lay torn apart on the floor, its contents strewn about the room by someone who had been furiously intent on finding something. I absently gathered up her ripped chemise and so too her hooded russet cloak. Clutching them, I sat on the little bedstead in the corner, the pit of my stomach in a wrenching knot. A chair had been dashed to pieces and the bed itself had been pulled away from the wall. I could almost see her being thrown about the room by Fludd, and she, in turn, lashing out like a cornered beast.

And then, horrid confirmation of what my mind had summoned up. A tuft of long brown hair, my Maggie's, lay at the foot of the bed, and my heart was stabbed straight through. Tears welled up and I could not drive from my head ever more dreadful visions of what had befallen her. I rubbed my face with the back of my sleeve. I had little time to track her, find her before it was too late. I took a deep breath and even as I did so, felt anger welling up to replace the tears. Then, by chance, I spotted a sheet of paper upon the little round table across the room. I put her things on the pillow and rose, making my way to the table. It was just some ha'penny broadsheet, but the thick pencil-scrawled message along the margin, bold and stark, was meant only for me. Whether Gideon Fludd had written it before or after he and his minions had accosted me, I knew not. Nor did it really matter.

Bring it to Whitehall Park.

He had her. And his bargain was clear. Give him the pentacle, and he would free her. I also knew that my life was part of that deal as well.

I dropped the ultimatum back to the table and was about to gather Maggie's things, but when I looked up, someone was standing in the doorway. I did not know who he was but he was studying me intently—and in some confusion from the look on his face. He was in a black suit with a plain collar, no weapon in hand. A man with an unspoilt face and gentle eyes, obviously having seen little of war or hardship. His long hair fell to his shoulders, swept to either side of a high forehead and a narrow nose. He looked like a lawyer.

"Who the hell are you, sir?" I growled, suddenly realising I too was weaponless.

"I am someone who has been looking for you for some time... a considerable time," he replied. He then shook his head sadly. "Leastways I *think* you're the one I'm searching for. I had expected more... presence of quality." And he then nodded to someone else in the hallway. In an instant, three burly redcoats piled in, pushing me back. One stuck his forearm against my throat and pinioned me to the opposite wall. My limbs were still weak and shaking from my rooftop fight and I gave no resistance as my back and head hit the plaster.

"My name is John Thurloe of the Council of State. And you, I presume, are Colonel Richard Treadwell." He moved deeper into the bedchamber and threw back his dark cassock off his shoulder as he reached for the paper on the table. He was still looking me up and down in open disbelief at my shabby, stinking condition. "I thought the Royalists were paying better than this. Christ's wounds! Look at the state of you, man." He scanned the paper but gave no reaction to Fludd's message.

A fourth soldier came in jangling a set of rusty manacles.

"Put him in irons," said Thurloe quietly.

He was still shaking his head in disappointment as they bustled me out the door. As I was swept past, I heard him mock me. "And he's a new knight of the realm, to boot. Sad times indeed."

Chapter Sixteen

Twice before I had seen the palace of Whitehall and both times it was a gloomy ramshackle place, full of endless passages and built without rhyme or reason. More so now that the king was dead. He had been led out to his execution on a scaffold from the window of his own banqueting hall. And the palace died with him. The place was empty, cold, and full of shadows and distant echoes now. Empty that is except for a few buildings near to the street of Whitehall where I found myself being driven: the old gate and guardhouse between the palace and Scotland Yard.

Without a word, my guards took me down from the coach and marched me underneath the archway of the brick gatehouse that led into the old courtyard and the heart of the old palace. I craned my head back to glimpse Thurloe emerging from a second coach that had followed. On either side were two great doors that I remembered were the chambers for the royal guard. It was here that they pushed me into the door to the left and I found myself in a large unadorned chamber, plaster falling off the brick walls in huge slabs, and the floor made up of large flagstones, cracked and uneven. It contained just a few tables and benches, some guttering tin lanterns and a great fireplace at one end, unlit. Leading off from this was another door—one with an iron grate and locks. Two redcoats stood up as we piled inside, looking a bit confused at my arrival and leaving their tankards upon the table.

"Sit him down over there," ordered Thurloe as he came into the room and removed his gloves. "And get a fire going."

"I thought I would be going to the Tower," I said, standing in the centre of the bitterly cold room. A soldier grabbed my arm and shoved me down onto a cracked and wobbling bench.

Thurloe pulled his cassock closer about himself and shut the door. "Oh, you'll find yourself there soon enough, Sir Richard. But let's not get ahead of things." He came over to me and pulled up a chair until it was but two feet in front of me. "I'm not inclined to turn you over to the charge of the Lieutenant of the Tower until we've had a chance to discuss your little journey of late."

Bad enough I had been captured, but to be but a stone's throw from where Cromwell was no doubt at that moment eating his soup and bread was bitter indeed. Two soldiers busied themselves with firewood while the others stood near the door. I stretched out my legs and absently rattled my irons in my lap. "Whatever intelligence you have is wrong. That I can tell you."

Thurloe didn't reply straight away. He was just sizing me up, his slightly flabby face shining yellow and sweaty in the dim lamplight. If those jaded eyes of his could have looked into my mind and seen what I had fought and sent tumbling off the rooftops of London Bridge he would have taken off my chains himself. I looked away. There were a few small casement windows in the chamber and I could see it was fully evening now, probably near eight o'clock.

"Where is that simpleton of a Ranter you've been travelling with?"

"He's the least of your worries," I replied. "Can I have a drink?"

Thurloe pursed his thin lips, but nevertheless motioned to one of the redcoats to bring me a tankard. I cupped it with my shackled hands and drank a swig of beer. It was rank stuff but it wet my throat and mouth.

"I cannot fathom," he said, hands clasped and elbows resting on the arms of his chair, "why you would come back here and risk your neck for nothing. You must realise that your life is now forfeit. What could they possibly have offered you?"

"You don't understand."

"Enlighten me, Colonel."

I took another swig before I began telling him my tale—or at least the lion's share of it. It didn't really matter whether I trusted him or not but I had to convince him of what was about to befall all of us.

"I assume it was the French ambassador who relayed the news of my arrival. He probably told you of the plot in the West Country that I was to help lead. But that is only a fraction of the whole truth."

Thurloe nodded slowly. "Yes, the ambassador gave us a warning that you were here on a mission for Herbert or Hyde. But I already knew full well about the rising in the west. I am more concerned with your *personal* mission here."

"My personal mission is to safeguard the life of the Lord General. Shortly after I arrived in Plymouth I stumbled upon a plot to assassinate him. A plot you are still blissfully unaware of." Guffaws from the guards sounded behind me.

"You three can wait outside," said Thurloe, his voice all ice and authority. "And you two," he turned to the redcoats labouring over the hearth, "get on with that fire!"

He looked annoyed, maybe even anxious, and I could tell he was already thinking that I was spinning him a fairy tale to try and save my skin.

He leaned forward, the chair creaking under him. "The only plot I am concerned with is the one you have against General Cromwell."

I just about managed a croak of amusement. "This rising you are so concerned about was nothing but a poor jest from the beginning. A band of drunkards and braggarts is what I found when I landed. And I was the bigger fool for believing there was half a chance. I'm not surprised you knew of their plans. But you've missed the real danger to the kingdom." And so I told him of how I had run into Gideon Fludd at Exeter, and, while leaving out the most fantastic details for the moment, revealed that this band of rogue Fifth Monarchy men meant to kill Cromwell in less than twenty-four hours. I told him the truth, but decided at this point in my creaky situation to omit how I had chanced upon and killed Israel Fludd. Things were difficult enough without a charge of murder being added to my woes.

Thurloe just sat there, silent and expressionless, taking in my words. His eyes betrayed nothing of the cogs moving in his mind. At length, he leaned back and placed his hands on the ruined turnings of the poor abused chair, a ruder piece of furniture than he was no doubt accustomed to.

"It was Major Fludd, I understand, who rounded up your co-conspirators in Exeter last week," he said. "From my vantage he and his men are in line for reward and not censure. And now that you've been caught you spin out a story that it is Major Fludd who should be under arrest. You expect me to believe that sort of bollocks, sir?"

It was my turn to lean forward. "Fludd is convinced he's on a mission from God to destroy Cromwell and usher in the Second Coming. I have heard him say this. His plan was to move as soon as Cromwell dissolved Parliament. As we speak he is already here in London, ready to strike."

Thurloe chuckled quietly, genuinely amused.

"If you won't believe me," I persisted, "then find the French ambassador's man, Lieutenant d'Artagnan. He was attacked by Fludd and his men this very afternoon. Know also, that Fludd has kidnapped a lady in the care of d'Artagnan."

"Fantasy, sir. It would seem that Gideon Fludd is at war with *everyone* in London. Why don't you just confess your plot and give me the names of your associates?"

I sighed. "But you saw the note... on the table at the inn. I have something he wants in return for the woman."

"Yes, I read it. But anyone could have scribbled that, even you. And what do you claim he wants of you?"

I opened my mouth to answer, but stopped. Down that path lay ruin.

"Can't think of anything fast enough, Colonel?"

I had to get the spymaster curious, curious enough to start asking questions. "Mister Thurloe, has not William Lilly come to see you today? To tell you about these Fifth Monarchy men?"

"Who? Lilly the astrologer? Come now, you really are grasping at straws. What could that gentleman have to do with this? I'm sure he's happily calculating the stars as we speak."

Now this was ill news indeed. If neither Lilly nor any of the other brethren had made the approach, I was truly left dangling. "I assure you, Mister Lilly will be looking for you to tell you. He promised me."

"We keep an eye on the Fifth men—like any of the radicals. If there was a plot afoot I would know about it... Like yours."

I hefted my manacles in frustration. "I beg you... seek out the Frenchman. He will tell you all. All I will admit is I came here to raise the West Country. Not to do murder. It is by pure chance that I uncovered Fludd's plans to assassinate the Lord General. And I have risked my life to come to London to stop it."

Thurloe slowly got up, his eyes boring into me. He was trying to decide whether I was just mad, calculating, or really telling the truth. "You offer me no proof of any of your assertions. And as a known enemy of the state, I have no reason to offer you a thing. And as for talk of assassination, well, I'm sure we will get the answers we seek once you're chained in the Tower. We have a Moor there who is most skilled at getting results from the uncooperative."

"Consider this then. If you don't ask the Frenchman and you don't question Fludd himself—and something *does* happen— who will bear the responsibility for that? I'll be hanged for rebellion but you'll be the man whose overconfidence killed the Lord General... I'm sure there is special punishment for that."

Thurloe looked down at me, unmoved but for a twitching of the corner of his mouth. A fire was now crackling away in the hearth, the smell of smoke blowing back into the room. The last two remaining musketeers had taken up stations at the door.

"Captain Poxwell!"

One of the soldiers approached Thurloe.

"Detain Colonel Treadwell here in the adjoining chamber for tonight. I want the rest of your men to remain as well. Lock yourselves in. I will return in the morning to escort the prisoner to the Tower." He gave me one last long look but I could not tell whether the spark of doubt was lit or not.

As one of the soldiers opened the door for him, he paused, and turned back to shoot me another long look. "Captain, keep a good eye on this fellow, do you hear?"

Poxwell sprung up straight as a ramrod. "Yes, my lord!"

THAT DREAM AGAIN. I was instantly awake, lying on the cot in the little adjoining chamber. It was a dream that came to me in times of trouble, always the same short but vivid scene. I am back in the wilds of Saxony, in the mountains. And I am fleeing as fast as my legs will carry me. Fleeing from the horde of Croat mercenaries that have just slaughtered my comrades on the field below. And the undergrowth tears at me, almost reaching up, binding me and pulling me like I am knee deep in mud. And the deep laughter of the Croats grows closer as they reach me... And I open my eyes.

Faint lamplight spilled in from the little barred window on the door to my cell. The room was no more than ten foot square. It reeked of stale piss from the bucket that sat upon the floor in the corner. This had to be a dossing place where the guards would bring their whores from Charing Cross for a little diversion. The one window to the outside, at head height, was iron trellis work. It would have made little difference were it open; I couldn't have fit through it if I were a child. I sat up on the cot and scraped my boots on the stone floor to warm my numb feet.

On the broken down table that was propped against the far wall lay my silver pentacle and the lump of chalk from my pocket. Thurloe must have been distracted by something, for he had not even bothered to search me. But the pentacle had become a curse. Somehow I knew that it drew the enemy to me, guiding them no matter where I hid. But so too was it probably the key to destroying them.

At least Poxwell had had the decency to feed me: a hunk of cheese, more rind than anything else, and half a loaf of black bread. And he had taken off the irons from my wrists. I could hear them all snoring in the next chamber, their bellies full of beer. The echoes of the nightmare had now passed. Always the same dream of when I was twenty-one and raw to soldiering. And always the same rank fear. But I had survived that episode. And others that few could even dream of. And I was not about to let Marguerite die in Fludd's hands. I would find a way to beat him.

I judged it was well past midnight. The soft, silver glow of the near full moon poured through my cell, spilling a pool of light upon the wall above my cot. I felt strangely rested, even after just a few hours sleep and the abrupt intervention of my little nightmare. Running my hands through my tangled locks, I started to think of a way to escape, by ruse or by desperate gamble. I thought I saw the light upon the wall fade out and in again. Probably the clouds passing by the face of the moon. And as I sat there, I became uncomfortably aware of a presence. My talisman almost pulled at its chain, seeming to grow heavier. I glanced up at the window. I could see ivy gently swaying with the gusts of wind outside, clinging as it did on the outer wall of the old gatehouse. That would explain the shadow fall and I quickly put to rest darker thoughts.

So then, a stratagem was needed. Perhaps to feign illness? That might get Poxwell into the room again. If he was wearing his short blade as he had earlier, I stood a good chance of taking him by surprise, snatching the weapon, and making for the door before the others could react. And then, for the second time, I felt I was being watched. I could not see Poxwell or his comrades at the door grate but the feeling persisted. And though it was cold in the room, my locket was pressing warm—oddly warm, against my chest. I slowly stood up, listening intently in the darkness. There was only silence and the ringing of my own ears. Still, that tickling feeling lingered. Something was not altogether right, and apprehension grew even stronger as my imagination began to play with me, pulling up memories of things I had tried to keep deeply submerged. And as my eyes passed by the little high window for the third time, I saw it. Saw it sitting quietly on the window ledge.

It was in a crouch, no more than a foot or so high, and nothing of it was truly visible other than its outline in the moonlight. But its large white eyes, like those of some frightened waif, looked right into mine and then blinked slowly, the lids rising up from the bottom of its orbs. It was a black homunculus, more baboon than man, bent over to fit in the small opening. I watched its tiny, long-fingered hands wrap around the wrought iron grill and saw it lean inwards. It was every inch a living imp, the likeness seen carved in stone in a hundred churches. But when it spoke I nearly leapt out of my skin.

"I can hear you in there."

Its voice, the tone of a creaking hinge, carried clearer and further than it should have from a creature only the size of a doll.

"I can hear what you think," it said. "Not as good as my brothers... but I am getting better."

I slowly stood up, my eyes riveted to the thing. "Leave, hellspawn! Get back to your master and tell him I shall meet him soon."

It tilted its head to regard me better through the grating, its small flat ears twitching. "The woman, she is very afraid. I can hear what she thinks too."

I approached it, looking about quickly for a stick or anything to strike it with. "Hellspawn or not, I shall twist your little head from your body if she is harmed. Mark me well on that."

And then it laughed, laughed like a coughing dog. "You talk brave but you're a'scared. I can hear it in your head. She is afraid we will eat her... and we will. When it is time."

I slammed my hand against the grate but it merely pulled back its hands and blinked at me, barely troubled. "My master says tomorrow we rule the night. It matters not whether you get out of here."

"You can tell Gideon Fludd that I will see him tomorrow night and finish this."

The creature laughed again, a fat black tongue protruding from its yellow-toothed grin. "The man is not my master. You are thinking that Fludd is the master! The Fludd is the *vessel*. The Fludd is the tool. The lord Andras is the master."

I stepped back from the window. "Why is he come? Why now?"

"To confound you all, sons of men. To confound you all."

"I will get out of here. I'll come for my Maggie. And I will slay you all."

The imp shook its head at me. "Piggy was weak. But we are stronger. Andras is coming."

"The Lord Jehovah will protect us!" I spat, more in desperation than conviction. But as soon as I spoke, its ears flattened like those of a cat struck with a broom. It grabbed the ironwork anew and hissed back at me.

"We will vex your world, man. The Crom man will die and we will multiply."

"There are many who guard Cromwell. You will not succeed."

"If your friends let you out then you can come and see. And then my brothers will eat you too. They are bigger than me."

I ran to the door and banged away to wake the guards. But they slumbered on—unnaturally so. This little thing was childlike but it knew much. And if the Fifth Monarchy men took over the kingdom with Gideon Fludd at the fore, they would be ushering in hell on earth. And I remembered the rabbi's warning: this demon's sole purpose was to sow dissent and discord in the hearts of men.

"They're all sleeping. Sleeping the night away. They cannot hear you. But I can hear you."

"You vile creature!" And I went for it again. As I touched the grating, it lashed with the speed of an adder and its claws scratched the top of my hand. I cried out and pulled back, the burning pain running up my arm as if I had been touched with a red poker.

"And I can *see* what you see... in your dreams." It blinked again and then slowly smiled like a little old man, turning my blood to ice. And then it vanished. But then I saw the ivy that draped around the edges of the window. It was rustling as if shaken by some unseen hand. First one, and then another vine poked through the rusting ironwork, like black-green worms, feeling their way over the brick sill. And just as quickly, more came through at the top, shooting through the grating. They poured through the opening and spilled down the floor and into the room. And they kept coming even as I jumped back against the far wall. The rustling noise was maddening loud, filling my ears. One strand found my ankle and instantly whipped its way around it. The wall was a mass of rippling green leaves and vines, and this soon was flopping its way across the floor, seeking me out. And it was climbing up the table legs too.

I looked to the table and saw the lump of chalk. And the pentacle. And I remembered.

Tearing off the vine that was already pulling me towards its brethren, I seized the silver pentacle just as two large quivering vines wrapped themselves around the wobbling table like a kraken upon a ship. I then grabbed the chalk and jumped to the opposite corner of the room, hurling the piss bucket at the writhing pile of greenery. I rapidly began drawing a circle around myself upon the stone tiled floor, my hand shaking so much I could barely keep the chalk lump firmly on the stone. I stood up straight, and looked about my feet. Christ! It was hardly a circle at all. And then I stumbled over the words that da Silva had told me. Hesitant, wrong, mixed-up, yes—but they came out. And by the third try, I had them in my mind, fully formed and true. And then they were upon my bone-dry lips.

"Be split, be accursed, broken and banned, you son of mud, son of an unclean one, son of clay, in the name of Morigo, Moriphath and his seal."

Again, again, over and over, until I was nearly screaming the words. Half mad with fear, I dared not stop. The ivy was still whipping frantically, the room was filled more than knee-high. A powerful stench of mould, the air of a tomb, filled the chamber. A few large vines slapped at my face but I could already see that not one strand had crossed the circle at my feet. The whole writhing mass broke upon me like a wave upon a jetty, surging and then falling back. I don't know how many times I repeated the incantation, that Hebrew charm, but my voice was soon hoarse.

And then I perceived the motion of the sea of ivy to lessen, its thrashing seeming to slow, to quiet. And just as quickly, so too did the smell change. Where the rotting musty odour was but a minute ago, now the smell of trodden plants, sweet and acrid, lay upon the air. And the ivy was now what it had been before—peaceful and at rest, companion to the stone.

The chamber was still. I felt for the pentacle in my pocket

to make sure it was still there. And then I cautiously inched a toe beyond the chalk line of the circle. I prodded the tangled thicket in front of me. No movement followed. I stepped out of the circle, gingerly, afraid to draw breath. But all was silent except for the crush of my boots upon the leaves.

And I can see what you see... in your dreams.

The Croats. The forest on the mountainside. The undergrowth pulling at my feet, defeating me. The thing had seen into my fevered mind as clearly as if I had told it aloud what I was dreaming. I stumbled through the vines to the cot, swept away the mass that lay there and fell upon the bedstead. I reached into my pocket and pulled out the Pentacle of the Moon. Curling up like a beaten child, I clutched it to my chest and passed into a mercifully dreamless sleep, a sleep of the dead.

"Sweet Jesus Christ!" Captain Poxwell was standing in the open door, mouth wide open. The sea of tangled greenery was still there on the floor, nearly waist high near the window. I turned over on the cot and looked at him, not knowing even what to say. It could be plainly seen that the ivy had grown in through the window opening as if five years had passed in a single night.

Poxwell looked at me. He was still bleary-eyed from his deep slumber but I could tell he was trying to figure if I could have pulled in all that ivy through the iron grating over one night. He looked at the window again. The alternative was too alarming to contemplate and he turned back to the other room, stuttering. "Mister Thurloe, sir... something's gone on a bit strange here... think you should have a look in."

I didn't await the arrival of the spymaster but instead rolled out of the cot and entered the main chamber. Thurloe was standing there, dressed as he had been the night before (had he even slept?), but he was not alone. Next to him was my sometime comrade and pursuer of late, the Lieutenant d'Artagnan. He had a thick linen bandage wrapped about his head, piled up so high he could not wear his hat. With his thin, drooping moustache, and fine velvet suit, he looked like some lugubrious Turk. His eyes met mine for a moment, then he lowered his gaze.

John Thurloe looked grimmer than he had the previous evening. "Colonel, it is time to continue our conversation," he said, giving no mention of the Frenchman who stood next to him, or of his intentions.

"Mister Thurloe... my lord..." Captain Poxwell was straddling the threshold to my cell, seemingly incapable of taking his eyes off the forest of vines. "I think there's witchcraft here, sir. Meaning no disrespect sir, but please do have a look inside."

"What is it, man?" said Thurloe. He pushed past me and entered the little room. He quickly reappeared, stepping somewhat slowly across the main chamber. "Poxwell, shut that door and lock it this instant." He turned to me, his face perhaps a little more flushed than a moment ago. Pulling his kerchief from out of his sleeve, he dabbed his mouth before continuing.

"My curiosity got the better of me after we last spoke," he said. "I sought out Mister Lilly as you suggested. He sends his greetings... and commiserations upon your arrest, by the way."

I nodded, knowing my fate rested on his next few words.

"He has told me the entire tale. A fantastical one to be sure, but I forbore it, listening in full. He confided that he had intended to seek me out yesterday and warn me of this alleged plot by Major Fludd but that his courage failed him. He says he believes your story though you offer no proof." Thurloe then gestured to d'Artagnan. "That is why I then sought out the French ambassador again. And there, I met this gentleman who I believe you are well acquainted with."

D'Artagnan stepped towards me, his hat gripped tightly in both hands, his mouth almost trembling with emotion. He extended one leg, elegantly slipped the other behind, and bowed his head to me. "My dear Colonel, I beg your forgiveness for doubting your word. You were right, and I have failed the lady St. John as well. My honour is gone. Gone until we restore her."

I looked at the young, once cocksure, musketeer and gave him a nod of acceptance. But I could not forgive him for his recklessness in losing Maggie. That he would have to earn, if it was even possible to do so. Cromwell be damned. I was going into battle against Fludd and his devils to free her. To free her and take her back home, away from this blighted place.

"So where do we stand now, sir?" I asked Thurloe. I held out my arms towards him. "Am I to be transferred to the Tower? Or do we seek out Fludd and his men instead?"

Thurloe gave me a hard stare. "Against my reason, I am inclined to give you the benefit of the doubt—for the moment. What I have just seen in that room adds some weight to what Mister Lilly has told me, that I will admit. But consider this only a furlough. The army and I will look for Fludd—if he is to be found. And you are coming with me. *Monsieur* d'Artagnan if he chooses. And you can share with me your intentions, Colonel, on where and how Fludd will strike. No more secret sorties, do you understand?"

"Very well, sir. I give you my word I will aid you. But we must act quickly and you must have faith in what I shall ask of you no matter how fantastic it sounds to your faculties for reason."

"I shall do what is in the interest of the State, sir, have no fear. But do not cross me." He extended his hand to me. "So then, let us give our bond to this little agreement."

I took the hand of the enemy in mine and my eyes widened as I felt the subtle but definite pressure of his forefinger and then his thumb as he gave me the secret sign that I had just been initiated in a day ago. Dazed, I reciprocated as expected of an accepted Mason. The spymaster betrayed nothing as he looked at me.

"And what do you propose we do first, Colonel, to expose this plot?"

"First, I advise you to double the guard on the Lord General's apartments. And you need to meet and listen to a few of my new friends, Mister Thurloe. Tell your musketeers to be ready for a fight against a new enemy." Captain Poxwell, standing next to his master, was ashen. I watched as his eyes darted to his comrades across the room, the same fellows who had smirked at me the night before. Now, the tune was a different one.

Thurloe retrieved his tall and plain hat from the table and placed it on his head. "I take it you refer to whatever did that to your cell last night," he said, nodding towards the far room, bolted shut.

"Tonight you shall see such things with your own eyes," I said. "And we will need God's help to stop them."

Chapter Seventeen

"SAINTS ABOVE!" SHOUTED Billy as I walked into the shop of Roderigo da Silva, somewhat stiff with pain. "It does my heart good, Fellow Creature, does my heart good indeed! Jesus knows we didn't expect to see you again." Billy came over and grasped my arm and shoulder, clapping me gently when he saw my poor state.

"How's your noggin, Billy?"

Billy smiled, scratching at the tuft of hair that stood up on the top of his skull. "The young woman here found a salve for that. No real harm done."

I smiled back. "And I can tell you that d'Artagnan has one double the size of yours."

The rabbi, too, entered the front room at the sound of the door, and looking at me, took more than a few moments before realising who it was. "Bless me, Mister Falkenhayn! We had heard the tale of your capture by the army. How—" He stopped himself and flapped his hands about like a flustered hen. "It matters not. You are here and safe. Mister Ashmole, come down here!"

Billy looked me up and down. "You look a might worse for wear, Mister Eff. Come now, take a seat over here and tell us what has happened."

I didn't refuse. I noticed that Billy was in but his shirt and breeches, sleeves rolled up and some sort of stinking yellow-coloured poultices wrapped about the wounds on his arms.

"I went back to the Bear later last night. Heard you'd been snatched away by some redcoats and assumed you were done for. But I did what you said and came back here again to the Portagees, Mister Eff. Like you said."

Elias Ashmole appeared through the curtain of the doorway to the back, took one look at me and swore an oath. "They let you go! Please tell me they believed your story, sir."

I stretched my legs out in front of me, a heavy cloak of fatigue finally settling over me now that I was back among friends. "Aye, they half-believe me. But Thurloe's men have me under watch and the man himself will be here within the hour. He wants to know our plan."

Ashmole tilted his head and cocked an eyebrow. "Our *plan*? Well, dear fellow, we were waiting for that from you. The rabbi here has been busy though, consulting the texts."

Da Silva nodded. "And we have the silver we need thanks be to Mister Ashmole. We'll have some means at our disposal for the work that lies ahead."

Ashmole reached for a brown bottle of Canary and brought it over to me. "*Senor* da Silva's silversmith should have the work done in a few hours from now. A very dependable man, we're told."

I wiped my face, took a swig straight from the bottle, and looked up at my companions. "Last night, in my cell... I spoke with one of *them*. One of the demon's minions. They have Maggie—alive, it told me. The damned thing actually spoke to me. Some sort of infernal imp—like a monkey."

"See! I told you just so!" Billy started waving his bandaged arms out of frustration and fear. "Goddamned creatures from hell itself!"

"My God," Ashmole muttered, looking over to the old Jew. "Can we really do this thing?"

"We must," da Silva said. He slammed open another one of his ancient mould-covered books to continue his search for divine assistance. "There is no one else to do what must be done."

"Thurloe has agreed to redouble the guard on the Lord General," I said. "And he will come with us tonight to confront Fludd." I glanced over to Billy. "And d'Artagnan is with him. He vouched for at least some of my tale."

Billy looked as if he was about to spit on the floor. "We can trust that Frenchman about as far as Thurloe."

"Aye, that may be so. But we'll need numbers to take on Fludd's Fifth Monarchy men."

Billy was having none of it. "Bah! Once they get a sight of the apes and the black dog they'll run for home. And then it will be us buggers on our fuckin' own."

Da Silva contemplated me again and shook his head slowly. "Isabel! Come down here!" He stood back from his table, arms stretched forward as if he too was suddenly stricken with weariness. "Your man is correct, Mister Falkenhayn. They will not know what to do when they confront the unholy as large as life." He raised his head and called out again shrilly. "Isabel!"

"No, I suppose they won't," I said. "But nor did I until I had to. We need the redcoats."

Da Silva's tiny eyes, surmounted by drooping lids, paper-thin and grey, looked into mine without wavering. "And what will you tell them about me?"

I had not thought of that. The Council of State might be turning a blind eye to the Jewish merchants of London when it suited, but Hebrew magic was something that Thurloe would probably find hard to stomach.

"Thurloe has already spoken with Mister Lilly," I said. "He may have already mentioned you and the Grand Pentacle of Solomon."

"Which is the property of Mister Lilly and not *Senor* da Silva's," added Ashmole. "Good Protestants may use these ancient Hebrew symbols as much as anyone. There is no secret in this. *Senor* da Silva is merely the owner of some old medical and religious texts. If you take my meaning. And besides, the government seems more preoccupied with Catholic conspiracies at the moment."

"Very well, then," I said. "*Senor*, I suggest you keep whatever cloak you use these days and leave the discussion to Mister Ashmole. We'll have to steer a delicate course with Thurloe."

I looked back over to Ashmole. "Elias, what of Lilly and the Craft? I had expected them to join you."

Ashmole shook his head. "I went to Mister Lilly's house this morning. It took some amount of banging on his door before one of his servants answered. They told me he had urgent business in Berkhamsted and would be gone for a few days. I cannot fathom it."

Somehow I was not too surprised by this disappointment. "And the others?"

Ashmole shugged. "Alas, they all seem to have flown the roost. The Lodge is empty but for we two."

"I suppose they didn't have the stomach for it."

Ashmole, ever the diplomat, was more sanguine. "Fearful or not, the others are not military men as you and I are... or were. At least we have Solomon's pentacle in our hands."

I noticed that Ashmole was in his country clothes: riding boots, heavy kersey breeches, and a grease-stained leather doublet. At least he was taking seriously the mission that lay ahead of us. I smiled at him, thankful for the steadfastness of a man who hardly even knew me. "We few, we happy few... eh Elias?"

"Father?"

The girl entered through the curtain, more subdued than when last we saw her, barely looking at me as she reached her father's side.

"Ah, daughter, there you are. Fetch Mister Falkenhayn a basin and some hot water that he may refresh himself. Bring him to the back and assist him."

She bowed her head swiftly and turned to me, her olive-toned face highlighted by the bright white scarf that entwined her head.

I looked at da Silva. "That is not necessary, sir, your hospitality is enough as it stands."

"Nonsense. You must be prepared for the trial yet to come. It will do your soul good."

The reminder of what I faced that evening did not ease my mind, but I nodded in agreement and followed Isabel into the next room, a connecting chamber with an empty hearth, just as sparsely furnished as the main hall. She led me onwards, quickly looking to see that I followed, into the back kitchen and scullery that looked out onto a courtyard garden barely the size of a skittle lane. The sun was shining and I could see many green herb beds and bushes through the open windows, carefully tended. Rosemary grew in great quantity, spiky and tall compared to the pale parsley and lemon balm that struggled in the April chill.

I watched her as she moved rapidly about the kitchen, filling a copper basin from the steaming kettle that hung suspended over a little coal fire that hissed and sputtered. She set this down next to me at the big oak table and set about getting linens and oils from a tired, sagging sideboard in the corner. I reckoned she was barely twenty and for all her industry, there was something very sad and melancholy about her.

She stood next to me and poured out some fragrant oil into the basin, mixing it with a small cloth that she dipped in, oblivious to the heat.

"What are you looking at?" she asked, although she was intently looking into the copper.

"Why, you, girl. Isn't that allowed?"

"It's rude to stare."

"Then I shall contemplate your garden instead. You grow a prodigious amount of fine rosemary, I see."

There was silence except for the gentle dripping of the water, its pleasing scent rising up to my face and already renewing my spirit. Such a little thing. And then, she spoke, her voice soft.

"It is from Lisbon. A variety that does not grow here in England. It reminds me of our old garden on the hillside there... before times became bad." She raised the dripping cloth and squeezed it over the copper bowl. She paused, cupping the damp linen in her hand. "I must apologise to you, sir, for my outburst yesterday. I was wrong. And I shamed my father by behaving so."

"You're rightly concerned for his safety. I see that as something admirable, not wrong."

She dipped the cloth in the copper again and swirled it carefully before raising it and wringing it a little. "Here, hold still, while I wash your face. You have been bruised upon your cheek?"

I started to protest, but she pushed my hand away and continued. "Don't fuss so. I wash my father's head and he doesn't make half so much noise."

The warmth felt good and I shut my eyes as she dipped and wrung out the cloth again, bringing it up to my forehead and cheeks.

"And when I've finished your face you must dip your head into the basin to rinse your locks."

I smiled under the veil of the cloth. "I shall protest no more."

I then dutifully dipped my tired head into the water and she handed me a linen square to dry myself. She was now contemplating me, hands upon hips.

"I thought you said it was rude to stare."

She smiled at me, a pretty mouth, but careworn for such a tender age. "I'm sorry. Now face the other way that I may comb out your locks, sir."

And as she was teasing out the tangled mess of my hair, occasionally drizzling some oil to smooth out the combing, she addressed me again.

"Father says that someone you love has been kidnapped by this Gideon Fludd. I'm sorry for that."

"Yes. She is very dear to me and I fear for her life."

"Is she your wife?"

"No... she is my mistress."

There was a long pause then. "And you love her very much?"

I found myself nodding, seeming to remind myself of that truth.

"But you're married to someone else?"

Lord, she was a curious creature. But I went along. "It's a complicated situation, Isabel, but the short answer is yes."

I felt the comb lift from my head. "There you are. It's finished. I shall look for some clean linen of father's for you to change into."

I got up and faced her. "Thank you for your kindness."

She looked at me, nodded, and then set about carrying the basin away. "Can you not divorce your wife?" she asked as she hurled the water into the garden.

"It is a difficult thing to do in this country," I replied, somewhat amused by her brashness. "I would need an act of Parliament and since, as of yesterday, we no longer have a Parliament that would be difficult to accomplish indeed."

"In our faith, it's enough for a husband to say 'I divorce you' and for the rabbi to hear it. Then it is done."

I nodded. "Now that is a simple solution to a difficult problem."

Isabel carefully strung up the wet cloth near the hearth. "My father wishes to accompany you this night. And I will let him go. I will do so because this woman's life depends upon you all. And she must not be made to suffer or to die."

I felt my throat tighten and I swallowed. "I'm grateful to you for this. And I will do everything to bring your father back to you."

She hung the kettle back on its hook and then slowly turned around again, wiping her hands on her skirt. "Oh, I will be bringing him back. Because I am coming with you too. For if he's meant to die, then I shall die with him rather than remain here alone."

"My word, I know this shop!" John Thurloe, secretary to the Council of State, looked around at the stacked bottles on the shelves of the wine merchant. "But who would have guessed I would be meeting here on this kind of business." He stepped into the room, Lieutenant d'Artagnan at his side. I could just glimpse Captain Poxwell lurking in the doorway, his hand resting on the hilt of his short hangar. Thurloe looked at me and then the others in turn.

"Sir Richard and I have exchanged greetings this day already." He pointed to Billy Chard and looked at me. "The Ranter, I presume?"

Billy held tight but looked ready to burst.

"And the celebrated Mister Ashmole..." Thurloe touched the brim of his very Puritan hat in a salute. "And, *Senor* Roderigo da Silva... my wine merchant from what my servant tells me."

Thurloe stepped lightly to one side and gestured with his hand towards the Frenchman. "And this, gentleman, is *Monsieur* d'Artagnan, on diplomatic assignment from the King of France and, as I understand it, a former comrade of Colonel Treadwell. Lieutenant d'Artagnan has graciously volunteered to assist in our little foray."

D'Artagnan, his hat now back on his head, *sans* bandage, gave a little bow and I was now beginning to wonder just how much command of the English tongue he really had. The musketeer quickly met my eyes and gave me an honest sort of smile as if to say we were once again on the same side. That remained to be seen.

"Sir," said Ashmole, nodding his head, "we're most grateful that you have answered our alarm. And for you seeing fit to release our good companion here upon hearing his tale."

"Let's just say that I've heard enough from several sources to get my attention," replied the spymaster. "But what I'm waiting for is proof of the plot... and a glass of wine if one is in the offing."

Da Silva scrambled to the back, and just as quickly re-emerged with a few glasses and began pouring from the open bottle on the table.

I was more concerned about other things. "Have you strengthened the guard around the Lord General's residence?"

Thurloe turned his attention back to me, a broad smile on his lips. "Your newfound devotion to the Republic is invigorating, Colonel. And yes, I have sent another squadron of troopers over there. The Lord General's own regiment. You may rest easy on that account."

"And have you told the Lord General about the threat on his life?"

"What? Tell him that a pack of hobgoblins are about to descend upon him? I think not. If Gideon Fludd and his rabble make an attempt to break into Whitehall, we'll stop him before he gets very far."

The little rabbi handed a full glass of ruby liquid up to Thurloe, who gingerly took it and saluted me. "And now, sir, I would invite you to enlighten me further about what intelligence you say you possess of these Fifth Monarchy men."

I began to feel my face flush in anger. "Mister Thurloe, I warn you not to underestimate what Gideon Fludd is capable of. He's convinced that by killing Cromwell he'll bring about the Second Coming. And I've seen with my own eyes these otherworldly powers that he summons forth. Shot and steel may not be enough."

Thurloe finished sipping his wine and stifled a chuckle. Elias Ashmole looked at his boots, his own wine glass untouched and still in his hand. "Colonel, there may be some evidence for a plot—certainly *Monsieur* d'Artagnan has supported *some* of what you claim. You, Mister Ashmole, have you seen any of the creatures that the Colonel maintains are stalking us?"

Ashmole began to stutter a reply. But Billy spoke up first.

"I've seen these things sir. Just as Mister Eff—the Colonel— says he did. Fearsome beasts, unnatural things from the pit of hell."

Thurloe barely looked at Billy. "Ah, the *Ranter* is the only one who can support your evidence then? No one else? I know the Lieutenant here has seen nothing demonic, have you sir?"

"I have not, sir, but I believe the Colonel just the same." D'Artagnan's English was heavily accented but clear nonetheless. He was a crafty player indeed. Or maybe just a fast learner in his few weeks in England. But Thurloe seemed to place little weight on the musketeer's words.

"Even Mister Lilly—who spoke most eloquently in support of you, Colonel—has said he has seen nothing unnatural or beyond rational description. If you're to help prevent the assassination you claim is imminent, it would be better to have knowledge of the numbers and arms of the enemy. And where they are hiding."

"Without the aid of the Lord your men will be swept aside like corn under the scythe." Da Silva's words were strong and clear, his knuckles bluish white around the wine bottle.

Thurloe's glass suddenly stopped halfway to his mouth. "Now that does beg a question. What does a Portuguese wine merchant have to do with this little circle of intrigue?"

Da Silva's sunken cheeks quickly became as white as his knuckles. And I was momentarily wrong-footed, my mind racing to cobble a reply. Thank God, Ashmole jumped in.

"*Senor* da Silva happens to be a collector of ancient tomes including some books that the enemy is believed to be consulting. His knowledge of Latin and Hebrew are of use in understanding what Fludd and his men are themselves using against us."

Da Silva nodded, jaw clenched.

"Indeed," said Thurloe quietly, and I knew then that he already was well aware of just what da Silva was, maybe even of the secret Hebrew congregation down the lane.

"Look here," I said, my impatience getting ahead of my reason, "Lilly must have told you that Gideon Fludd is a conjuror. He's using some ancient book of magic to summon forth a demon and its minions."

"Hardly what one would expect of a godly man of Christ, radical or not."

"That is true. But he believes he is summoning forth an angel to help him. And this angel has ordered him to kill Cromwell. It is, in truth, a demon called Andras, appearing as a being of heavenly light." I decided then, to show him at least *something* about what I spoke. I reached into my breeches pocket and pulled out the silver Pentacle of the Moon. And I handed it to Thurloe.

"This is what he had in his possession. It is the key to calling forth unholy forces."

"Or holy ones," added da Silva, bravely.

Thurloe handled it and flipped it over as if he was examining some large coin. "This signifies nothing, Colonel. What would you have me say?"

"I tell you I used what you now hold to save my life last night. That forest of ivy you saw with your own eyes would have strangled me otherwise. This charm held it at bay." It was a lie to some extent but I was desperate to convince him of its power.

Ashmole stepped forward to point out the inscription. "He is correct, sir. I have established this with the help of *Senor* da Silva. Gideon Fludd is using a similar one to conjure his black magic." And he proceeded to translate the Hebrew phrases upon it and show Thurloe the symbolic gateway etched on its face. Thurloe tilted his head slightly to the left, his lips pressed together in obvious scepticism. At length, he handed the pentacle back to me.

"There is another matter. The Lieutenant here has told me of this woman... a woman of quality... who has been abducted by Fludd. What is her involvement in this?"

I looked at d'Artagnan. "She is my mistress, Marguerite St. John. She followed me here from Paris without my knowledge. She's innocent of any involvement, sir."

"Then what does Fludd want with her?"

"You already know that," I told him. "You saw the message he left for me at the Bear in Southwark. He proposes her life in trade for the pentacle."

Thurloe nodded slowly. "If that is the case then it is behaviour most base. But I told you I need useful intelligence: numbers, weapons. As a soldier, you should know that better than most, Sir Richard."

It was all poor Billy could stand. "This is all stuff and fucking nonsense! We've told you the fucking truth and you spit it back at us!"

Thurloe was already two steps back, eyes wide, and Poxwell leapt in front of him, eager to throttle the wild-haired frothing Dorsetman.

"Stand down, boy!" said Thurloe to Billy, setting his glass on the table. "Lest I put you in irons and have the magistrates bore out your tongue tomorrow."

I grabbed Billy's shoulder. "Rest easy. We're in truce."

He quickly wiped his palm across his mouth, nodded wordlessly and I felt his shoulders sink a little in defeat under my hand.

Now, though, John Thurloe was riled. "Well, Colonel? How many men does he have? Swords and pikes? Pistols, carbines?"

"I don't know. He had three men with him last night on London Bridge when he attacked me. In Exeter he had at least half a dozen. Swords and pistols in the main."

"Well, that's a start. And why do you think they will strike tonight?"

I looked over to da Silva and Ashmole before I gave answer. "Because tonight the moon waxes in full. Fludd believes his power and that of his... followers... is strongest then. He will come to the Cockpit sometime before or around midnight. I'm sure of it."

"With his infernal horde in tow?" Thurloe's voice dripped disdain.

But it was d'Artagnan who answered him. "*Je suis Catholique.*" And then he tried his hand at English once again. "And the Faith... it tells us the Devil he walks among men to do his work, just as," and he glanced at me, "*les Anges?*"

"The angels."

"Like the angels, they do their works. Disbelief is sometimes the Devil's greatest friend."

Thurloe looked at d'Artagnan, somewhat lost for a reply, and simply shook his head before turning his attention back to me. "If that is all you can tell me then I shall return to Whitehall. Meet me at sundown at the Cockpit. I'll be there with the squadron. In the meantime, I will see what my informants can tell me of this Gideon Fludd and his whereabouts." And he pointed a long finger at Billy. "And keep *him* on a short leash, sir."

He touched the brim of his hat, met the eyes of all of us, and then turned on his heels as he motioned to Poxwell. But he paused just as he was about to leave the shop, half turning back to me. "By Jesus, we're in league with Papists and Jews against good Protestant Englishmen who you say have gone to the Devil... The whole world has gone to Bedlam!" He laughed and left. Captain Poxwell shot each of us a surly glance before stepping after his master and slamming the door behind him, rattling the windows.

But Lieutenant d'Artagnan remained where he stood, contemplating me.

"So *Monsieur*," I said, "Is it not time to return to your master? To tell him what a shambles you've made of things?"

"He remains *your* master, as well."

I laughed at his doggedness. "I think the Cardinal has little use for outlaws. You should consider your mission here at an end."

D'Artagnan closed the distance between us. "I told you

that I have pledged my sword arm to free your mistress. The Cardinal's mission can wait. Besides, we have done good work together before, have we not?"

"You brought her here in the first place," I said, my throat tightening. "And it was you who lost her."

"Fuck him!" said Billy softly as he moved a step forward.

D'Artagnan held his ground. "What can I say or do to prove I am yet your comrade?"

"Sir Richard, accept the gentleman's word." Elias proffered the bottle of wine to me. "Charge his glass and then your own and make amends. You yourself said we need every man who will stand against this enemy. That was good counsel."

My head knew that was right. But my heart was still wounded by my Maggie's fate and my own role in it, not just the Frenchman's. I looked over to the old Jew, his wrinkled hands pressed upon the work table. He was nodding to me, urging me to accept the advice of Mister Ashmole. I took the bottle from Ashmole's hand and extended it towards d'Artagnan's glass.

"Sir, will you drink with me?"

"*Bien sur, colonel.*"

We raised our glasses to our lips as the others watched. I heard a growl of discontent from Billy's throat but he kept silent.

I kept silent too, praying that our strange little band would be strong enough, and hold together long enough, to save Maggie, preserve old Coppernose, and send Gideon Fludd and his minions to hell.

Chapter Eighteen

We ascended the dusty, creaking staircase one after the other. In front of me, Isabel's skirts swished along the steps, try as she might to lift them above her ankles. The glow of the single rushlight taper she bore was barely enough to show our way. As I entered the hall of Roderigo da Silva, my eyes instantly went to the oaken dining table where he was standing, waiting for us to join him. Over his head, a brass chandelier blazed and sputtered away, its light dancing upon the objects that he had carefully laid out on the Turkish rug covering the table.

"Come gentlemen! Gather 'round. Sir Richard, over here, near me if you please."

At one end, da Silva had arrayed three naked blades: sturdy basket-hilted broadswords. The hilts of each were as mirrors, dipped in pure silver. And along each blade, from forte to point, the fullers were filled with an equally fine shining strip of silver. D'Artagnan's mouth fell open. Billy whistled loudly while I leaned in for a closer inspection. I saw that each blade had Hebrew characters engraved upon it.

יהוה

I turned to da Silva.

"The name of God?"

The old man nodded. "And each sword is blessed by my words."

Beyond the swords, I spied a dish containing musket balls—each one pure silver. I picked one up and saw that it too had the powerful Tetragrammaton etched upon it.

"Can we say this word, as a charm if we come under attack?" I asked.

"Never. The name is not spoken. *Adonai* is all we may utter: the Lord. And..." His hand reached out to the hilt of one of the weapons, his fingertips barely touching it. "I fear I may have sinned even in this."

I glanced over to Ashmole who had lost the ruddiness in his cheeks. He looked at me.

"In folklore, both Hebrew and Christian, this is a most powerful charm and protection. We must not take this lightly."

D'Artagnan pulled out a golden crucifix that hung inside his shirt and gently kissed it before placing it outside his doublet. "I have my own talisman, gentlemen."

Da Silva smiled at him. "Then you have the protection of the Father *and* the Son, *monsieur*." He then pointed his bony hand at me. "And you must not profane these weapons by using them against mortal men. They are to defend you from attack by the Fallen Ones and their minions alone."

"But what of Gideon Fludd?" I asked. "Am I to use my bare hands?"

Da Silva lowered his gaze. "I fear that he who once was Gideon Fludd is more Devil than man now. He has been in the presence of a demon for so long he may be wholly possessed by now, a mere shell for Andras to control."

"You mean he's a puppet for that creature?" asked Ashmole.

"That comes as no surprise to me," I said. "The little hell ape told me as much last night."

Billy picked up one of the swords and hefted it. "Scabbards and belts?" Da Silva gestured to the corner of the room where they lay upon the floor. Billy looked over to me. "Mister Eff?"

"Aye, Billy."

While Billy stowed the weapons, da Silva drew my attention to the Great Pentacle of Solomon that he had spread out upon the other end of the table. I now noticed that this had been tacked onto the front of a large linen shirt.

"I cannot bear arms against the enemy. But what I propose is to create a sanctuary for you, even in the midst of the unholy ones."

"Wait now, *senor*," said Ashmole, coming round the table end. "You've done enough to get us this far. Mister Thurloe and his soldiers, and we four here, we will go to Whitehall."

Billy spoke up from the far side of the room. "We've only got three of these holy swords. Who draws the short straw?"

Billy was right. One of us would have to fight with plain steel.

"We shall face that challenge when the time comes," I said, not really knowing how we would decide the question. "But let us hear out *Senor* da Silva first."

"I must go with you to the palace," said the old man. "I am the only one who can create the circle that you can retreat to if all goes ill. I have read the texts. I know the ways and means. Nothing else will save you. Consider it your invisible redoubt to sally from and to return to."

"A magic circle," said Ashmole softly. "I too have read of these... in the old grimoires. That is why you need the Grand Pentacle. You will use it as a shield, a shield upon your own body."

Da Silva folded his hands in front of him. "That is so."

From the edge of the stairwell, I watched Isabel's face, remembering her vow to stay at her father's side. She was as stone. Her mouth was closed tight, jaw clenched. But her large dark eyes were calm, almost sleepy. I understood, then, the strength in her gentle frame. The strength of her belief in her God and in her father. There would be no swaying this girl from what she set her mind to.

"Sir Richard," said da Silva, "you must know that the enemy has many weapons it can employ against you and your comrades. You must never let your guard down. I will do my best to keep the circle unbroken but you must never stray more than a quick dash away from it. Far better that Gideon Fludd comes to us where we can fight him on our terms."

"Very well," I said, doubts welling up inside me even as he spoke. This was as much of a forlorn hope as I had ever volunteered for. But in every other at least I knew I was facing flesh and blood that a good sword thrust or pistol ball could defeat. This night, we were about to go into battle against an enemy altogether new and terrifying. I could not rid my mind of the image of that horrific great black dog that had stared me down at the inn in Brent. I'd need a boar spear to stand a chance of taking the thing down.

"And there is one thing more I must ask you, Sir Richard," said da Silva. "Do you intend to hand over the Moon Pentacle to Fludd? If you do so, no door will remain unopened to him—anywhere."

"If he doesn't," said Billy, wrapping the swordbelts around each scabbarded weapon, "Fludd will kill her."

"And what makes you think he won't murder her anyway?" replied the old man.

"I cannot give Fludd the key he wants to enter the palace," I said.

Billy stopped, the cradled weapons in his arms jostling and clanking. "Then you've signed her death warrant, Mister Eff."

"No, there's another way. A decoy. We haven't much time though. Elias, can you obtain a pewter plate or a medallion the same size as the pentacle? Perhaps something from that collection of yours?"

Ashmole dropped his chin to his chest. "Lord, there is little time indeed... I'll have to return to Lambeth. But, I think I can find something that would pass muster. If you give me another look at that disc, I can measure it and then be on my way."

"Good. I suggest we meet you at the steps of Saint Martin's at seven of the clock. The sun sets at around half past the hour... that should give us time to proceed down to Whitehall and meet up with Thurloe."

"I am sorry, Colonel," spoke up d'Artagnan, "but this is no plan. What you propose is just to walk into the enemy's embrace."

"Shut your hole, you goddamn coxcomb!" Billy dropped the swords upon the table.

I held out a finger towards him. "Enough! D'Artagnan speaks like a soldier. And I cannot say that he doesn't speak the truth. But the fact is we must walk into the jaws of the enemy to meet them. We stay close to Cromwell and we'll find them soon enough. That is the only plan we need. The rest is in the Lord's hands."

No one said a thing. After what seemed a long silence, Ashmole moved towards the stairwell, turned and touched his hat. "I shall meet you at front of the church. God keep you, gentlemen." And he was gone, pounding down the staircase.

Da Silva's voice was small. "Isabel will get the serving girl to find you three some fare. You need full bellies to face this evening."

Isabel had not moved from her station near the staircase. "I will see to it, father." But then, she looked at me and inclined her head, motioning for me to follow her.

When we were down in the shop, she pulled me by the arm into the kitchen. "I must speak with you, sir, about your servant."

"Christ, what has he done now?" I asked, half a dozen possibilities rushing through my exhausted mind.

"He has done nothing, sir. It is what has been done to him. I tended those wounds he has on his arms."

I knew exactly what she was going to tell me.

"His wounds are not deep, but they're not healing either. They're growing worse, suppurating with poison. I have done my best to clean them, to salve them. But they are no ordinary wounds."

"Aye. I fear they are not."

"And this morning, I heard Billy retching in the privy out back. He's growing sicker though he hides it well."

I held up my left hand that she could see the single black welt and cut that ran over the top and across the knuckles. I had noticed it had begun to weep droplets of blackened blood.

Isabel grasped my wrist and examined the wound, her face grave. "Yours is the same. A cut this shallow should not be as it is." She looked up at me. "I have no physik that will cure this."

I withdrew my hand. "Do what you can for Billy. It's enough that we get through tonight in one piece. I'll worry about anything else after the sun comes up tomorrow."

WE WERE AN unusual party that stood outside the tower of Saint Martin's—an old man in black, black cap upon his head and a large satchel over his shoulder. A young maid supporting his arm, beautiful in black cloak and white coif, her face a delicate mask of apprehension. Then there was Billy Chard and me. We looked like two highwaymen who had strayed in from Hampstead Heath, dressed in old cracked buff leather, baldrics and swords over our chests. It was almost a wonder that we had not been stopped by soldiers, but oddly we had seen none all the way.

And then there was the young Frenchman, wearing a good suit of fancy grey silk, and a high starched collar. His baldric held one of the silver swords, but also too, a slender *main gauche* tucked into a belt loop at the small of his back. His boots were the finest I had seen since leaving Paris, sleek black Spanish leathers pulled up high. His only other concession to armour was a stout pair of leather gauntlets. D'Artagnan had been sullen most of the way, having argued loudly that Isabel should stay behind. I could understand his reticence. His conscience still tortured him for having let Maggie be taken. He raved in French for some time before I could convince him she would no doubt follow us anyway even if her father ordered her to stay. Besides, she could assist her father, and otherwise one of us would have to do. "So be it," he had mumbled.

Ashmole was late. The sun was now very low in the west, its dying light painting an orange halo over Westminster. The sky was clear; a darkening purple in the twilight. Not a single cloud disturbed the firmament—the moon would shine brightly this night. I could not keep the thought of Maggie from my mind as we stood at the base of the bell tower, waiting. The more my mind spun round and round, the more I felt an almost choking sense of dread rise up. Was she still even alive? Worse thoughts intruded as I remembered the threats of the black imp the previous night. The imaginings grew so vivid that I felt sweat pouring down my back and sides. She might even now be just half a mile away from me. I tried to console myself by the thought that Gideon Fludd had up until now shown great restraint in taking innocent lives. If he truly believed he was a man of God then he would not harm her. But even as that small solace came to me, I could not hide something else that clawed at my gut: that Gideon Fludd might no longer be his own master.

"He is come!" Billy bounded past me and walked up to welcome a thoroughly red-faced Elias Ashmole. His cloak was spattered with water and mud and he had yet to catch his breath.

"Forgive me. It took me longer than I hoped to find a suitable changeling for our silver pentacle and then... well, I ran afoul of a clumsy waterman and an oar that seemed more intent on catching me than the river."

I clapped him on the shoulder, relieved that our little army had not become any smaller. "No matter, you've made it. And you have something we can use to fool Fludd?"

Ashmole pulled out a round medallion of sorts. Not silver, but something that looked more like pewter. "It is some sort of medal struck by the city fathers of Augsburg in my grandfather's time. Let's hope Major Fludd doesn't stop to examine it."

"I won't give him the chance," I said, taking it and dropping it in the right pocket of my breeches.

Ashmole smiled. "Just don't forget which pocket the real one is in."

I looked at the others. "If we're all at the ready, then? Time to search out Mister Thurloe and his men." Billy sidled up to me. I could see his pallor was white as a shroud, a tiny droplet of snot poised to fall from the end of his sharp nose.

"Where do we go, Mister Eff?"

"We must find a way into the old Tilting Yard to the right of the Cockpit and the Lord General's apartments. I expect Thurloe will have thrown a cordon around front and back. They ought to find us before we find them."

They did. We had barely made it to Banqueting House when a party of dismounted dragoons at the great gate saw us from afar and made a beeline. I smiled, doffing the hat Ashmole had gifted me, and told their sergeant that John Thurloe was expecting us on the grounds of the palace. He didn't seem convinced and ordered us to give up our arms. Billy looked at me—I knew what he was wordlessly asking. His hand was already on his hilt. And then d'Artagnan shot forward, brandishing a flapping scrap of paper, which he offered to the dragoon.

It was a pass, a pass from the French ambassador. And obviously in English, as the sergeant pushed his nose into it and read, aloud for the benefit of all. He looked up at us, clearly puzzled at the presence of the old man and young woman, but then gave a shrug and handed d'Artagnan back his papers.

"I'll take you to the captain of the guard," he said, slowly, as if only half trusting his decision. His eyes had trouble shifting away from Isabel. So did those of a much younger trooper who practically toppled forward into her. "What are you looking at!" The sergeant cuffed the boy on the head with the flat of his palm. "Back to your post, all of you!"

And so it was the bowlegged sergeant alone who escorted us to the small gate that led into the old tilt yard. At our left the ancient Tudor brickwork of the old palace soared up four floors high as we made our way west, towards the back and the old deer park. The sergeant stopped us near a ramshackle wooden staircase that wound its way up the brickwork to the second level. His face wore a confused look, heavy brows falling together as he swivelled his head around.

"He was hereabouts not more than a short time gone by. He and the rest of the squad." He poked a finger into my chest. "Wait here—all of you. I'll go inside and fetch him. Understood?"

Ashmole grasped one of the rotten newel posts which wobbled alarmingly in his hand. "To think, this was once the playground of the court. Tennis, bowls, theatre for cockfights or plays. And then the masques of the king and queen at Twelfth Night. All turning to ruin now."

"The new landlords don't give a turd for all that," I said. I looked out across the park as the light faded away, sky graduating from dark azure to purple blue. I could just spy the great brick hunting lodge of King James, half a mile distant. The park was wild now with long brown grass, scraggy bushes and tall hogweed, lonely stands of oak and beech scattered here and there like small groups of frightened children gathering for comfort in the descending gloom. And not a single deer to be seen.

"Elias, has the brotherhood abandoned us? You told me those who meet upon the square do not take their duty lightly."

Ashmole looked at me, almost hurt. But he shifted his gaze

down after a moment. "I cannot say why Lilly and the others have gone off suddenly. They must have discovered something. They would have had good reason I am sure..." He went quiet. "But I would have expected to have been confided in just the same." His hand began to worry the butt of the pistol shoved in his belt. "You are correct, friend. This is not at all on the square."

From our vantage, to the right of the cupola domed Cockpit, we could see the rest of the palace extending into the deer park, flanked by a wall some ten feet high that ran west as far as the eye could see. Somewhere inside this corner of the palace Oliver Cromwell and his family sat in ignorance of the tempest that was gathering. At least there were no doors or windows at ground level, only these wooden staircases tacked on the side. I told the others to wait while I disobeyed the guards and had a scout around the back. As I reached the rear of the palace and looked around the corner, I saw that the park wall abutted the far side of the palace, thus securing that elevation from entry. I looked up to the windows above but saw no signs of life.

"*Senor* da Silva," I called out once I had made it back to our little party, "I suggest you fashion your magic circle right here next to these stairs. If the enemy comes not by King Street, then they must come through here."

Isabel whirled around away from her father and confronted me. "Don't you dare use that word! Would you see us condemned by your people? My father uses the power of prayer to serve the Lord, not some empty conjuror's tricks."

"It's all right, daughter," said da Silva. He gently pulled her back by the arm. "We have come this far by His will and we must play our parts. I will begin straight away, Colonel." He opened the sack he bore and walked a few paces toward the palace wall. He held the sack in front of him and bending over, proceeded to pour out flour in a long line upon the ground. Working backwards, he shuffled along, fashioning a circle some fifteen feet across as we watched.

Isabel came up beside me and spoke quietly. "I'm afraid that when the soldiers see this circle they will take us away."

I touched her forearm. "I won't let them, mistress. Nor will Mister Ashmole."

Elias nodded and smiled at her. I saw da Silva with a different small sack, pouring out a second white substance along the line of flour.

"What is this he does?" I asked.

"Salt," she said. She reached into her purse and pulled out a small square of linen. "Quickly, sir, while I can still see. Let me pin this upon your coat."

As she held it up, I could see that she had embroidered the Tetragrammaton in red thread upon the square. "And now you, Billy Chard."

Billy came forward, his neck craning to watch as she deftly fitted the pin through his collar and patted the linen square upon his chest. "May the Lord bless you," she said.

"Thankee, ma'am," Billy mumbled.

After she had affixed the talisman to Ashmole she turned to d'Artagnan. "And would you take the amulet as well, *monsieur*?"

D'Artagnan smiled thinly. "I fear that I may not, good lady. With respect, my monsignor would object."

She nodded and moved to help her father as he struggled to pull on a fulsome white shirt over his doublet. And my heart suddenly felt heavy for the girl, trapped in a land that she could only exist in as a wraith in the shadows, living a lie, forever a *marrano*. And we all watched as she affixed the Great Pentacle of Solomon to her father's chest, holding the pins in her mouth and delicately tacking the large square as she held it gently upon his shirt. I watched d'Artagnan's face as he observed Isabel. His eyes seemed to narrow as if some old distrust was bubbling up.

Christ above. She is right. They'll arrest us all for this.

Ashmole stood just outside the circle, cradling a pistol in the crook of his arm as he poured a charge down the barrel.

"I see you chose the firearms and not steel," I said.

He smiled, but his hand was shaking as he fumbled with the loading. "Well, I'm an old artilleryman after all." He took out a silver bullet, studied it between thumb and forefinger, and then dropped it down the barrel of the doglock. He looked at me, his trepidation showing. "Do you really think he'll come here? It would be madness."

"He'll come."

We all stood there, with nary a word, and watched as da Silva walked the perimeter of the circle, lips moving rapidly in silent prayer. Slowly, I became aware of moonlight casting shadows along the palace and on the wooden staircase. It was nearly bright enough to read by, a silver-blue illumination that was both cold and clean. He would come soon.

"All of you! Listen to me." Da Silva raised his arms, beckoning us to gather around him. "Those who wish protection must enter the circle, and stay close to the centre."

D'Artagnan and Billy exchanged hard looks and it was clear they did not relish standing side-by-side. But it was Elias Ashmole who stepped inside first, guiding Isabel by her arm.

"Allow me, young lady."

And then d'Artagnan and Billy stepped in. Da Silva looked at me and inclined his head. "You are not convinced, sir?"

I stood near the staircase, my palm rubbing the pommel of the silver sword at my hip. "Something is not right. I can feel it. That sergeant never came back. And where is Thurloe?" I turned to look back along the wall of the palace towards the Whitehall road. There wasn't a soul or a sound. I walked towards the park, skirting the magic circle. The stands of trees took on new and sinister shapes as I scanned them. And I became aware that it was as quiet as a tomb—not a single snatch of sparrow song, no cackle of a crow. No cry of a gull from the Thames. No whistle of wind over the roofs and chimneys above us. Nothing.

I slowly drew my blade and ran my right hand along the silver fuller. The four letters of the Tetragrammaton twinkled in the reflected moonlight. I knew we were being watched. I could feel it. And then Billy was at my side.

"Mister Eff?" he whispered. "Are you all right? What is it?"

"Gideon Fludd is already here."

Billy drew his sword. "Where away, Mister Eff?"

I looked from left to right, slowly watching for movement in the trees. And then, almost as if he had heard me, I saw a lamp light awaken out in the park, off to the left a few hundred yards ahead. They had surely been there for some time, waiting until now to raise the shutter of the tin lamp. To signal the meeting. Billy grasped my forearm.

"Fucking hell. They *are* here."

"Get into the circle. I'm going to meet him alone."

Billy stepped in front of me. "Not a clever idea, Mister Eff. We're both going out there."

"Listen to me. I need you here with the others. God knows what he has with him and outside the circle he could pick us off one by one." Billy swore and protested again but I cut him off.

"I won't take any chances. I've got to find out if he has Maggie with him. And don't worry—I'll leg it back here if it gets hot."

"I don't like it one fucking bit."

"Tell the others to stand ready."

His eyes met mine. Challenging me. But then he relented, gave a curt nod, and ran back to the circle.

I let my sword arm fall into a wide, open guard, the point brushing the ground. And then I started walking across the scrub land, towards the twisted trees and the flickering orange light.

Chapter Nineteen

THREE FIGURES HOVE into view. Two tall, one short. The lamp lay upon the ground a few paces in front of them. Fludd was to my right, easily recognisable with his white hair, hatless as I had always seen him. To my left, one of his men, sword drawn. And the man was holding a woman up by her arm. She was cloaked and hooded but the form was right. It had to be Maggie. But she was not struggling, she was not even moving. Just standing as if frozen. I stopped a few paces from them and took my stance; feet spread, knees slightly bent and ready for a spring.

Fludd looked at me, his eyes unblinking. He appeared even gaunter since I had met him last, his skull bones showing through his veined parchment-like skin. His black cloak, cinched up tight on his neck, hid most of his body and I could not then tell if he bore naked steel. His voice was sharp and carried a whiff of impatience.

"We have unfinished business, Mister Falkenhayn. And the hour grows late."

"I have come. Now give me the woman."

"When you give me what is mine, sirrah."

My fingers tightened on my swordgrip. "I have what you want. But I want to see her face. Show me!"

"Go ahead, Snook. Show him it is she."

Fludd's man pulled back the woman's hood. Marguerite St. John was there before me, her eyes wide open and looking out—past me, into the darkness. She was expressionless and wooden as if she was not there at all. I swallowed and felt an invisible fist in my chest. What had they done?

"Maggie! Maggie, look at me!"

"She is not harmed. Give me the pentacle and she can go." Fludd then took a step forward, slowly folding back his cape to free up his sword arm. "But I'm afraid you and I have to settle the blood debt."

I reached into my breeches pocket and drew out Ashmole's old medallion, closing it in my right palm. "It is here. Now release her."

Fludd gave a thin smile. "Not so fast. Hold it up that I can see it."

I obeyed, hoping my splayed fingers would obscure the falseness of it. "I shall place it here... on the ground... and step away. You will step away from the woman and move back towards those trees a few paces."

Fludd shook his head slowly. "You're a trickster I feel I have long known. And I would know why you killed my brother."

I didn't answer his question. I carefully knelt a little, enough to toss the medallion a yard or two off to my right. "There it is. Release her, Gideon."

I glanced over to Snook and now noticed that the man was near upon shaking with fear. His face was dripping with sweat. He licked his lips nervously and, oddly, kept glancing *behind* him. And his shoulders twitched like he was warding off a chill. He was terrified of Fludd—and something else.

"Where are the rest of your comrades, Gideon? They seem fewer each time we meet."

Fludd looked at me with a look so poisonous it nearly stole my courage. And when he replied his voice was icy calm.

"Their faith failed them. Some men are not able to treat with the angels."

"Or demons."

The poor ignorant soldier next to Fludd looked ready to jump out of his skin. He had moved his grip upon Maggie to her shoulder, more than ready to push her towards me so he could make his own escape.

"And I reckon your men have come to a sticky end. At the hands of your angel's companions."

Fludd's boyish face contorted, his jaw clenching with rage. "Eistibus commands a terrible army. But his cause is holy. And I serve that cause."

"You fool! You serve the Devil. It is Andras and his minions that do the bidding. You must see that!"

Fludd's rapier rasped from its scabbard. "Blasphemer!"

I stepped back, raising my blade. "For the love of God, man, open your eyes! What angel of the Lord would command you to do murder!"

Fludd hissed out his reply. "Vanquishing the enemies of Christ is not murder. I am opening the road for the new kingdom and no one will stop me. Least of all you." I saw his eyes dart down to the medallion lying in the grass.

I fell back again, and towards my left, to get closer to Maggie who still stood as if a statue. "I won't let you kill General Cromwell. For pity's sake get out of here now before it's too late."

Fludd had sidestepped closer to the medallion. Once he seized it and saw the ruse, Maggie would be in mortal danger.

"Who are you, sirrah, to talk of murder? Why did you kill my brother?"

It didn't matter anymore. "I fought to defend my life. And I was in my own house. A house he had stolen."

I watched as Fludd slowly raised his chin, the import dawning. "Now I have more than one reason to kill you. Richard Treadwell the malignant. I was a fool not to have realised sooner." The anger was roiling up inside him, I could see it. He was almost quivering as he glared at me. "The angel has given me power of his dominion. I want you to see the dark army that he has hired from hell." He extended his blade towards me and slowly crouched until his left hand encircled the medallion. He did not even have to pick it up. The moment his fingers touched it, his face suddenly dropped. He stood up quick and backed away, smiling at me.

"Trickster, trickster."

I tensed my legs, ready to make a rush for Snook and to seize Maggie. But Fludd was speaking to himself now, mumbling some words, foreign words that sounded harsh and clicking.

"Major!" The reluctant trooper released his hold on Maggie. "I beg you, don't do it! Don't call them again, for God's sake!"

And a blur of cloak blew past me from behind, straight into the poor man, a blade slashing down into his skull with a muffled crunch. In a heartbeat, d'Artagnan had gathered up Maggie in his free arm and hefted her over his shoulder. I jumped to put myself between them and Fludd, before he could strike. But Fludd was walking backwards for the trees, still praying aloud, sword held high in guard. I advanced on him even as I saw the Frenchman stagger off with Maggie flopped over his back. I had to give him time to get her back to the circle.

"Gideon, this creature has bewitched you. It has deceived you. Open your eyes, man! You're doing the Devil's bidding."

He was past listening. He was looking at me but not seeing me, lips forming some abominable chant. From beyond him, a thick fog moved towards me, about a foot high, and it carried a carrion stench with it. It was unnaturally rapid. The tendrils swirled about the tree trunks like a phantom river and kept on moving, sweeping around my knees and spreading across the park towards the palace walls—and the circle.

Gideon Fludd stopped his mumbling. He raised his sword and looked straight into my eyes; once again a soldier facing his enemy. "It was the angelic host that threw down Lucifer and his servants into the Pit. And it is the angels that hold the key to that prison." He had stopped retreating and was standing, feet firmly placed and cloak thrown back over his shoulder. "And that key they have given to me."

I became aware of a dull pounding, rising up from the ground. At first, it sounded like a herd of deer that had been alarmed and set into flight. Yet I quickly realised that this was the sound of something much larger than deer. And it was coming towards us.

Fludd looked at me, a strange sort of smile appearing on his face. "You had better start running... *Now*."

And something inside me told me to obey. I bolted. Fast as my feet would carry me. I twisted around to glance behind and immediately wished I had not. Two huge infernal black dogs were bearing down on me, loping in great strides. I glimpsed their open jaws and wild rolling eyes before snapping my head round again and redoubling my flight. I was gasping already, the back wall of the palace looking very far away indeed, bobbing up and down as I pelted forward. I knew the beasts were closing because I could hear them now, deep rasping and growling sounds that grew louder. A loud snort at my back acted to spur me forward. I could just make out the little group gathered together. I yelled out. Less than fifty yards to the circle and now I could smell the creatures behind me, a horrid stench of wet fur and rotting meat. I dared not look behind now for they were nearly on top of me. I expected at any second to feel my back rent by great claws.

I had a blurred view of da Silva and Billy and then I saw and heard a great muzzle flash from the circle. Elias had given fire. And with a final great cry I flew into the circle and rolled onto the ground. A second pistol shot reverberated across the palace yard and I rolled onto my back and looked out. The dogs stood some twenty feet away, side by side, motionless and staring straight at us. No one said a word and I watched my companions as each tried to make sense of what they were seeing. And then Billy was helping me up.

"You brought our old friend back with you, Mister Eff," he whispered. "And he's brought his brother."

We all watched as the wave of low mist came to the circle us from all around. It rolled up fast, and then, as it reached the line of flour and salt, it rolled back on itself like the sea against a jetty.

Da Silva stood at the circle's edge, facing the beasts, his arms spread wide. I could hear the Hebrew words flowing from him as he prayed. Ashmole's mouth still hung agape. I grasped his arm.

"Elias, reload the pistols!"

He looked at me, suddenly recovering himself. "I cannot believe what I'm seeing."

D'Artagnan muttered something in Gascon as he went into a fighting crouch. He was probably already worrying that a circle of flour would not stay two dogs the size of bears. I looked down again. There was Isabel holding Maggie, brushing back her long hair and rocking her gently.

"Isabel, keep her warm."

The girl looked at me and nodded. She pulled her cloak about them both as they huddled. Elias worked furiously to reload his two doglocks and I noticed that all of us had bunched together, unconsciously seeking safety.

"I'm sorry I didn't stay with you," said Billy darkly. "I couldn't stop the musketeer—he said something about his duty and honour and was off like a shot."

I could not take my eyes off of the hellhounds. "You did the right thing, Billy." But I was glad that the Frenchman had come when he had. His debt had now been repaid.

"Where is Fludd now?" said Ashmole as both hammers clicked loudly into place.

"I don't know. But he's not giving up on what he has set out to do. He'll have to get through us though." I thought I would then try something. I moved to the edge of the circle. I raised my sword and then took two steps outside, towards the black dogs. In an instant they began moving forward, and in the bright moonlight I could see the juices from their fangs dripping down the corners of their wide mouths. I retreated back into the circle. The dogs stopped, motionless as if stone, and did not move.

"Elias, give me a pistol."

I levelled the barrel at one of the creatures and fired. A howl of pain erupted and one of them dropped down on its front legs, its huge head shaking. It was up again after a few moments but clearly chastised as it slunk behind its companion.

"They can be hurt!" Ashmole said, clearly relieved we had some means of defence against the netherworld.

"Aye, but we don't know if we can kill them. *Senor* da Silva, are you well, sir?" I saw that the rabbi was, like the hellhounds, frozen to the ground.

The old man kept looking outside the circle and towards the evil that stared us down. "I must concentrate on the prayer and the words from the grimoire. I will not be able to converse with you. The circle will fail if I do not keep my mind upon it." He sank to his knees and folded his arms to his chest. Again I heard him chanting and he began to rock forward and back as he spoke.

"Now what shall we do?" said Billy. "No sign of the regiment anywhere and us trapped here in this circle."

A cry from d'Artagnan brought Billy and I around. Isabel gave a muffled shriek. From the other side of the circle, a new threat was emerging from the shadows. It was what I had feared since that night in the cell when the imp had spoken to me. Ashmole had now turned as well to see what was coming.

"Dear God," he muttered.

D'Artagnan's voice rose up. He was saying his Pater Noster.

They had come to the very edge of the circle. Curious, snorting and sniffing, three great demons stood there contemplating us. They were the size of men, walking on two legs that ended in a cockerel's talons instead of feet. Each was different but all were equally terrible in appearance. And I had seen these creatures before: painted in countless murals and carved in stone across the cities of Europe. They were blackish grey in hue and naked, seemingly fashioned from parts of men and beasts. One had the head and long muzzle of a dog while another had a large goat-horned head with a bulbous nose and feline mouth. Their eyes were black as pitch, glistening and unblinking, without whites or pupils. Scale, fur, and skin covered their muscled frames and their hands bore long bony fingers, almost delicate, but sprouting scythe-like claws.

The largest of the three extended a burly leg to the line of flour and salt, his three toes flexing up and down. Then he pulled it back fast, as if burned. The creature had no manhood, but instead, the head of a large toad-like thing grew from his loins, its tongue lolling out obscenely, probing the demon's rippling thighs. And all sprouted great leathery wings from their backs, rising up and curving forward, making the creatures look even taller than they were.

A fourth emerged from the darkness to join his brethren. And I watched in horror as I saw that it was dragging the body of a man behind it, held firmly about the ankle in its claws. It was the soldier Snook, Fludd's last companion, the man that d'Artagnan had killed. While the dog-headed demon pinned the corpse down, sinking its leg talons into poor Snook's chest, the bearer proceeded to twist and crack the man's leg at the hip joint like a glutton tearing a drumstick from a capon. The rending noise was enough send me a step back—I was too stunned to do a thing.

The largest of the demons, its enormous nose quivering, just stood there at the thin white line. It regarded us, openly curious and disdainful, then slowly crossed its arms as if resigned to a wait. Such a human pose was more than chilling; it told me that these things could think as men could. And then it spoke. With a voice that sounded strangled as if it was never meant to speak the tongues of men, the creature said: "Come out."

Its companions were tearing into the corpse now, rending arms and legs and ripping chunks of flesh with beaks and fangs. Behind me erupted a cry of defiance and Billy pushed past. And I watched as he threw a tremendous sword cut straight from the shoulder, aimed at the neck of the demon who stood an inch from the circle. I saw its arms shoot out but Billy's blow came faster than it could react. With a dull thump, I saw the creature's head fall to the side, nearly severed. A fount of black blood shot up, Billy's sword hissing loudly as the liquid ran down the blade. And the demon fell back and collapsed among its brethren. The horde sprang up almost as one, roaring in fury at the sight of one their own somehow slain.

"And *that's* for what your little friend did in Exeter, you bastard!" Billy shouted, swinging his sword in front of him and daring the others to have a go.

"Huzzah!" said Ashmole in a hushed tone.

Da Silva pushed through, shaking. "Please, all of you, stay in the middle of the circle! More of the creatures are appearing!" As soon as the demons caught sight of the Pentacle of Solomon on da Silva's chest, they ceased their clamour and moved back, leery of the rabbi. Perhaps some memory of a previous encounter with a conjuror had come back into their hate-filled brains. Billy's victim was fast disappearing, melting in a puddle of steaming black corruption, but the sound of beating wings, low and slow, grew louder around us.

"Colonel!" D'Artagnan pointed to the black dogs, which were cautiously on the move again. Still some distance from the circle, but moving around to where the other hellspawn had assembled. And so too, I could feel the ground beneath me tremble as footfalls sounded, a horde of creatures moving fast from the park beyond. A loud thrashing noise sounded to my right; a huge demon landed just outside the circle, its knees bent in a crouch. Slowly, it stood and rose to full height, wings folding behind it. It had a face like a lion but with great ram horns, and a long tail that thrashed away behind it, cracking the air. A pair of hag's breasts hung from its hairy chest and it raised its arms as it bellowed its displeasure at finding the protective circle.

Billy was taunting them all now. It was as if by screaming at them he was purging himself of all that he had believed before. Now he knew hell did exist. He stamped again, swung his sword around his head, and before I could reach him, I saw his foot fall outside the circle. Even as I cried out a warning, I watched as one of the demons seized Billy's ankle and pulled him out as easily as if he had been a child. And then I was outside the circle too, landing a downright blow to the creature's arm. D'Artagnan gave a cry behind me and followed. Ashmole's pistols exploded into action; he must have been firing at the hellhounds. I was swinging like a madman, whirling to keep them off, as were Billy and d'Artagnan. A clawed hand raked the front of my thick leather buff coat, ripping it like taffeta.

But the blessed silver swords were biting and I saw the creatures hesitate when they caught sight of the Tetragrammaton on our breasts. So too, there appeared to be some surprise that our weapons could do them hurt. There was some small hesitation from them now, maybe enough to give us a fighting chance. A great bat-like thing tackled d'Artagnan from above, the two of them tumbling to the earth. The Frenchman sprang up and severed the demon's wings from its back, a horrible screech coming from the creature. I pushed Billy back into the circle and yelled for d'Artagnan. A black dog was loping towards him now and if it had not been for a demon landing between him and the beast, he would have surely been in its jaws.

Something hit me from behind, knocking me to my knees, and I instinctively rolled to the side, raising my blade up to shield myself. An ape-faced demon stood over me, grinning, then fell on me, trying to wrench the sword from my grasp while using its other hand to try and claw my face. I think I was roaring just like the creatures, a mix of fear and desperation. I glimpsed Billy again, saw his blade descend, and the creature screamed and stumbled off of me.

"Get back into the circle!" cried Ashmole, letting off his pistol again at a black dog. This hound must have been hit several times by now for it was hunched over and moving slowly, spit pouring from its mouth, eyes rolling up in pain. But then I saw it catch sight of d'Artagnan, and some new power must have driven it forward, intent on its victim. The musketeer was almost at the edge of the circle when the thing leapt a full ten feet and knocked him down with its shoulder. As I ran to him, I heard d'Artagnan scream as the hound took his leg in its great jaws. I plunged my blade into the hellhound's side, a great overpowering stench rising from the beast. I felt the blade slide in as if it was slicing a pudding. The hissing of the silver as it singed the creature's wet fur was like some angel's cry. I yelled as I drew it out and thrust it into the wound again. A great howl went up from the dog; I could feel the vibration through my blade as the beast shuddered.

Now free, d'Artagnan crawled, nearly enveloped in the unnatural fog, until Billy grabbed him and pulled him back into the circle. The hound turned on me and lunged with its long neck. I twisted away behind its tail but a cloud of its hot fetid breath enveloped me, and I gagged. Something sprang into vision on my left side. A long-eared creature with a pig's snout and yellow tusks was already reaching for me. In the same instant, I heard a report and saw the creature's head jerk to one side, steam and black blood shooting from the wound. It placed a claw to its head and gave a strange cry like a baby. The hellhound sent it sprawling as it whirled around to grab me.

I dived for the safety of the magic circle and rolled inside, just as the black dog, roaring with pain and dripping gore, rose up on its hind legs and reached the invisible wall. It was a hellish scene inside our sanctuary. Ashmole was furiously stabbing his ramrod into a pistol, ranting to himself as he reloaded. D'Artagnan lay screaming in agony, arms sprawled in the thin grass while Billy tried to hold his leg to wrap it in a sleeve he had ripped from the musketeer's doublet. And the look of unbelieving shock on poor Isabel's face cut me to the heart. She still clasped Maggie tightly in her arms, giving comfort and trying to draw out some for herself. But I could not see Maggie's face, pressed as it was into Isabel's bosom. Only Roderigo da Silva stood unbowed. He faced the horde of Andras's minions, the very cutting prow of our symbolic little ship, praying loudly as if in song.

And they jeered at him, snarled at him, and rent the air with their claws. I saw one turn and bare his arse. But not one dared violate the circle and the Great Pentacle of Solomon. In spite of all their abominable strength and howling rage, they still feared the power that lay behind it. Yet, here we were and there they were—at least a dozen of them, capering and watching us with hungry eyes.

"How bad is he?" I leaned over Billy's shoulder as the Dorsetman finished knotting the scrap of fabric around d'Artagnan's leg.

"His calf is bloody mincemeat," said Billy. "And he has passed out from the pain. Guess that's lucky for him." He looked up at me. "We're fucking trapped in here, aren't we?"

"It's stalemate," Ashmole said quietly. He hefted his freshly loaded pistols and looked out into the demon horde.

And that's when it struck me. I swore aloud despite the fact that we were hanging by one thin holy thread of prayer. I was a soldier. Gideon Fludd was a soldier. His very absence should have told me what he was up to.

"He's outflanked us," I said.

"What do you mean?" said Ashmole.

"He's bottled us up here while he is making his way to Cromwell. I'd wager my life on it."

"Wager?" Billy chuckled darkly. "We've got no more credit, Mister Eff."

Isabel was still rocking the bundle of ragged clothes that was Maggie. I knelt down next to them and gently pulled

Maggie's shoulder so that I could see her face. I leaned in towards her, whispering her name. Her eyes were open, and looking into mine, but she was looking through me. She was not seeing me. She was not seeing anything around her. Whatever horrors she had glimpsed in the last day and night had robbed her of all sense and speech. I cupped her cheek with my hand.

"Maggie, come back to me."

But there was nothing from her. She stared on, motionless. Her flesh was chill to my touch. Isabel was watching me, her large dark eyes glistening with tears. Slowly, she gathered Maggie up again and pulled her close.

I stood and turned to Roderigo da Silva. He looked at me, a strange calm on his deathly pale face. "*Senor*," I said, "The Moon Pentacle. How do I work it? How does it open doors?"

His sunken eyes seemed to widen a bit. "You cannot attempt to use this thing! You must not dare."

"I already have, *Senor*. Tell me what I need to know and hurry, I beg you."

"Why, you must be pure... pure in spirit," he began, stuttering with surprise. "That is the most important thing. Without that, the pentacle will fail you and the evil ones will overwhelm you."

"And the charm? The words?"

Da Silva turned to face the demons that were slowly encroaching on the circle again. "You must speak the names of the Lord, for that is whence the power derives." And in a loud voice he cried out: "Adonai! Elohim! El Shaddai!"

As one, the devils clapped hands to their misshapen ears, cringing and jumping, scalded by the only thing that could burn them. Da Silva reached out for my wrist and gripped it tightly.

"If you do not believe, sir, you will surely die!"

I nodded, fully understanding what he was telling me. "The Lord will bear me up in his hand, sir."

I had seen what the pentacle had done to the pig man. And tonight, under the influence of the full moon, it was at its flood tide of power. Fludd had wanted it to redouble his control over the minions of his pretending angel. I could do the same thing.

"Keep the others safe," I said.

Billy was still in a crouch, his silver sword across his knees. He was looking at me, waiting for the command.

"Billy Chard, you and I are going upstairs to pay a call on Mister Cromwell."

Chapter Twenty

"A LITTLE MORE haste, Mister Eff!"

Billy's wrist snapped his sword sharply in an upwards slash, ripping open the black neck of a thing that possessed the head of a gargantuan wasp, great mandibles clacking as it tried to bite his blade. It thrashed at the top of the wooden steps, wisps of steam or smoke pouring from its wound, and tumbled back down the staircase, taking with it another devil.

I stood, forehead pressed to the oak door of the palace entrance, the pentacle in my shaking hand. Though I had said the names of God, as da Silva told me, the door had not moved an inch.

Ashmole's pistol thundered again below us. Two more creatures had bounded to the top of the shingled landing, and Billy sent one sprawling with a curse and a boot in its belly. The other snatched at him but he leapt back and brought his blade smashing down into its skull.

He called out again, his words expelled between great gasps of breath. "They've latched onto us now, Mister Eff. We can't get back down again so you better get us in!"

I stepped back and looked down the great staircase to see more than a dozen glowing eyes bobbing below, moving slowly upwards, the rasp of claws on the wooden treads enough to freeze the marrow.

I turned to the iron-bound door again. This time I placed the pentacle against the centre of the boards, my palm spread wide. And I cleared my mind and then quietly said the names of the Lord in the Hebrew tongue. And then in English. But there was no reward for my efforts; no sound of turning bolt or lock. Suddenly, Billy cried out and I wheeled to see him falling back with two devils on him, one the size of a child. I struck the head from one and Billy managed to free himself from the small one, scratching and screeching before punching it away with a gloved fist. I caught a glimpse of Billy hauling himself up again against the railing and then I was knocked off my feet by a black hissing winged ape. I tumbled backwards and into the door—which opened under my weight as easily as you please.

I was inside the palace, but with the creature on my chest and pinning my sword arm. It thrashed and jutted its head, pressing hard to sink its hooked yellow fangs into my throat. My right hand flew up, the pentacle firmly in my grasp, and with a punch I shoved the silver disc into its jaws. There was a tremendous burst of steam and stinking blood as the devil's head exploded. The thing flopped sideways to the floor, twitching. Billy stood firm in the doorway, dispatching another demon with a savage cut then flinging the massive door shut. And I finally breathed when I heard the bolt slam home.

I propped myself up on an elbow, rubbing the gore from my face with the back of my gauntlet. The pentacle lay next to me, still sparkling despite the black blood that was spattered upon it. I reached out and grasped it, then slid it into my breeches pocket. Outside, the demons began to pound on the thick door, its hinges rattling with every blow.

"Aye, batter away, you bastards," spat Billy. "They'll not get through wood that stout." He came over and helped hoist me up, his eyes momentarily fixed on the corpse of the demon. Already it seemed to be congealing, melting away as if its skeleton had somehow vanished inside it. "Come on, Mister Eff. Are you still whole?"

I nodded, glancing around the hallway. It was not totally dark. A large brass wall sconce threw out some light from its three candles, still flickering though nearly burned away to nubs. More candlelight spilled from around a corner a few yards away. But the ancient wood panelling, dark as sable, gave the hallway a sinister appearance, all the more alarming because there was nothing but silence within.

"You suppose the guards have fled, or gone over to Fludd and the Fifth men?" Billy hefted his blade and took a few steps towards the north end of the hallway.

"I fear it's worse than that," I replied.

There was something in the air inside the palace. Not a smell, but more a heaviness that brushed the nape of one's neck like the hand of a ghost. I knew it was more than mere imaginings. It was a presence of the unholy, of something dreadful. Billy could sense it too.

"We're being watched, I swear it," he said, voice low.

"We may be too late. Pray that Fludd has not discovered Cromwell's apartments yet." I moved past Billy, sword at my waist, level to the floor and held back like a spring. I knew only that the Lord General's lodgings faced onto the deer park. So long as we continued along the corridor, we would eventually find them. Billy moved up to my right, two steps behind as we approached the corner. Rounding this, the corridor turned again on itself left. Here, our way was lit by moonbeams through the long windows that lined the hall.

"Look!" Billy was at a window, the basket hilt of his sword slamming into the frame. Below us, outside, we could see the magic circle and the small cluster of figures inside it. And it was surrounded by moving shadows, black things that capered and crawled about, giving no peace to those who sheltered within it.

"We can only help them by killing Fludd, and quickly," I said. "Keep moving!"

I had never been in this part of Whitehall before. It was damned old, the wainscoting cracked right through with age in places, the floors creaking so loudly we could be heard in Westminster. We moved on, and soon came to a large panelled door. This was unlocked and we found ourselves entering a large square chamber, devoid of furnishings but lit by more wall sconces. A railing to our right overlooked a vast open room below—the old Cockpit theatre. It smelled of wood rot and mould, harsh moonlight shining down from the windows along the cupola above it. We carried on, passing through another open door at the far end of the chamber. There upon the floor, propped up in a sitting position, chin upon chest, was a man.

Billy pulled the hat off the figure, who didn't even flinch. "By Jesus, it's Thurloe!"

I knelt down next to him. "Is he dead?"

"Why... I think he's fucking pissed!"

Thurloe moaned a bit, his head flopping to one side. Billy gave him a shake but Thurloe only slid further down the wall.

"He's not drunk," I said. "He has been magicked—enchanted by some unnatural sleep."

Billy's hands jumped from Thurloe's doublet as if he too might be caught by the spell. Looking into the next room, another antechamber by the look of it, I could see a pile of bodies stretched out on the floor. "Roundheads," I said.

"So much for the bloody army then," said Billy. "Looks like we're too late."

Sweat was pouring down his long face, his complexion the colour of his buff leather jerkin. His chest heaved deeply—he still had not caught his breath from the fight on the stairs outside. He was dying before my eyes.

I smiled a little and touched his forearm. "More campaigning than you expected when you signed up?"

He gave me a grin, dropping his head a bit. "As recruiting sergeants come, Mister Eff, you were damned convincing."

I stood up and looked back along the hallway. "Something's coming."

It was a shuffling kind of noise, the sound of soft-shod feet accompanied by the clicking rasp of claws as if a dog was padding its way towards us. Billy was up fast, raising his sword and settling his grip anew. "You reckon they knocked their way through?"

I took a few steps towards the large square chamber we had just come through, trying my damndest to peer down the black panelled hallway with its gutting candles. And then they walked into view from around a corner. Two of the strangest creatures I had ever seen, straight out of a wine-soaked nightmare. They were walking side by side, like two old friends and neither taller than three foot. One was akin to a great hedgehog, a long snout protruding down, prickles covering its head. It had long arms and even longer claws and it walked upright with a kind of loping gait. All the while it was speaking some sing-song tongue to its companion, harsh and lisping, its long fingers flexing open. Its palms were pink as a man's.

The other was a man, but as misshapen as any farm-born monster. It had a huge bald head that sat atop a stocky naked torso. No neck, the thing had to turn its entire body to look at its nattering friend. But it was its horrid mouth that struck me. It was like a wound from ear to ear, filled with yellow teeth and unnaturally wide. Its pug nose and small black eyes were a far cry from the creature next to it; the hedgehog had large orange orbs like a snake, black slits for pupils. So intent were they in their infernal conversation, they did not see us until they were nearly upon us. They stopped up short, the hedgehog's claws scrabbling loudly. They stared, fearless. From between them emerged an even smaller creature. It was black as coal, a monkey with leathery wings that rose up from its hunched back. And I recognised it for the black thing that had visited me in my cell the previous night. It extended a long thin arm at me and let out a screech to wake the dead.

Billy swore and suddenly pushed past me. "I'll send these little shits back to hell!"

"Billy, no!" I grabbed at his baldric to pull him back but he was moving too fast. I fumbled in my pocket for the pentacle but even as I drew it out, I saw the man-like thing open its huge maw, the top of its head practically falling backwards. It crouched a little, spindly arms and legs tensed, and then unleashed a gale of rank breath down the hallway straight at Billy. The force of this unholy wind knocked Billy backwards and blew him along the floorboards. I heard him hit the far wall with a sickening crunch. And he moved no more. Before the demon could aim a blast at me, I raised the Pentacle of the Moon and held it out before me.

"In the name of the Lord Almighty, get thee hence!"

And I heard a voice from someone behind the creatures, further back along the hall.

"You've done well to make it this far, Colonel. But that *lamen* will do you no more good here." The small demons moved aside and Gideon Fludd stepped into view. The bat-winged ape, bold as brass, pranced closer to me. Its face cracked open into a grin, as if it knew something that I did not.

"These creatures are also creatures of God," said Gideon, moving out in front. Even in the poor light, I could see he looked terrible, every bit as sick as Billy Chard. His skin was drawn tight as a drum over his skull, voice reedy thin. "They are sent to torment sinners like you, Colonel. Those who would thwart the Will of King Jesus."

The little ape looked up at me and spoke, its hissing voice freezing my blood and sounding like it was at my very ear. "Perhaps he will listen to a friend, a friend who knows better."

I backed up, the pentacle still in my right hand, my sword poised and shaking in my left. I looked straight at Fludd. "Don't speak your blasphemy to me, sir. You serve a false angel that has cozened you like a Southwark whore. And I'll not let you pass me. Not while I live and breathe, sir."

The ape demon looked back to Fludd. "He needs his friend."

And I saw Fludd nod his agreement to the demon. I moved back again to put myself between Billy's prostrate form and the enemy for fear they would enchant him while he lay senseless.

That was when a new voice floated down the hallway from beyond Gideon Fludd.

"You're making a mistake, *Rikard*. It's you that has been cozened by evil, turned away from the true path."

And he was there before me, his boots sounding as real as life as he rounded the corner and stood next to Fludd. He was as flesh and blood and looking at me with that old mischievous smile of his. Andreas Falkenhayn took a slow step forward, slipping his beaten broad-brimmed hat from his head and scratching at his long salt and pepper curls.

"There's so much I have to tell you, old friend. Wondrous things you would not believe possible."

"Andreas," I breathed. "I saw you die in front of me. I *watched* you die."

Andreas smiled at me again, as if he had just caught me out again with one of his practical jokes. "I can explain that to you. If you let me, *Rikard*."

And it *was* Andreas. As big as life, just standing there, in his best black doublet and lace, hand on hip and rapier. My heart leapt at seeing him again but just as quickly I knew this was all very wrong. If Gideon Fludd wanted to reunite me with my old comrade, it was in death, not life.

"Andreas... go back to where you've come. I cannot follow you, old friend."

Andreas extended his hand. He was so close now I could see every line on his weathered face, glowing like he had stepped in from a long ride in the cold. "You don't need that bauble any longer. We're on the same side now. Give it here."

The pentacle in my hand was dull and heavy, just a disc of old metal. Beyond Andreas I could see Gideon Fludd, nodding, encouraging me to listen to the words of an old comrade.

"It is over now, *Rikard*. Give it here."

Clinging with one arm to the edge of Andreas's right bucket-top boot was the little ape, wings pulsing silently like a butterfly on a branch. Andreas's hand stretched a little further, his fingers curling up in a gesture of beckoning. His nails were black and grubby from a soldier's toil.

"Andreas, you must go back... don't make me hurt you."

But how could I kill my friend? A friend who was already dead.

"We can go back together, *Rikard*. We can leave this place."

The tail of the ape demon whisked as if irritated.

I raised my right hand slowly, the pentacle gripped between thumb and forefinger. And then I struck with the left. I stabbed downwards with all my strength and skewered the black ape, nailing it to the floor. It screamed amidst a cloud of steam as the silvered sword melted it, the inscribed name of the Lord searing it back to hell. I heard Fludd yell out "No!" even as Andreas fell back, his hand flying up to his head as if in a swoon. My sword sprang into a guard position as I readied to take on the rest.

It was then my eyes met with Andreas's. And it was as if he had just woken from a long slumber. The look he gave me was one of pure confusion as if to ask: *Where am I?* This then slowly changed to awareness and his eyes widened.

"*Rikard*, I'm not meant to be here. I know this."

"Sweet Jesus, Andreas. You're dead now. Months gone by."

The German nodded, understanding returning to him. "I know." And he looked at me with such old tenderness as if in that one moment all remembrance had flooded back to him.

The sound of Fludd's blade flying out of its scabbard brought me back to reality. He made straight for me, the other demons scurrying to the walls. I raised my blade to parry him. But in an instant, my old dead comrade ploughed into Fludd, sending them both crashing into the wooden wainscoting. Dead or alive, Andreas was back to his feet, his rapier shooting from its scabbard in one deft draw. I saw the little man-thing gape again, ready to belch another fetid tempest. I dived forward and thrust it clean through its chest just as Andreas parried a downward blow that Fludd had aimed at me.

The demon thrashed about screeching on the floor, all arms and legs, and I found myself staggering back in a cloud of stinking steam. Gideon was fighting Andreas now, a look of utter shock on his ghoulish face. The hedgehog thing had wisely retreated back around the corner and I saw Gideon back pedal to follow it. His lips started moving rapidly, an incantation of some sort, and I remembered this was how he had conjured the things outside. And the fell creatures came again. Crashing down the hallway, the floorboards bouncing under my feet, they howled and squealed as they came. Andreas stood firm, between me and Fludd, sword raised high. He half turned to me.

"*Rikard*, see to your friend and get out of here! I'll hold them off."

I joined him, my sword raised next to his. He looked so alive, so real. And we were facing the enemy again, together, as we had done countless times before.

"*Rikard*, don't be a fool. Do as I say."

"I never abandon a comrade."

And then he turned to look at me again. "Then do not abandon the living. See to your friend." His face took on an expression that nearly broke my heart. A look that said he knew exactly where he was and what fate lay ahead. He spoke again. "You cannot defend the dead, old friend. *Jetzt... geht!*"

I locked eyes with him for but a moment, nodded, and retreated to where Billy lay sprawled. My sword still drawn, somehow I managed to haul him up with one arm across his chest. Half dragging, half carrying, I stumbled backwards along the corridor, deeper into the old royal apartments. My last sight as I rounded a corner was Andreas Falkenhayn giving a battle cry and bringing his blade down upon some black shadow of a thing that rose up, more than a head higher than him. Then it was only the terrible sounds of the fight, the screeches and crashes, which came to my ears. I dragged Billy past the bewitched redcoats and further down another corridor. And I found my way barred by a locked door.

And again, it was time to put my faith in the pentacle and my God. I prayed loudly, pressing the disc to the thick, ornate panelled door, all the while the sounds of the legions of hell echoing down the hallway. I closed my eyes, my will bent on getting through before we were set upon by the horde. Without a sound, the door fell inward under my gentle pressure. I whispered a hallelujah and hauled Billy in by his arms into yet another antechamber. The door I slammed and bolted, just as I heard the sound of flapping feet and grunts from the other side.

Into the main chamber, I set Billy down and propped him against the wall. We were in a large room, well-lit. I took in my surroundings: a large sideboard, table and chairs, books strewn about on smaller tables, leaded windows letting in the bright silver glow of the night.

I knelt next to Billy. He was still alive. I tapped his scarred jaw, trying to rouse him, but was rewarded by only a feeble groan. There was nothing for it now. I was truly alone. I shut the second door to the antechamber and bolted that as well. Strangely, there was little noise on the other side except for what sounded to me like the snuffling of rooting pigs. When I turned again, sword in hand, there was a man standing next to the great table, watching me.

"Have you come to kill me, sir?"

I just stood there, staring at the man I had sworn to assassinate only weeks before. And now I was here. My great enemy was but a few paces from me. And I knew at that moment, I could cut him down before he could move a muscle.

Oliver Cromwell's eyes moved to a scabbarded sword that hung from a chair at the end of the table, and then they moved to me again. "Well, sir? I can't abide men who dither. Make up your mind."

"General, I am here to protect your life." They were words I never thought I would utter.

"Forgive me, sir, if I take a sceptical view of your sudden appearance in my lodgings." Cromwell took a few steps towards his sword but did not reach for it. I had never before seen him in person. He looked very tired, his heavy-featured face puffy, nose as red as his reputation. His doublet lay open, unbuttoned, a plain simple shirt underneath.

"Sir, there is a plot against you under way even as we speak. Fifth Monarchy men are here in the palace. They are aided by..." And how was I to explain that the very gates of hell had opened up in St. James's Park, spewing out an unholy host of devils?

"How did you get past the guards?" Cromwell carefully placed both hands on the back of the chair, his eyes fixed on me.

"Your regiment—and Mister Thurloe, I might add—are lying outside your apartments, on the floor and senseless. How else do you think I would have gotten past them?"

"Your name, sir?"

I told him. His eyebrows rose, the name sparking a damp memory, not quite igniting recognition. And then, after a moment, it came to him.

"I do remember you, Colonel," the words came out slowly, laden with distrust. "And as a king's man you have more cause to kill me than to aid me." He now reached for his sword, drawing the blade free as he stepped back, the table separating us. "So I will take the course more prudent and summon the guard."

I shook my head and kept my blade lowered. "They will not come, sir, and I beg you not to go through that door to find them. Your true enemy is Major Gideon Fludd and he stands ready to strike you down here and now. He has conjured up the Devil himself to help him."

Cromwell snickered at me. "God, you are bold, sir! Major Fludd of Okey's dragoons? You will have to do better than that."

"Christ! Have you heard nothing of the din outside this room! The gunfire in the park?"

"It's been quiet as the grave, sir. So lay down your sword and yield."

"He's speaking the God's truth, General." It was Billy, doing his utmost to pull himself to his feet. "I fought for Parliament. And I swear to you, this here Cavalier is the only thing between you and Satan's host." Billy's shoulders were pressed against the wall, his feet spread wide. "For Christ's sake, believe him."

Now it was Oliver Cromwell who seemed confused. But the sound of the door being rammed brought him around to the nature of things. A second crash brought the sound of splintering wood and crashing iron furniture.

"Do I smell... burning sulphur?" A gentleman in a black skullcap holding a small book close to his chest had wandered into the room from an adjacent chamber.

"Mister Milton," said Cromwell to the newcomer, "we are under attack."

John Milton looked at Billy and me, squinting and holding up a hand to cover one eye. "These fellows?"

There was a pause. "No," replied Cromwell. "Someone... something else."

I looked at the doorway. "Sir, is your family here with you?

"No, they are in Cambridge."

"We must get out another way. Can you show us?"

Cromwell nodded just as another crash shook the room. I took Billy by his arm but he shook me off.

"I can manage, Mister Eff. But lost my blade back there, I'm afraid."

"General, *now* if you please! We cannot fight what is coming through that door."

We headed for the room from which Mr. Milton had emerged. Cromwell pointed to Billy, the commander in him now coming alive. "You, sir, assist my secretary Mister Milton. He is nearly blind."

We entered the Lord General's bedchamber even as the first outer door burst in, the howl of the demons reaching our ears.

And Cromwell looked at me, his eyes suddenly grown large with surprise. He pointed to another door at the side of the bed and we all four poured through it into an outer corridor. Cromwell slammed the door behind us and grabbed me by my coat.

"Why, sir?" I somehow knew he was asking me why I was helping, not why he was under attack.

"Because there is the matter of a debt of blood, General. A life for a life. And it would seem I owe you mine."

His grip relaxed. "So mercy and justice has its reward, it seems."

A shriek issued from the room behind us, a cry of such strength and otherworldly horror that I felt the Lord General flinch as it pierced the door.

"We can get down these stairs here," he said, gesturing with his sword. "They will lead us to the Cockpit and thence outside."

And even that was no certainty. Billy dragged along a spluttering John Milton by the elbow and we all began pounding down a wide ramshackle staircase. "Where is the army, my lord?" Mr. Milton said, neck craning. "And just what is it that's pursuing us, gentlemen?"

I was bringing up the rear, the skin on my back crawling in anticipation of a black winged thing sinking its talons into me. "We are hunted by hell itself, sir! For pity's sake, don't stop moving!"

True to his word, Oliver Cromwell led us to the old theatre, throwing open the double doors and rushing through, sword in hand, before I could urge him to hold back. The moment the doors had cracked open, groaning on their lazy hinges, I knew it was for ill. The Cockpit had been in near darkness when Billy and I had passed by the mezzanine minutes before. Now we were met with brightness, the light of a hundred candles spilling into the corridor. The stage had been set for our arrival.

Cromwell gave a cry and disappeared from view, sailing into the air. I heard him crash into the benches beyond. Billy and Mr. Milton pulled up short, but they too were flung to the left as if by some great invisible hand. Behind me, the demon horde had made the staircase and already I could hear them howling and screeching as they arrived. The pentacle was in my right hand even before I crossed the threshold, my blade raised high in the other. But no tempest caught hold of me as I entered. I walked into the soaring chamber, my eyes locked on the figure of Gideon Fludd standing at the centre of the stage. A quick glance to my left showed me that the others were sprawled upon the floor, still stunned by the force that had beset them.

The flip-flop of bare feet, mixed with the occasional clop of hooves, now reached my ears. I crouched, turned halfway to the doors behind me. The horde had now arrived, baying for flesh. I shot out my right arm and thank God the sight of the pentacle halted them in their tracks. Gideon's laughter bounced across the round hall. I turned to see that he had extended *his* arm and that it was this gesture that had really stayed the advance.

"Colonel, you have wielded the First Pentacle as surely as if it had been in my own hand. And now you have brought to me the object of the task I must complete. Just as I was told you would."

I slowly moved to where the others were. Billy was up on his feet, lifting up a squinting Mister Milton, but Cromwell was still on his knees, leaning on the wobbling point of his sword. Blood was running down his forehead in tiny rivulets.

"General, are you whole, sir?"

Cromwell looked over to me and nodded. I reached his side and raised him up to his feet. He leaned into me, shaking his head like a hunting dog that had been swatted by a bear.

"I suppose... this is your Fifth Monarchy man, then?" He wiped his brow, blood smearing his sleeve. He looked up at Fludd. "Treason and sorcery both, sir! You are doubly damned. I'll see you gutted alive—"

"I serve the king who is to come!" Fludd's voice rang out, high-pitched and full of righteous joy. "Not the petty Tyrant who thinks he can thwart the will of God. And King Jesus will come when I do what I have been bid to do!"

Mister Milton had turned to gawp at the black monsters now crowding the threshold of the theatre, their weaving eyes yellow and orange, jaws dripping. He placed a hand over one eye, then switched to the other, all the while moving closer to the doorway. Billy dragged him back to us, Milton's mouth moving wordlessly, one finger pointing back to the legion of hell. I now saw that the light of the candles was far brighter than it should have been. They burned like sparking gun match, as brilliant as the sun. It was a light not of this world.

"Come down and try and take us!" I said. "Or send in your hell beasts. I've sent enough of them back to the pit this evening. I can do it again."

Fludd strode across the stage towards where we stood. He was unsmiling and radiating disdain. "It is as it should be, a godless Cavalier defending an old enemy who is no better than he. Your debt will be paid after his, sir. My brother's blood demands it."

If I was to fight alongside an old enemy and to do it here in this place, amidst gilded columns and dusty swags, an audience of heaven and hell alone, then I would do it. And I smiled. Smiled because it was as good a way as any to finish things and because my faith had been given back to me, handed to me on the sly, like a playing card under the gaming table.

"General," I said softly, "I'm not certain that plain steel will afford you much defence but I have something more up my sleeve if you fancy giving a fight."

Cromwell looked at me and for the first time I saw how truly old he was. His wispy, thinning forelock was matted with blood. "I have fought the Devil all my life, sir. I'm not about to stop now."

"Fludd is convinced that killing you will bring the end of days as the Bible tells. It is the Devil that has bewitched him and given him these powers."

Cromwell's brow creased as he locked eyes on Gideon Fludd. "I should never have signed his damned commission."

I turned to see Billy clutching Anya's charm, his hand to his chest, preparing for the onslaught. Milton was loudly intoning the Lord's Prayer, hands clasped. Billy looked at me, long past fearful, his hair plastered with sweat to his sallow face. "Orders, Mister Eff?"

"Hold on, Billy. And hold fast."

He bent down and lifted a bench with which to defend himself. "Aye."

Gideon Fludd raised his chin, looked around the cavernous chamber and spoke. "O Eistibus, my guardian! Show yourself that I may fulfil your holy command." He turned around in a circle, arms on high, and I instantly felt my stomach drop past my knees. I remembered the last time I had seen him summon his false angel.

Cromwell lifted his sword up to take his guard. "Colonel," he whispered, "If we both rush forward, one of us might be able to strike him down!"

I nodded, recognising it might work, but knowing full well that the moment we ascended the stage, Fludd would unleash the minions upon us.

"On my mark, sir." I whispered. Fludd had closed his eyes, his lips moving fast.

"Now!"

I leapt ahead, reaching the low set of steps even as Fludd riveted his wicked gaze on me. But Oliver Cromwell had not moved an inch. I saw his eyes grow wide in disbelief as he strained to lift his feet.

"I'm unable to move, sir!"

I did not stop, but even as I mounted the stage, I saw the ball of white light take form behind Fludd. So blindingly brilliant, it caused lights to dance before my eyes. I stumbled forward, sword and pentacle raised, and then tripped over a loose board. I dropped to my knees, the wind knocked out of me as if I had been kicked by a horse. The Moon Pentacle flew out of my grasp, tumbling through the air and pitching over the front of the stage. It rang crisply as it struck a bench below, then bounced and rattled its way to a floor thick with years of dust.

Fludd possessed his own pentacle that he held before him, a talisman to control what he conjured. I scrambled to regain my feet—I was only two steps away from striking distance—and promptly was knocked down again by the force of the vivid white orb. It shifted shape suddenly, growing larger even as Fludd backed away towards the rear of the stage. This was no mechanical sleight of hand from Cardinal Mazarin's theatre. This was real. The light was taking form. It towered over me, the form of a man but monstrously huge: legs, arms, slender torso, and a great set of spreading wings at its back. Still too brilliant to see clearly, I shielded my eyes as Andras arrived into the world.

The glare began to dissipate a little, and, as I lowered my hand I found myself looking up ten feet into the face of the demon. Its golden hair, large flowing curls, seemed to float about its head. I could not tell if it was seeing me for its wide eyes were utterly milk white, like those of some marble statue. But it was its awful mouth—the beak of an eagle—that froze my heart. It was a pitiless visage. Andras slowly swivelled its huge head, taking in everyone in the chamber. I gagged as the overpowering scent of lilies engulfed me. The demon seemed to hover somewhere between solid form and dense white fog, long arms, horribly elongated hands and fingers moving excitedly. They played in the air like the limbs of a monstrous white spider, probing its surroundings.

"O Eistibus, great and dread angel!" Fludd's voice trembled, not with fear, but with ecstasy. "Your enemies are delivered unto you! Fulfil the prophecy!"

I somehow managed to crawl backwards, reaching the edge of the stage near the small set of stairs. That's when I saw the face of Andras look down on me.

"The angel knows the weaknesses of all men," yelled

Fludd, his self-righteous voice rising. "And yours he knows well—as do I!"

And it started. Rising up in my belly, seizing my chest in a vice of iron. I felt my arms go weak in an instant, shaking like I was some palsied cripple. My breaths came faster and faster, my heart pumping so fast I thought it would burst. My own Beast had been summoned up from inside of me. I could feel myself sinking down on the steps, as helpless as a babe fallen from its crib. From the centre of the floor of the stage, directly underneath the hovering demon, I watched as what appeared to be a pool of tar spread outwards, perfectly round. It grew to nearly cover the stage. Pearlescent and jet, it first appeared to be liquid but then took on the appearance of highly polished tile.

Gideon Fludd walked towards me, his rapier now drawn. I could not even lift my silver sword. He merely booted me aside, carefully stepping down to the theatre floor.

"You may watch the prophecy fulfilled before I send you to hell."

And the dark angel remained floating, barely moving over the stage, more observer than participant. I could not stop the tears from welling in my eyes as despair, naked despair, washed over me and swallowed me up.

As if in some dream between sleep and wakefulness, I saw Billy move to step between Fludd and Cromwell. And so too, I saw another figure walk into view. It looked to be an old man with a crutch, a one-legged man, in rags. I raised up my head. It was the old veteran I had chanced upon in Fleet Street, the strange wizened man who had known so much about me, things by right he could never have known.

Fludd halted and turned towards the newcomer. And I saw Andras shimmer more brightly, the heat burning my face. The thump of the crutch was the only noise in the chamber. I saw Billy lower his makeshift weapon in awe of the old beggar's entrance. The little man stopped suddenly as if stricken. And then his eyes were filled with golden light. So too his nostrils and open mouth. Rays of sunlight shot out from the gaps in his rags, growing in intensity until the beggar was one shimmering firework, growing larger and larger as we watched.

And he took on new shape. There before us was another being of the ether, on bended knee with one hand placed flat upon the floor. Every inch as tall as Andras, he was more man than wraith. His hair was long and white, his face beautiful to behold but the expressions shifting faster than I could perceive. From his back unfolded four huge white wings and he stretched his arms upwards, the muscles of his giant alabaster torso flexing and pulsing. He was real. He slowly rose up and stood, facing the monster on the stage. A great silver sword, rippling with purple flame, appeared in his right hand and the room was filled with the sound of a great whirlwind rushing in. The curtains and swags around the theatre flapped and began to rip as the tempest increased.

Fludd kicked me again as he remounted the steps to shelter behind his angel. Andras shook like a tree in a storm, its arms flailing, beak opened in a silent scream at the newcomer. In one great leap, the glowing ethereal giant was upon it, striking again and again with its burning blade. Andras thrashed, wrapping its serpent-like arms around this beautiful being that I knew to be the true angel. The sound of the wind grew to such a roar that my ears began to ring and both combatants grew brighter and brighter until I had to avert my eyes. The room was near upon white, all shades of colour dissipated. I could see Cromwell and Billy, side by side watching dumbstruck at what was unfolding. John Milton was on his knees, hands clasped in prayer, his sickly eyes huge with wonder.

I pushed myself away from the stage and the battle. Fludd was still cowering at the back, his face a mask of pure terror and confusion. Already, I could feel my Beast within subsiding, the panic ebbing away, my reason returning. I turned my head to where Cromwell had stood. He was now on his back upon the floor. A boy, just an ordinary boy, sat upon his chest, hands wrapped about the Lord General's throat. Billy was a few paces away, his head shaking with disbelief at what he was seeing. I could see Cromwell struggling to pull the hands from his neck, his legs twisting and turning as he tried to throw the boy off.

"Billy!" I pushed myself up onto my feet, leaning on my sword, head swimming. Billy's jaw was slack and he stood, rooted. And then, the boy turned to look at me. It was my son.

I staggered towards Cromwell. "No, sweet Jesus, no."

Thomas beheld me with a look of innocent love, a sweet smile upon his lips. But still his hands worked upon Cromwell's neck. The Lord General was beginning to go limp. I reached the pair and raised my sword over my head. My darling boy's expression turned to fear.

"Father! Do not strike me!"

My arms shook. I hesitated. "It's not you, Thomas," I whispered.

Cromwell wasn't moving anymore. I wrapped both hands around the sword grip and shut my eyes. And I brought my blade down with all my might, cleaving the boy's skull. Instantly there was the loud hiss of steam and an unholy screech. My eyes open, I saw that now there was nothing but the prostrate form of Oliver Cromwell. Billy fell on his knees next to him, grasped his shoulders and gave him a shake. Cromwell gasped, and retched. And looking beyond, towards the doorway, I could see the great horde still held back, all of them transfixed by the battle that still raged upon the stage. I turned around, my sword slipping out of my hand and clattering to the floor. And I sank to my knees as I watched what was happening.

The flaming purple blade of the angel rose and fell and I faintly seemed to hear the sound of an unearthly wailing, of many creatures in great pain. And so too, I began to see that Andras was being forced down into the mirror-like pool upon the stage with every blow that rained down on it. The sound of an unearthly trumpet filled the theatre, reverberating from the rafters, and Andras sunk completely into the black pit, the angel rising above it with one great push of its wings. The legion of devils cowering by the threshold of the theatre, caught up like so many straws in the wind, somersaulted across the room and plunged into the dark abyss.

The whole stage shook as if it had been picked up and dropped. Fludd fell, the torn curtain he had clung to falling with him. He hit the stage floor, rolled and fell into the blackness. But it was not liquid, this pool. It sent out no ripples as he fell. He disappeared completely for a moment, then suddenly, his head and shoulders surfaced, his hands reaching for the edge. I was on the stairs again, staring unbelievingly at what my eyes were showing me.

"Jesus, help me!" Fludd was scrabbling at the edge of the stage, fingers desperate to find purchase. He screamed again. "Please, help me! I've seen it!"

I shall never forget his face for as long as I shall live. Fludd had seen his mistake as well as his fate.

"Treadwell! For pity's sake... your hand!"

I leaned down, my arm moving out to him, to save him from the abyss. I looked at his hands. One wore the ring I too had briefly worn, the pentagram. But the other, the other bore a ring I had not noticed before. Upon it was the square and compass of the Craft. I grabbed him by both wrists and began to pull. He was crying like a child now. I could feel him rising up and rapidly his breast emerged from the pitch. But then I felt a tug, like a great fish pulling on a line. Fludd erupted into a long drawn out cry; whatever was tugging at his legs was bigger and stronger than me and I felt myself beginning to follow him down. As my chest fell level on the stage, I had to let go, and watched his face disappear beneath the surface, down into the ebony Pit. His last look was one of stark terror and disbelief. And then the Pit shrank, retreated as it had formed, until it too was gone.

I twisted around, my back sliding along the stage steps. The true angel had glided silently to where Billy stood, shaking. It reached out its hand and touched his head but a moment. Billy gasped aloud and collapsed as if pole-axed. Then the angel came to me. I looked up into his eyes, as human as any, and they were smiling. He lightly touched my head and I too swooned but stayed upon my feet. And he spoke to me without voice.

Your Faith has held you up. Be at peace!

The great glowing sword he held seemed to melt away in his hand and he raised himself up with a downward beat of his white wings, up towards the ceiling rafters and in a flash of golden brightness he was gone.

No one said a word. The Lord General of England collapsed down on a bench, staring up at the ceiling while he rubbed at his throat. Billy Chard looked numb. He slowly began to unlace his buff coat, hands still shaking.

"Billy Chard?" I said, my voice quavering, "Are you whole?"

Billy nodded to me. "I almost stopped you, Mister Eff. I almost... went for you. It was—I mean, it looked like my mother. And then you swung...."

I reached out and grasped his shoulder. "I saw someone there too. But our eyes were bewitched. It was not what it seemed."

Billy's voice was hardly above a whisper. "I know. But it was a terrible hard thing to see."

And then John Milton raised his voice up, triumphant.

"We are as Joshua and Daniel, gifted among men! For we have seen the Lord's Captain in battle!"

Cromwell turned to Mr. Milton, looking confused as to his own sanity.

Milton nodded and smiled. "It was the Archangel Michael, of course!"

And suddenly, my heart in my mouth, I remembered Maggie.

Chapter Twenty-One

"SAINTS, ABOVE, RICHARD! You're alive!" Elias Ashmole burst into the Cockpit, a pistol in each hand. He spotted Cromwell and checked his rush forward. With a bow from the waist, arms outstretched, he did a quick reverence.

"My Lord General, thanks be to God, you're safe!" He bowed awkwardly a second time. "Eh, Elias Ashmole, your servant, sir!"

Ashmole thrust his weapons into his belt and reaching me, squeezed my shoulder. "It was beyond extraordinary, sir. A rustic little fellow on a crutch came across the park. The creatures fled at the sight of him. He bent down near the Lieutenant and... well, he healed his wounds quick as you like—before my very eyes. Then he was gone, hobbling off, towards you here."

I looked at the back of my left hand where the black imp had sunk its teeth into me. It was now unblemished, no sign of any wound.

I gripped his forearm. "Maggie, how fares Maggie?"

"She follows with the others," replied Ashmole. "See, here," and he pointed to the door he had come through, wedged open and partially obscured by a heavy brocade curtain. Roderigo da Silva entered and right behind him was Isabel and my Maggie, arms supporting each other as they made their unsteady progress into the theatre. And poor d'Artagnan followed them all, his face sombre and pale, silvered sword in hand.

I ran to Maggie. If the archangel had healed d'Artagnan, then, there was a chance. I pulled her to me, Isabel pushing her to my embrace.

"Maggie! Look at me, my dear!"

She raised her round, plump face to me. She was worn down, her eyes red-rimmed and her cheeks grey, all colour lost. But she gave a valiant little smile, like a maiden, and gently pushed me back, now contemplating my blood-smeared face.

Her brow creased. "Do I know you, sir?"

I took a step back. "Maggie, you're still dazed. Look at me."

She moved a lock of hair that had fallen into her face. "I cannot remember you," she said. She looked around at the others. "Nor any of these people. Nor how I came to be in this place."

I took up her hand. "You are Marguerite St. John. Surely, you must remember? You must remember all that has happened these last days?"

"I do know who I am but..." And she shook her head, her fingers brushing her temple.

I felt like stone. Ashmole put an arm about my shoulders.

"She has suffered greatly. Her mind will return soon enough in the light of day. You must not worry."

I nodded. She would remember. Her mind surely had closed to save itself from madness. Time would heal her, I told myself. But for now, I was still a stranger to her.

"Fear not, mistress," said Isabel, moving in again to comfort her. "We will look after you until you are yourself again."

Billy came alongside and pushed something cold into my hand. It was the Moon Pentacle.

"Here, Mister Eff. It might set her to rights again, if you can use it."

I contemplated it for a second and then proffered it to Ashmole. "Nay, Billy. This thing has done its dreadful work and I would not play with it further, for any reason. Here, Elias. A donation for your collection of curiosities."

Ashmole took it gingerly into his hand. "And one I shall never catalogue."

"Colonel Treadwell, sir," said Cromwell, limping towards us, grimacing from his tumbles and from the demon's throttling. "I owe you my life. But some explanations are in order. I'm a God-fearing man but I am not sure of what I have just witnessed. And who are these people?"

I could feel my last strength ebbing away, fatigue nearly overwhelming me. I weakly raised my arm and indicated da Silva, who stood, silent, next to his daughter. "Lord General, sir, meet the architect of your deliverance, *Senor* Roderigo da Silva."

Cromwell's eyes widened as he took in the little old man with the skullcap and white tunic with Solomon's pentacle emblazoned upon it.

Roderigo bowed, hips cracking. "At your service, my lord."

Cromwell nodded his head. "I know you, sir. But in very different circumstances."

"That is true, my lord."

I pointed to the Frenchman, who yet stood off to the side, looking worse for wear. "And may I present to you the emissary of His Eminence, the Cardinal Mazarin—Lieutenant d'Artagnan."

The musketeer swept off his battered hat, slowly putting his right leg forward. He inclined his head to the Lord General, but said not a word.

Cromwell, looked about the chamber, now dimmed, the supernatural glow dissipated. He shook his large square head, incredulous. And then he turned to me directly. "I want to hear everything, from the beginning. We shall return to my apartments upstairs. All of you." He wiped his brow and observed the drying blood that covered his fingers. "And I have a few words for Mister Thurloe, once I find his useless carcass."

* * *

THE LIGHT OF a most welcome, nourishing sun entered the leaded windows of General Cromwell's private rooms. There was not a trace of the demons we had slain, all blood and gore vanished like smoke. Only the sundered doors gave witness to the battle of the night before. We were surrounded by redcoats, all having woken with the first light of dawn and now sheepish and nervous for their failures. They bustled like housewives bringing more food and drink from the pantry and buttery, carefully setting the fare upon the table we all were gathered at.

Try as I might, I could eat nothing. My mind was sore distracted by my Maggie's plight. Her words had stabbed me deeply. Cromwell had sent both women home with an escort and I could not rid my mind's eye of Maggie's confused, questioning glances as she desperately sought to understand where she was, and why. And I was bitter besides. My wounds and those of d'Artagnan and Billy—all surely destined to be mortal wounds—had been healed by the archangel (for Mr. Milton was undoubtedly right). Why had the angel not come to her aid?

"My lord." John Thurloe's voice sounded as if he had drunk a hogshead of wine the night before. "We have sent out riders to apprehend any further known associates of Major Fludd. I am working to establish this very morning the degree of complicity of others in the Fifth Monarchy."

"You do that," said Cromwell from his high-back chair, fixing Thurloe with a glare. He then beckoned to one of the redcoats. "Take your men outside and shut the doors." When the last soldier had scurried out, he looked at the faces around his table, each in turn. "You are undoubtedly brave men, gentlemen. But these events of late and all you have told me this last hour, make necessity of some grave decisions." He raised a red Venetian goblet to his lips, took a sip, and set it down again. "I find at my table a Cavalier, his Ranter servant, an alchemist, a Frenchman, and a Jew. Strange company indeed. And I am beholden to each, it seems."

Ashmole stood up. "My lord, as you have heard, it was Colonel Treadwell who learned of this plot and risked his life to come to your defence. He sits here still a condemned man... unless you change that."

Cromwell did not reply straight away. He slowly pushed his chair back, stood up, jaw clenching with pain, and walked to the windows. "First things first," he said, half to himself.

Ashmole hurriedly sat. "I meant no offence, my lord."

Cromwell turned to us again. "First, I would tell you that *Senor* da Silva is known to me. We have had several discussions these last few months."

I looked over to da Silva, who was nodding as he watched Cromwell. Everyone had secrets, it did seem.

"*Senor* da Silva knows it is my intention to open the way for his people to live in England freely again. No less do we, as free Englishmen, owe the people of the Book. His personal courage last night means that my political intention now becomes a vow." Cromwell touched his hand to his breast.

Da Silva bowed his head in return.

"Second, I must tell all of you: what happened here last night must never be revealed. The line between miracles and witchcraft is a fine one. Last night I saw both. But those that have not seen with their own eyes will never understand. The guards, even Mister Thurloe here, remember nothing leading to their bewitching."

John Thurloe flashed an embarrassed grimace and slunk further beyond Cromwell.

"But my Lord General," stuttered Milton. "Surely we must reveal this wonder to the people that we may bring them to closer to God's wisdom. Already in my mind, an ode, a poem, is taking form. The battle against Lucifer and his fallen angels. *Paradise—*"

The sound of Cromwell's crashing boot brought silence.

"*Never* revealed, Mister Secretary!"

Milton sank down on his bench, blinking.

"That leaves us with the question of your fate, Colonel Treadwell."

I looked over to the ruler of the new republic. "I would only ask that you give Billy Chard, here, free passage to wherever he chooses and, to Mistress St. John, passage and safe conduct to Paris, to rejoin her father."

"These things I can do. But that does not solve the question of your fate, sir."

D'Artagnan had barely stirred throughout. He was looking at me now; his face heavy with remorse for all that had come to pass.

"It was your own free will that brought you back to these shores—under pain of death," said Cromwell. "I will not guess your original purpose, but I'm no fool. Even so, you have saved my life as I saved yours eight years ago. The slate is clean."

He was right. Our slate was clean. And maybe I had saved England by saving him. But I had betrayed my king, endangered my kin, and caused my dear Maggie the theft of her own memory and with it, her love for me. And I suddenly felt very, very old.

"And there is the matter of your outstanding business with the Cardinal, as *Monsieur* d'Artagnan has so plainly laid out for us." Cromwell scratched at the mole that dwelt between his eyebrows. "That leaves me with the choice of throwing you into the Tower, handing you over to the French, giving you a pardon, or... doing nothing."

Billy sat up, a slice of gammon falling from his mouth back into his trencher.

"*Monsieur*," continued Cromwell, "speaking as the Cardinal's representative, what would you counsel?"

D'Artagnan looked straight at me, his green eyes moist. "I would say, let Colonel Treadwell decide. As my comrade, he's earned that choice. One can always tidy the affairs of state later, *n'est ce pas?*"

Cromwell growled. "Somehow, I doubt the Cardinal would see it that way, sir."

"I'm sure I can concoct something to convince His Eminence," replied d'Artagnan, not taking his eyes from me. "I was once told that, sometimes, loyalty trumps practicality. To my mind and my heart, that is sound counsel here." And he gave me a knowing smile and a nod. I nodded back to him. Honour was restored.

"So, my Lord General," said d'Artagnan, turning back to Cromwell, his face full of handsome vigour, body restored by an angel's grace. "The fate of Colonel Treadwell must lie with you, and your conscience."

BILLY AND I stood once more in the hall of Roderigo da Silva, this time brightened by glorious morning sun through the large leaded window. The vivid blue and yellow glass at the centre of the diamond panes set the reflected rays to dancing upon the great table. But even this simple pleasure could not alter the atmosphere in the room. It was as if we were all on a death watch; a great unspoken truth hovered over all of us.

The old rabbi placed his hand on my forearm. He looked far older now than when we had set out to do battle at the palace two nights ago, and it was clear to me that his vigil in the sacred circle had come at a price. But it was the question of Maggie's fate that set the pall over things.

"There is a deep wound in her mind," said da Silva, quietly. I looked over to Isabel who stood near the staircase, gravely silent. Her eyes met mine and I could see little hope in them.

"I have prayed for her," he continued. "Prayed for healing deliverance. I felt sure that after she had slept for a day and a night that she would have been restored."

"And she remembers nothing still?"

Da Silva shook his head. Isabel moved to join us, placing an arm around her father.

"But she did not know us to begin with," she said as she guided the old man back to a chair, "And she has been here resting since the other night. She seems happy... without concern. Almost as if she is trying hard *not* to remember what has befallen her. It may be that she needs to look upon you, sir, to restore her memory."

It was Billy who was bold enough to ask what I held back.

"What if them creatures, the demons, took something from her?" He gesticulated in his awkwardness. "I mean... took away what makes her like us. She's not said a blessed thing since what happened."

Isabel looked up at Billy. "You mean her *soul*?"

Billy looked at his boots. "Aye, I reckon that's my fear, mistress."

"I will not believe that," said the rabbi, his voice filled with sudden strength. "The Lord would not permit such a thing."

I was not so sure. The Archangel had restored us all: saved us from our infernal wounds and maybe even banished my secret Beast forever. But it had left Maggie untouched and lost to me. Perhaps it was my punishment for this adventure, not hers.

"She *is* restored in body," said Isabel. "And she can be restored in spirit too, in time. But my father and I are worried that what you propose to restore her memory carries much risk. You must have great trust in this person... this *apothecary*."

"I do. It is a trust that is long-earned."

"Very well, then. Let me bring her down to you now." And she quickly ascended the stairs.

Billy gave me a worried glance and I edged closer to the stairwell to await the arrival of the woman I loved. When Maggie came down she looked straight at me and smiled. But it was the smile of a gentlewoman entering a room and not a smile of recognition. Her chestnut tresses were tucked in a white crocheted cap that sat far back on her head. Isabel had thrown away Maggie's torn and soiled clothes and dressed her in her own: dark madder skirt, white chemise and green woollen bodice cinching in her bosom modestly. Isabel gently placed an arm about Maggie and slowly guided her to me.

"Do you know this man, Marguerite?"

Again, Maggie looked at me. She dipped her head in a gesture of greeting. "Sir, I cannot recall if we have met... but you must forgive me as I have not been well these last days. Indeed I cannot even remember how it is I have come back to London. These good people here have told me I bumped my head... and this is why I have forgotten things."

I nodded and smiled even as my heart was run clean through.

"How about me, mistress?" said Billy like some cheerful clown, sweeping his battered hat from his greasy noggin.

Maggie laughed and shook her head. "I would remember *you*, sir, I am sure!"

I reached out and grasped her hand gently. "If you would allow me, mistress, I think we know someone who can help you to remember. Will you let us take you there?"

Maggie looked confused and I saw a brief wave of fear wash over her face. She turned to Isabel. "If Isabel comes with me, and if she thinks I should..." The words trailed off as she sought support. And I looked straight into Isabel's eyes so that she could see this was all I wanted with all my heart.

The girl turned to her father. Da Silva, sitting hunch-shouldered in his high-backed oak chair, nodded his head twice. He then raised his chin off his starched collar and gave me a look as if to say whatever was to follow was now all upon my head. Isabel took Maggie's other hand. "I will come with you and make sure that you will be safe."

OUR LITTLE PARTY made its way across the uneven cobbles of the Covent Garden, anticipation and worry hastening our pace. My cloak was thrown about my chest and over my shoulders, the silvered sword that had saved my life bounced against my hip as I stepped; my right arm was tightly entwined about Maggie's. Isabel held her right hand. Billy was a pace ahead, loudly clearing a way for us among the costermongers with his usual Ranter manners.

We were momentarily stopped by the throng that swirled around us. "You don't sound surprised," I said to Ashmole, who was getting jostled by a little old man bent double under a wicker basket. I had just told him that I had spied the ring of the Freemasons on Gideon Fludd's hand, moments before he was pulled down into the abyss.

"Richard, I was going to tell you. I received a letter this morning, from Mister Lilly. He has arrived back this morning from the north."

"How convenient."

"You don't understand, Richard. He and the others left because they had heard that Gideon Fludd was of the brethren. They went to Berkhamsted to learn the truth of it. Alas, too late."

"Would it have made a difference?"

Ashmole looked at me. "It might have. But time was not on our side. You know that."

We started moving forward again. The crowd seemed vast, surging along to market. I pulled Maggie closer to my side but instantly felt her body tense under my grip. I relaxed my hand and loosened my hold upon her arm.

"We're nearly there now," I said. "You mustn't worry. All will be well. Billy! Slow down there!"

I leaned closer to Ashmole so that he could hear me over the roar of traders. "Forgive me. I have not had the chance, until now, to give you my thanks. For believing me."

Ashmole smiled broadly. "I know an honest man when I see one, and one who is worthy of assistance. And brotherhood."

Into the Seven Dials now, we had turned down a narrow street, no more than an alleyway, and now stood in front of our destination.

Ashmole placed a hand on my shoulder. "We are all mortal men, even those of us in the Craft. Sometimes courage and faith fail even the best and bravest of us. I suppose even Gideon Fludd did not expect to take the path he ended up upon."

"Mister Ashmole," I said quietly, "You're a gentleman true and among the most generous of souls in London. Will you not come in with us?"

"Nay, you don't need me any further than here. I will pray that you find the aid you need. And I shall remain outside no matter how long it takes. God be with you."

I took his hand. "I thank you, sir."

Billy looked to me and I nodded. He pushed open the door and we entered the strange little shop that we had visited not three days ago. And Anya was waiting.

She stood near her work table, wiping her hands upon her moss-green skirt, a baggy linen smock masking the leanness of her brown body. Upon her head, a white turban was coiled, covering all of her raven hair except for two long strands that fell down each side of her long neck.

She looked at me, eyes sparkling despite the feeble light that fought its way into the room. "Sooner than you expected, man?"

"Aye, but no surprise to you, Anya. It never is."

Billy swept his crumpled felt hat from his head and touched thumb and forefinger to his brow. "Mistress."

Isabel stepped back and stood behind Maggie, a hand gently placed on her back, a gesture to let her know that she was still with her. Anya's bare feet moved silently across the floorboards. She stopped in front of Maggie and drew back the hood of Maggie's cloak. I could hear Maggie's breaths coming faster as Anya's eyes bored into her. Anya raised her long-fingered hand to Maggie's cheek and offered a caress. "Child, what have you lost?"

Maggie hesitated, her weak voice quavering. "I've lost... part of myself." And she turned to look up at me, her eyes filled with apprehension.

Anya dropped her hand and looked at me in the strangely cold way she had. "You and I must speak together, man."

I followed her into the darker confines of the house. Over my head hung a veritable forest of dried plants and wizened things that looked vaguely like they had once been alive. Anya stopped and turned to me.

"You have succeeded against the evil, that is proved by your presence. But your victory has come at a cost."

"I know that. You have to help her. I know that you have the power to heal."

"She has seen things that no one should ever see. How did you let this woman come to such grief? You were careless, man!"

I felt my face suddenly burn and I moved towards her. She held her ground and met my glare with her own.

"It was not my doing!" I said.

"Bah! What has come to pass is all your doing, man. It always has been."

I growled and swiped my hand at the festooned ceiling, pulling down an armful of stinking vegetation. Anya laughed, my shoulders sank, and my rage melted in an instant. I was defeated and she knew it. Anya undid her turban and tossed it onto a table. She gave her head a shake, long black hair spilling down to her shoulders. Even in the dimness of the room, I could see her pale eyes shine.

"Can you bring her back to me?" I begged, my voice a thin, reedy whisper.

Anya put her hands on her hips. "There are ways. I have a draught I can give her. I can push my way into her mind and force her to look too. If I have to. But there are risks. You know that too, don't you, man?"

I nodded like a scolded schoolboy. "What is your price, woman?"

Anya raised her chin as the old phrase left her lips. "One silver thaler... deferred." And I knew then that whatever happened next, our business together was not at an end.

We emerged together into the daylight of the shop room. I

drank in the picture of Maggie, beautiful and lost, her companions standing by her.

Anya took up Maggie's hands in hers. "Will you trust in my medicine and my craft, girl?"

Maggie stuttered.

"Girl!" said Anya, the tanned leathery skin of her neck tightening. "Will you open yourself to me?"

"Yes, yes, I will!" The explosive reply set her to shaking.

Anya gave a slow steady nod. "Then let us begin." She pulled Maggie along and I made to follow, but Anya reached out and placed her hand firmly on my chest, her eyes commanding my attention.

"No. The girl and I must be alone. You know this."

"She is... dear to me."

"That matter is plain to see. Wait here."

I nodded and the two vanished behind a red curtain that took them into the recesses of the house. I let out one long and heavy breath.

"Then *I* will go with her!" Isabel stepped forward to follow them in.

I grabbed her arm. "You will not, girl! What must be done must be done alone by Anya."

Isabel twisted out of my grip, "Who knows what that witch will do!"

I instantly relented my action. "I beg you. Give her this chance. I need her back."

The girl's fire diminished. She blinked, glanced at Billy, and then nodded.

"Have faith, Mistress," said Billy with all the confidence of an old sage. "She's a proper Cunning Woman, she is. Mister Eff knows."

"I pray you are both right in that," she said, her voice subdued.

Silence fell among us, an awkward stillness with doubt, unseen, but still heavy, in the strongly scented room. Billy plucked a posy of dried lavender from a ceiling beam, made a few cautious steps, and handed it to Isabel. She took it from him with a raised eyebrow, a small shake of her head, and then a wisp of a smile.

"What will you and your father do now, mistress?" he asked.

And the look on his face made it clear to me, as I suppose I should have known from the beginning, that he was love-struck for her. He stood square, well-illuminated by the warm sunlight of the front window. He had sprung back to health in but a day it seemed. His features remained hard-favoured, as always, but now his complexion shone hale and hearty as when I had first met him. And it was as if years had passed since our meeting in Plymouth town, so much dark adventure had we shared together.

She inhaled deeply of the purple flowers and then offered the posy back to Billy. "We will do what we have always done. We will do what needs must to survive. We are *marranos*."

Billy reached out again and took it back. He gave her a smile, trying to hide his disappointment, though his face flushed pink. "But General Cromwell has promised to look after you. Look after your people. I heard him say it."

"A promise remains only that, a promise, until it is fulfilled. And we have waited a very long time. I'll not depend on anyone but myself." Isabel turned to me. "I will wait outside with Mister Ashmole. Forgive me, but there is something dark about this place, something uneasy."

I gave her a slight nod and she smiled and moved to the door, pausing to briefly touch Billy upon the arm.

Once she had gone, Billy let out something between a sigh and a grunt and pushed his crumpled brimmer back on his head.

"What will you do now, Billy Chard? Will you go back to the Ranter colony?"

He shook his head. "Nah. They got it wrong they did. At least now I have my answer to the truth of their creed." He looked at me. His grey eyes were somehow older, more tired than the rest of his face. The price of what he had seen. "There *is* evil and sin in this world, Mister Eff. And it comes by the cartload. But there is good too, in men. And I have seen Heaven's Grace with my own eyes." He scratched at his long crooked nose. "I guess you can't have one without the other, can you, Mister Eff?"

"Did I do what was right, Billy?"

"You did the best with the cards we was handed and you can't ask better than that. General Cromwell is pretty much all this sorry kingdom has left these days. Why didn't you accept his offer of pardon?"

"And give up one death sentence in exchange for a new one from the Royalists? No, I'm happy with the lot I chose."

"But you didn't choose nothing, Mister Eff."

I folded my arms, set my backside against the opposite wall, and dropped my chin to my chest. "I'm my own master, Billy. And that is no small treasure in these times."

Billy let out a chuckle, as light and free as I had heard from him these weeks gone by. "Guess that means I'm a rich man too!"

An hour passed. And then another. Light and shadow slowly altered the little room as the day wore. My mind wandered, filled with hope one instant and despair the next. And then Billy bolted upright off the floor where he had sat cross-legged. I heard Maggie's shoes clopping and scraping along the gritty floor as she returned, Anya at her side.

I turned to meet her, struggling to glimpse her face in the darkening chamber. And slowly, she came into my view. I saw that there were tears streaming down her face. Tears that I had not seen since the day I had wounded her, abandoning her to d'Artagnan and fate. But she was looking at me, and she was seeing me. *Remembering* me. She rushed to my arms and I swallowed her up. I pushed my lips to her ear.

"Can you forgive me? For everything?"

She hugged me tightly. "I remember everything, or nearly everything... But I can forgive you for all. If you can forgive me my foolhardy adventuring."

I lifted her away and cupped her face in my hands. "Maggie, you're as brave as any man I have ever known. And I will not let you from my sight again."

"But what will happen to us now? Where shall we go?"

I smiled, feeling freer than I had since I was a boy.

"Maggie, my love, we can go anywhere!"

About the Author

Clifford Beal, originally from Providence, Rhode Island, worked for 20 years as an international journalist and is the former editor-in-chief of *Jane's Defence Weekly* in London. He is the author of *Quelch's Gold* (Praeger Books 2007), the true story of a little-known but remarkable early 18th century Anglo-American pirate.

UK ISBN: 978 1 78108 018 4 • US ISBN: 978 1 78108 019 1 • £7.99/$9.99

Alice isn't having the best of days – late for work, missed her bus, and now she's getting rained on – but it's about to get worse.

The war between the angels and the Fallen is escalating and innocent civilians are getting caught in the cross-fire. If the balance is to be restored, the angels must act – or risk the Fallen taking control. Forever. That's where Alice comes in. Hunted by the Fallen and guided by Mallory – a disgraced angel with a drinking problem he doesn't want to fix – Alice will learn the truth about her own history... and why the angels want to send her to hell.

What do the Fallen want from her? How does Mallory know so much about her past? What is it the angels are hiding – and can she trust either side?

 WWW.SOLARISBOOKS.COM

Follow us on Twitter! www.twitter.com/solarisbooks